Sizzling a
ultimat

PASSIONATE

Playboys

Strong and sensual—the
ultimate temptation...

PASSIONATE

PASSIONATE
Playboys

Kim LAWRENCE
Ally BLAKE
Nicola MARSH

MILLS
BOON

All the characters in this book have no existence outside the imagination
of the author, and have no relation whatsoever to anyone bearing the
same name or names. They are not even distantly inspired by any
individual known or unknown to the author, and all the incidents are
pure invention.

Harlequin Mills & Boon Limited, Eton House,
18-24 Paradise Road, Richmond, Surrey TW9 1SR

PASSIONATE PLAYBOYS © by Harlequin Books S.A. 2011

The Demetrios Bridal Bargain © Kim Lawrence 2007
The Magnate's Indecent Proposal © Ally Blake 2008
Hot Nights with a Playboy © Nicola Marsh 2008

ISBN: 978 0 263 88727 3

024-0511

Harlequin Mills & Boon policy is to use papers that are
natural, renewable and recyclable products and made from
wood grown in sustainable forests. The logging and
manufacturing processes conform to the legal environmental
regulations of the country of origin.

Printed and bound in Spain
by Litografia Rosés S.A., Barcelona

THE DEMETRIOS BRIDAL BARGAIN

Kim Lawrence

Kim Lawrence lives on a farm in rural Anglesey. She runs two miles daily and finds this an excellent opportunity to unwind and seek inspiration for her writing! It also helps her keep up with her husband, two active sons and the various stray animals which have adopted them. Always a fanatical consumer of fiction, she is now equally enthusiastic about writing. She loves a happy ending!

CHAPTER ONE

ANDREOS DEMETRIOS, his erect posture making no concession
to the whirling blades of the helicopter from which he had just
alighted, looked around, his piercing dark glance moving pointedly over and past his reception committee—a younger man
standing beside the helicopter pad.

It was a deliberate snub, but nothing in the waiting man's
expression suggested that he was affronted by the action. His
only response at all was the faintest of sardonic smiles as the
older man pointedly turned his back to him.

People did not, as a rule, overlook Mathieu Demetrios. It
wasn't just his height—Mathieu topped six four—or his face,
though more column inches than he cared to recall had been
devoted to his classical profile, which many writers claimed, with
what Mathieu considered a lack of originality, could have graced
a Greek coin. No, what Mathieu Demetrios had was far less quan-
tifiable; he had that rare indefinable quality—he had presence.

When Mathieu spoke people listened. When he walked into
a room heads turned, people watched him—people, that is,
who weren't his father. The same father who was at that
moment delivering a string of terse rapid instructions to the
bespectacled man who had just disembarked with him from the
helicopter.

Mathieu's patrician features gave no hint of his feelings as, silver eyes narrowing, he silently observed the interchange. He held himself with natural grace, his body language relaxed as an updraft from the helicopter blades plastered his thin shirt against his body revealing the clearly defined musculature of his powerful shoulders and chest, the same squall tugging at his dark hair.

The man nodding respectfully as he listened to Andreos Demetrios was the only one of the trio who was made visibly uncomfortable by the tension and simmering hostility vibrating in the disturbed air.

Keeping one wary eye on his employer, he risked the Greek financier's wrath by sending the younger man a tentative smile of sympathy before he hurried past him. It was hard to tell whether the gesture was either noticed or appreciated. Unlike his father, Mathieu Gauthier, or Demetrios as they must learn to call him, kept his cards pretty close to his chest and he definitely was not prone to the uncontrolled outbursts of emotion for which Andreos was famed.

If Mathieu Demetrios had been a different sort of man, the sort who looked as if he would appreciate well-meaning advice, he might have taken the younger man to one side and explained that the older man's mood changes, though abrupt, could sometimes be diverted if you learnt to read the danger signs.

Even simply showing a little reaction to his father's outbursts, excepting Mathieu's usual cynical amusement or boredom, would help.

Opinion amongst employees who had to witness the conflict firsthand was split into two camps when it came to the subject of the uneasy relationship between Andreos and his heir apparent. Personally, his logical accountant's brain could not allow him to believe that anyone would deliberately go out of his way to provoke Andreos Demetrios. No, he joined those who said it was a matter of perception, and someone who had hurled a formula-one car at speed around a track for a living as Mathieu Gauthier had could not be expected to perceive danger the same way normal mortals did.

It was only after the third man had left that the Greek financier faced his son. Andreos had read and reread the comprehensive report he had requested during the flight from the mainland searching for errors.

If there had been flaws in the report he would have found them; there were none. It was clear, concise and drew some unexpected but challenging conclusions, which only seemed obvious once they had been pointed out.

Challenging about summed up his eldest son. A nerve jerked in Andreos's heavy jaw as his eyes, dark and contemptuous, swept upwards from the feet of the younger man to his face.

Only once in all their years of marriage had Andreos ever broken his vows of fidelity to the wife he adored; it was a moment he had regretted and been ashamed of ever since.

But to have the physical proof of that infidelity appear in the form of a sullen, self-contained male adolescent who did not further endear himself to his reluctant father by outperforming his legitimate half-brother in every way both intellectual and athletic had been a nightmare situation.

Ironically it had been his wronged wife, Mia, not Andreos, who had been able to welcome the motherless boy into their home with genuine warmth.

The noise of the helicopter engine faded at the same moment the men's eyes locked—smouldering brown with cool grey.

They stayed that way for a long time.

The older man was the first to lower his gaze. A dull angry colour dusted his cheeks and heavy jaw and he addressed his son. He did not waste time on preliminaries.

'You will cancel your little trip to…' a spasm of irritation crossed Andreos's heavy swarthy features as he trawled his memory '…wherever it was you were going.'

There was no trace of warmth or affection in his curt demand, but Mathieu did not expect it. His father had never made any pretence of affection, but before Alex's death Andreos had not been as overtly hostile as he was now. But then before Alex's death twelve months had been able to go by without father and his elder son meeting.

But Alex's death had changed that.

It had, Mathieu reflected bleakly, changed a lot of things.

'Scotland.'

'Well, you can change your plans.'

It was not a suggestion. But then the head of Demetrios Enterprises, a global giant that had major interests in amongst other things IT and telecommunications—things had moved on since the days the family were merely Greek shipping million-aires—did not make suggestions.

Andreos Demetrios spoke and people jumped.

The recipient of this peremptory decree wasn't showing any signs of jumping. Mathieu wasn't doing anything; in fact he achieved a level of stillness that very few people ever managed. His eyes narrowed but it was impossible to tell what emotion lay concealed beneath the mirrored silver surface and his enigmatic expression was equally uninformative.

Not that Andreos in his turn seemed interested in his son's response. After issuing his pronouncement the older man began to walk briskly up the winding white marble path that led to a massive villa complex that was built into the pink rock above the sparkling turquoise waters of the Aegean.

Andreos had reached the edge of the lush landscaped grounds that surrounded the villa when Mathieu caught up with him.

'I am going to Scotland to stay with a friend; the plan is not flexible.'

The trip was only partly pleasure; Jamie had asked for his help. The banks were making unhappy noises and the fate of the highland estate his friend had inherited from his father the previous year hung in the balance.

Unless I come up with one hell of a business plan they won't extend the loans, Mathieu. That means I won't just be the MacGregor who couldn't hack it as formula-one driver, I'll be the MacGregor who lost the estate that has been in the family for five hundred years.

The older man swung back, his expression antagonistic. 'Were going. Sacha and her mother are arriving tomorrow.'

Mathieu repressed a sigh, reflecting that he really ought to have anticipated this.

'A fact you neglected to mention when you summoned me.'

The older man gave a thin-lipped smile. 'It would be an insult to them if you are not here. There have been links between the Constantine family and ours for generations. My father and—'

'And,' Mathieu inserted, interrupting the history lesson, 'there is no son in this generation to inherit and you hate the idea of the Constantine fortune slipping through your grubby fingers.'

A flash of anger darkened the older man's heavy features. 'And I suppose you would turn your nose up at it?' he grunted.

'I wouldn't be prepared to marry a girl of nineteen to get it.' A girl who had coincidentally been engaged to his younger brother. When he had first heard of the engagement, Mathieu had been inclined to view it with cynicism.

Not so much a marriage as a merger.

But Mathieu's view had changed once he had seen the two youngsters together. They had been very obviously in love.

'Sacha is a mature nineteen and you could do a lot worse. That actress, for instance, who was plastered all over you at that première. What was her name?'

Mathieu, not explaining it had been a stunt staged to gain

publicity for a low-budget movie, dismissed the young starlet with a contemptuous shrug and admitted, 'I have not the faintest idea.'

She had been and still was a total stranger, despite her offer to show him how grateful she was, a proposal he had said thanks, but no, thanks to.

His taste had never run to that sort of gratitude. The formula-one racing circuit attracted groupies like a magnet. Women who in his opinion represented everything that was bad about today's depressing shallow, celebrity-obsessed society.

Mathieu had frequently been tempted to say to them, Go away, get a life, get some self-respect, but he hadn't—any attention at all they took as encouragement. So he had gained a reputation for being aloof and unapproachable. He had changed careers but the reputation persisted. It was on occasion useful.

'I read the wedding plans were at an advanced stage.'

Mathieu angled a dark brow at the sarcasm in his father's voice and retorted lightly, 'I should review the sort of newspapers you read if I were you, Andreos.'

'You are not me.'

'Nor even a paler version.' He knew he took after his mother; he wondered sometimes if looking at him reminded his father of the young woman he had used and discarded.

'So there is no one—you are not in love?'

Mathieu was not in love or actively seeking it. On the contrary, if he saw it coming he had every intention of running or at least walking swiftly in the opposite direction.

What was the all-consuming attraction of love anyway? A form of temporary insanity that made your happiness reliant on someone else's smile?

The allure baffled him.

And anyway, the people he loved had a habit of dying.

No, falling in love was not on Mathieu's list of things to do.

The only person he relied on was himself and that was the way he liked it.

'I fail to see what business that is of yours, regardless of which I can think of few worse fates than to be married to a teenager, even a mature teenager.'

Andreos's face darkened with displeasure. 'I am not telling you to marry the girl.'

'But you wouldn't exactly be displeased if I did either, and in the meantime you will take every opportunity to throw us together. You are embarrassingly transparent.'

Andreos looked at him, his face dark with frustration. 'The girl is Vasilis's only child, his heir. Her husband would—'

Mathieu lifted a hand to still the flow. 'I hardly need it spelt out; you are empire-building.' His lips thinned in distaste. 'Does the girl have any say in this?'

'Do not look down your nose at me,' Andreos barked. 'And do not pretend you could not make this girl love you if you chose to do so. I have seen you with women.'

'She is not a woman; she is a child.'

'She was good enough for your brother.'

'They were in love.'

'You have taken everything else of his—why not his woman?'

The words hung in the air, building the tension between the two men, until Mathieu shrugged. 'I never wanted anything of Alex's.'

Except a share of their father's love, but that desire had only lasted until Mathieu was sixteen. He had been living with his father for a year when an overheard conversation had made him recognise that was never going to happen.

Mathieu's thoughts drifted back to the occasion in question. He had been walking past a half-open door. It was hearing his own name and the anger and frustration in his normally softly spoken stepmother's voice that had made him pause outside…

'The boy tries *so* hard, does everything you ask of him and

more. Could you not just occasionally give him a word of encouragement? Would it kill you, Andreos, to smile at him? All
Mathieu wants is your approval. He's desperate for it. I can see
it in his eyes when he looks at you. It breaks my heart.'

'What you see in his eyes is naked ambition, Mia. Why can
you not see that? The boy is hard, he is confrontational—'

'You say you wish that Alex would stand up to you more.'

'That is not the same thing. Mathieu doesn't need love and
kisses; he needs a strong hand.'

'Not one raised in anger, I have told you that. If you ever—'

'No, of course not. I told you I was sorry about that, Mia. You
know I have never raised a hand to Alex; it's just Mathieu lied
and then, caught out in the lie, refused to apologise.'

'Oh, for pity's sake, Andreos, are you blind? It was Alex who
broke your precious statuette and he was too scared to own up
so Mathieu took the blame.'

'No, no, you're wrong! I don't know what story he has told
you, but—'

'Not Mathieu, he didn't say a word. It was Alex who told me
about the beating and the broken statuette.'

'Oh, goddamn that boy…he made me…the thing is, Mia, when
he looks at me all I can think is that I wish he'd never been born.'

He had heard enough. Mathieu had moved on, in more ways
than one. It had hurt at the time to hear the truth, but it was better
to face bitter reality than live in false hope.

'You will have to pass on my apologies. I'm expected in Scotland.'

A dark mottled colour rose up the older man's neck until his
face was suffused with angry colour. Mathieu watched the effect
of his words with clinical detachment.

The truth of it was he had returned just over a year ago at his
stepmother's request, not his father's. 'Give it a year, Mathieu,'
she begged. 'Your father needs you, though he'd never admit it.'

Mathieu was reluctant to shatter the illusion that he cared what his father needed, especially when she added, 'And when I am gone he will need you even more. The company and the family,' she reflected with a rueful roll of her eyes as she spoke of the Demetrios clan. 'They both need a strong hand at the helm. He was grooming your brother for the role…'

A memory had surfaced in Mathieu's head—Alexander sliding his small hand in his and saying earnestly, 'I want to be just like you when I am older, Mathieu, even if it means Father doesn't like me.'

'Alex would have done it well,' Mathieu lied.

Mia smiled and shook her head. 'I appreciate your loyalty, but we both know that isn't true. Alex hated business. He tried, of course, to please his father, but…' She shrugged. 'One day Andreos would have had to accept that Alex would never take his place, but sadly for us all that day never came.'

As Mathieu moved to enfold her in a comforting embrace, hiding his shock at the fragility of her birdlike frame, she grasped his hand tight and said fiercely, 'Promise me, Mathieu, to help him even if he doesn't want your help.'

So Mathieu had promised, and he had stayed after his promise to her had been fulfilled, not out of a sense of duty, but because against all the odds he was enjoying what he was doing.

'You ingrate, you will do as I say or…or…' Andreos raised his clenched fists from his sides and glared at the younger man with every appearance of loathing.

Mathieu, his calmness increasing in direct proportion to his father's furious incoherence, raised a satirical brow. 'You will disinherit me?' he suggested.

'And do not think I won't.'

'That is your decision.'

'You expect me to believe you don't care?' Andreos let out a loud bellow of scornful laughter and shook his head. 'That you don't care about losing an empire worth billions?'

'I don't ask you to believe anything,' Mathieu responded calmly. 'Your empire is yours to give to whom you wish. I know you wanted to give it to Alex—'

'Don't you dare say his name. He was worth ten of you.'

Mathieu continued seamlessly in the same even voice as though there had been no interruption. 'That is no longer possible. Alex is dead.' An image of his half-brother's smiling face flashed into his head and for a moment his sense of loss was so acute that he could not speak.

Alex, the indulged and adored only son, could have, should have, resented the bastard older brother who had suddenly appeared like a cuckoo in the gold-lined nest. But he had not. Alex's disposition had been as sunny and generous as his smile.

'I am the only son you have left,' he said bleakly. 'You wish to mould me into someone you think is fit to carry on your line.' Mathieu's smile revealed his total lack of regard for the illustrious family name he had inherited in his mid-teens. He had deliberately chosen to use his mother's name when he began his racing career to distance himself from that name.

'Well, I think we owe one another some honesty. I am not interested in your name, your line…your empire. I have a name of my own, and I am not some malleable child, Father. I was moulded, for better or worse, into what I am today a long time ago.'

The ruddy colour on the older man's cheeks deepened to an alarming purple. 'It is not my fault I did not know you existed…your mother…I brought you into my home after her death.'

Like a surgical knife Mathieu's deep, clear voice cut across the older man's blustering protest. 'Her name was Felicite, and you will not speak of my mother. You lost that right years ago.'

The older man's jaw dropped. He was not accustomed to being on the receiving end of commands. Nor was he used to seeing the glow of passion in the eyes of the son he had not known existed until he was fifteen years old.

'I gave you everything…'

Except love. 'I am not the son you want.' Mathieu gave a philosophical shrug. 'And you are not the father I would have chosen. But the fact is,' he continued calmly, 'I am the only son you have.'

The older Greek flinched as though struck and Mathieu added in a softer voice, 'We both wish it otherwise.'

Anger flared in the older man's eyes. 'Wish it otherwise?' he echoed, his lips twisted in a scornful grimace. 'Your brother being killed as he was left you the sole heir…yes, your tears were most apparent at the time,' he observed bitterly.

This was a subject they had tiptoed along the edge of many times and this time, like the others, it was Mathieu who drew back, though emotion surfaced and flared for a moment like silver fire in his heavy-lidded eyes before he responded with a moderate, 'We both wish it otherwise but this is the situation we find ourselves in. I suggest we both learn to live with it.'

'How dare you speak to me this way?'

Mathieu had learnt the hard way that showing emotion gave people the upper hand, but for once his iron control slipped and his emotions spilled out. 'You mean not like the puppet dancing to your tune?'

Andreos visibly recoiled from the blaze of fury written in every line of his son's patrician features. 'I have given you everything.'

'And everything you gave was given out of a sense of reluctant duty. You tolerate me only because it was Mia's dying wish. Has it not occurred to you…Father, that my actions are similarly constrained?'

It was clear from the older man's expression that he had not.

'She was always kind to me even though my very existence must have caused her pain.' He sucked in air through his flared nostrils and fought to regain his control. 'And it is only in respect of her wishes that I did not leave after her death.'

Both men were silent as they simultaneously recalled the last painful months of her life, which Mia had endured with cheerful dignity that had humbled those who had been lucky enough to be around her.

'As far as I am concerned the only thing you ever had going for you was the fact that a woman like that could love you. She must have seen something in you that I have not.'

'I will be leaving for Scotland tomorrow. You must do as you wish, Father…'

CHAPTER TWO

HER family's and friends' opinions were unanimous; Rose had lost her mind. Only a total lunatic, they reasoned, would leave a comfortable life in the capital where she had friends, family and a stimulating job she enjoyed to bury herself miles away from anything that remotely resembled civilisation, not to mention any place that served a halfway decent coffee.

Her twin sister had been particularly vocal in her opposition. In fact, initially Rebecca had been unable to believe her twin was serious about the move. Then, faced with the black-and-white reality of her sister's letter of resignation, she had stopped being amused and adopted a firm manner.

'This is a massive overreaction, Rose. You fell in love with your boss.' She lifted her slender shoulders in a so-what shrug. 'Who hasn't?'

Rose winced at the casual reference to Steven Latimer, protesting, 'Becky!' as her twin, who did dramatic with style, ripped up the letter and held out her hands as though her action settled the matter.

And Rose could see why she might think so. It was a classic case of someone believing their own press. Since they were children, people had been calling the more flamboyant Rebecca the dominant twin. It was probably only Rebecca's husband, Nick, who recognised the true dynamics of the twins' relationship.

'Sure, Rose gives in to Becky, but haven't you noticed it's only on the little things?' the shrewd New Yorker had observed. 'Things that don't actually matter. When it comes to something important, that she cares about, Rose could give a mule lessons in stubborn, though you don't realise it because she says no with such a sweet smile.' He had flashed his sister-in-law one of his own laconic smiles and winked.

At that moment—Rebecca had dragged him along to convince Rose of the error of her ways—he earned himself a black look by observing when appealed to for support by his wife that it was pretty much up to Rose what she did.

Rose would have been more grateful if he hadn't added, for the record, that, yes, he did think that Steven Latimer was a lower form of human life.

Rose glared at her brother-in-law and picked up a piece of torn paper from the floor. 'All I have to do is print out another copy, Becky.'

'Is this about Latimer, Rosie?' Nick interrupted. 'Are you leaving because he is putting pressure on you? Because you don't have to put up with it, honey. Nowadays employers take a very dim view of sexual harassment.'

Rose shook her head firmly. 'Steven isn't like that, Nick. He's a very honourable man.'

'I wonder if your marvellous Steven would be quite so honourable if his wife wasn't the boss's daughter?'

'Becky, that's not fair.'

'Was it fair of him to tell you he was desperately in love with you?'

'It wasn't something he planned.'

'In my opinion Steven Latimer plans everything. The man hasn't a spontaneous bone in his body—which I admit isn't bad.

He's also the most calculating person I've ever met…and I've met a few.'

'Steven might come over as a little ambitious sometimes.'

Her twin didn't mince her words. 'He'd sell his grandmother for a seat on the board.'

'He went to Eton with a guy I know.'

Rose turned her head at the interruption. 'Eton?' Anyone else she might have accused of lying, but her brother-in-law was as straight as they came. 'No, your friend must be mistaken. Steven went to an inner-city state school.'

'Is that what he told you?' Rebecca snorted, bending to pick up the shredded paper from the rug. Looking at her twin, she began to thread it between the perfectly manicured fingers of her right hand.

'Why would he lie?'

'Because he isn't a nice man. The man you fell in love with only exists in your head, Rose,' Rebecca said, tapping the side of her own blonde head with its new gamine crop. 'He's a self-serving bastard and you're such a hopeless romantic.' She sighed. 'You know, I think you prefer a tragic unrequited love because it's safer than the real thing—you're a coward, Rose!'

Rose shook her head. This had been a hard decision to make but she knew it was the right one, no matter how Rebecca tried to twist things.

'I've always wanted to go to the Scottish Highlands,' she reminded her sister.

'*Go*, not *live*,' Rebecca exploded, running a frustrated hand over the hair. 'I can't believe you're actually serious.'

'I just need a break. This man needs his book collection catalogued. I only fell into the marketing job. I originally trained as a librarian—'

Rebecca gave an impatient snort. 'Don't try and pretend this is about musty old books, because we both know it isn't. You're running away; it's a big mistake. For God's sake, it's not like anything happened…' She stopped and gave her sister a sharp look. 'Is it…?'

'He's married.'

Rose's outraged expression had seemed to amuse her sister. 'It has been known, Rose, for married people to have affairs,' she taunted gently. 'You do know you're something of a rarity in the twenty-first century, don't you?'

Rose had been stung by her sister's affectionate mockery. 'Because I won't sleep with a married man?'

'No, actually that doesn't make you totally unique—even with my colourful history I might have a few qualms about that.'

Despite the levity in her sister's tone Rose knew that she had strayed on sensitive ground. Rebecca could be pretty touchy about what she liked to call her 'summer to forget'. It was a subject that by tacit agreement neither referred to.

'Sorry, I didn't mean that you're…'

'That I'm an abandoned hussy?' Rebecca suggested with a twinkle. 'Relax, Rosie, Nick knows all about my chequered history, don't you, darling?'

Her tall husband stretched laconically and offered her a lopsided grin with his nod of wry agreement. 'A paragraph,' he announced with a hint of complacence. 'My past would fill several volumes.'

Behind his teasing there was profound love and commitment that brought an emotional lump to Rose's throat. Her sister had found the man of her dreams too. Why couldn't Rebecca recognise that the only difference between them was that Nick had been available?

Was everything in life merely down to timing?

'The Scottish Highlands! You know I can't believe you're actually serious about this. You're mad, totally insane!'

* * *

Rose had defended her sanity but as a second sickening splintering sound issued from under her feet and the crack in the ice spread rapidly she was forced to consider the very real possibility Rebecca might have had a point.

Mathieu had risen early, long before anyone else in the house was awake. He enjoyed solitude, time to recharge his batteries and gather his thoughts without the distractions of phones and faxes, but moments like this one had become increasingly rare over the past months.

Not that he was complaining. Against all the odds he found he loved what he was doing, and he was learning all the time.

It was a steep learning curve, but he relished the challenge and knew that even if it ultimately proved impossible for him to work with Andreos he would take these new skills with him when he left.

And, on a less charitable note, in the meantime he had the pleasure of knowing Andreos, who had never disguised the fact that he didn't think his bastard son had what it took, was struggling to hide his frustration when he hadn't fallen flat on his face.

Yet, he corrected himself with a mocking grin. You know what they say about pride and falls, Mathieu.

Someone had recently asked if he hadn't found the restrictions of riding a desk after the freedom of the racing circuit crushing. They had not understood why he had laughed, but like many they hadn't had the faintest idea of the sort of physical and mental discipline both required to compete at the level he had.

They saw the glamour but not the struggle to remain at the peak in a competitive environment.

He slipped his rucksack from one shoulder to the other and rotated his neck to ease the tension that still remained in his shoulders. The chair in Jamie's study was not designed with human posture in mind and he had worked long into the night, poring over the accounts, a flattering description for the collection of papers and illegible scribbles in the ledgers that Jamie had supplied him with.

They did not make for happy reading. Far from exaggerating the situation as he had suspected, Jamie had if anything underplayed the seriousness of his position.

It had been dawn when he had tackled the climb so, with any luck—his glance skimmed his watch—yes, he ought to make it back in time for breakfast and to place a few calls.

The post-climb general sense of well-being combined with the dregs of the adrenaline rush were still circulating in his blood as he made his way to the spot where he had parked the Land Rover. He glanced once more at the metal-banded watch on his wrist and quickened his pace already planning his strategy, though he suspected it would come down in the end to plan B…it was always good to have a plan B.

He was about half a mile from the Land Rover when movement in the periphery of his vision made him turn his head in time to see a red-hatted figure moving below. Someone else who enjoyed the morning, he thought, moving off again. He had reached a steep slope of scree directly above the loch when some instinct made him stop and seek out the distant figure.

'Nobody is that stupid…' He held his breath for a moment as the figure stepped out onto what he knew to be paper-thin ice.

He hit the ground running. He didn't waste his breath shouting, knowing the person below would never hear him above the wind that whistled through the valley.

He was fifty yards away when the stillness was rent first by a loud cracking sound, then a woman's scream. A final sprint brought him to the edge of the ice in seconds.

A girlfriend had once accused him of having too little imagination to be sensibly scared of anything, but she was wrong.

He just saw little benefit under the circumstances of wasting time to linger on the lurid details of death by drowning in cold, icy water. Instead as he pulled off his light padded outer jacket he scanned the ice estimating his chances.

His actions were swift but not hurried, his brain working out all the factors. It was his ability to think clearly in situations like this that had made him a successful racing driver. That combined with lightning reflexes, nerves of steel and, according to some of his competitors, more than his fair share of ruthless cunning.

Mathieu didn't think of it in those terms, but he did know that his thought processes were at their sharpest when the stakes were high. Right now they were as high as they got—a life.

The situation did not allow for further preliminary evaluation so, sucking in a breath, he tucked his ice axe into the belt of his trousers and lay down flat on his belly to distribute his weight as evenly as possible on the thin ice. Then Mathieu began to crawl as quickly as possible towards the hole that stood like a gaping black wound in the silvered surface of the frozen water.

He saw the top of a red hat surface, heard the stifled yell and pushed himself faster regardless of the warning creaks of the fragile ice underneath him. He reached the edge of the gash in the ice in time to see the white hand vanish beneath the water.

He hauled himself to the edge of the hole and thrust his ice axe into the water. Relief flooded through him as it snagged on something. His face set in lines of grim determination, the sinews in his neck pulling taut, he began to pull.

Even as she opened her mouth to scream for help Rose was very aware that the chance of anyone being around to hear her was, at the most optimistic, remote.

The second scream of visceral fear remained locked in her throat as the ice beneath her feet opened up and she fell. She had never imagined that cold could be this extreme. It enveloped her, freezing the air in her lungs, its icy tentacles infiltrating every cell of her body. After the first paralysing shock she began to struggle, kicking out wildly in panic as she fought her way to the surface.

Rose was a good swimmer but the extremely low temperature of the water sapped her strength within minutes.

'Help me,' she screamed as she felt herself sliding beneath the surface. Cocooned in the icy darkness, aware only of the heavy thud of her own heartbeat as it continued to pump the oxygen-starved blood around her body, she refused to accept the inevitable.

I am not going to drown.

But she was.

Still Rose refused to accept the reality of it. Clinging stubbornly to the last flicker of hope, she kicked weakly for the surface even though she knew she wasn't going to make it.

Only she did. Just as she had used up the last reserves of strength and her lungs were burning she felt something snag in her coat, then she was being dragged upwards.

Holding the bedraggled girl's head above the icy water, Mathieu could just about make out her muffled words. The damsel in distress had reached the inevitable 'what happened?' phase. He didn't waste his breath replying, though if she asked, 'Who am I?' he would have a harder time restraining himself. People called him a risk-taker, but any risks he took were of the clear-headed, calculated variety. If this girl wasn't suicidal to pull a stunt like this she was…she had to be one of the most criminally stupid women ever to draw breath!

'It is important to stay calm and not struggle,' Rose heard the deep voice above her say.

Struggle. Was he joking? At the moment breathing required all her energy and each raw breath she dragged in through blue lips hurt.

'When I pull you clear…'

Now that sounded like a good idea. It was also good that he

hadn't suggested she do this herself as her limbs were not responding to any requests; she couldn't even feel them.

'I'm just going to—'

'Wait!' Rose protested, lifting her head in panic as she felt herself pushed briefly clear of the relative security of the ice. 'N-no…don't.'

Her warning went unheeded.

'I'm just going to put this rope around you. It's all right, just be still.'

Rose felt the rope her rescuer had just looped under her arms tighten.

'That's it, you're perfectly safe now.' Mathieu said this with a confidence he did not feel.

He shot a glance over his shoulder towards the shore and safety. As he had crawled out there had been several moments when the ice underneath him had threatened to give way.

She could feel the heat of her rescuer's breath on her icy cheek as he bent closer. Her nostrils flared in response to the clean male scent of his body overlaid with a light citrusy scent. He represented safety but she really felt she ought to warn him that pulling her out of the water might not be so easy.

'S…s…seven to ten p…pounds…' Shut up, Rose, you sound unbalanced.

'Seven…?'

'Doesn't matter.' Still, it would be kind of ironic in a dark sort of way if the amount of excess the magazines said she needed to shed if she wanted any shot at happiness in this world was the amount that tipped the balance.

What if her determination not to end up a victim to the prevailing fashion for unrealistically thin women ended up being the reason for her demise?

She laughed and above her a man's voice advised her once more to stay calm. She opened her mouth to tell him she wasn't the type to have hysterics when the ice gave another loud warning creak and she changed her mind.

Perhaps she was the type to have hysterics? Under these circumstances perhaps everyone was the type. Then she remembered the sound of her rescuer's deep, calm voice, and thought maybe he was the exception, which was lucky for her.

The situation was better than he had dared hope—there were no new major cracks visible. However, only an insane optimist would expect this situation to last for long. The window of opportunity for this rescue was small.

He took a deep breath and, totally focused on the task ahead, smiled slightly. He knew what he had to do; there were no fuzzy lines, no protocol or politics to consider. It was a simple matter of survival; these were factors he felt comfortable working with.

Mathieu braced his knees on the thin ice beside the woman who had given a scared whimper. 'Let's do this.' She had reason to be scared. He probably ought to be, but the adrenaline pumping in his bloodstream sharpened his reactions and dulled his caution.

Do what? Rose thought.

'Are you ready?'

Roused by the sheer inanity of this comment, Rose lifted her head. 'No, I'm not ready!' The indignation died from her face as her full lower lip quivered. 'I don't want to die…' Her voice trailed away as her eyes connected with those of her rescuer.

They were the palest grey, almost silver, slanted upwards in the corners, the heavy lids fringed by long, curling, sooty lashes. Even this close to descending into gibbering fear she registered in some portion of her brain that they were the most excruciatingly beautiful eyes she had ever seen in her life.

The sort of eyes that a doctor might prescribe for someone who had just had a near-death experience to look into: beautiful. The rest of his face was a blur as she concentrated on those beautiful eyes, but she had the impression of sharp angles and intriguing hollows.

There was a fractional pause before he responded calmly and for a moment she imagined she saw something flicker in the silvered enigmatic depths…*recognition*…? Which made no sense, because if she had ever met a man with those eyes she would not have forgotten!

'Nobody is going to die. I'm going to lift you out of the water.'

He made it sound so easy. She nodded, thinking again of that seven to ten pounds. 'What do you want me to—? Oh!' The breath huffed out of her chest in a noisy gasp as she landed face down on the ice. She lay there and felt the tears leak from her eyes. 'I'm not going to drown.'

'Not if you do exactly what I say,' came the not exactly comforting response. 'Are you injured? Do you have pain?'

She lifted her head, wiping the water-darkened strands of hair from her cheek…the shore seemed an awful long way away. She shook her head. 'Just cold and tired. If I could just rest for a minute…'

A hand under her chin jerked her head up. 'Open your eyes. Now!'

She obeyed the imperative command and saw the man with the beautiful eyes was totally unmoved by the tears that welled up in her own eyes. She blinked; she wasn't after a sympathy vote.

As her misty vision cleared she registered properly several more details of her rescuer's appearance beyond his spectacular eyes. The hair that waved smoothly back from a broad brow and fell silky straight to his collar—had he been wearing one—was dark. The sable shade echoed in his dark winged eyebrows was complemented by a clear olive-toned complexion.

His patrician face was long with high, razor-sharp cheekbones and an angular jaw that was lightly dusted with a dark shadow of stubble. His nose was strong and aquiline and his mouth wide and mobile. Rose found the overtly sensual outline of his lips almost cruel.

He was the most incredibly good-looking male she had ever seen or even imagined and yet when she looked at him she found herself almost repelled by his male beauty. Well, what other emotion could be responsible for the uncomfortable, lurching, shivery sensation in her belly when she looked at his saturnine face?

'You will not fall asleep.'

Rose wanted to ask if he really thought she was that stupid. But she didn't have the energy and, besides, he probably did think just that. Instead she just nodded and asked, 'What do I do?'

'Keep flat, move slowly.'

'I'll try.'

'Trying is not good enough if you don't want to kill us both. I will be behind you, but it is most important that we distribute our weight evenly, stay low and flat…' he made a sweeping horizontal motion with one hand to indicate how he wanted her to move '…commando-style.'

'Commando?' Rose repeated, wondering if he did something along those lines for real.

Her glance skimmed the muscle-packed length of him. He had that lean, hard look that made it easy to imagine him being part of some élite group trained for covert operations. And then there was the air of authority. Not many people could give, let alone maintain, that kind of authority when lying belly down on thin ice!

'You understand?'

She nodded. 'But the rope…is it such a good idea…?' She looked from the rope looped around her waist and followed it to his washboard-flat middle. 'If anything goes wrong we are tied together.' She didn't want to be responsible for pulling this good Samaritan into the icy water.

'Then we shall just have to make very sure that nothing goes wrong, won't we?' he inserted with the impatient air of someone not used to having his instructions questioned. 'You are ready?'

She nodded, thinking there were some things a person was never ready for, but he had made it pretty clear she had very little choice.

The progress they made seemed torturously slow, though she knew it couldn't have taken as long as it felt. Each time she felt she could go no further because her legs were shaking or she just couldn't feel them her rescuer was there, encouraging her, though his encouragement at times bordered on coercion.

CHAPTER THREE

FINALLY on solid land, Rose simply lay there for several moments, too euphoric at being safe to even register the cold that every flutter of wind was driving deeper into her bones. Then, pulling her shaking knees up to her chest, she heaved herself into a sitting position, hugging her arms around her body.

The dark stranger was beside her. He had hunkered down to her level and was casually balancing on his heels with the inbred grace of a natural athlete.

'Thank you so much; you saved my life.'

She found it slightly off-putting that there was not a flicker of expression in the spooky silver-grey eyes trained on her face.

'I'm Rose, by the way, Mr…?'

Mathieu looked into the incredible amber eyes brimming with gratitude and innocent as a kitten, which could not be more different from the reckless, sexual challenge he recalled last seeing in those same eyes. If she intended to pretend they did not know one another it was nothing to him. He supposed it was *just* possible that she didn't—his upper lip curled in fastidious contempt—she had been very drunk that night.

The win had clinched him the champion's medal for the fourth year running. So for that reason alone the evening of the gala reception at the embassy would have lingered on in his memory, even if he hadn't returned to his hotel room later that night to find a naked woman in his bed.

A woman who had smooth skin like cream, long hair the colour of pale caramel and golden eyes.

The golden eyes that were looking at him now.

'Can you walk?'

She blinked at the abruptness of his question and the smile faded from her face. She was philosophical about the hostility in his manner. His life had just been put at risk because of her. He was bound not to look too kindly on the person responsible for his close encounter, although the level of cold disdain in his body language did seem excessive. He was looking at her as though she were something offensive on his shoe!

She attempted to struggle clumsily to her feet. 'Of course.'

Mathieu, who had realised the moment he had formed the question that she could probably barely feel her limbs, never mind walk, ignored her optimistic assertion and bent to scoop her up. As he gathered her to him he was aware first of softness, then, before he had time to wonder at the heat that exploded inside him—cold, icy cold.

A glance revealed her skin had an unhealthy bluish tinge, which was hardly surprising considering what she had been through. He was well aware of the danger of hypothermia. It was imperative that she warmed up quickly.

'I…what are you doing?' Rose stuttered as she found herself slung unceremoniously over his shoulder.

'Preventing you getting hypothermia. The Land Rover's parked just up on the track,' he explained, mentally assessing the time it would take him to reach it.

He didn't say anything. Not another word until they reached the vehicle, which did not surprise her. What man could speak with an overweight—and that was dry—blonde over his shoulder? What did surprise her was that he could keep up a brisk running pace the entire way and still not be breathing very hard.

Pulling open the door, Mathieu dumped his shaking burden in the back seat before going around to the driver's side and switching on the engine, sliding the thermostat on the heater to full.

'Get the wet things off.' He barely glanced in her direction before leaving the front of the Land Rover.

He returned a moment later carrying a metallic survival blanket and a heavy cable-knitted sweater, which he flung in the seat beside her. His dark brows drew into a straight line as he assessed her progress.

'Did you not hear me? I said take those things off,' he said, sliding into the driver's seat and turning around.

Heater on full, the cab was hot, but Rose was still shaking. She actually couldn't imagine ever stopping, ever being warm again. 'Sorry. My fingers,' she said, holding out the slim, pale tapering items under discussion apologetically; like the rest of her they were shaking. 'I can't f-feel them.'

His dark eyes slid from her face to her fingers. There was a tiny pause before he heaved a sigh that suggested exasperation. 'Then I suppose I'll have to do it for you.'

'Do what?' The dumb routine was a self-defence mechanism, because she knew if she let herself consider in any serious way what having this man remove her clothes, even in a totally clinical, I'm-saving-your-life sort of way, might feel like, she might do or say something terminally embarrassing.

There was a blast of cold air in response to her question, then another as the passenger door opened and he slid in beside her so close that their thighs touched and slammed the door shut.

The thigh beside her own had all the give of a steel bar. He was an extremely tall, athletically built man and pretty much all of him looked equally hard. He was the sort of man who could make an auditorium seem small!

This was not an auditorium, it was a hot, steamy tin box on wheels, and it wasn't just his physical presence that made it uncomfortable to share the enclosed space with him, it was the raw sensual energy that cloaked him like a second skin. Though she couldn't help noticing that his first skin was pretty special.

Embarrassed by the direction of her thoughts, she flicked a sideways glance at his classical profile, her nostrils quivering as she tried not to inhale the subtle male scent of his body. His presence made it impossible to concentrate on anything else but…well, anything but him!

He was totally overpowering and not at all, she reflected, trying to co-ordinate her actions, a comfortable man to be around. When their glances connected, his slightly impatient, she looked away biting her lip because she knew she was acting like some gauche schoolgirl.

For God's sake, Rose, anyone would think from the way you're acting that the man is trying to seduce you.

She swallowed and lifted her head determined to match his pragmatic manner as he shifted in his seat so that they were facing one another.

She suddenly laughed.

One dark brow lifted. 'What is so funny?'

She shook her head. 'Nothing.' It was hardly the right moment to inform him that she'd just realised this was the first time she'd been in the back seat of a car with a man.

Rebecca would say her education had been sadly neglected. Rebecca would probably have a point. Some people were simply not born with the reckless, exciting gene and she was one of them. Neither was she particularly highly sexed.

This man probably knew his way around the back seat of a car, she mused, studying his lean, autocratic face through the shield of her lashes, though he had probably moved on from the nursery slopes of fumbling long ago. Nowadays she doubted her imagination stretched to cover the things he could find his way around.

It was some comfort that he definitely didn't seem as if he wanted to do any of those things with her. She stared at his sinfully sexy mouth. Of course, she didn't want him to leap on her or anything, but she wouldn't mind knowing just once what it would feel like to be the sort of woman who made a man's mind turn to such things.

She could always ask Rebecca, who was such a woman, or maybe lose half a stone...? His terse voice broke into her rambling thoughts.

'Lift up your arms.'

Rose would have broken contact with those disturbing eyes if she could have but they exerted a strange, almost hypnotic hold.

'Look, this really won't be necessary.' She was dismayed to hear her voice emerge as a breathy whisper without a trace of the amused competence she had intended to inject into it. 'I'll change when I get home.'

To her consternation, instead of taking the opportunity to rid himself of her, his body language having made perfectly clear that was what he wanted, he sketched a cynical smile that lifted the corners of his wide mobile mouth.

'Don't worry, *yineka mou,* I'm quite willing to take it as read that you're incredibly modest.'

Rose was bewildered both by the smile and the distinct undercurrent of scorn in his voice. But the drawled endearment explained the fascinating but faint foreign inflection in his voice she would have puzzled over later when reliving the encounter.

He was Greek, and rude.

Her smile was warmer than it might have been because the latter observation made her feel pretty much an ungrateful wretch—if it hadn't been for this rude Greek she would most likely now be in a watery grave.

The acknowledgement sent a shiver, stronger than the others that intermittently overcame her, down the length of her spine. She looked at his mouth—it was frankly hard not to—and smiled without as much conviction this time because somehow she found his mouth deeply disturbing, and said, 'You're Greek?'

'Half Greek, half French…did you not read my bio?'

'Your bio…?' she parroted, no longer even trying to follow him.

She closed her eyes and leaned back with a weary sigh. Even though she was no longer looking at him she was still very aware of his presence. Considering she had only studied his features briefly, she appeared to have memorised every detail of his extraordinary face. Even with her eyes closed every strong angle and plane was etched into her brain.

'Most do,' he observed drily.

And having read all the stuff on the websites, and the reams of nonsense that were printed about him, these women thought they knew him.

He had never fathomed why these women were so drawn to celebrity; something, he reasoned, had to be missing in their own lives that they spent so much of their time fantasising about a total stranger.

'Sorry, I don't read as much as I'd like to. If you could just drop me off…' Her voice trailed off.

Curses sounded like curses in any language and presumably the ones that fell fluently from his lips would have made a less unrestrained Greek blush.

He dragged a hand through his dark hair and regarded her closed eyes with exasperation tinged by concern. 'You cannot fall asleep!'

'Sorry…no, of course.' Her blue-veined eyelids lifted as she gave her head a little shake. 'I'm really grateful, you know,' she told him as she tucked her hands under her legs. The circulation was returning to her fingers, and they were throbbing painfully.

'I think you saved my life,' she said, rocking forward as the throbbing intensified.

'What you did was criminally stupid.'

Rose bit her lip, but she supposed that under the circumstances he had earned the right to speak to her as though she were some not too bright child.

'I'd ask what you were thinking of, but clearly you weren't thinking.'

'There was a fox…' She could only assume that when the ice had cracked it had escaped, or maybe it had never even been stuck…?

'I saw no fox.' He dismissed the animal in question with a regal wave of his hand. Clearly he hadn't seen it, so it couldn't have been there—not a man who spent a lot of time agonising over self-doubt.

'Which doesn't mean it wasn't there,' she pointed out.

'I saw no animal.' Just a woman determined, it seemed, to end her life. Mathieu relived the moment he had seen her vanish beneath the icy water and his simmering anger surged. 'What sort of person would walk out onto paper-thin ice to rescue a *fox*?'

The sort of person who had to switch channels when there was a wildlife programme where the makers did not intervene—and they could have—even though the weak, injured or just unlucky animal was about to meet a slow, lingering or occasionally violent and savage end.

She could have explained this, but she doubted he would be interested. Clearly what he wanted, and given the circumstances deserved, was a grovelling apology along the lines of, 'I'm insane and you're incredible.' Which he was if your taste ran to macho alpha males.

'If this was some sort of stunt to get my attention again…? It worked.'

'Stunt?' she echoed, blinking up at him. 'Again?' she added, her voice lifted in confused enquiry.

'I'm assuming this act is because I hurt your pride?'

'Pride…?' She was too confused to do anything more than echo what he said as she met his laserlike stare warily. The man really did have eyes that looked as though they could see into your skull and read your thoughts, which was disturbing because some of the thoughts that popped into her head when she looked at him were not ones she would have felt comfortable sharing.

Least of all with the person they concerned.

Did he inspire lust in all women he met or was she particularly susceptible? Maybe a person could only suppress their libido for so long before it rebelled?

'When I threw you out,' he prompted. It was a pity she had not displayed a little of this pride when she had offered herself to him.

Her eyes widened. 'Threw me out…?'

'Of my hotel room, my bed…'

Her jaw hit her chest and for a moment she forgot about her throbbing fingers. 'Why would I be in your room or…' she swallowed and gulped '…bed? I don't even know you.'

'Look, I'm willing to humour you and pretend if that is what you wish—we've never met before, OK.' The scornful smile that twisted his lips vanished as he added, 'But I'm not willing to let you die of hypothermia, not after all the effort to get you out of the loch.'

Rose swallowed. He really did have the hardest eyes she had ever seen. 'I think you must have mistaken me for someone else.' She struggled not to show her concern.

Had she just got into a car with a dangerous lunatic? It was starting to seem like a strong possibility.

A hissing sound of exasperation escaped his white, clenched teeth. 'Look, if you want to pretend you did not bribe your way into my hotel room, that is fine by me, and I'm not suggesting for a moment that you don't do this gushing, sweet, innocent act very well,' he conceded nastily. 'But it might be more productive if you save it for a man who hasn't seen you naked.'

'What? Naked?' Her hands came up in a protective gesture across her breasts. It would take a woman who was either very brave, or very beautiful, to parade naked in front of a man as physically perfect as this man.

And she was not that woman.

'You have never seen me naked.' It didn't matter how many near-death experiences she had, that was something she would not have forgotten.

'Well, if you're going to be pedantic I wasn't counting the stockings and stilettos.'

The visual image in her head that accompanied his husky concession sent the mortified blood rushing to her cold cheeks. 'Look at me.' Her shrill invitation was unnecessary because he already was and not in a way she liked. 'I've never worn stockings in my life, not even hold-ups…' He's accusing you of being a predatory tart and you take the time to tackle the stockings issue—sure, that makes perfect sense, Rose.

'I do not forget a face or a body,' he added, his eyes dropping to the upper slopes of her full creamy breasts. 'Your body has…ripened,' he admitted. 'And the blush is a new addition to your repertoire…it's good.'

'I do not have a repertoire.' The smouldering sexual insolence in his bold stare started a chain reaction that began low in her belly. In a matter of seconds her entire body was involved. If she hadn't been sitting down her legs would have folded under her. She couldn't believe that she had reacted this way to a casually lecherous stare.

'The weight suits you.' The woman in his bed at the hotel had possessed the lean, angular, borderline androgynous build that models aspired to. It had crossed his mind at the time that she would have undoubtedly looked more attractive with her clothes on.

The same could not be said now.

'Look, you've had your joke, but enough is enough,' she said,

even though one look at his expression made it clear he hadn't.
It seemed probable, going on what she had seen of him so far,
that he wouldn't know a joke if he fell over it.

'We've never met, I promise you.'

'I've encountered a lot of groupies but you stood out.'

'Groupie…' Best to treat this all as a joke. Co-operate, keep
him happy and the quicker she'd be back at Dornie House, and
after that she'd never have to see this man again.

She wasn't getting very far with denial so she tried a different tack. 'Sure, I eat men like you before breakfast.' Her mocking
grin slipped as an erotic image flashed into her head.

A man, his face hidden by the curtain of hair of the woman
who sat astride him, lying naked on the tumbled silken bedclothes of a vast bed. His fingers were wound into the bars of a
metal headboard and entwined with those of the woman. Deep
fractured moans were issuing from his throat as the bed creaked
under their combined weight. The woman's hair fell back and…

Rose sucked in a sharp breath. Oxygen starvation, that was
the only explanation she could think of for the lurid erotic fantasy
that had crawled out of her subconscious.

'But you'll be pleased to hear that drowning has had a damp-
ening effect on my libido.'

Mathieu, dragging his eyes from the heaving outline of
her breasts, swallowed. It was a pity he could not say the same
for his own libido. He could only assume it was the adrenaline
that was still circulating in his blood now the danger was
past…though adrenaline caused a flight-or-fight reaction and he
felt no compelling urge to do either.

'It's put me right off my daily diet of reluctant men. So you're
quite safe.'

He gave a triumphant smile. 'So you admit that you are that
woman.'

She clamped her lips together. 'No, I damned well don't.'

'There's no need to yell. Your secret is safe with me. Relax.'

Was he mad? 'Would you relax if someone suggested you were their rejected one-night stand?'

'What do you object to—the one-night-stand tag or the rejection? And for the record I do not do one-night stands.'

She saw the spark of anger in his eyes and thought, Great, it's all right for him to take offence. 'That's what I'm saying, neither do I. I don't…' She stopped, remaining immobile as he bent forward and unzipped her jacket.

He lifted his head and their eyes connected. Without a word he slid it off her shoulders.

'Lift up your arms.'

Without thinking Rose obeyed his command this time and her sodden sweater was peeled away. Brushing a heavy hank of water-darkened caramel-blonde hair from her eyes, she looked at the sweater as it fell onto the floor of the Land Rover. The tee shirt she had worn underneath had come away with it.

She was sitting there stripped to the waist in nothing but what felt like acres of bare goose-pimpled flesh and her pink lace bra that had definitely seen better days. She saw his eyes drop and like a tide the hot, mortified colour washed over her skin.

Mathieu's gaze slid upwards over her body. By the time he reached her heavy breasts encased in a light lacy bra through which the dark circles of her nipples were clearly visible the dull throb of blood in his temples had become a pounding roar.

Every instinct Rose possessed made her want to cover herself but that would be as good as saying she was not comfortable with her own body, that she had something to be ashamed of, whereas it was him, the sleaze, she thought wrathfully, who should feel guilty for ogling.

'I thought you'd seen it all before,' she snapped when the moment of paralysing embarrassment had passed.

His head came up with a jerk. Rose registered the dark

colour scoring the crests of his sculpted cheekbones and then their eyes connected.

His smoky stare sent a fresh quiver of sexual awareness through her body. This had to be about the near-death experience; she didn't react like this to men…not even Steven. And they had worked in close proximity most days.

Very close sometimes, which was part of the reason she had left. But a small part, because she had never feared not being able to control herself. The real reason was she felt guilty, ashamed because she had feelings for a married man.

If she had to work with this man on a daily basis, have his hand brush hers, feel his breath on her neck as he bent over her desk to read a report as Steven had done many times…? Rose shuddered. The horrifying imaginary scenario made her want to crawl out of her skin.

'Don't be embarrassed. The extra padding has gone to all the right places.'

Padding! Rose gritted her teeth. She was comfortable with her weight. She knew she was never going to be a size eight, basically because she would never starve herself and become a gym junkie like Rebecca to achieve it, but there was a line. And he had just crossed it.

She embraced the anger, gritting her teeth, and gave him a steady look. 'You're too kind.'

'No, I'm not. I'm not kind at all.'

Looking into his spooky pale eyes, Rose believed him. She shivered and lowered her gaze.

CHAPTER FOUR

IGNORING him as best she could, Rose pulled the heavy dry sweater over her head. It reached her knees and acted as a screen as, still shaking feverishly, she peeled away her jeans.

Before she had managed to wriggle them down to her ankles he had opened the door and returned to the front seat without a word. He started the engine with a curt instruction for her to belt up.

*Belt up…*he probably, she decided, meant it in both senses of the word, which was no problem for her. The last thing she felt like was making conversation. They'd been driving for a couple of minutes before she realised he couldn't know where she lived.

'I'm staying at Dornie House, that's the last turning after—'

His impatient voice cut across her. 'I'm not taking you there.' His eyes met hers in the rear-view mirror. 'You need to get checked over; there's a cottage hospital in Muir.'

'I don't need to see a doctor.'

'Need or not, you're going to,' came the autocratic retort.

Short of jumping out a moving vehicle, she didn't have much choice but to go along with his plan. The man was obviously a total control freak.

'There's a blanket on the back seat if you don't mind a few dog hairs. It should only take five minutes or so.'

She lasted three. She was wasting her breath, she knew that, but how could she let him go away thinking that she was someone she wasn't? She really wanted to hear him admit he was wrong.

'I've never slept with you, you know.' Or anyone else, though Rebecca's theory on this sad state of affairs was wrong—it wasn't because she was a hopeless romantic who couldn't deal with real emotions. That was the problem. She *wanted* emotions; she didn't want soulless sex.

It was just her luck that the one man she had met whom she could imagine sex not being a cold, mechanical exercise with had already been taken. Her brow wrinkled as she recalled Rebecca's suggestion that it wasn't accidental she had fallen in love with someone who was inaccessible. Then she found herself recalling that one time when Steven had kissed her...it hadn't been what she had expected. She hadn't been carried away by passion; in fact, she had felt oddly removed from the event.

'Only because I threw you out.'

His scornful observation cut like a blade through Rose's rambling reflections.

'Why? What was wrong with me?' Rose closed her eyes and bit her lip... Could I have sounded more like a rejected lover if I tried?

'I do not sleep with drunk groupies,' he announced with disdainful hauteur.

The blood that had returned to her tingling extremities now rushed to her head. 'Now hang on, I know you probably saved my life, but—'

He cut across her with a sardonic, 'Probably?'

'All right, then,' she conceded crossly. 'You saved my life, but that doesn't give you the right to invent stories and virtually call me a tramp.'

'It was not a term I used, but what would *you* call a woman who targets famous men with the purpose of adding another scalp to her belt? An icon of modern female empowerment?'

'Famous?' she echoed, getting seriously angry. 'Am I supposed to know who you are?'

Dark brows elevated to an incredulous angle, he shot her a look of sardonic amusement in the rear-view mirror. 'You are trying to tell me you don't?'

'I have never laid eyes on you before today,' she snapped angrily.

'Fine.' He sighed, sounding like someone who was bored but prepared to go through the motions for a quiet life. 'I am Mathieu Gauthier...'

Of course she knew the name even though she didn't follow formula one. Well, it explained the arrogance—the adulation those drivers got was ludicrous. He had probably started believing his press releases.

'Is that meant to mean something?'

It was obvious from the brief look he slung her over his shoulder that he didn't swallow her pretended ignorance for a second, but to her relief he didn't challenge her lie, but sounded lazily amused as he said, 'If you are a fan of formula one it might.'

'I thought you were Greek. *Gauthier* doesn't sound very Greek to me.'

The lazy smile faded from his face. 'Half Greek. I used my mother's name professionally.'

'So you are actually...?'

'Mathieu Demetrios. Look, you don't need to do this. I'm not going to tell anyone if that's what is worrying you. Maybe your life has moved on and you're ashamed of your past...though in my opinion you'd do better to come clean with whoever is in your life now.' He didn't doubt for a moment there would be somebody; for women who looked as she did there was always somebody.

'Thank you for the advice,' she gritted, thinking it was so not asked for. 'But I'm not ashamed. I have nothing in my past to be ashamed of.' Which makes me one of the most sad twenty-six-year-olds on the planet. 'I don't even know where or when I'm supposed to have tried to…to…seduce you.'

'Monaco.'

'Well, I've never been to Mon—' She stopped. She hadn't, but Rebecca had. She had the postcard to prove it.

Rose closed her eyes, a silent sigh leaving her lips. The woman he was talking about, sneering at, the woman who had tried to seduce him, was none other than her twin.

Rebecca who had been dumped literally at the altar and gone a little crazy. It all fitted, the timing, everything. They were talking about Rebecca's 'summer to forget' when she had by her own admission done a lot of things she would like to forget. It looked as if jumping into the bed of a formula-one champion driver had been one of them.

It was like seeing the last piece of a jigsaw slot horribly into place—she had always hated jigsaws.

Oh, God, Rebecca, how could you? Rose felt guilty for the selfish question the moment it popped into her head. If anyone had had a reason to go slightly off the rails that summer it had been her sister.

Simon with the floppy hair and the sweet smile had been the boy next door quite literally. He and Rebecca had been child-hood sweethearts, dating since they were sixteen and engaged at nineteen.

Rose had been one of six bridesmaids—the wedding had *not* been a low-key affair—in a dress that had made her look almost slim. The sun had shone, the babies had refrained from crying, Rebecca had looked stunning like a dream bride.

The only thing missing had been the groom.

In response to a desperate phone call Rose had jumped in the vicar's Mini and gone to Simon's house. She had found the best man looking stunned in the driveway.

'Is it nerves?' she asked him.

He just looked at her, shook his head and asked for a cigarette. Rose reminded him he didn't smoke and went indoors. When she'd dragged the reason for his no show from the groom she briefly contemplated starting smoking herself.

'You have to tell her, Rose, I can't do it. Tell her I'm sorry and I love her, just not that way.'

'Oh, sure, that will make her feel much better. Shall I tell her before or after that her fiancé has waited until his wedding day to admit he's gay?' Rose wasn't in the mood to feel much empathy for anyone else but her twin that day.

Rose fully anticipated that Rebecca would collapse or lose it totally when she told her about Simon, but her sister was calm, almost surreally so considering the circumstances.

It was Rebecca who had taken control, which was good because their father was almost catatonic and their mother was stressing about the protocol of returning the gifts.

She insisted on telling the guests personally. Rose would never forget the image of her standing there like a serene goddess in her frothy white wedding dress explaining in a few dignified sentences that the wedding would not be going ahead.

Watching her, knowing how much she had to be hurting, broke Rose's heart; she knew that if the roles had been reversed she could never have been as brave.

It was about four days later that it actually hit Rebecca, then there were the tears, the anger…and a few weeks later she announced she had swung a refund on the honeymoon and some of the reception and planned to travel for a few months with the money.

It looked pretty much as if her travels had at some point taken her to Mathieu Gauthier's bedroom.

'It's gone quiet back there. Could it be your amnesia has been cured? Is it all coming back?' he suggested in a silky sneery voice that made Rose fantasise about wiping the superior smirk off his face.

'For your information…' She stopped the words playing in her mind—the tramp in your bed wasn't me, it was my twin sister.

It didn't matter how much she wanted to squeeze an apology out of the awful man. Her loyalty to her twin was more important. It was the very least that Rebecca deserved.

It wasn't as if it mattered one way or the other what Mathieu Demetrios or whatever he called himself these days thought of her.

She drew herself upright and, glaring at the back of his neck, shook her head, closing her mouth firmly on the retort. 'I've never been to Monaco.'

'Then you have a twin out there somewhere.'

Yes, I do, and I could give you her address, though I doubt her husband would be too happy about it. 'If you say so,' she agreed, shivering as she turned her head to look out of the window. 'I don't think the cottage hospital even has a casualty department.'

'It's a hospital. There will be a doctor.' If there wasn't it would have to be Inverness.

'I'm fine and I'm late…' She grabbed the door handle to steady herself as he took a corner clearly under the impression that he was still at the wheel of a formula-one car, not a battered Land Rover.

'We'll let the man who trained for six years decide if you're fine, shall we?'

Rose pursed her lips and didn't say another word. What was the point? He was clearly going to do what he wanted no matter what she said.

It turned out he was right, there was a doctor at the small community hospital—one of the local GPs who said they had done exactly the right thing when she related her story, apologising repeatedly for wasting his time.

When she returned to the waiting area a few minutes later she thought at first that her racing-driver rescuer had left…then just as some of the tension was leaving her spine he peeled himself away from a wall.

'Oh, I didn't see you in the shadow.' The tension was back with a vengeance. She had never met anyone who aroused such feelings of antipathy by doing nothing more than drawing himself up to his full and admittedly impressive height. It was lucky really—if she'd liked him she'd have felt that in some irrational way she was being disloyal to her twin.

'I said I'd wait.' His brows drew together in a straight line when she shivered.

'And I said it was not necessary. I'm quite capable of making my own way back.'

He arched a brow. 'Dressed like that.'

He had a point, she conceded, glancing down. The sweater covered as much as a dress, but it was a bit short and quite drafty. As for the man-sized woollen walking socks he'd dug out of the boot when she'd refused point-blank to allow him to carry her over the gravelled forecourt—well, they weren't exactly ideal footwear for public transport.

There was also the slight problem of her having no money.

She hated to be even more in his debt, but what choice did she have? 'I'm sorry to put you out. I'm sure you have more important things you should be doing.'

'Yes.'

Rose bit her lip. Clearly he was not into making people feel comfortable.

'Sorry,' she said again.

His lips quivered. The word was 'sorry' but the sentiment behind it was clearly 'go to hell'. His eyes slid to her feet encased in an old pair of Jamie's walking socks. To get there he had to move past her legs—they were very fine legs. They were the sort of legs a man could not look at without imagining himself between the soft, smooth thighs.

You passed, the voice in his head reminded him. It sounded disgusted and he could see why.

'What did the doctor say?' He found her more attractive in this weird get-up than he had that night in his hotel room. Did that, he wondered, make him twisted?

'He said what I said all along, I'm fine. He also said I was lucky.' She took a deep breath; not liking the man was no excuse for bad manners and he had risked his life to save her. 'And I am, thanks to you.'

He looked at the hand she had extended to him for a moment, then, just when she thought he was going to ignore it, he reached out and clasped it in his.

Rose's eyes flew wide and a small startled gasp escaped her parted lips before she could prevent it. She grunted something guarded and snatched her hand away. It was difficult to stay in denial about being wildly attracted to someone when you had a reaction like that to a simple handshake. She swallowed as she wondered about the electrical thrill that had shot through her body.

Did he feel it too?

She pushed aside the thought, ran her tongue over her dry lips and, still not looking at him, directed her words to the wall over his left shoulder. 'I really need to get back,' she said, her voice cracking with nerves.

He bowed his dark head slightly in acknowledgement of her request. 'Dornie House, you said…?' His eyes narrowed in concentration as he sketched a mental map of the area. If it was the place he thought he could stop by the estate and reassure Jamie that he hadn't dropped off the face of the earth.

'That's right.'

'The place off the Inverness road?'

'I think so.' She lifted a hand to her head.

As Mathieu watched the intensely weary gesture he was startled to feel his protective instincts stirring. He reminded himself who and what this woman was, but found it hard to re-concile the predatory man-eater of his memory with this ex-hausted and white-faced figure who had just narrowly escaped death…and there hadn't been a single tear.

You had to admire that. Whatever she was, she had guts.

'You walked a long way this morning. Come on.' She had to be tired because she didn't object when he placed a light guiding hand on her arm.

CHAPTER FIVE

'YOUR adrenaline levels are dropping,' Mathieu said, studying Rose's pale face with an expert eye. 'The delayed shock is kicking in,' he explained as he waited for her to swing her legs into the Land Rover before closing the passenger door. 'Are you sure the doctor said you were OK to leave?' he added when he slid into the driver's seat beside her.

You had to wonder about the competence of someone who sent a woman who looked ready to collapse home.

Rose nodded, but did not mention that the medic had only released her on the understanding she had someone to take care of her once she got home.

Home…it was ironic, after she had had such a fight to leave, that she had been suffering dreadfully from homesickness ever since she had arrived.

She knew it would pass, but at that moment she was feeling it particularly acutely. So acutely that she had to clamp her teeth into her lower lip to stop it trembling. The idea of showing that sort of weakness before this man horrified her.

'Have you moved here or are you visiting?'

With anyone else she would have suspected they were making conversation to give her time to compose herself. She lifted a hand to blot the moisture at the corner of one eye and sniffed. 'I'm working. I'm cataloguing Mr Smith's book collection.'

'*You're* cataloguing books?' He doubted she could have given a reply that would have surprised him more.

'Yes, when I'm not seducing men in their hotel rooms I'm a trained librarian.'

'Librarian?' He gave a sudden bark of laughter that brought a militant light to her amber eyes.

'What's so funny?'

He slid her a quick sideways glance. 'Well, you must admit it's not…well, a person doesn't look at you and think…' He turned his head again, the sweep of his eyes this time slow and sensual. Facing the road again, he grinned and shook his head. 'Well, he doesn't think librarian, *ma petite.*'

Why did French sound sexy even when a person was being sarcastic? And he must have been because nobody would call her his little one and be serious. 'You appear to have a very stereotypical image of a librarian, Mr Demetrios.' Did he make love in that language too?

Well, you're not going to find out, Rose, she told herself sternly. He threw Rebecca out of his bed and she's the size eight sexy one.

Was Rebecca right when she claimed being sexy was a state of mind? If she had meant thinking about sex, then that might well make me the sexiest person on the planet just now, Rose thought, embarrassed by her sudden preoccupation with the subject.

Meeting this man was going to put her in therapy.

'I won't ask what you think I look like.' Knowing what he thought she was was more than enough information.

'I try as a rule not to judge a book by its cover, but then you know all about books, don't you? You don't mind if I just swing by the estate to let Jamie know what's happened?' Without waiting for her response he took a sharp left. The entrance gates they passed through were grand but the tree-lined driveway beyond was potholed.

Rose had been here long enough to know that the estate, or Castle Clachan given its correct title, was occupied by the laird, a pretty important person hereabouts. She supposed it figured that someone like Mathieu would be on first-name terms with the man.

'You're staying here?'

He nodded and negotiated a particularly deep pothole. 'Jamie raced for a season.'

'Was he injured?'

'No, he just…you need…Jamie was a brilliant driver, but he lacked the…he wasn't, I suppose, ruthless enough. Jamie,' he explained, 'is much nicer than me.'

'An unnecessary explanation, I promise you.'

This drew a laugh from him. Rose couldn't help but notice what an attractive laugh he had.

They drew up on the gravelled area in front of the house. Well, actually there wasn't much gravel left, but there were a lot of weeds, though the house itself, a large sprawling Victorian pile in dressed stone, was impressive.

Mathieu seemed to read her thoughts. 'The original one dated to the fifteenth century; it burnt down, I believe. You wait here. I'll just let Jamie know…oh, there he is.'

Rose turned her head in time to see two men walk around the side of the house. One was tall, sandy-haired and, she assumed, the laird; the other was her employer. She began to struggle with the door handle. Now she knew why the car they had pulled up beside looked familiar.

Mathieu leaned across and caught her arm. 'What are you doing?'

'That's Mr Smith,' she said, drawing back into her seat as far as she could. 'I'm cataloguing his books.' Do not hyperventilate, Rose.

Mathieu turned his head. His mental image of Rose's

employer had made him a good twenty years older than the one
talking to Jamie.

'You live in?'

Rose nodded, puzzled by the odd inflection in his voice, but
relieved she was no longer pressed into her seat by his arm. It
didn't even cross her mind that Mathieu might be wondering
about the sleeping arrangements and if she had guessed she
would have laughed. Robert Smith, despite the fact he was
youngish and quite good-looking, was peculiarly sexless and a
humourless cold fish to boot.

'You stay there. I'll explain what's happened.'

Jamie greeted him with his usual hearty good humour. Though his
expression sobered when Mathieu explained what had happened.

'Lucky you were around, old mate.'

'Yes, most fortunate,' Robert Smith agreed. 'But you say that
Miss Hall is not hurt—the doctor gave her a clean bill of health?'

'She's shaken, obviously.'

'I'm sure once she's working she'll forget all about it.'

'Working?'

The other man flushed under the sardonic stare. 'Well, I
thought…I have a schedule and—'

'She needs to rest.'

Robert Smith visibly recoiled from the blaze of fury in the
other man's eyes. 'Oh, well, if that's what the doctor recom-
mends, of course I'll make sure she—'

'Robert,' Jamie drawled, clapping the man on the back. 'Why
don't you just toddle along in and look at those books? I left them
on the hall table.'

The other man accepted the invitation with alacrity.

'I'll just go and speak to Miss Hall first.'

'I think you scared him,' Jamie said in an amused undertone
as the other man began to walk towards the Land Rover.

'I think the man,' Mathieu said scornfully, 'is an idiot.'

'Yes, that came across,' Jamie said drily. 'Rich, though—made a bomb in the City and retired young. I thought I might sell off a few old books, seems he's mad about them. So the girl…do I get an introduction?' He glanced curiously towards the Land Rover. 'Why don't I ever get the opportunity to play the white knight to damsels in distress?' he complained.

Mathieu's glance followed the direction of Jamie's stare. Rose, presumably at the suggestion of Smith, was getting out of the Land Rover. His brow furrowed as she nodded at the other man and began to walk towards them. 'She's changed a lot…since Monaco.'

Mathieu wasn't even aware he had verbalised his thoughts until Jamie spoke.

'You know her! My God, what are the odds on that?' Jamie, his eyes widening in appreciation, gave a low whistle under his breath as Rose got closer. 'Any chance of an intro, Matt?'

Mathieu flashed Jamie an irritated look. 'I hardly know her…we met—' he began, then stopped as Rose came within hearing distance. She stood there looking, despite her outlandish outfit and gloriously tousled hair, dignified and beautiful enough to offer some excuse for Jamie's childish outburst.

'Hello.' Rose nodded towards Jamie, her smile dimming perceptively as her eyes reached Mathieu. 'Mr Smith is giving me a lift back. I just wanted to thank you…again…for, well, saving my life,' she said awkwardly. 'And I'm sorry for putting you to so much trouble.'

'Saving your life?' Jamie interrupted, stepping forward, hand outstretched, to introduce himself. 'Played that part down, Matt.' He flashed his friend an amused sideways glance. 'But then that's our Matt all over, the modest hero.'

The modest hero in question looked uncomfortable and irritated and his grin broadened. 'We've not met, though in a place this size it was only a matter of time. I'm Jamie.'

'I know—the laird.'

'For the present, but I'm hoping Matt here will do something brilliant and keep the bailiffs from the door.'

Rose found it hard to tell from his tone if he was joking or not, but what did come across was his confidence in Mathieu's ability to pull off the odd miracle in his spare time. She found herself hoping that on this occasion Mathieu did so because it was hard not to warm to the young laird.

'I'm Rose. If you'll excuse me—' she glanced expressively down at her clothes before extricating her hand and wrapping her arms around herself '—I'll just go wait in the car. It's warmer.' Rose smiled once more before turning away.

'I think she likes me,' Jamie said under his breath as she walked back to the parked vehicle. 'No so sure about you, though.'

'So what books are you selling?'

It seemed for a moment that his change of subject might work, but, mid-description of a book, Jamie stopped and angled a sharp look at his friend. *'Monaco...'*

Mathieu shrugged and pretended ignorance.

'You said you knew her in Monaco.'

'It might have been.'

'My God, it's her, isn't it? The blonde that got into your room the night of the embassy party.'

Mathieu, his expression schooled to neutrality, held his tongue, though he suspected rather too late in the day.

'I take it that silence means yes.' Jamie let out a long silent whistle followed by a cackle of laughter. 'Someone who works for Smith doesn't seem the type...she didn't seem the type. Though, to be honest,' he admitted rather regretfully, 'I've not had a whole lot of experience of the sort of women who try and seduce men they've never met. Was she totally naked?'

Mathieu flashed him a flat look.

Jamie held up a pacifying hand. 'All right, no need to implode.

You sure nothing happened? I mean, was there a frisson out there on the ice?' Grinning, he raised a speculative brow.

Mathieu did not smile back. 'You have an overactive imagination, Jamie,' he said coolly.

This time Jamie did read the warning in the other man's manner. 'If you say so…' he said in his easygoing way. 'But I suppose you do know, Mathieu, that you're one of the few men in the universe who would get mad about finding a naked beautiful blonde in his bed.'

'I don't like surprises, I suppose.' His dark brows drew into a straight line above his hawkish nose. 'I don't know why I ever told you about it,' he added, the exasperation in his voice aimed mostly at himself.

'You didn't have much choice after I heard you lambasting the hotel staff on their security,' Jamie reminded him. 'Weren't you even slightly tempted to take what was on offer? I mean, the delicious Rose is pretty hot…' His wistful sigh was accompanied by a lecherous grin.

It was a grin that Mathieu had a problem with.

His long fingers tightened until his knuckles turned white. His dark lashes came down in a veil as he took a deep breath that did little to reduce the angry pounding in his temples.

'Do people here have nothing better to do than gossip?' he asked coldly.

'Not really,' Jamie admitted. Then, oblivious to the fact his friend was fighting violent urges, he continued to speculate about the blonde.

'I wonder if she'd like to come and catalogue my book collection after she finishes with Smith?' His comic suggestive leer faded dramatically in the face of the flash of livid fury on his friend's face.

It was at that moment that Robert Smith announced his presence by clearing his throat.

Both men turned in unison.

'I'm afraid, James, that the books…well, they're not quite what I'm looking for.'

Jamie took the news with a philosophical shrug. 'Oh, well, not to worry.'

'I have a friend who might be interested and I'll mention them to him if you like? I'm afraid, though, they're really not that valuable.'

'I'll buy them,' Mathieu heard himself say.

Jamie looked as surprised by the offer as Mathieu felt. 'You don't know what they are,' he pointed out.

'I have a bookshelf to fill.'

'Right, then, I'll be off.'

Mathieu's lip curled into a contemptuous smile. 'The schedule?' he suggested.

The other man struggled to smile back. 'Just so…and thank you once more for helping Miss Hall.'

Mathieu watched, his eyes narrowed, as Smith got into the car beside Rose. 'I don't like that man.'

Jamie fought a grin. 'And you hid it so well, Matt,' he said, clapping a congratulatory hand on his friend's arm. 'As you're on a roll with the saving-people thing…about my finances—is it hopeless?'

Seeing the real concern behind his friend's levity, Mathieu dragged his thoughts from the unlikely librarian and back to his friend's financial situation.

CHAPTER SIX

ALL the way over in the taxi Rose kept going over the morning's scene in her head.

'I'm afraid, Miss Hall, that I must let you go.'

Jaw clenched, Rose turned her head and stared out of the window not seeing the stunning Highland scenery, dusted that morning by a sprinkling of snow. She squeezed her eyes tight and shook her head. She hadn't had an inkling of what was to come even after that opening, but then she hadn't woken up expecting to receive her marching orders.

'Let me go?'

'I no longer think we can work together.'

'You're giving me the sack?' She was too astonished to be angry…that presumably would come later—*and it had*. 'But I don't understand. The job is only half done. Have you some complaint about my work? Is this because I spent the rest of the day in bed yesterday, because I would have worked if—'

'Your work has been adequate,' Robert Smith conceded stiffly. 'However, certain other matters have been brought to my attention.'

'What matters?'

He started moving objects around his desk, not quite meeting her eyes. 'I have given the matter some thought since yesterday.' He gave a sigh and lifted his head. 'And unfortunately I have concluded it would be quite unsuitable for a woman of your…' He stopped, clearing his throat.

'A woman of my what?'

Lips pursed, his eyes cold behind the horn-rimmed glasses as they slid from hers, he said, 'This is a small community; there are no secrets. Your exploits, Rose, will soon be common knowledge.'

'Exploits?' Rose echoed, still in the dark.

'The people here are old-fashioned and as an incomer I have to respect their values. I did have some concern initially about having such a young woman living here,' he admitted, and Rose thought, God, does every man I meet think I'm out to ravish him? 'But as you are well qualified I put my concerns to one side. Now, of course, that is out of the question given your dubious history…'

Rose laughed. She couldn't help herself, the idea was so ludicrous. Then it hit her in a blinding flash. Her eyes narrowing, she asked in a dangerously calm voice, 'Have you been talking to Mathieu Demetrios?' So much for 'your secret is safe with me'— he hadn't been able to wait five minutes to spread his vile lies.

The worm! Not content with humiliating her personally, he had set out with what had to be deliberate malice to ruin her reputation, or, as it happened, Rebecca's. What a sly, vindictive bastard. If she had ever needed confirmation on her decision not to reveal the case of mistaken identity, she had it.

All she stood to lose was her job and she had.

'Of course, I will pay you until the end of the month.'

She would have been the first to advise anyone who found themselves in a similar situation to maintain a dignified silence, take the money that she was due and put the entire episode down to experience.

It was excellent advice, but Rose had found herself unable to refrain from telling her erstwhile employer that she wouldn't touch his money with a bargepole, and he wasn't likely to repeat the offer—not after she had been pretty frank when she had offered her opinion of him.

Rose asked the driver to wait, which was probably reckless considering her financial situation, but when she made her big exit she didn't want to have it fall flat because she had to beg a lift to the station.

It was not a uniformed flunky who opened the vast oak-studded door, but Jamie MacGregor's sister home for the school holiday. Her look of shock when she saw Rose morphed into a wary smile.

'Oh, hi. I saw you yesterday. You might not have seen me,' she added awkwardly.

Rose was too preoccupied to wonder at the teenager's odd manner. 'No, I didn't.'

'You work for Mr Smith.'

'Not any more.'

'Do you want Jamie?'

'I want Mathieu.'

The young girl registered Rose's gritted teeth, angry eyes and flushed teeth and gave a nervous giggle.

'I'm afraid…the thing is I don't think that…'

Rose cut across her. 'I don't give a damn if he's busy or un-available or anything else because I intend to see him whether he wants to see me or not.'

'I, really, they're—'

'I want Mathieu.'

'I am quite naturally flattered.'

'You shouldn't be,' Rose snapped, tilting her head up to a combative angle to glare at the tall figure that had materialised at the girl's shoulder.

She blinked as her gaze travelled up from his gleaming

handmade leather shoes to his glossy head. This was the first time she had seen him dressed in anything so formal as a suit and tie. And not just any suit. She was no expert, but it was obvious even to Rose that the dark grey single-breasted number was no more off the peg than the body it covered, and she had to admit Mathieu looked nothing short of breathtakingly spectacular in it.

Some men relied on power suits to give them presence. Mathieu didn't need to; he had more presence than any man ought to be allowed.

Enough presence to make her slightly dizzy when she stared at him.

Then don't stare.

Damned good recommendation, but not one Rose could observe. It would have been nice, she thought wistfully, to find something…one tiny flaw she could criticise.

But there was none.

He looked tall and impressive, the discreet tailoring of the dark, beautifully cut jacket emphasising the powerful breadth of his shoulders. It hung open revealing a crisp white shirt made of a fabric fine enough to show a faint shadow of the body hair on his chest, sending her stomach into a lurching dive.

'What are you doing lurking like that?' Her nerves found release in snapping antagonism.

He arched one brow sardonically. He loosened his tie and allowed his eyes—actually, it was not something over which he had much control—to wander over her soft feminine curves before explaining. 'I'm on my way to Edinburgh.'

There were occasions when being a Demetrios had its advantages, and he had the financial clout that went with the name to arrange a meeting at a few hours' notice with the bank that was threatening to pull the plug on Jamie and the ailing estate.

The phone calls had gone pretty much as he had anticipated. The money men had been negative initially. They'd liked his plan, called it innovative and daring, but the bottom line, they had explained, was it was too late in the day.

'Of course, Mr Demetrios, if someone else was willing to invest…share the risk the bank has already taken…?'

That too had been a response Mathieu had anticipated. He had made only one stipulation. Jamie, he had explained to them, must never know who his new investor was.

Mathieu looked thoughtfully down at the flushed angry face of his visitor and bent his head. 'Fiona, I think Jamie was looking for you,' he said without taking his eyes off Rose.

With a show of reluctance and several curious looks the young girl left them.

'Can I come in or should I go around to the tradesmen's entrance?'

He bowed slightly from the waist and stepped back for her to enter the hallway. 'I think, yes,' he said, pushing open one of the heavy doors that led off the vaulted hallway, 'we can be private in here.'

'Oh, very big on confidentiality all of a sudden, aren't we?' she muttered, following him inside the room.

She vaguely registered the oak-panelled walls, and the obligatory stag's head on the wall, but her attention was concentrated on the figure who preceded her.

Nothing she could say was likely to make him feel guilty; wrecking lives was probably one of the highlights of his day.

She watched as he bent to throw a log from the stack beside the vast stone fireplace on the fire that brightened the gloomy room.

The log crackled into fiery life. So did her temper when he turned around, set his shoulders to the jutting stone mantle and said politely, 'Is there something I can help you with, Rose?'

'You could drop dead.' She clamped her lips to prevent any further childish retorts that gave him the opportunity to look down at her in that superior way from escaping.

'How things change,' he bemoaned, his eyes glimmering mockery as he casually pulled the tie from around his neck. 'And I thought you were different, Rose.'

Rose dragged her eyes from the small vee of brown skin revealed at his throat as he slipped the top button of his shirt and glared up at him with renewed venom.

'Once you liked me a good deal better, but a man learns who his real friends are when he leaves behind the glamour of the racing circuit.'

'I'm sure you still have an entourage of hangers-on and people willing to treat your every stupid pronouncement as wise and wonderful. Men like you always do.'

'Have you known a lot of men like me?'

'No, I've been lucky that way, though if I saw any coming I'd cross to the other side of the street.'

He pursed his lips and loosed a long silent whistle. 'Someone got out of bed the wrong side this morning.'

'This morning I had a bed.'

He levered himself off the stone mantle and took a step towards her. 'And you don't now?'

'No, I don't. No bed, no job.'

'You quit?'

'No, I was sacked.'

'Smith sacked you.' He shook his head, his expression one of mild contempt as he thought of the other man. 'I didn't see that one coming.' That certainly explained her mood, but not her presence.

The rueful amusement in his expression made her see red. 'Liar!'

He froze, the lines of his lean face moulding into a mask of chilling hauteur. 'What did you call me?'

Rose lifted her chin to a belligerent angle and placed her hands on her hips. She had no intention of allowing herself to be intimidated, even though he did have the look of a jungle predator about to pounce.

'You heard me.' She lifted her chin and ignored the sound of hissing outrage that escaped through his clenched white teeth. 'You're many things, but you're not stupid.'

'Thank you,' he said, his voice dripping with mockery.

'You must have thought of the consequences when you told everyone I'm a drunken nymphomaniac?'

'I did not tell anyone anything of the sort…' He stopped, an expression of pained comprehension passing across his face as he slapped a hand to his forehead and swore.

Rose's head came up with a jerk. 'Well, it's the sort of thing that could slip anyone's mind, I suppose.'

He bit back a cutting response to her sarcasm and watched, his expression softening, as she rubbed a hand wearily across her eyes with the back of her hand.

'I hope, incidentally, that it makes an amusing after-dinner anecdote.'

'I can't believe he actually sacked you.' He regarded her with frowning concern.

'And I can't believe you actually care,' she cut back. 'But I really don't see why the concept is so hard to get your head around. What did you expect my boss to do when you told him I was a groupie—give me a raise?' Her lip wobbled and a tear escaped from the corner of her eye. 'Damn,' she muttered, brushing it away. 'Why does this happen when I'm mad?' Her head dropped as she fought to regain her composure.

As he studied her bent head and watched her hunched slender shoulders shake Mathieu experienced an alien and compelling urge to take her in his arms. It was followed by an almost equally violent need to throttle her idiot employer.

'I did not relate the story.' He half expected her to resist when he put a hand in the narrow of her back and steered her towards the nearest chair, but she didn't. 'Sit down before you fall down.' Impatience masked the concern he didn't want to be feeling.

Why should he feel responsible? It was not his fault that she had worked for someone who was parochial and intolerant. Neither, despite what she thought, had he been telling tales.

'I did not relay the story at all. I suppose it's possible he simply overheard something that Jamie said.' Mathieu looked doubtful.

'*Jamie…?*' Brushing her hair from her face with her forearm, Rose tilted her head and looked up at him, rolling her eyes in disbelief. 'My God, is there anyone you didn't tell?'

'Jamie was in the hotel that night. He heard me complaining about the hotel security and he wormed the story out of me. When he saw you he guessed…'

'Guessed,' she echoed. 'You must have dropped some pretty heavy clues.'

'I didn't need to. Jamie doesn't miss much. If it's any comfort, as a consequence of seeing you my standing in his eyes has plummeted.'

With a dry laugh she lifted her head. 'That I doubt.'

'It was me, I think.'

Both turned in unison as the door swung inwards to reveal Fiona standing there. Jamie's sister looked the picture of guilt.

Mathieu's brows twitched into a straight line of disapproval. 'Fiona, have you been eavesdropping?'

'Yes…no, that is, it wasn't deliberate the *other* time.'

Mathieu's brows lifted. 'Other time?'

Fiona's eyes slid from his as she shuffled her feet miserably and mumbled, 'I heard you and Jamie talking about Monaco and the hotel and…' her eyes lifted to Rose '…you. Grace said—'

'*Grace?*' Mathieu ran a hand along his jaw, looking impatient. 'Who is Grace?'

'Who is Grace?' Fiona echoed, sounding indignant. 'You know who she is. She's been my best friend for ever, or since we were four anyway…her dad runs the climbing centre. I texted her and, well, she might have texted Ellie and Ellie probably sent an email to a few other people.'

'Oh, my God,' Rose breathed shakily. 'I think the mystery of how Mr Smith knows the story is solved,' she said in a shaky voice. 'The only mystery is how there's anybody left this side of Inverness who doesn't know.' Hearing the note of hysteria in her voice, she bit her lip.

Presumably Mathieu heard it too, because he looked at her oddly before he jerked his head at the teenager and snapped, 'Out.' A tearful Fiona fled and he walked across to a bureau, out of which he produced a bottle and a glass. 'Jamie's best malt,' he said, filling the glass.

'If that's for me,' Rose said, shaking her head as he walked towards her, 'I don't like whisky.'

'It's medicinal,' he said, handing it to her.

With a sigh of irritation she took the glass. 'I've lost my job. I'm angry, not ill.'

'It's true, you know. Take a sip, it'll steady your nerves.'

Not while you're standing this close, she thought, lifting the liquid to her lips. 'What's true?' she asked, giving a shudder at the taste the sip of peaty malt left in her mouth.

'It's true Jamie thinks that any man who threw you out of his bed needs therapy.' Maybe he was right, Mathieu thought as his eyes were drawn once more to the soft lush outline of her pink lips.

'I wouldn't mind,' she mused, staring into the bottom of the glass, 'if I had actually done anything...no, actually, I would mind,' she burst out, levelling a burning resentful glare at Mathieu. 'So long as I did my job well, my personal life is none of his business, the narrow-minded, pompous little bigot. He said people might get the wrong idea about our relationship. Can you imagine?' she asked, her voice rising in an incredulous note, before she added with a bitter laugh, 'Sleep with that cold fish. God,' she muttered, 'I'd rather sleep with *you*!'

'I'm flattered.'

Rose put down the glass very carefully. This interview was not going as planned; by now she ought to be making a grand sweeping exit. The alcohol and fire, she decided, were having an undesirable mellowing effect.

'Don't be,' she advised. 'If there's one thing I despise more than a sanctimonious prig, it's a man who can't resist boasting about his conquests to the boys.'

'Conquest?' His dark brows rose. 'Your memory of the occasion is no doubt hazy, but we didn't actually—'

'No, because I wasn't good enough for you!' Almost before the words were out of her mouth Rose was struck by the incongruity of her reaction to his jibe.

While she felt indignant about the rejection on her twin's behalf, she also felt relieved. Relieved that Mathieu had resisted Rebecca's advances, because if he hadn't… Her thoughts skittered to a halt as a look of stupefied shock spread across her face.

I'd have been jealous!

She skimmed a look up at the man responsible for this foreign emotion. She had never been jealous of her twin even though there had been ample cause. Rebecca was always the talented one, the slim one, the passionate one. The one that men were drawn to.

But Mathieu hadn't been.

'You were drunk.' Mathieu dragged his eyes from the heaving contours of her bosom at that moment outlined in heather-blue angora.

'It wasn't me,' she snarled through gritted teeth. 'How many times do I have to tell you? My God, but you are so judgemental. Haven't you ever done anything you regret?'

'I suppose it is something that you can regret it.'

'Did it ever occur to you that there might be a reason for her behaviour? A reason that had nothing to do with you being totally irresistible for what she did that night? Did it ever occur to you that she might have been going through a really traumatic time in her life? That she might have found out the man she was engaged to, the man who dumped her at the altar, was gay?'

Mathieu watched as she stopped to catch her breath. Presumably her use of the third person was part of the denial thing she had going on.

'You were engaged to be married?' There was an inflection in his deep voice that she couldn't quite pin down, but Rose immediately knew that she had made a tactical error.

Her instinctive desire to offer an explanation for Rebecca's uncharacteristic behaviour had only resulted in him believing she was trying to excuse herself.

Eyes shut tight, she groaned in sheer frustration as she bellowed, 'Not me; we are not talking about me.'

Mathieu, it seemed, was.

'Of course not.'

This was said with such obvious insincerity that she wanted to scream.

Mathieu looked down at his hands and saw they were bunched into fists at his sides. It was irrational to feel the sort of violent antagonism he was experiencing for a total stranger. He took a deep breath and forced his tensed muscles to relax.

'Who was he?'

'Look, I really don't want to discuss my personal life with you.'

'At least you now admit it is your personal life.'

Rose rolled her eyes in frustration. What was the point denying it when he obviously wasn't going to listen?

'I can see that it must have been a shock, but I'm sure you will agree in retrospect that getting drunk and sleeping with strangers was not the wisest response,' he continued.

'You have obviously never been in love.' She studied his lean face with dislike, and thought it was a safe bet that there had been droves of women who fancied themselves in love with him.

Blinded by his exotic heritage, dark devastating looks and charismatic smile, not to mention the raw sex appeal he exuded from every pore.

'You feel equipped to make this assumption because…?'

Rose blinked. 'You've been dumped?' She gave a laugh of total incredulity as her glance travelled up the long, lean length of him. 'Now that I don't believe.'

His lips twitched and a gleam that she deeply distrusted entered his dark eyes. 'It might be that not everybody finds me as irresistible as you do.'

'For a man with power, position and money a lot of women would be willing to overlook a good many flaws.'

'You are not very charitable to your sisters.'

'I doubt if I have anything in common with your lovers.' Thinking of them did not improve her mood. 'You know, it would serve you right if I went around telling everyone that you were awful in bed…' If she had a reputation she might as well use it.

Rose was startled when her threat drew what seemed like a totally genuine laugh from him…genuine and attractive, she thought, very conscious of the butterfly-wings sensation low in her belly. It was the brandy on an empty stomach, she told herself.

'You think I'm joking?' she asked him belligerently. 'I would, you know.'

He shook his head. 'No, I'm sure you would. The only problem is I think you're assuming I have a fragile male ego. I don't. I imagine,' he mused, not smiling, 'it is partly to do with genetics and—'

'And partly,' she cut in contemptuously, 'to do with every woman in your life telling you how perfect you are.' Poor deluded idiots. 'Newsflash, Mathieu, women lie.'

'You being the exception.'

'Well, I'm not about to tell you you're perfect,' she promised grimly as she rose to her feet with slightly wobbly dignity. 'I've said what I came to, I'm going now and I just…no.' She broke off and lifted her blazing eyes to his before placing her shoulder bag very firmly on top of her case beside the chair. 'I'm not going anywhere.' No way, that would be letting him off too easily.

She had come here to vent her feelings and hopefully prick his conscience, but she could see now that it had been naïve of her to expect him to exhibit some remorse. The man was a total stranger to compassion.

'You messed up my life—you can put it right.'

The smile was wiped from his face. A spasm of distaste contorted the perfectly proportioned contours of his lean features. 'And how much will this putting right cost me?'

'Cost?' She stared up at him in bewilderment. Then as his meaning sank in the colour left her cheeks as a wave of revolted fury washed over her. This hateful man couldn't open his mouth without insulting her.

'You think I'm asking you for cash? I wouldn't take money off you if I were dead,' she declared in a quivering voice.

He looked down at her for a moment, his expression considering. 'If that were the situation money wouldn't do you much good, but as you are very much alive…' His eyes moved from the sparkling scorn in her bright eyes, and touched the soft fullness of her lips before sliding slowly across the smooth opalescent skin of her slender throat.

'I don't want your money; I want a job,' she declared.

He looked perplexed by her explanation. 'A job?'

CHAPTER SEVEN

'YES, I want a job, the thing I had until you decided to slander me to anyone that would listen.'

'I haven't slandered you to anyone, I told you—'

Rose cut off his weary explanation with a bored wave of her hand. 'Yeah, yeah… It seems to me that under the circumstances it's the least you could do.'

'Slander is a crime.'

Rose shrugged, lowered her eyes from his lean face and thought looking sinfully seductive and dangerous ought to be one too.

'And I'm sure you have a team of lawyers who make damned sure that nothing you don't like ever gets said or printed about you.'

'That might not be such a bad idea,' he conceded.

'Are you laughing at me?' she asked, studying his solemn expression suspiciously.

He took a step closer and looked at her with his dark head inclined to one side. The expression she didn't trust was still in his eyes, but she was no longer sure it was laughter. Whatever it was it made her heart beat a lot faster against her breastbone.

'You could sue me,' he suggested softly.

Rose held her ground even though every instinct she had was screaming at her to run. The charge that he gave off was electrical, almost physical; her own reaction was definitely physical. Just being this close to him made her toes tingle and her stomach quiver.

'And don't think I wouldn't if it wasn't for…' She stopped, biting her lip.

'If it wasn't for what?'

Rose dropped her eyes and shook her head. 'Just thank your lucky stars I'm not litigious,' she gritted back huskily. 'The legal system is loaded in favour of people like you, anyway.' Even as she said it Rose knew the stereotyping was flawed; this man might be despicable, but he was not part of the herd. He was unique.

'Like me?'

His dangerously low-voiced query made Rose wind her anger around her like a protective scarf. 'You know, if you possessed a fraction of the moral fibre you like to shove down other people's throats,' she yelled, 'you'd own up to the fact it was your fault I lost my job and want to put it right.'

Mathieu watched as she sucked in a wrathful breath causing a good deal of quivering under the soft angora. The blazing gold eyes that meshed with his were shimmering with tears of anger. 'Want…?' he echoed thickly and swallowed.

The truth was at that precise moment the only thing that he wanted to do was drag her into his arms and kiss her senseless. The raw, primitive nature of the response she drew from him was like nothing he had ever experienced before.

He had had the opportunity to do a lot more than kiss her and he had walked away. When offered on a plate what his body now craved, he had been able to reject it with no difficulty.

What had changed?

Four years ago he had been aesthetically aware of the beauty of the woman who had offered herself to him, but he had not been tempted. There had been no chemistry.

Yet now he could not be in the same room as her, or even think of the scent of her perfume, without feeling the stirring of desire.

A bemused groove between his darkly defined brows, his brooding glance drifted speculatively across the soft contours of her face. Emotional and physical control was something he pretty much took for granted, he was master of his appetites and he had met women who were more beautiful, so what was it about this one, beyond the obvious, that ate away at his discipline? And why now and not four years earlier?

'But, of course, someone like you wouldn't understand what it is like to lose a job.'

He arched a dark brow as he met her scornful glare. 'What exactly am I like, Rose?' He liked the way her name felt on his tongue; it led him to wondering how she would taste.

'I'd tell you if I thought it would do any good, but no matter what I say you'll still carry on thinking you're God's gift to the human race and the female part of it in particular.' Her angry gaze grew distracted as it stilled on his lean dark face. Wouldn't anyone who looked in the mirror and saw that face every morning be arrogant?

'But basically you're someone who wouldn't have a clue what it means to lose a job. We don't all have a private income to fall back on.'

'You have a family to go home to—you won't exactly starve.'

'I have a family and I have savings, but that's not the point. I'm twenty-six. I don't want to sponge off my parents.' And neither did she want to go back and have everyone say *I told you so*.

'You assume that I have led a rich, pampered existence?' Anything less pampered than his life up to the age of fifteen would have been difficult to imagine.

Yet in many ways those years when there had been just himself and his mother living what many would consider a deprived, hand-to-mouth existence had been in the ways that counted the happiest of his life.

Mathieu was in a position to know firsthand that money and

material possessions did not buy happiness. He had wanted for nothing materially when Andreos had recognised him as his son. But that first year there had been many occasions when if someone had offered him the chance to return to the life he had had before Andreos he would have taken it without a second thought.

Rose felt a rush of anger. Surely he wouldn't be hypocritical enough to suggest anything else. 'Now why should I assume that when you're standing there in your fancy suit and handmade Italian shoes?' she drawled sarcastically. 'I suppose you've spent no end of nights worrying about paying bills.'

'Not lost sleep,' he conceded. 'But I have needed to—what is the expression? Rob Peter to pay Paul.'

Suspecting his mockery, she glared. 'Oh, yes, I'm sure you had it tough.'

A flicker of sardonic amusement flashed into his eyes as he lifted his shoulders in a minimal but expressive shrug. 'You might be surprised.'

Rose looked at him in disgust and he looked back with a faint smile and cool confidence that went bone-deep. Was that confidence a result of his privileged upbringing or was that inherent in the man?

Rose suspected the latter was true.

'Surprised that a man who is wearing a watch that costs more than some houses knows what it's like to be hard up,' she tossed at him scornfully and folded her arms across her chest. 'Frankly, yes, I would be surprised. Very surprised. You're heir to a huge fortune…squillions!'

And even if his wealth hadn't been common knowledge it would be obvious just by looking at him, she reflected, her gaze travelling up the long, lean, supremely elegant length of him, that he was part of an exclusive élite.

'I wouldn't be surprised if your silver spoon was encrusted with diamonds,' she speculated bitterly. 'What's so funny?' she demanded indignantly in response to his dry laugh.

The satirical glitter faded from Mathieu's eyes, leaving his expression sombre as he said, 'I didn't always have a silver spoon, Rose.'

She slung him an irritated glare and swung away, or she would have if he hadn't caught her by the shoulder and twisted her back.

'Do you mind?' Her breath was coming in painful little gasps as she forced her eyes away from the disturbing image of his brown fingers curled over her upper arm. 'I don't enjoy this hands-on stuff,' she claimed, even though her entire treacherous body was doing its best to reveal her as a liar.

She mentally crossed her fingers and hoped he would put down the tremors that were rippling through her body to her re-vulsion. Fortunately there was no way he could know anything about the warm, squidgy, fluttery feeling low in her belly. And unless she fell down in a heap the weakened state of her knees would remain on a strictly need-to-know basis.

Even so she half expected Mathieu to respond with a scornful laugh, but he didn't. As their eyes connected she stopped struggling.

'Mathieu…?'

'I was born in a single-roomed apartment in an area of Paris that the tourists do not visit.'

Rose stared. The words that had literally shocked her into silence had erupted from his lips with an intensity that made her take an involuntary step backwards. In the split second before she saw his smooth urbane mask slide into place she saw a flicker of shock in his eyes. It was almost as if he was as surprised as she was to hear what he said.

'Actually nobody visits there unless they have no other choice.' His taut smile did not reach his eyes and his previous stark announcement hung in the air between them. 'But that is not relevant.' The words, his manner—they both signalled his intention to draw a line under the subject. A subject you introduced, Matt.

'But I don't understand.'

Mathieu's jaw tightened. Neither did he. He didn't understand what impulse had made him volunteer personal information that way. He might as well have handed the woman a gold-edged invite to tramp around in his head.

It was bizarre. Andreos had said a lot worse and utterly failed to get under his guard, but for some reason Rose's silver-spoon jibe, not to mention her assumption of moral superiority when she had made it, had really got to him.

Since when did he give a damn what anyone thought of him? It didn't matter to him if Rose Hall dismissed him as some spoilt, pampered rich kid who had grown into a spoilt, pampered man.

'What are you talking about?'

His lashes lifted from his chiselled cheekbones. 'I'm not.'

'You can't say something like that and leave it,' she protested.

He gave a very Gallic shrug. 'Why not?'

Rose rolled her eyes. 'Are you serious?'

'I am not the subject of this conversation.' His sanity possibly should be. For the first time in his life he was worried that if he started talking he couldn't guarantee where the cut-off point would be. He had already let this woman have a glimpse of himself that should have remained private. That was a pretty heavy price to pay just for the pleasure of the look of smug superiority wiped off her face.

'Your father is Andreos Demetrios, isn't he?' Just about the richest man in Europe and Mathieu was his heir. How could what he was saying be true?

A growling sound escaped Mathieu's clamped lips as he bared his teeth in a ferocious smile and glared down at her. She was like a damned terrier with a bone.

Rose, who didn't have a clue what she had done to earn such seething resentment, kept her chin up but regarded him warily.

'You want the salacious details? Fine.' His lip curled contemptuously as he punched the air in a gesture of frustration and asked himself, 'Why not?' before dragging a hand through his hair. 'Andreos is my father; I have the DNA results to prove it. But my mother,' he continued in the same driven manner, 'was not his wife. My mother was a young girl who gave birth nine months after a one-night stand.'

'Then you were a…'

'A bastard—yes, I am.' Her embarrassed flush brought his mocking smile to the surface.

'And you had no contact with him…your father…when you were young?' A pucker appeared on her smooth brow. 'Surely he gave your mother financial support.'

'It was only after my mother's death that I learned who my father was.'

'Didn't you ask? Weren't you curious?' It seemed inconceivable to Rose that anyone would not want to know their roots.

He shook his dark head, his expression remote as though his thoughts were in another time and place. 'We were fine as we were, just the two of us.'

'Did he know?'

'About me? Apparently not. I went to live with him six months after she died.' He related the information in a flat, expressionless tone…well, having revealed this much there seemed very little point holding back now. *Dieu*, what was it about this woman that activated some previously dormant soul-bearing gene in his make-up?

She met his eyes. All she could see was her own reflection in the mirrored silver surface. His expression, in stark contrast to the blaze of white-hot emotion that had been written there moments earlier, was inscrutable. 'It is sad, your mother being alone…'

'She wasn't alone; she had me.'

'How old were you when she died?'

'Nearly fifteen.'

'And that six months before you went to live with him?'

Mathieu ran a hand over his jaw and nodded. It was years since he had even allowed himself to think about that time in his life. There was something almost liberating about allowing himself to share these private recollections.

'I stayed on in the flat and I worked as a construction labourer to pay the rent.' These were things he had never told anyone— not even Jamie, his best friend.

'But you were fifteen,' Rose exclaimed, her eyes round with shock.

'I was tall for my age.'

'That's not what I meant. You were a child—you shouldn't have been alone that way. You should have been at school.'

'I didn't go to school when she got ill, and afterwards...' He gave a careless shrug. 'I suppose I fell through the cracks. Look,' he said, changing the subject abruptly, 'whether you believe it or not, I am sorry you lost your job, but I have no vacancy that would suit your qualifications.'

'I'm a qualified librarian, but I haven't always worked with books.' As she looked at him Rose was unable to shake the image from her head of him as a lonely little boy forced first to care for his dying mother and then to fend for himself. Her tender heart ached when she thought about it.

'I know what you're good at,' he said, his eyes lingering on her lush mouth as he once again was overwhelmed with the urge to kiss it, 'and that I can get it for free.'

Mathieu moved his head to one side just a split second before her hand would have connected with his cheek. He caught her wrist and surprised her almost as much as he did himself by bringing it up to his mouth and brushing the smooth blue-veined inner aspect of her wrist with his lips.

Eyes wide, she released a small cry and pulled back. Mathieu released his hold and watched as she nursed her hand against her heaving breasts.

'Sorry, that was a cheap crack.' And he had made it to drive the look of compassion from her face… If there was one thing he could not tolerate, it was pity.

Rose's head came up; he had sounded genuinely regretful.

'And not true,' he continued. 'Nothing is for free in this world.'

This cynical outlook caused her brow to furrow, but she bit back her instinctive protest.

'We all of us do things we regret in life. It is not helpful to be reminded of them constantly, especially when you have obviously made an effort to turn your life around.'

My God, this was priceless. Rose Hall, the fallen woman, trying to live down her past…what would he say if he knew the truth?

Rose would have laughed if her ironic appreciation hadn't been severely dented by her response to the light seductive touch of his lips on her skin. Being this close to him short-circuited any sense of self-preservation she had left.

She pulled her hand away, but the sensitised skin of her wrist carried on tingling.

'You're offering me some sort of grudging pardon?'

Forgiveness from Mathieu Demetrios. A man who by all accounts had hardly led a blameless existence.

'That's really big of you,' she responded with a smile of dazzling insincerity. 'But for your information I haven't done anything I'm ashamed of…well, not the anything you're talking about anyway.' She stopped. 'Are you listening to me?'

The disturbing smile twitched the corners of his lips as he shook his head and confessed, 'No…I was having a Eureka moment.'

'What are you looking at me like that for?'

'I have thought of a position that you might be suited for… Yes, the more I think about it…' His narrowed eyes travelled from the tip of her glossy fair head to her toes and back again. He slowly nodded. 'Yes, you might just do.'

'Do what? What are you talking about?'

'You need a job; I need...' He paused, a smile that filled her with deep distrust spreading across his lean features. 'I have a vacancy.'

'A vacancy for what?' She had demanded a job on impulse and had not for an instant expected him to come up with the goods. She still wasn't sure he wasn't just messing with her.

'You're choosy suddenly.'

'What is this position?'

'I need a fiancée.'

In the act of brushing a strand of hair from her cheek, she froze dead. 'You need a fiancée?' she repeated flatly. He said it the same way someone else would say they needed more petrol.

'Before you get excited...' Too late, she already was if the heaving bosom was any indicator. 'The position,' he explained, dragging his reluctant gaze upwards, 'is purely temporary.'

Rose pointed to her face with a not quite steady hand. 'What you are seeing is not excitement,' she told him. 'This is fear of being in the same room as an insane person.'

The man was quite definitely off his head, but, that being a given, his mental state was apparently more stable than her own. For a split second there she had almost allowed herself to consider his offer. Not in a serious way but thinking about it in any way at all was worrying.

'If you need a fiancée I suggest you put an ad in the situations vacant column.'

Or announce it on any street corner and you'll be mobbed, she thought, watching as his lips curved into a smile that was almost as dangerous as the gleam in his incredible metallic eyes. As her eyes lingered on the sensual curve of his lips heat exploded somewhere deep in her belly and radiated outwards and downwards.

Deeply ashamed of the heavy ache low in her pelvis, she struggled to school her features into a bland mask that gave no hint—she hoped—of the physical reaction over which she had no control. The wave of colour that washed over her skin she couldn't hide; she just hoped he attributed it to anger.

'Let me explain…'

Rose didn't want explanations; she wanted the nervous excitement fluttering in her stomach and causing her mouth to grow dry to subside.

Feeling the panic rise, Rose assured herself what was happening was no big deal. It was normal. He was an incredible-looking man. It was just shallow physical attraction, nothing to get worked up about…just biology. Something over which you had no control, like a sneeze.

Think sneeze, Rose.

It wasn't easy to stand there and think sneeze when you were looking up at someone who was just possibly the most incredible-looking man on the planet.

'Save your breath,' she advised tersely. 'I'm not enjoying the joke.'

'It isn't a joke. There is a girl that my father wishes me to marry.'

Rose looked at him in exasperation. He wasn't even attempting to make this plausible.

'And you, I suppose, always do what your father wants.' She rolled her eyes, relieved that she had her hormones back in check. Mathieu being a dutiful obedient son was about as likely as him asking her to marry him for real.

'Don't,' she said, picking up her case, 'say another word. I'm leaving.'

CHAPTER EIGHT

HAD Mathieu really expected her to say yes to such a crazy idea?

'My God, I'm not that desperate!' Rose muttered, slamming the taxi door and in the process trapping the hem of her ankle-length coat in it. 'Damn,' she groaned, opening it and rescuing her coat that was now liberally coated with mud along the hem.

After a second definitive slam that made the driver wince, she slumped back in the seat and, eyes closed, exhaled a heavy sigh.

'The station, please.'

The past half an hour had all been slightly surreal.

She still wasn't totally sure if he had even been serious. If it had been his idea of a joke. People just didn't go around asking other people to pretend they were engaged. Though she was learning fast that Mathieu Demetrios was not exactly a man who felt obliged to follow the rules. In fact he seemed most comfortable making them up as he went along.

And he had a way of making the most outrageous suggestion sound almost normal. She sighed and straightened up. Pulling a compact from her bag, she flicked it open.

'If you'd stayed around a minute longer,' she told her reflection, 'you'd have ended up agreeing with him.' She rolled her eyes and laughed at her joke. Then frowned because her laughter had a slightly hollow ring to it—also the driver was looking worried.

She hadn't been tempted, not for a second.

Turning her frowning glare on the dour grey stone façade of the house as they drew away, she reached inside her bag for her mobile. The sooner a line was drawn under her Scottish misadventure, the better.

Her twin picked up straight away.

'Is this a good time?'

'Rose, of course, I was just thinking about you. How are things in bonny Scotland?'

Rose didn't waste time wrapping it up. 'Terrible. I'm coming home. As you and Nick are in New York until March, would it be all right if I stayed at your place for a couple of weeks?'

There was a pause that grew longer.

'This is where you say *I told you so* closely followed by *I can't wait to see you.*'

'Of course I can't wait to see you…'

'But?'

'But the thing is, I was going to call you, but Nick said I should leave well enough alone and…the thing is, Rose, Steven's wife is divorcing him.'

Rose's eyes opened wide.

She screwed up her face as she made an effort to visualise his face. Should a person have to make an effort to see the face of the person they had decided was the unrequited love of their life?

Even when she had formed a mental image to go with the name his eyes kept switching from blue to silver-grey and another mouth, one that was both sensual and cruel, kept superimposing itself over his.

'Are you still there, Rose?'

Rose gave her head a little shake and forced a smile even though there was nobody there to see it. 'Yes…so Steven is getting a divorce?'

Which made him available and ought to make her deliriously happy.

Only she wasn't, which probably meant that Rebecca had been right all along and whatever she had felt for Steven Latimer hadn't been love. And *had*, she realised with dawning shock, was the key word. Whatever it was she had felt for Steven was simply not there.

Which made her shallow and superficial—even worse than that, he was getting divorced because of her and she could barely remember what the poor man looked like.

'Steven is divorcing his wife?' This is all my fault.

'No, Rose, she's divorcing him.'

The hand with the phone in it fell into her lap as she sighed. 'Thank God for that.' Feeling light-headed with relief, she lifted the phone back to her ear.

'Rose…Rose! Did you hear what I said?'

'No, sorry, I lost the signal,' she lied cheerfully.

'God, does that mean I have to tell you again?'

'Tell me what again?' Rose asked, her curiosity roused.

'Steven's wife is divorcing him because she found out that he's been having an affair.'

'No…no, there was no affair, you were right, I—'

'Not with you, Rosie. The reptile has been having an affair with the nanny.'

Rose's jaw dropped. 'The nanny!'

'And the thing is, Rose…' the pity in her twin's voice made Rose half suspect what was coming next '…well, the thing is, it's been going on for two years. I wouldn't have told you, but if you're coming back to London you'd have been bound to have found out.'

Rose closed her eyes. 'You both warned me, didn't you? And I didn't listen.' The memory of one of the last conversations she had had with Nick and Rebecca before she'd left began to replay in her head.

Rebecca and Nick had seen what he was like all along.

Eyes bleak, she lifted the phone to her ear. 'Well, it's easy to see why he found it so easy to keep his hands off me.' They were all over the nanny. She closed her eyes and allowed her head to fall forward. 'I thought his love was *pure*. Tell me, Rebecca, is there much insanity in the family? God, when I think about how he must have been laughing at me.' She scrunched up her face and swallowed the humiliation burning like bile in her throat.

'I could kill him,' Rebecca said at the other end of the line.

Releasing a strangled laugh, Rose raised her head and, phone pressed to her ear, she pushed her hair back from her face with the crook of her elbow. 'Not if I get to him first,' she said, allowing her head to sink into the backrest.

'Just don't do anything crazy. I'm catching the next plane over there. Planes do go up there, don't they? I'll ask Nick. Nick…' Rose could hear the sound of a muffled conversation. 'Nick says—'

Rose cut her off. 'Calm down, there's no need to fly over here from New York. I'm fine.'

'Liar, but if it makes you feel any better he's had the push from his job…even before the affair came out. He made a major and very costly mistake and there was no Rose there to cover it up for him.'

'I did cover up his mistakes, didn't I?' she said with a groan as she thought of all the unpaid overtime she'd put in to make sure that he looked good. 'You must think I'm a total fool.'

'Who am I to throw stones, Rose? It's not as if I have a brilliant track record when it comes to men.'

'You've got Nick.'

'I wish you had a Nick.'

'You and me both. But the Nicks of the world are pretty rare.'

'Rose says you're rare.'

'I'm unique…how is she? Tell her I'll beat the skunk up for her if she—'

Rose, who had been listening with half an ear to the conversation between husband and wife, suddenly cut in. 'I'm not.'

'Rosie,' Rebecca said, sounding worried. 'You sound really odd. You're not what?'

'I'm not coming back to London.' She didn't love Steven. The Steven she had loved had never actually existed outside her fertile imagination, but she could tell Rebecca this until she was blue in the face and it wouldn't do any good. And sympathy and understanding were the last things she needed right now. They would only remind her of what a prize idiot she had been.

What did she need? That was the question…

'So you're staying there?'

'Can't. I got the sack.' Rose barely registered her sister's shocked gasp. She was considering her options—they were rather limited. She'd sublet her flat. She wanted to avoid her sister flying back from the States, her parents' searching questions, and she was reluctant to dip into her meagre savings.

Was this the moment to throw her customary caution to the wind? Well, being cautious and doing the right thing hadn't got her very far except in the geographical sense.

'You got the sack?' Rebecca could not have sounded more incredulous, but Rose barely registered it. Her thoughts were racing.

There was a way out… Mathieu had offered it her, but it was just too crazy… She couldn't do that, *could she*? When you'd stopped waiting for Mr Right because the penny had finally dropped that he didn't exist—wasn't that the totally right time to take a leap into the unknown, and if that leap brought you into intimate contact with a man who made bits of you quiver you didn't know you had wasn't that a plus? So far avoiding temptation and being a good girl had made her a pathetic laughing stock.

She sucked in a decisive breath. 'I'm going for it.'

'You sound strange, Rose. Rose is going for it. No, Nick, I've no idea what she's going for, and will you stop interrupting? Rose, what are you—?'

'Why not?' Rose's unexpected whoop had her twin lifting the

phone with a wince from her ear. 'You're right, Becky, I'm a coward. But no more.'

'I didn't say that,' her twin protested.

'Yes, you did, and you're right. I hate being nice. Nice people just get kicked in the teeth and laughed at. You know, I didn't sleep with the wrong man because I'm too nice. Is that good or bad? I can't decide,' she mused. 'When you think about it you might as well sleep with someone you don't give a damn about because they can't hurt you and I might actually find out what I've been missing.'

'Oh, God,' Rebecca groaned down the other end of the phone. 'Are you thinking of anyone particular you don't give a damn about?' she asked warily. 'Look, Rosie, now might not be the best time to make big decisions…you're feeling hurt and—'

'I'm not hurt.'

'Of course you're not hurt.'

Rose brought her teeth together in a frustrated grimace. Her twin had obviously decided that she was being plucky and brave trying to hide her broken heart. It was deeply frustrating that nothing she could say was likely to convince Rebecca otherwise.

'There is no need to humour me. I was already completely over Steven.' Rebecca had had her 'summer to forget' before she had found Nick. Maybe she was due a winter to forget—or remember, depending on how things turned out…?

'That's great.'

'It's true—I'm not heartbroken, I'm just mad and I feel like a total idiot.'

'Look, you don't have to put on a brave face for me. I've been there. These things take time.'

'Not for me. I've met someone else.' The moment the words were out of her mouth Rose regretted introducing a face-saving lover. The chances were Rebecca wouldn't believe her anyway.

'You haven't mentioned him before…?'

'It's early days and I didn't want to tempt fate,' Rose improvised brightly, pretending not to hear the sceptical note in her sister's voice.

'So what's he like?'

'Like…?'

'Yes—tall, short, dark, fair? Married or single?'

'I do not make a habit of falling for married men and he's tall.' She closed her eyes and leaned back into her seat. A faint smile curved her lips as the image in her head solidified. 'Tall and very dark, with grey eyes that have a dark ring around the iris and really long dark lashes. His mouth…well, he's got a really great smile…when he does…smile, that is…'

'Wow, does he have a brother?'

The laughing query jolted Rose from her contemplative silence.

'Look, Rebecca, I have to do something and, don't worry, it's not crazy…well, it is, but good crazy. I think. I'll get back to you.' She slid the phone back in her bag and leaned forward to speak to the driver, who had been unashamedly eavesdropping. 'Could you turn around and take me back to the estate, please?'

CHAPTER NINE

'So do you want me to wait?'

Rose took the notes from her wallet and handed them over. 'No, thanks.' She was burning her bridges—no escape route to allow her to chicken out.

She stood, her case at her feet, and watched as the taxi vanished. When it was gone she stayed where she was, staring after it.

'Have you any idea what you're doing, Rose?'

Good question.

She spun around. Her heart gave a lurch as she looked at Mathieu… He represented all the reckless excitement she'd been avoiding all her life.

And if you wanted to learn about sex he would probably be a pretty good guide. And there would be no possibility of emotional complications because it didn't seem a big leap to assume he wasn't into deep and meaningful relationships.

'I came back.'

'So I see. Is there a problem?'

'Not really.' Only if you count the fact I've gone insane as a problem, she thought as his tactile voice sent an illicit shiver down her spine… That alone should have warned her she was making a mistake. 'I came back.'

'We covered that. I'm surprised.'

'Good surprised or bad surprised?'

'That kind of depends if you're going to take another swing at me.'

'That depends on how rude you are to me. Do you find me attractive?'

The question seemed to throw him; she suspected not a lot did.

'Or do you say the stuff you do because people expect you to?'

'Is this,' he asked, 'some sort of test? Multiple choice, perhaps?'

'It doesn't matter, you don't have to say. I was thinking…'

His winged brows lifted in the direction of his dark hairline. 'I'm not sure if I should ask…? But what were you thinking about?'

'Were you serious?' she blurted out.

'Rarely,' he admitted solemnly. 'But few people appreciate my sense of humour.'

She slung him an irritated look. 'About the job.' If you could legitimately call pretending to be engaged to a Greek million-aire a job. 'Were you serious?'

His expression sharpened. 'You'll do it?'

'Don't look smug just yet,' she warned quickly.

Mathieu watched her hair blow in the wind and struggled to control a sudden overwhelming compulsion to mesh his fingers into the silky strands…then he could draw her face up to his and… He sucked in a deep breath.

'But you're thinking about it…?' he suggested while his own thoughts stayed stubbornly fixated on the soft lush outline of her lips.

'I'm thinking about it.'

'Just thinking? Why the sudden change of heart?'

She shrugged. 'I'm assuming it pays well.'

'You expect me to believe your motives are purely mercen-ary?' He laughed, baring his white teeth in a wolfish grin.

'And what is so funny about that?'

'I meet people every day of the week who would sell their

souls for a profit margin. I can smell avarice a mile away…'

Around her the only scent he was aware of was the light floral scent of the shampoo she used. Brow creased, he shook his head positively. 'No, this isn't about money.'

'I'd be touched if it wasn't for the fact you were accusing me of trying to screw money out of you twenty minutes ago.'

'I jumped to the wrong conclusion,' he admitted, drawing a hand across his jaw.

'Jumping to the wrong conclusion is a lifestyle choice with you. Look, do you want me to do this or not?'

Something flashed into his eyes that Rose couldn't quite put a name to. There was a pause. 'I want,' he agreed.

Rose swallowed. 'There will be conditions,' she warned.

Amusement flickered in his eyes, but his expression was sombre as he nodded his head and wondered who or what had put that reckless glow in her golden eyes. 'Fine.'

'You can't say that when you don't know what they are,' she retorted.

'When a man wants something badly enough he is generally prepared to take the rough with the smooth.' And she was smooth, very smooth, and he wanted her. He glanced at his watch and did a quick mental calculation. 'I have to be in Edinburgh this afternoon. You'll have to go on ahead to London. I'll book you on a flight and—'

'Today? But I thought…' No, Rose, you didn't think, and that, she reminded herself, was the point of the exercise. You're being spontaneous. Oh, God, leaps into the unknown were a lot easier when they weren't real.

'And on to Nixias in a couple of weeks. I'll arrange the rings and the itinerary,' he said, taking her elbow and urging her towards the entrance.

'What? But,' she protested as she was hustled forward, 'what is Nixias?'

'It's where I'm going to show off my blushing bride-to-be to my family.'

'But two weeks…I thought…'

He stopped on the steps of the entrance and raised an enquiring brow. 'You thought what, *ma douce amie*?'

'What did you call me?'

'*Ma douce amie*…my sweet love,' he helpfully translated. 'Just putting in a little practice, but don't worry, you don't have to reciprocate.' Their eyes connected and a sardonic smile twisted his mobile mouth as he added, 'I'll settle for you not calling me a bastard.'

'I've never called you that,' she protested.

'Not out loud,' he agreed, casually tucking her heavy case under his arm while he dealt with the big door that swung inward with a loud creak. 'But you have very expressive eyes,' he observed, wondering what expression he would see in those eyes at the moment her climax peaked and sent ripple after ripple of pleasure cascading through her taut body.

He was not a man normally inclined to think or speak in terms of destiny or fate, but in that moment he truly believed that one day he would find out.

His molten silver eyes focused on her mouth and her eyes and hoped for the sake of his mental health that it was sooner rather than later.

'This is all so fast,' she said, stepping past him into the hallway. 'I wasn't expecting this to be so fast.'

'What can I say? A man in love doesn't let the grass grow under his feet.'

'Well, as you asked, you could try not saying that again for a start,' she grumbled, feeling the rush of blood to her cheeks.

He laughed, then said, 'Well, at least you won't have time for second thoughts.'

And he was right. The next hours flashed by in a blur: the

private flight down to London; being installed in a swish hotel suite—apparently his London flat was undergoing a total renovation—and having her dinner alone in the same suite.

That next morning the memory of the previous day's events seemed like a dream.

The dreamlike quality vanished the moment a hotel employee delivered a small red box with the compliments of Mr Demetrios.

There was an envelope with her name on it handwritten in a bold scrawl. She opened the envelope first. It was short and to the point.

'Be ready for dinner at nine-thirty. Wear this.'

He had signed his signature at the bottom. It was about as personal as a cheque, which was not a problem—she had not expected him to send love and kisses—but his Christian name would have been nice rather than the damned squiggle of his signature.

She was still frowning with discontent when she opened the box. The breath left her lungs in one shaky gasp.

On the red silk lay a ring, and not just any ring. The square-cut emerald surrounded by diamonds that stared back at her was exquisite.

Wear it, he'd said; the very thought of it scared her silly. It had to be worth a small fortune.

There was a slight tremor in her fingers as she slid it onto her left hand. It was a perfect fit. The tears that filled her eyes were, she told herself, ludicrous. It wasn't as if she were self-deluded enough to wish this were for real.

The woman who became Mathieu Demetrios's wife would have the eyes of the world on her every move. Rose wouldn't be surprised to see a candid shot of her unshaved leg change hands for tens of thousands on the open market.

While Rose was prepared to admit her take on the subject might lack balance, one thing she was sure of was that the woman who married Mathieu would have a husband other women coveted. God, she'd spend her life on a permanent diet and develop a nervous tic from keeping a watch out for younger, hungry women with designs.

It wasn't a job description that appealed to her.

She had to ring Rebecca. She would be economical with the truth, or Rebecca would be jumping on the next plane. Their parents, enjoying a second honeymoon aboard a cruise ship, she could deal with at a later date.

'It's just a marvellous opportunity,' Rose enthused.

'Marvellous. But what exactly are you going to be doing on this Greek island? For that matter, what Greek island?'

Rebecca, who had interrupted several times during her twin's rambling and deliberately vague description of her new and exciting opportunity, sounded suspicious.

'And who exactly did you say you will be working for?'

Rose hadn't, and the omission had not been accidental. She grimaced down the phone. 'Oh, you wouldn't have heard of him…the family is called Demetrios.'

'Demetrios! You're working for *the* Demetrios family?'

'It's probably a very common name in Greece.'

'Do they happen to own the island you're going to?'

'I think they might,' Rose admitted uncomfortably.

'And which Demetrios are you working for, Rose?'

'The son, I think…I really have to go, Rebecca,' she said hurriedly. 'But I'll be in touch,' she added brightly.

The dismay and shock echoed down the line as Rebecca said blankly, 'My God, Rose, you're working for Mathieu Demetrios. He used to be known as Mathieu Gauthier.'

'I think that was his name,' Rose admitted uncomfortably.

There was an audible sigh of relief. 'Then you haven't met him…if you had you really wouldn't have forgotten his name or anything else about him.' This wry aside was muttered. 'The thing is, Rose, there's something I have to tell you...'

Rose was desperate to spare her twin the embarrassment. 'Actually I've met him, but I really don't think I registered on his radar. Reading between the lines, I doubt if I'll actually see much of him once we're there.'

'Really...?' The relief in her twin's voice echoed down the line.

She hung up pleading an early night and was just putting the phone back into her bag when there was a sharp rap on the door.

'You are ready?'

She turned and saw Mathieu standing in the doorway wearing a pair of faded blue jeans, black tee shirt and worn leather jacket. The violent stab of lust that slammed through her body with the force of a sledgehammer left Rose momentarily both breathless and speechless.

The indentation between his darkly defined brows deepened as he studied her pale face. 'Are you sick?'

Rose sucked in a deep breath and thought, Oh, you have no idea how sick! But it was just physical, she told herself, determined to maintain an objectivity about the entire knee-trembling, pulse-racing thing she suffered in his presence—after all, pretending something wasn't happening implied you were scared of it.

And she wasn't; she had it under control. It wasn't as if her emotions were involved—she barely knew the man and what she did know she didn't much like.

Not like him and yet you planned to sleep with him...?

The guilty colour flew to her cheeks and her eyes fell from his.

Sanity had returned about two-thirty in the morning when she had sat bolt upright in bed, a horrified groan escaping her lips.

The only crumb of comfort she could take from this momentary madness was that Mathieu would never, *ever* know the underlying reason she had agreed to go along with his scheme. Neither he nor anyone else would ever know that she had ever got it into her head that she would throw caution to the wind and sleep with a man she didn't love, and not just any man, this man. She schooled her features into a smile and lied. 'No, I'm fine. Am I overdressed?' she asked, hating that she was asking for his approval, but it was preferable to saying she was immobilised with lust.

Mathieu's eyes, concealed from her behind the dark fringe of his lashes, slid down her body.

In his opinion she was overdressed only in that she was wearing anything at all.

He toyed briefly with and almost immediately discarded the idea of explaining to her that she was the sort of woman who looked better without clothes.

It was quite irrational to keep a guard on his tongue around a woman who he knew was more than capable of adopting the male role of sexual predator. Maybe it was because the air of wholesome sexuality she seemed unaware she exuded was tinged with vulnerability.

It was not as if he would be telling her something she did not already know. Something many men had told her before him… The thought of these faceless men who had looked with lustful longing at her lush curves brought a frown of dissatisfaction to his face.

'You look fine. I thought we'd dine somewhere casual the first night. The rest of the week, I thought…in fact, here—I made you a copy of the itinerary.'

'Itinerary?' she echoed, staring at the paper he'd handed her as she stepped out into the corridor after him.

'Unfortunately I've a full diary, the next ten days or so, but we should be able to take in a première, dinner three nights and a couple of lunches.'

'But won't people see us?' she asked as the lift door closed behind them. She took a deep breath. Oh, God, but enclosed spaces with him in were so much more, well, *enclosed*.

Mathieu looked down at her with the advantage of his superior height and shrugged. 'Being seen, Rose, is the idea. This is about photo opportunities, establishing us as a credible couple before you meet my family.'

'Oh…'

'What did you think it was about—getting to know the real me?'

The angry colour flew to her cheeks. 'Well, if you're as two-dimensional as you seem that shouldn't take long.'

'Well, if you struggle, the back page has a few pertinent facts.'

'You think of everything,' she snapped irritably. It was a good thing she had given up on the idea of seduction because Mathieu seemed to have this job laid out along very formal, businesslike lines with no room for anything more spontaneous. 'But actually you don't. I have nothing to wear at these sort of places,' she pointed out, tapping the top sheet of his so-called intinerary with her forefinger.

'The new wardrobe should be delivered in the morning.'

Her chin came up. 'New wardrobe?'

He seemed not to notice the dangerous note in her voice, though several people they passed as they stepped out of the lift did.

'If there's anything else you need don't hesitate…'

Outside in the air Rose took a deep sustaining breath and counted to ten. She'd have still been mad if it had been ten thousand. 'Listen, because I'm only saying this once, but I'm not taking clothes from you. I'm not taking anything from you.'

Mathieu threw back his head and laughed. 'Why, you sweet old-fashioned thing, you. But relax, *ma petite*, this is not a gift— it is a uniform. Don't get me wrong. I like the sexy librarian look, but not everyone has my imagination,' he drawled. 'And they will expect you as my future wife to look a certain way. When we are alone you can wear what you wish…or nothing at all…though we will have little time to be alone before we leave for Nixias.'

She could hear his laughter as she got into the waiting car. She clenched her teeth and didn't stop clenching them all evening until he said goodnight at the door of her suite.

'No, I won't come in,' he said.

'I wasn't about to ask.'

'But you did think I'd expect it?' His cynical smile deepened at her expression. 'I want my father to realise that you are not a casual pick-up, but the woman I want to be my wife.'

'You don't intend to have sex with the woman you marry?'

'After an appropriate courtship I intend to have a great deal of sex.'

Rose, her face aflame, almost threw herself through the door. 'Not with me, you're not,' she yelled, before slamming the door in his grinning face.

Rose discovered Mathieu hadn't been joking. Other than the events he had listed in his precious intinerary she barely saw him at all and as on all of those occasions they had been in the full glare of the press—she had blinked at more flash bulbs than she would have dreamt existed—it had not been exactly relaxing.

The morning of their journey to Nixias arrived and there had been only one occasion when she had seen a tiny glimpse of the real man. Or was that wishful thinking on her part?

They had been getting into a car after a meal, the paparazzi had been snapping happily, when a stray dog had appeared from nowhere. One of the photographers had tried to kick the mangy creature out of his path and that was probably the last thing he had known until Mathieu had hauled him off his feet, practised smile gone as he'd said something that had made the man's colour retreat.

'I take it you like dogs.'

Mathieu had smiled grimly and said simply, 'I dislike men who kick anything that is weaker or unable to hit back.'

If that night he had suggested coming in when they got back to her hotel suite she would have said yes, but he hadn't.

* * *

They reached the airport around ten in the morning. One brow lifted as Mathieu's silver eyes swept her face before he took hold of her left hand. 'You are not wearing your ring.'

'Not *my* ring...*the* ring. If it was my ring I'd be keeping it when this contract is over. I didn't wear it for the journey because it is obviously valuable...what if I lose it?'

'Then *obviously* you will spend the rest of your life paying me back,' he said, leading the way towards the terminal building.

Trotting on her four-inch heels to catch him up, she caught his sleeve. 'I'm serious, Mathieu,' she said. 'People who walk around with jewellery like this have bodyguards.'

'What makes you think I'm not serious?'

She met his silvered gaze, flushed and as things tightened low in her belly complained crossly, 'Don't you ever give a straight answer?'

'Relax, it's a prop.'

'You mean it's not real.' Rose didn't know whether she was disappointed or relieved.

'My father would spot a fake at twenty feet.'

'Then it is real. You father sounds scary.' Considering his son, genetically speaking this was pretty much a foregone conclusion.

'This might help,' he said.

Rose glanced with a frown at the file he had placed in her hand. 'What is this—another itinerary?'

'Some things about my father...his likes, his dislikes, things you might find useful.'

Rose, her expression incredulous, shook her head. 'Are you sure you don't want me to learn Greek on the flight over as well? Mathieu, if you wanted covert operations you took on the wrong person,' she told him bluntly. 'If I was your fiancée I wouldn't be interested in pleasing or impressing your father.'

'Just me.'

Rose pretended not to hear his sly insertion. 'It would

probably be more useful if I knew something about you other than how you like your steak and how prettily you smile for the camera. It's all so…*shallow*…'

'It or me?' he said, sounding unconcerned. 'I'm sorry if you feel neglected, but you can spend the next few days learning all my unplumbed depths.'

Rose rolled her eyes while her heart did a double flip. 'I can hardly wait,' she grunted. What had she let herself in for?

He accepted the file without comment when she distastefully handed it back to him, though he actually sounded serious when he said, 'You've got a point—it is probably best if you try as much as possible to be yourself.'

'Well, it would be kind of hard to be anyone else, wouldn't it? And what would be the point?'

He gave her a strange look. 'Most people, Rose, spend most of their life pretending to be someone they're not.'

'Well, I—' She stopped dead as she saw the private jet that was waiting for them. 'Oh, God!' she groaned. 'This is so not me. I will never carry this off. I'm just not billionaire's bride material.'

Mathieu grinned at her dismay and nodded to the man who greeted them. 'Don't knock it until you try it, *ma petite.*'

Rose slung him a disgruntled look. 'Some things, you know, don't fit without trying.'

'Oh, I think we fit perfectly.'

Not unnaturally his purred comment reduced her to red-cheeked silence. It was a silence that Mathieu seemed in no hurry to break.

By the time the private helicopter circled the island five hours later she doubted that she and Mathieu had exchanged more than a dozen words. He had been immersed in his laptop for the entire journey totally oblivious, it seemed, to her growing resentment.

It wasn't as if she expected him to hold her hand, but neither had she expected him to tune her out. Every time she had made an attempt to initiate conversation he had given a monosyllabic response. In her opinion it would have occurred to anyone with an ounce of sensitivity that she was nervous, that she required a little reassurance.

'So we're here, then.' Mathieu looked up as if finally remembering she was there.

She looked in the direction he indicated, taking in the long, low, sprawling villa built into the rock and surrounded by acres of manicured grounds.

The private jet that had brought them to Athens, the transfer by helicopter, and now the private island retreat—it was just hitting home how seriously off-the-scale rich the Demetrios family was.

Her smooth brow pleated as she caught her full lower lip between her teeth and nibbled nervously. Nobody, she thought, staring down at the island retreat—not the other guests and, more importantly, Andreos Demetrios—was going to swallow the engagement story.

Mathieu lived in a different world from the one she inhabited. She fought to maintain her calm as panic nibbled at the edges of her composure.

She slid a surreptitious sideways glance towards her travelling companion, who had abandoned his computer and was also looking through the window. She supposed the wealth thing should have been a consideration earlier. Rose supposed she hadn't really thought about it earlier because, unlike many people who needed to flaunt their wealth and position to establish their superiority, Mathieu didn't labour the fact he was staggeringly wealthy.

Not because he had any leanings towards modesty and self-deprecation. In fact, thinking of Mathieu and those worthy qualities in the same sentence made her lips twitch into a wry smile.

No, Mathieu didn't need to remind people of who he was

because he was one of those rare people who possessed a confidence that went bone-deep—a confidence that would have been there if he hadn't had a penny to his name.

Besides, far from wanting to be an object of envy or surrounding himself with fawning flunkies, he had a genuine disregard for what anyone thought about him, too arrogant to much care what anyone thought about him.

'I can see now why you don't just tell your father to mind his own business...' Honesty was the best policy in theory, but it would take an unusual man to risk losing all this.

'There's no chance of me losing all this,' Mathieu said, his voice just loud enough for her to hear above the noise. 'I own it.'

'You own what?'

'The island.'

She turned and tilted her head back to look into his face. 'You own the island...' she echoed, shock stripping her voice of all expression. Her eyes slid to the vista below and she gulped. 'All of it?' she added faintly.

He nodded and explained. 'It never belonged to Andreos, it belonged to my stepmother's family. She had originally intended that Alex and I share it, but he...' He stopped, swallowing, the action causing the muscles in his brown throat to ripple, and said, 'It came directly to me after she died.' Andreos had been furious, taking the bequest as a personal slight.

Her head was spinning. 'It didn't occur to you to mention this to me?'

He raised his brows and looked mildly surprised by the heat in her husky enquiry. 'Why should I? It isn't relevant.'

'I like that you thought it might be relevant for me to know what your father's favourite colour is but you didn't think it relevant to mention you own a whole damned island paradise.' She flung up her hands in exasperation and glared at him.

'It is only paradise now that you are here, *mon coeur*,' he drawled, clasping a hand dramatically to his chest.

Rose took an irritated swipe at him, which he evaded with a laugh. 'If you keep that up I will just laugh in your face,' she warned him, wishing with all her heart that laughter, instead of the heavy weakness that affected all her limbs, were her response to his mocking endearment.

CHAPTER TEN

'NO RECEPTION committee,' Rose said, sounding relieved.

'No,' Mathieu agreed, not sounding as though he shared her relief.

She shot him a curious look. 'You're annoyed?'

Mathieu's eyes, cold as steel, flickered briefly over her face. 'You're my fiancée—not to come out to meet you is a deliberate snub.' Andreos could be as rude as he liked to him, it was water off a duck's back, but Mathieu would make sure that his father treated his future wife with the respect she deserved.

'But I'm not.'

Mathieu flashed her a strange look, then retorted, 'He doesn't know that.'

He probably will about five minutes after seeing us together, she thought, pressing a hand to her churning stomach.

'There's no need to be nervous.'

Rose tried to smile. 'And here I was thinking that I was hiding it well,' she quipped.

'Come in, it's been a long day. You'll feel better after a shower.'

It was silly, she knew, but the light pressure of his hand in the small of her back made her feel more confident.

Halfway up the path to the villa they were met by a man in uniform. He bowed slightly to Rose, then turned to Mathieu and made what sounded to Rose like a profuse apology.

Mathieu responded to him in the same language and he walked a little ahead of them the rest of the way. When they reached the entrance, a glass atrium from which several corridors radiated, Mathieu turned to her and said, 'Spyros will show you to your room.'

'You're not coming?' Hearing the sharpness of anxiety in her voice, she frowned, but she need not have worried. Mathieu appeared not to notice anything amiss.

'I need to speak to Andreos.'

She watched him stride away and tried not to feel deserted.

'Miss…?'

She turned to the uniformed man smiling encouragingly at her and followed him further into the villa.

His father was in his study. He glanced up when Mathieu walked in, then almost immediately returned his attention to the newspaper he was reading.

Mathieu walked straight across to him, grabbed the newspaper and threw it on the ground.

The older man looked at him in open-mouthed astonishment. 'What do you think you are doing?' he thundered.

'I'm laying down a few ground rules, Andreos.'

'You're laying down rules to me?' The older man gave a snort of scorn.

'Rule one…actually there is only one rule,' he revealed, flashing a cold smile that made the other man look wary for the first time. 'In future you will not slight Rose in any way; you will treat her with the respect she deserves.'

Andreos got to his feet. 'You are very sensitive all of a sudden. Who is this Rose, anyway?'

'The woman who is wearing my ring…that is all you need to know. Do we understand one another?'

'Oh, I understand you. You march in here as if you own the place.'

'I do.'

The soft intervention caused the older man's already high colour to deepen. 'If Alex had been alive none of this would be happening.'

'Alex isn't alive.'

'You were always jealous of him,' Andreos accused, stabbing a finger towards his first-born.

'If he had been someone else I might have,' Mathieu conceded. 'But he wasn't, he was Alex.' It was hard to explain but nobody could be jealous of Alex—he just didn't inspire negative emotions in people.

Or hadn't. Sometimes even after eighteen months Mathieu still expected him to breeze into a room with that grin that was impossible to resist.

'I've stepped into my brother's shoes because you asked me to, Andreos.'

The reminder earned him a dark scowl.

'But this is one area where I am not prepared to step into my brother's shoes…not even to see the Constantine fortune swell the Demetrios coffers. I will marry the woman of my choice, not someone you chose for me.'

'She's half in love with you already.'

'She thinks she is.'

And that was the problem. She'd been hurting after Alex's death and he'd been there. He'd shown her a little kindness and she had developed a crush. In the natural course of things the crush would have died a natural death. But their respective parents kept it alive by continually contriving to throw them together.

The poor kid was so vulnerable. Couldn't the old foxes see how cruel they were being to the girl? In his opinion they needed their heads banged together, but that not being an option, all he could do was not play their little game.

Hand on the door handle, Mathieu turned. 'Just don't try and manipulate me, Andreos. I don't bend.'

Outside the room Mathieu almost collided with a still figure. Hands on her shoulders, he steadied Rose before firmly pushing her away from him so that he could look into her face.

'What are you doing here?'

'I was looking for you.'

'Well, you found me. How much,' he asked, nodding towards the door behind him, 'did you hear?'

'Pretty much all of it.'

Enough to know he had loved his brother; she could hear it in his voice. She was just amazed that his father seemed deaf to his remaining son's pain. As for Mathieu's relationship with his father, that was even rockier than she had imagined. Ironically if his father had not pushed the union it was entirely possible that Mathieu would have fallen in love with the eligible Sacha, if she was beautiful, and Rose was sure she would be.

Maybe he already was in love with her?

'I didn't mean to, the door was open and...'

'You decided to listen in.'

He didn't look annoyed, which surprised her. 'Well, you weren't exactly quiet.'

'So why were you following me?'

'I asked Spyros to tell me where you were.' She nodded towards the man who was standing by the wall being selectively deaf. 'My phone was charging on the plane; you put it in your pocket. I want to ring my sister.' Want was actually the wrong word, but she did feel obliged to assure Rebecca she was all right.

'So I did,' Mathieu said, digging the phone from his pocket and handing it to her.

Rose sucked in a tiny breath when his fingertips—was the contact accidental?—brushed hers. It was easier to hide your reaction when you knew what was coming.

'You have a sister?'

She nodded, wondering what Mathieu's reaction would be if he ever discovered he had already met Rebecca.

'Just the one?'

She nodded.

'And you're close?'

'Pretty close,' she agreed, 'though she's married now, so…well, we don't see as much of one another.'

Mathieu said something to the waiting Spyros, who vanished. 'Come, you look exhausted. You should lie down before dinner.'

Rose couldn't pretend the idea did not appeal; the day was beginning to catch up on her with a vengeance. She had to make a conscious effort to put one foot in front of the other.

'This is my suite.' He pushed open a door and preceded her into a large, elegantly furnished sitting room. 'Your room is there.' He pointed towards a closed door to her left. 'And that is mine,' he added, indicating the one next to it. 'And your parents— they are alive…?'

For a moment the edit function on her vocal cords disconnected and Rose was horrified to hear herself say, 'Is Sacha beautiful?'

'Yes, she is.'

'Then why don't you want to marry her?' she wondered as she moved around the room looking at the artwork on the walls. 'Are these all genuine…?'

'I should think so,' Mathieu said, not looking at the artwork. 'You should know—they're yours.'

'Then, yes, they are genuine.' The soft wide-legged trousers she wore clung to the warm womanly curves of her hips and thighs as she moved.

'You're a beautiful woman too.'

Startled, Rose spun around, the heat rushing to her cheeks. 'Are you trying to change the subject?'

Her beauty was a subject that was never very far from his thoughts, but he judged that this might not be the best moment to mention it.

'No, I am trying to give you a compliment. Who would have thought,' he murmured, moving towards her, 'that it would be this hard?'

'Well…all right, thank you. I think,' she added cautiously. 'Why don't you want to marry her?'

Mathieu sighed and sank into an upholstered armchair. He propped his chin on steepled fingers and looked at her. 'Are we talking about Sacha again?'

'Well, if she's beautiful your children would be winners of the genetic lottery,' she mused, a frown of dissatisfaction settling on her soft features as her thoughts lingered on a mental image of golden-skinned little boys with grey eyes and jet hair. And pansy-eyed little girls with curls and sweet cupid-bow mouths.

'I think that was a compliment.'

'Like you're totally unaware that you're good-looking,' she retorted, having some sort of heat rush and not the good kind— if there was a good kind. Concentrate, Rose, she told herself, sucking in a deep breath and saying crossly, 'What are you doing?' as he grabbed her wrist and pulled her down onto the arm of the chair.

'I am looking at your neck,' he explained huskily.

'Well, don't. I don't like it.' Like wasn't the last word she would use to describe the slow-burning heat that was invading every cell in her body.

'You want to know about Sacha? I will tell you. She loved my brother. She needed someone after Alex died and I was there.'

'Your father said she loves you.'

'It is a crush, nothing more,' he said, sounding irritated. He loosed his grip on her arm and Rose got hastily to her feet.

'I think that I'll take that nap if you don't mind,' she said, backing quickly towards the door.

The interconnecting door between their rooms was ajar, Rose presumed left this way by the maid who had just brought fresh flowers into her own room.

Lips compressed, she tapped on the interconnecting door loudly. It made her feel odd to know that Mathieu could have walked in any time when she was asleep.

Not that she could imagine he would have unless he had a thing for snoring women.

'It's open.'

Rose stepped inside. 'I have a slight problem with that.'

He was standing at the window gazing out to sea.

'There is a key if you're worried for your virtue.' Mathieu, who had been standing at the open French doors, turned as he spoke.

Rose was conscious of her already tumultuous pulse giving several loud erratic thuds as it banged against her ribcage. Mathieu looked conspicuously sexy in a beautifully formal dark dinner jacket, and she barely noticed the stunning backdrop of the turquoise sea crashing onto the rocks below.

Her lashes came down in a protective sweep and she swallowed, ashamed of the silky heat between her thighs.

'And don't think I won't use it.' She could only hope he'd do the same because it would be good to have temptation removed.

And there was no point pretending that Mathieu wasn't temptation. Head tilted a little to one side, Mathieu looked her up and down. Being the subject of his silent and critical perusal made Rose's temper fizz, but she fought to control it, aware that flushed cheeks would ruin the aloof but sexy look she'd aimed for.

'Pity.'

Her head came up. 'I'm so sorry if I don't meet with your approval.' Anxious not to give him the totally false impression— she actually wanted it—she refused to ask him what was wrong with the way she looked.

'Oh, you look fine,' he said, his glance dropping once more to skim the pale blue silk shift dress she had taken a good deal of care to select.

She had also taken care with her hair and make-up and until he had turned up his nose she had been feeling confident that whatever else let her down it would not be her appearance.

Rose's temper flared to the surface as she fixed him with a hostile look. 'I look fine?' she repeated in a dangerously quiet voice.

She didn't want to look fine, she wanted to look outrageously gorgeous, although on a more realistic level she would have taken presentably pretty.

The dangerous note in her voice awoke a gleam of humour in his steely grey eyes, but his expression remained serious as he observed with a note of regret, 'It's just a pity you didn't choose something that showed…' His glance sank significantly to her breasts, which began to heave against their covering.

'Show what, exactly?'

'A little more cleavage. My father would have been too distracted to ask any awkward questions.'

'Have you never—' she choked '—heard of political correctness?'

'Heard of it, but I don't have an awful lot of time for it. Don't take it personally, Rose, I'm just being practical.'

'*Practical*,' she spluttered, practically shaking with outrage.

'I don't think there's anything incorrect in using what assets you've got, and don't tell me you never have.'

This cynical suggestion made her temper fizz. 'No, I haven't.'

She knew she shouldn't respond to his sceptical shrug

because he was obviously trying to needle her, but Rose couldn't bite her tongue.

'As for encouraging anyone called Demetrios to leer at me,' she said, 'I don't think so—just being around anyone of that name for any length of time is enough to make me want to go lie down in a quiet, darkened room.' She would have felt a lot happier if the mental image that accompanied that hot statement had her lying alone in the quiet, darkened room.

'I had no idea you felt that way…' He glanced at his watch and sighed. 'Unfortunately my father does not like tardiness. Otherwise I would be perfectly willing to oblige.'

The colour flew to her face; he had an uncanny ability to read her mind. 'I meant *alone* in a darkened room with a cold compress on my head, not you…' On top of me…inside me… What would that feel like, she wondered, to feel the weight of his hard body on top of her? His silky hardness filling and stretching her?

Glazed eyes half closed, her glance drifted to his mouth and a fractured sigh shuddered through her body. She expelled a second, deeper sigh and bit her lip. His raw masculinity and what it did to her was terrifying.

Face burning, she slammed her hand against her forehead, which even as she spoke was beginning to pound ominously.

'If you want to distract people, Mathieu, and it's legitimate to use what you've got—' and he certainly had quite a lot, she thought, tearing her eyes from the hard, supple contours of his muscle-packed torso and feeling a bit dizzy as a consequence '—why,' she suggested, sucking in a deep restorative breath 'don't you take off your shirt to go to dinner?'

She folded her arms across her chest, causing the silk across her hips to tauten, and fixed him with a tight-lipped smile.

'See how you like being treated as a sex object?'

'You would find me taking off my shirt distracting?' He was definitely finding the way the subtly shiny fabric clung to the peachy curve of her hips and thighs more than distracting. In his mind he could hear the swish of the fabric as it fell in a silken pool around her feet. The image made his body temperature rise a notch and as his imagination lingered over the soft curves the ache in his groin became more difficult to ignore.

He was asking if she would find him performing a striptease distracting…?

Rose's feeling of superiority vanished faster than her protest had the time he had kissed her. Now this was what was called shooting yourself in your own foot and then stamping on it for good measure.

She laughed nervously, her eyes sliding away as she attempted to treat his suggestion as the joke.

'One naked man is much the same as another,' she dismissed, smiling faintly.

Well, what else could she say?

She could hardly go into gratuitous detail about how she turned into a drooling, sex-starved imbecile every time she considered the hard body that filled his superbly cut clothing.

Swallowing hard, she lifted her chin and pinned a fixed smile to her face. She had heard that lust was undiscriminating, but she had not imagined how undiscriminating until she had met this man.

'So you would be bored?'

'For God's sake!' she snapped. 'That wasn't a challenge. You're an incredible-looking man with a great body,' she admitted, her attitude see-sawing between exasperation and desperation. 'But I happen not to be one of those women who go for beefcake. A six pack does nothing for me.' Well, not up to now it hadn't, anyway.

Not that Mathieu could be categorised so neatly. Beefcake was just visual candy. Nice, but instantly forgettable, and he was neither.

What he had was far more complex and dangerous than simply the combined appeal of a great body and a charismatic smile. He had an earthy sexuality that evoked an almost visceral response in her. And there was nothing even faintly contrived about it; it was as much a part of him as his fingerprints and equally unique.

A dangerous smile lurking in the back of the platinum eyes still holding her gaze, he slid the unfastened tie from around his neck. 'In that case,' he mused, 'it wouldn't bother you if I...'

Rose watched, her eyes saucer-wide in horror as he began to slip the buttons of his shirt revealing in seconds a segment of golden skin sprinkled with dark body hair. Unable to tear her eyes from the erotic spectacle, Rose ran the tip of her tongue across the outline of her full upper lip and sucked in a shaky breath as illicit excitement clutched at the quivering muscles low in her pelvis and shot down to her curling toes.

'Not in the slightest,' she agreed hoarsely. 'Although if your father doesn't like tardiness this might not be the moment to allow your exhibitionist tendencies full rein.'

'You would not find it that distracting, then?' he questioned with a show of silky smooth innocence that was in stark variance to the sensual, mocking glitter in his deep-set eyes as they moved from her parted lips and fastened onto her wide, dilated amber eyes.

Another button followed the first two and Rose, fighting for composure, felt the sweat break out on her forehead as he pulled the hem from the waistband of his trousers. 'N-not in the slightest,' she said with what she suspected was the most unconvincing show of indifference this century.

'You should never, ever play poker, *mon ange*.' His shirt hung open to the waist, revealing a large proportion of his powerful chest and a tantalising section of muscle-ridged flat stomach.

Rose was shocked and horrified by the shaft of lust that struck to the heart of her. Eyes glazed, she ran a tongue over the dry outline of her lips. The impulse to reach out and touch him, place her hands on the golden glowing skin that looked like oiled silk, was so strong she could physically taste it. She stood poised on the balls of her feet to take flight, but was unable to summon the strength to break the hypnotic hold of his smoky eyes.

Then finally she managed to turn her head sharply. Her hands clenched as she fought to calm her erratic shallow breathing and drag enough air into her lungs to stop her head spinning.

'I prefer poker to the games you play,' she husked, feeling the unexpected sting of emotional tears fill her eyes…which was crazy because she simply wasn't a crying person.

'I don't play games, Rose.' There was a note in his voice that she hadn't heard before. It made her want to search his face, but she knew that would be a bad idea. Looking at him made her mind mush…actually, her mind was permanently mush at the moment.

He covered the few feet that separated them in seconds. Framing her face between his hands, he tilted her head up to his.

Rose's knees sagged; the sexual smoulder deep in his eyes made things shift and tighten with painful intensity low down in her pelvis.

He's going to kiss me.

This alarming realisation was almost instantly followed by one that was even more alarming—I want him to!

Wanted him to so badly she could taste it—not, of course, that she was going to let him.

It would have been easy to defuse the situation—she could have laughed in his face, pulled away or told him he was taking the role play a bit too seriously. She did none of these. Rose took an option not on the list. Shaking like someone with a fever, she gave an inarticulate little moan, wove her fingers into silky raven strands of his glossy hair and dragged his face towards her.

Her fingers stayed tangled in his hair as he covered her mouth with his. She was sucking in a tremulous breath when his tongue slid into her mouth in a slow, sensuous exploration. Tugging gently at the pink fullness of her lower lip, he lifted his head slightly.

'I have been wondering how you would taste.'

The erotic, husky confidence sent a thrill of illicit excitement through her trembling body.

He freed a hand from her face to trace a lone finger along her cheek. 'I thought you might taste delicious…' He swallowed, the muscles of his throat working as he ran his tongue over the soft inner surface of her lower lip. Rose shivered and moaned softly. 'And now I know you taste even better than that…' he completed in a throaty husk.

Eyes dilated and glazed with passion, she lifted a hand to his cheek. As her fingers slid along the hard line of his cheek and jaw somehow she caught a glimpse of movement in the periphery of her vision.

The realisation that they had an audience swept through her aroused body like an icy chill; they were not alone. She would have pulled her hand away had Mathieu not held it there. Looking past her, he said casually, 'Hello, Sacha.'

'S-sorry, I didn't know…'

The girl, who was beautiful, sounded as miserable and embarrassed as she looked. If Rose hadn't been dealing with her own feelings of shame and humiliation she might have felt sorry for her.

'I just came to say that dinner…your father is waiting.'

'We'll be right there.'

The door closed and this time he made no attempt to stop her pulling away. Well, he wouldn't, would he? There was no one to see the tender scene of seduction.

And you thought he genuinely found you irresistible? Self-disgust churned in her stomach as she backed away glaring at him with loathing.

She could not, she would not, fall for Mathieu. This was just chemistry and chemistry she could deal with, she told herself. Who better? Twenty-six-year-old virgins were not renowned for their uncontrolled sexual appetites; she had reached the conclusion a long time ago that hers was underdeveloped. Any chemistry she could ignore.

'Now where were we?'

CHAPTER ELEVEN

ROSE backed away so fast she almost tripped over a low table. Hastily righting it and the porcelain figurine that she had just saved, she straightened up and hitched up the neckline of her dress a protective inch before smoothing it down.

A distracted expression filtered into her wide wary eyes as her hand remained flat on the gentle curve of her stomach. She could feel the heat of her skin through the thin fabric. Mathieu's body had felt hot when she had been crushed up against him—scorchingly hot. Hot enough to melt her.

Closing her eyes, she counted to ten—slowly. When she opened them he was staring at her.

'Was that really necessary?' she asked.

As he carried on studying her flushed face with an unsettling intensity she began to panic. What was he seeing? If he knew how and what she was feeling it would give him an unfair advantage because she as sure as hell didn't. She had never felt so confused in her life.

There was a noise outside the windows on the patio and his attention shifted briefly. Rose, who had been unconsciously holding her breath, released it on a shuddering sigh of relief.

'They are forecasting a storm tonight. It looks as if for once they are right,' he observed, walking across to close the window.

He turned as Rose was sinking into a chair. 'It felt like it at the time.' He was genuinely shocked to recognise how necessary it had felt. He was no stranger to lust, but not since his teens had he allowed it to rule him. A man could take pleasure from his appetites without becoming a slave to them.

'What?'

She looked so prim perched on the edge of the seat with her hands folded neatly in her lap. Her lips did not look prim—they looked swollen from his kisses. 'Kissing you felt necessary.' It still did.

Her eyes slid from the hunger in his; a man had never looked at her that way before.

'I'm wearing your ring.' She held out the hand in question where the square-cut emerald in its bed of diamonds caught the light. 'I think she's already got the message. That was just plain cruel,' she observed, thinking of Sacha. 'Or I suppose you'd call it being cruel to be kind...tough love...?' she ended on a sneer.

'You're shaking.'

The soft interruption cut short her heated diatribe. His voice made her shiver but not as much as his touch. As she stared at his long fingers, very dark against her pale skin, encircling her wrist, a febrile shudder worked its way along her spine, followed by a second and third as her throat dried. She closed her eyes, bit her lip and dragged herself from the fog of sexual inertia that wrapped itself around her.

'Of course I'm shaking,' she snapped, lifting her chin in an attitude of angry defiance. 'I don't appreciate being mauled for the benefit of your girlfriend.'

'You seemed to appreciate it pretty well at the time.'

Her fingers itched to slap the smugly complacent smirk off his face, they itched to do other things, but she wouldn't let herself think about those shameful impulses.

She was unable to deny the observation without looking like a total idiot—his normally sleek dark hair was still mussed from where her fingers had pushed into the rich, lush thatch. After a painful pause she played safe and ignored his comment.

'What is it about me?' she asked bitterly. 'Do I have a sign across my forehead?' she wondered, drawing a vicious imaginary line with her finger. 'Use me because I'm so stupid I'll probably just say thank you.'

The guy with the troubled sexual identity who had dumped her at the altar, Mathieu thought, a flash of contempt appearing in his narrowed eyes as he contemplated the faceless loser who was responsible for the defensive hard-faced pose, which frankly was pretty shaky.

Rose could talk the talk but he had met hard-faced, and she was not even close to it.

Whatever his faults, he had never made any promises he couldn't keep. What sort of weak idiot, he asked himself, backed away at the last minute after making someone believe you wanted to share the rest of your life with them?

Did she still love him, he wondered, this ex who had bolted? There was no trace of any emotion so tender in her face as she jabbed a finger in the direction of his chest and snarled.

'Well, newsflash, I'm not that stupid. Do you think I didn't know you were kissing me because Sacha was standing there? God, I hardly think it was necessary to go that far to get your message across.'

'You know what they say about anger, don't you, Rose? It's only fear turned inwards.'

Fear as in fear of the consequences was not a bad thing—not if it stopped you doing something really stupid. 'Very profound,' she snapped, giving him a slow handclap. 'Where did you get that one from, Mathieu, a Christmas cracker?'

'You're mad because you think I kissed you for Sacha's benefit?'

There were two tell-tale patches of colour on her cheeks as she rolled her eyes and said in a voice laced with sarcasm, 'No, I think you kissed me because I'm totally irresistible to the opposite sex.' At that moment she would have settled for being irresistible to one man, just to have the pleasure of rejecting him.

Sure, that's really likely.

Ignoring the snide voice in her head, she gave a contemptuous sniff and folded her arms tight across her chest, the action unintentionally pushing her breasts together and drawing his eyes to the modest neckline of her dress.

'I can't speak for the rest of the male sex, but you do have a seriously destructive influence on my self-control.'

Rose loosed a scornful laugh. 'What's the punchline?'

There was a pause as their eyes locked. Mathieu's voice was flat apart from a slight ironic inflection as he said, 'It isn't a joke.'

Or maybe it was, he mused. A joke on a man who had always prided himself on never being a slave to his basic instincts being so fascinated by a woman who, given the perversity of female psychology, was probably still hung up on a man who had broken her heart.

His jaw clenched as he struggled to contain the irrational explosion of anger that surged through his body at the thought of her still craving another man, he covered the space between them in one stride.

He pinned her with a molten stare and as he cupped one side of her face with his hand some of the anger seeped from him. Her skin was soft and warm…she was soft and warm. His thumb moved across the curve of her satiny cheek and with a tiny cry she pulled away.

'And you feel the same way,' he said as she swung away from him.

Rose froze, then slowly, sparks of anger flying from her eyes, she turned slowly back and planted her hands on her hips as she lifted her chin. 'Don't you dare tell me how I feel,' she snapped. 'You haven't the faintest—'

'Please,' he begged, cutting her off mid-rant. 'Don't give me that garbage about knowing Sacha was there; there could have been a twenty-person choir in full voice and you wouldn't have noticed.'

She bit her lip, knowing that no matter what she said the mortified heat was going to rush to her cheeks. Who still blushed at her age, and why wasn't there a pill to deal with this affliction?

'Because you're such a brilliant kisser, I suppose.'

'I've had no complaints so far.' His mocking grin flashed and faded. The sombre brooding expression that replaced it was even more disturbing. 'Look, I don't know why you have such a hard time accepting what is obvious, and there is an obvious solution. Sleep with me.'

Rose didn't say a word. She couldn't. The embarrassed flush that had coloured her face fled, leaving her deathly pale as her shocked gaze flew to his. If you took away the tension around his jawline there was absolutely nothing in his expression to suggest he had just proposed anything more momentous than picking up her dry-cleaning.

She would have treated it as a joke and laughed if her vocal cords and facial muscles had not frozen solid.

'Think about it.' Again his manner bordered on the offhand, but then deciding to have sex with someone was probably nothing he got worked up about…neither presumably would he lose any sleep if she said no…which obviously she was going to…

Responding to the pressure of the hand in the small of her back, Rose began to walk towards the door.

CHAPTER TWELVE

'SORRY we're late.'

There were seven people sitting around the table. Following the lead of the heavy-set grey-haired figure, presumably Andreos Demetrios, at the head of the table the men rose courteously as Rose approached.

It would seem he had taken Mathieu's demands to heart.

Rose carried on smiling—it could be that the pasted smile might have to be surgically removed at a later date—as Mathieu made the introductions.

It was always hard walking into a room of strangers. Walking into a room of strangers when you were pretending to be someone you weren't raised the stress stakes a hundredfold. But she was not, Rose realised, nearly as nervous about being the focus of six pairs of critical eyes as she was at the thought of being alone with Mathieu once dinner was over.

What was she going to say?

Andreos gave her a hard assessing glance. She smiled faintly back. If she hadn't been so distracted by the scene in the bedroom still playing in her head she might have managed a token display of the deference that Mathieu's powerful father obviously considered his due.

Now of course she could think of a hundred responses ranging from amused to cuttingly sarcastic that would have left Mathieu in no doubt that she was not interested.

Instead what had she done? Nothing. Nothing was only slightly less incriminating than the truth, which was his suggestion had excited and scared her. She hadn't said anything because she had been afraid that if she opened her mouth she might hear herself say something along the lines of, Yes, please.

The knowledge appalled her.

'Well?'

Rose, about to take her seat, stopped and glanced towards her host. She saw the flash of annoyance in his face. Damn.

'My father asked if we had a good journey.'

'It was an experience. I'm not used to travelling in such luxurious style.' She turned her head as she lowered herself into the chair that Mathieu held out for her. Their eyes brushed before he straightened up. She found his expression hard to read. He seemed tense. Did he think she'd gone out of her way to annoy the older man?

Besides the two cousins who were like paler, less bulkier versions of Andreos Demetrios, there was the man himself, an aunt, a lawyer who had been introduced as a family friend, the lovely Sacha and her mother, a thin woman who drank water and pushed her food around her plate.

The mother looked at Rose with a marked lack of the warmth and animation that was in her face when she addressed Mathieu, who sat opposite Rose.

Sacha's expression when she looked at Mathieu was equally transparent. Rose found it difficult to believe that Mathieu could be as indifferent to her shy adoration as he appeared. The younger girl looked gorgeous in a dress that showed off her smooth pale gold shoulders. The moment her glance lighted on the glowing young brunette, Rose felt like an ancient and overweight frump.

'Not hungry, Rose?' Mathieu asked in a voice intended for her ears only as he leaned towards her.

Rose's own hushed voice had a shaky quality due in part to the shock of having her foot nudged, which might have been accidental if her shoe, an elegant high-heeled court, had not been slipped off. There was nothing accidental about the fingers that curled around her ankle.

'I…' Rose gave a yelp as the fingers slid higher, and drew her foot back, blushing deeply.

'I bit my tongue.' She sent a look of seething reproach in Mathieu's direction while nodding fervently to the maid with the wine bottle who had materialised at her elbow.

She was beginning to suspect she'd need whatever prop was available to get her through this meal.

By the time the fish course was served Rose's initial discomfort had been replaced by a tipsy recklessness.

She was wondering if anyone would actually notice if she got up and left, when Andreos's deep voice cut across the quiet and slightly stilted chatter of the dinner table. 'So my son tells me that you met in Monaco.'

Rose lifted her eyes from her plate.

As she put her fork down on her plate Rose could hear the beat of her pulse in her throbbing temples. Her eyes moved past and beyond Andreos to Mathieu who was sitting directly opposite her.

She wondered for the umpteenth time since they had arrived how she had allowed him to talk her into this.

'Oh, I love Monaco,' she heard Sacha bubble happily. 'It's just about my most favourite place in the world.'

'I've never been there,' Rose said in a clear voice that carried around the table.

Mathieu didn't express panic or even moderate concern that she wasn't playing the game. Rather his lips quivered and she saw the amused glitter in his eyes before he bent his head, calmly reapplying himself to the food on his plate.

Rose, her eyes narrowed, looked at his dark head with dislike.

A man who had gone to the trouble of inventing a fiancée and kissing her senseless in front of a witness to prove a point ought, under the circumstances, to look less relaxed when it looked as if his elaborate charade was about to be blown.

Andreos, his manner interrogative, turned his attention to his son. 'She says—'

Mathieu's dark head came up. The warning reflected in his eyes was mirrored in his deep voice. 'She is called Rose, and she is sitting beside you.' His eyes swivelled in Rose's direction. 'I hope, *ma petite*, that you will forgive my father. He does not intend to give offence, but he manages it anyway.' His attention swivelled back to his father, who looked ready to explode at the thinly veiled censure.

Andreos opened his mouth to deliver a robust denunciation but Rose got in before him.

'Genes being what they are,' she retorted, reminding herself that Mathieu was only playing a role when he rode to her defence.

Not that she needed anyone riding to her rescue—she could look after herself. A notable exception to this rule of self-sufficiency being when she was about to drown in the middle of an icy loch. There were moments that she forgot that she owed him her life.

'It would have come as an enormous shock to me if *your* father had turned out to have manners that could be called faultless.'

The jibe drew one of Mathieu's lopsided and wildly attractive grins. His father was a few beats behind in interpreting her comment. When he did his jaw literally dropped. With no experience of guests who told him he was rude, he struggled to come up with an appropriate response, though she could see that his natural instincts leant towards throttling.

'Young woman—'

'Rose,' Mathieu inserted.

'Rose, you seem to be a very outspoken young woman. That no doubt is what attracted my son to you, but I do not appreciate—'

Mathieu's languid drawl sliced across his father's rebuke. 'No, I'm shallow—her ability to speak her mind was way down the list.' His grin broadened as his eyes slid suggestively down her body.

Rose, her face flaming, dropped her fork. It hit the floor with a clatter. 'I hardly think your father is interested.'

'Such innocence. Of course he is interested, Rose. I would be most surprised if there isn't a firm of private investigators working round the clock in search of salacious details. By tomorrow he will know your shoe size and favourite colour. I could have saved you the trouble, Andreos—there is nothing that you could tell me about Rose that would shock me.'

She thought he was joking until she saw the Greek entrepreneur's expression. The colour seeped from her face at the idea of strangers building a dossier on her; it made her feel physically sick.

'So you didn't meet in Monaco. I suppose you're not engaged to be married either,' Andreos said, not denying his son's charge.

'I wouldn't marry him if he was the last man alive,' Rose announced to the room at large.

There was a startled silence, broken when Mathieu put down his fork, threw back his head and laughed.

His reaction made everyone present treat her comments as a joke.

Rose glared at him with seething frustration.

'I'd be grateful in future if you did not bring your lovers' tiffs to the dinner table.'

'You're right.'

Andreos looked visibly startled by his son's agreement.

'Forgive us, it is not an appropriate place to air our differences. I can promise you,' Mathieu continued, his eyes holding Rose's, 'that it won't happen again.'

'Don't you dare apologise for me,' she breathed wrathfully. 'And,' she added, her gaze swivelling in the direction of the older

Demetrios, 'this is *not* a lovers' tiff,' she gritted from between clenched teeth. 'We are not even…' She stopped. She couldn't think the word in the same context as Mathieu, let alone say it out loud.

'Not even what?'

'Lovers,' Mathieu inserted.

The suggestion of unspoken intimacies in the warm velvet undertones of Mathieu's deep voice brought a rush of colour to Rose's face. The resulting laughter dissipated the tension around the table. People began to eat once more.

Mathieu didn't. He laid down his fork and looked directly at Rose. Her heart began to hammer as she read the message glittering in his platinum eyes—a combination of challenge and something more elusive.

With a last glare of fulminating loathing at his amused dark face she stared fixedly at her plate until the fragrant lamb was a misty blur.

She could not have said what else she ate during the interminable meal and when it was over the ordeal went on. The women retired to the salon.

Rose found the segregation slightly Victorian and the conversation stilted and awkward.

It could not have been much more than five minutes before Mathieu left the other men who were gathered on the terrace and came to join her indoors, but it felt like longer to Rose.

As he crossed the room looking like the archetypal dark brooding hero of fiction her heart started to throw itself against her ribcage. The sudden hush that fell amongst the chattering women and almost audible buzz of interest made it clear that hers wasn't the only heart to misbehave.

And was it any wonder? Even if you left the drooling sex appeal he oozed out of the equation, aesthetically speaking he was very easy on the eye—even the way he moved was riveting.

He touched her shoulder as he reached her side and left his

hand there, a proprietorial gesture that she had no doubt was for the benefit of the other women. 'It's been a long day.'

She nodded and wondered if there was any way she could make him move his hand without making it too obvious his touch was so disruptive to her nervous system that, given the opportunity, she would have crawled out of her skin to escape the nerve-tingling sensation.

His attention lingered on her face. 'You look tired,' he observed, sounding very much the attentive lover, and then the forceful lover as he announced casually, 'We will have an early night.'

Teeth gritted and trying very hard not to think about what an early night with Mathieu might entail if the circumstances were different, Rose responded to the pressure of the hand that was under her elbow and got to her feet.

An image slipped past the barrier. She wasn't sure if the groan was in her mind or if it had actually come out of her mouth. Then she saw the way everyone was looking at her—question answered.

The edges of Mathieu's deep velvet voice were roughened with concern as he searched her face and asked, 'Are you all right?'

She shrugged off his hand. 'Did it occur to you that I might not want an early night? I'm quite capable of deciding when I want to go to bed and,' she added grimly, 'who with.' She didn't add that normally the choice was between a good book and the cat from across the way that always came calling when she left her bedroom window open.

'The truth? No, it didn't occur to me,' he admitted. 'But don't worry—I take rejection well.'

'Like you'd know.'

To Rose's relief—she was still biting her tongue—Mathieu didn't react to her as good as telling him that he was too gorgeous for any woman to resist. She bit her tongue to stop herself explaining that she was an exception to the rule. She was, after all, meant to be engaged to him and, besides, it might just smack of the lady protesting too much.

'Rose,' he explained for the benefit of the women who were straining to catch each syllable of this lightning-fast exchange, 'is trying to reform me.'

'Reform?' Sacha, her dark curls bouncing attractively as she turned her head quickly looking in bewilderment from one to the other, echoed.

Rose could see the girl's dilemma. As far as she was concerned it was a case of why reform what was already perfect, and from the way her eyes followed Mathieu it was clear that she thought he could not be improved upon.

'It is her ambition to drag me into the twenty-first century,' he explained, 'and turn me into a modern man.'

Sacha flushed and lowered her eyes when Mathieu directed his ironic grin in her direction. Her mother, however, was not similarly tongue-tied.

'A modern man,' Helena Constantine echoed, her artfully pencilled brows lifting as she gave a contemptuous smile. 'Despite what they may say all women prefer strong men, not a puppy dog.' From the direction of her admiring stare it was not difficult to see whom she was talking about.

Rose rolled her eyes. 'For goodness' sake, it's not like he needs encouragement.'

The older woman's carmine lips tightened in response to Rose's flippancy. She glanced at Mathieu and seemed disappointed when, far from looking outraged, he was openly amused.

'A man should lead, a woman should follow,' she said firmly.

'Not this woman,' Rose promised, quite enjoying the novelty of finding herself cast in the role of staunch feminist. 'I'm not the following kind.'

'Mama says that the trick is making a man think the idea was his in the first place,' Sacha confided, glancing towards her mother for support, her smile wobbling slightly when she saw her parent's expression. 'She says that a clever woman can make a man do…' Her voice dried up totally in the face of an icy glare from the older woman.

It was Mathieu who came to her rescue.

'There you have it, a clever woman…that leaves you out, *mon ange*.'

There was nothing faintly angelic about the expression on Rose's face as she asked, 'Are you calling me stupid?'

'I have far too much respect for my well-being to call you anything of the sort. How fortunate it is I prefer feisty women to the clever variety,' he said, looking straight at her with an expression that in her mind was inappropriate outside the privacy of a bedroom.

'And as for turning you into a modern man,' Rose said, forcing herself not to break eye contact even though her stomach was churning with a volatile mixture of excitement and heart-racing fear, 'I'm a realist.'

And as a realist she knew that he was acting a part. He really didn't want to rip off her clothes, send the crockery crashing to the floor and make love to her on the table. Oh, yeah, Rose, hold that thought. It's really going to help you stay calm and in control.

'As a realist I don't attempt the impossible.'

'How about…?'

Rose closed her eyes. His manner suggested he had just had an epiphany, while the gleam in his eyes told her he was about to say something that would make her want to curl up and die from sheer mortification.

Unfortunately her reading of that gleam turned out to be spot on.

'If in the interests of harmony once the bedroom door is closed I will let you take a turn being in charge…'

A choking sound emerged from Rose's throat. Of course she was delusional to have thought even for a second that she could get the better of Mathieu in a war of words; he would always win in the end—he had no scruples.

In the sybaritic image playing in her head he had no clothes either. The only thing covering his gleaming golden skin was a fine sheen of sweat and her thighs where she sat astride him. She blinked and sucked in a shaky sigh as she tried to block the treacherous thoughts that made her skin crackle with heat.

'You like the idea?'

Rose liked the idea of a deep dark hole opening up at her feet for her to step into. She had never felt so embarrassed in her entire life. She flashed Mathieu a look of appeal, which he responded to with a warm and loving smile. Lowering her gaze, she gave a theatrical yawn before announcing she was actually quite tired.

She didn't meet anyone in the eye as she bid her fellow guests a hurried goodnight and headed for the nearest door.

CHAPTER THIRTEEN

SHE had gone a couple of hundred yards before Mathieu caught up with her. 'Well, I think that went well,' he observed with some satisfaction. 'Don't you?'

She stopped dead and spun around to face him. Had he been in the same room as she had?

'Went well! No, I don't damn well think it went well. I think it was a total nightmare and so were you.'

His long lashes swept down to partially conceal his eyes, but not before she had caught the wicked amusement dancing in the silvered depths. 'Did I say something to upset you?'

The innocent act made her grind her teeth. Did he get a kick out of baiting everyone or was it just her he liked to see squirm? 'Now what makes you think that? I just love having people think I'm into, into…bondage or something.'

There was startled silence before his warm laughter boomed out. 'I admit I am having trouble seeing you as a dominatrix.'

His taunting grin widened when she lifted her hands to her burning cheeks and choked, 'Shut. Up.'

'Relax,' he advised. 'I imagine they are simply thinking we have a healthy sex life.'

Relax. Was he serious? It was bad enough that her own imagination was running riot without the thought of other people speculating about what they got up to in the bedroom.

'You think that makes me feel better?' she asked. 'You may like to discuss your sexual preferences with all and sundry, but I prefer my sex life, even my imaginary sex life, to stay private.'

'It can hardly be private from your lover. Who is your lover, Rose?'

The twin bright spots on the apples of her cheeks deepened to carnation pink. 'I can't imagine a situation where that information would be any of your business.'

His sardonic smile widened and she got a flash of even white teeth. 'You can't…?'

'And it just so happens I don't have a lover,' she blurted. 'I've never had a—' She stopped dead and developed a sudden interest in the patina on the marble floor.

'Never what? Had a lover?'

She listened to him laugh softly at the idea and gritted her teeth. 'Now you know my little secret.'

His eyes drifted to her full lips. 'And now I'd like an answer to my question…' It was not the only thing he wanted… He had never in his life wanted a woman this much. He thrust his hands in his pockets to hide the fact he was literally shaking with need.

'What question?' She stopped as their eyes meshed. Mathieu raised one brow and gave a savage smile as he watched the colour climb to her cheeks.

'Oh, *that* question.' She dredged a laugh from somewhere. 'Don't worry, I didn't take you seriously.'

'Yes, you did, and I was serious, deadly serious.'

It was hard to maintain her flippancy in the face of his steady and disturbing silver stare but she did—just. 'Look, Mathieu, you're not paying me that much.'

His upper lip curled. 'Name your price. I might be willing to meet it.'

Something inside her snapped. Her response was pure reflex.

There was no conscious thought between lifting her hand and it connecting with a resounding crack with the side of his face.

'Oh, God, I'm so sorry…' Tears sprang to her eyes as she watched him rub a hand over the area on his cheek that was already discolouring. 'No, I'm not sorry, you deserved that. You've progressed from implying I'm some sort of tart to treating me as one.'

Mathieu's hand fell away. 'Yes, I did deserve it. That was an unforgivable thing to say and I'm sorry.'

The anger faded from her face. 'You are?

He nodded. 'It's no excuse, but I'm extremely frustrated.' He placed a hand on the wall beside her head and leaned in, his smoky eyes drifting slowly across her face.

Her chest felt so tight she could hardly breathe as two opposing instincts battled inside her. The sane area of her brain was telling her to back away; another was telling her to lean into him.

Rose couldn't back away because there was no place to go— her back was literally against a wall. The only thing preventing her from taking the second course was a fragile thread of control, but as the heat in her stomach spread and the hunger spiralled that control was stretching to breaking-point.

'Mathieu,' she groaned, turning her head and kissing the finger he trailed across the cushiony softness of her lips. 'You're…this is…' She swallowed, her eyes drifting to his mouth. She was willing him to kiss her when the distinctive sound of voices raised in laughter drifted down the corridor. The sound seemed to mock her.

What was she doing? With a horrified squeak she ducked under his confining arm and began to walk away at speed, praying as she did so that her knees would not buckle.

His chest rising and falling in tune with his rapid, shallow respirations, Mathieu watched her walk away. In some women he might imagine that the sexy sashaying sway of the hips was contrived, but not Rose. There was no calculating flirtation or fluttering eyelashes with her.

It seemed incredible to him, but she was genuinely oblivious to the fact she represented to the opposite sex a sexual ideal, the sort of woman that they dreamt about waking up beside in the morning.

No wonder he lost all sense of perspective around her—the woman was a mass of contradictions.

She had jumped naked into his bed and now she blushed like an inexperienced adolescent if the conversation turned to anything remotely intimate.

She showed him a cold face and claimed not to be interested in him sexually. Yet he knew she was lying. He knew she felt the crackle of sexual tension between them as strongly as he did. He had seen her eyes dilate until they were black pools, felt her body tremble at the accidental brush of their fingers and felt the heat under her cool exterior.

Had her idiot ex been too self-absorbed to teach her to enjoy her own body and celebrate her ripe sexuality? Humiliated by him, she had lost her confidence and tried to recapture it by getting drunk and having casual sex with a total stranger—him. Had his own rejection that night been the act that had made her retreat?

He raised his voice and called after her. 'You didn't read the small print, Rose. No time off, not even for good behaviour, and, let's face it, you were not good back there.'

Breathing hard, Rose swung back, her eyes dilated as she found him standing almost at her shoulder. 'I never said I'd lie for you and there is no small print, nor any print. You're just making up the rules as you go along.' She ached to wipe the taunting smile off his face, and it wasn't a recognition that violence solved nothing that stopped her, but a suspicion that if she touched him for any reason it might be hard to stop.

'You know what I think?'

'I'm shaking with anticipation.'

She was shaking too, Rose realised, registering with a scared frown this new development. Anger, she told herself. She was shaking with anger.

'I think things are going exactly to your plan. You don't want your father to approve of your bride.'

'Interesting theory. Just why would I want my father to disapprove of my future wife?'

'Because you take a sadistic pleasure out of doing the opposite of what he wants you to.' Before she actually said it Rose didn't have the faintest idea what she was going to say, but even before she saw the flicker of shock move at the back of his eyes she knew that she had intuitively hit the nail on the head.

'My father...'

'Oh, he's just as bad as you are, I can see that. I'm really not concerned with who did what to who.'

To hear his complicated and painful relationship with his father reduced to the level of a school-yard squabble reduced Mathieu to a stunned silence.

'I just want out of it.' She bit her trembling lip, cleared her throat and added in a flat voice, 'You chose me because you knew that I'd never fit in.'

Now why should that hurt so much?

Shaking his head, Mathieu reached out his hand. Rose pulled back, her eyes wide and wary. With a shrug and a twisted smile he let his hand fall away. His eyes were flint-hard as he said dismissively, 'I didn't choose you. This was an arrangement of mutual convenience, though I have to admit there has not been a lot of convenience involved so far. The irony is that you were the perfect choice.' His considering glaze slid over her. 'If I had turned up with one of the usual suspects...he would have smelt a rat immediately.'

'Usual suspects?'

'Well-groomed, articulate...'

'Everything I am not, presumably.'

'Oh, you scrub up pretty well.'

'You know, there being nothing in writing works both ways. If I choose to walk there's nothing you can do to stop me.'

'You underestimate my resourcefulness…'

She stuck out her chin. 'But not your total lack of scruples and ruthlessness.'

Mathieu's brows drew together in a dark disapproving line above his hawklike nose. 'That's what most people say about my father.'

Ironically it was the familial likeness that he appeared offended by, not the insult… Not that this mattered to Rose—her objective had been to annoy him.

'Most people haven't been forced to spend as much time in your company as I have recently.' She could think of more than a few who would pay for the privilege.

He pretended not to hear her muttered interruption and angled a curious look at her face. 'My father…you're not scared of him, are you?'

'Scared?' An image of the broad-shouldered Greek financier flashed through her mind. 'Why should I be?' Now his son, that was another matter. She turned her head sharply and gave a little shiver as her eyes brushed his profile.

'He's rich and powerful.'

'He has nothing I want or need—why should I be afraid of him? You, on the other hand…'

'You think I'm afraid of my father?'

She had expected the suggestion to produce an offended denial, but the only reaction she got was an amused quiver of his lips.

'I suppose you think fear is a sign of weakness.'

'No, I think fear is healthy.'

'Oh, will you stop sounding so impossibly well balanced? You made your living tied down in a metal box hurtling around in circles while people paid money for tickets to watch while they waited for you to crash. Someone who chooses to make their living that way—' she tapped the side of her head '—has a few screws loose.'

It was the families she felt sorry for—the ones who loved those men who risked their lives…and for what? The thrill, the money, the fame…or was it cheating death that hooked them? Either way it was the wives and mothers waiting at the sidelines that had her sympathy.

'I…' Mathieu closed his mouth with an almost audible snap, shock quickly followed by caution filtering into his expression as he realised what he had been about to do.

Why should he feel the need to justify his life choices, redeem himself in her eyes? Why, when he never asked for anyone's approval, should Rose's good opinion matter so much to him? A man who normally did not duck issues, but met them head-on, he found himself pushing this particular issue to the back of his mind.

'It was something I was good at.'

She lifted her eyes in mock amazement. 'You mean there are some things you're not good at? I thought you were brilliant at everything. Except,' she added with a wry twist of her lips, 'being pleasant to your father.'

'*Me*. You think it's my fault?' The resentment he told himself he had put aside along with other childish things surfaced and his jaw clenched.

'Well, it takes two, doesn't it? And you can't deny you don't go out of your way to be nice. There's an atmosphere you could cut with a knife when you're together.'

'He thinks the wrong son died.'

Mathieu, the most alive person she had ever met, dead. She shook her head in violent mute rejection of the idea and saw the floor moving up towards her.

She gave a sigh of relief when the world steadied, but didn't loose her grip on the ornately inlaid console table she had grabbed on to to steady herself.

Of course he regretted saying it the moment it left his lips. He sounded like someone looking for the sympathy vote and nothing could be farther from the truth.

He regretted it even more when he saw Rose's amber eyes fill with compassion.

She was just the sort of woman who would go for the damaged type, he thought irritably. It wasn't by accident that the women he ended up having relationships with did not want to heal or mother him.

Mathieu was scowling but, more significantly, he was avoiding her eyes. He wouldn't look at her—was he afraid of what she would see?

She felt like yelling, Your father hurt you, big deal, join the rest of the human race. She also felt like wrapping her arms around him and pulling him close, but she knew he was a man who would not appreciate the gesture.

No, that would mean admitting he wasn't totally invulnerable.

'I'm sure he doesn't think that,' Rose said, wondering why it was that some men found it so hard to talk about their feelings. Half the family rifts in the world would be healed if men actually did more than grunt and look noble. 'It's not like he actually said that…' She paused, her eyes sweeping his dark face. 'He did!' Her soothing expression melted into one of angry indignation.

How could any man, no matter how much he was hurting, say something like that to his own son? She'd like to give the selfish old man a piece of her mind.

'Alex was the exact opposite of me.' He made it sound as though this was a reason, an excuse even.

'Why does the memory of your brother have to push you apart? That's the one thing you and your father have in common,' she pointed out, shaking her head in exasperation. 'You both loved him.' You'd think that would draw people together, not push them farther apart.

'Look, I didn't bring you here to bring about a reconciliation between me and Andreos. I'm not paying you to be an agony aunt.' He saw her flinch and hardened his heart against the hurt in her liquid-gold eyes.

Rose stiffened. 'Don't worry, I won't forget my place again.'

'Your place is not in my head.' He clasped a hand to his head and gave a frustrated groan. 'Oh, for God's sake, don't look at me like that.'

'Where is my place, Mathieu? Just so that I know.'

His burning eyes swept her face. 'In my bed, damn you,' he said, turning on his heel and striding off.

CHAPTER FOURTEEN

ROSE knew Mathieu was in the room even before her nostrils flared in response to the scent of his body. His invisible presence was like an electric prickle under her skin.

'You've been crying.' The visible damage, her red-rimmed eyes and the tear marks on her cheeks made something inside him twist.

'I always cry when I get mad,' she said, keeping her eyes trained on the waves whispering on the moonlit shore. Behind her breastbone her heart was beating like a captive bird and as the last lingering effects of the wine at dinner had worn off she couldn't even blame that for her response.

'Did you cry because you thought I wouldn't be back?'

His voice warm like honey came from just behind her. Paralysed by the insidious weakness that was spreading through her body, she managed a negligent shrug and suggested coldly, 'You forgot something?' She turned her head and he nodded.

She wanted to look away but she couldn't stop staring. His glossy dark hair was sexily mussed as though he had just run his fingers through it. His jacket was gone, and his tie hung loose around his neck. But it was his eyes that made her stomach dissolve; they were burning like molten silver.

She cleared her throat, but the words wouldn't come. Her restless gaze moved over the shadow on his jaw following the line of his strong neck to the base of his throat, and lower then to the section of satiny golden skin revealed where the top buttons of his shirt had parted.

She sucked in a deep breath and stuck out her chin as she gave a shrug…a yawn would have been overkill, especially as she had a horrible suspicion he knew exactly what havoc he was wreaking on her nervous system.

The extra gust of wind that blew in from the sea ruffled his hair and made her shiver. The distraction enabled her to pull free of the sensual thrall that had held her immobile.

She turned her back on him and closed her eyes. 'Then get what you want and leave.' Before I touch you… In her fevered imagination she already was; her hands were on his ribcage and sliding lower to his flat, muscle-ridged stomach. She put a stop to her treacherous thoughts…

'That was my intention.'

She felt the warmth of his breath brush the side of her neck. A shiver of excitement chased a path down her spine as her heavy eyelids closed.

'What are you waiting for?'

Her eyelids lifted abruptly when a moment later he took her by the shoulders and spun her around to face him. The lines of his face were taut with anger and frustration.

'I'm waiting for you to stop pretending this isn't happening.' He looked down at her; the devouring hunger in his spectacular eyes sent a violent surge of bone-melting lust through Rose's receptive body.

'Nothing's happening except I'm catching a cold standing in this draught.'

He lifted a hand and made a stroking motion that traced the outline of her head but did not make contact, although her nerve endings reacted as though he had.

His voice normally had nothing more than the faintest trace

of an accent, but when he spoke it was now thickly accented. 'Your hair looks silver in this light.'

Rose swallowed and shook her head. Things were moving too fast. At this rate the point of no return would have passed without her explaining that this wasn't what she wanted.

It was, of course, but that was irrelevant. As intellectual exercises went, the one where she had felt empowered and daring enough to plan being seduced by a man she had no emotional connection with—a man like Mathieu—now seemed totally ludicrous.

For starters there was nothing intellectual about the things the scent of his warm body did to her. The danger in him aroused and excited her. Primitive, raw instincts, she was discovering, were not something you could intellectualise, and as for no emotional connection... As much as she wanted to believe he had just woken dormant sexual instincts within her, Rose knew what she was feeling was far more complicated than simple lust.

A sensible woman like her didn't waste feelings on a man who had no use for them.

And she was sensible...wasn't she? A month ago she would have had no problem replying in the positive, but now she knew, and it was a shocking realisation, that if she let herself she could fall in love with him... The question was could she stop it happening, and did she actually want to?

But those were questions for later; her mind could not deal with them now.

'And your skin looks like moonlight, so soft, so smooth.'

The throaty rasp shuddered through her and though she struggled she couldn't tear her gaze free from the burning silver of his deep-set eyes as they devoured her. A tremor rippled through her body as his fingertips grazed the side of her cheek. She closed her eyes and shook her head, desperately trying to cling to some semblance of self-control and sanity.

'I don't know why you're trying to fight it. We have no control. It is coded into our DNA.'

'Do many women fall for that "it's just chemistry" line, Mathieu?'

The lines of his chiselled face tautened with anger. 'I'm saying that what we are feeling is as basic as the colour of our eyes. You may not like it but you have to live with it.' His glittered like liquid silver as his restless glance roamed over the soft contours of her upturned features.

'Convenient fatalism, but I don't have to live with you and I definitely don't have to have sex with you,' she retorted.

There was a glow in his eyes that was sinfully suggestive as he bent close to whisper in her ear, 'Great sex.'

His sensuous purr had a catastrophic effect on her sensitive stomach muscles. She plucked at the neckline of her dress as her skin prickled with heat. Her heart thudding with nervous excitement, she swallowed and shook her head.

He drew back a sound that was close to a growl vibrating in his chest as he ripped the loose tie from his neck and threw it on the floor. 'Are you trying to tell me that you don't want to share a bed with me?' Actually the way he was feeling—the closest words in his extensive vocabulary that came anywhere close to describing that condition were *totally out of control*— meant the bed was by no means a prerequisite. Just about anywhere would do.

The urge to feel his skin in contact with her skin was overwhelming. If he wasn't able to satisfy the primitive instinct to sink into her softness and warmth and feel her tight around him it was possible he would lose what little sanity he had left.

'Well?'

The words of denial shrivelled on Rose's lips the moment she met the smouldering challenge in his. She swallowed and squared her shoulders.

'Just because you want something doesn't make it a good idea.'

'And you want me.' He closed his eyes as a shudder of relief vibrated through his lean frame.

She doubted he could have sounded any more smug or complacent if he'd tried, but it was hard to feel the proper level of indignation over this when he couldn't have looked more sexy or desirable either.

And on that front, to give the devil his due, he never tried, he just…

'If you don't, just lock the door.' Producing a key from somewhere, he held it out to her.

Rose caught her full lower lip between her teeth as she stared at it.

After a moment the key went the same way as the tie.

'You can hardly stand up, you're literally shaking and I haven't even touched you.' He swallowed, his voice dropping a husky octave as he added, 'Have you any idea what it does to me to know that? To know that you're weak with lust for me?'

'I am.' Rose stared into his eyes, seeing her own reflection there along with the combustible mixture of the emotions that gripped him.

Her heart was beating so frantically that she could hardly breathe as she lifted a hand to touch the spot in his lean cheek where a nerve jumped. He turned his head and caught her hand, pulling it to his lips, drawing one finger and then the next into his mouth.

A fractured gusty sigh escaped her lips and her knees disintegrated. She would have fallen in a heap at his feet if he hadn't caught her at the last moment, wrapping an arm around her waist and drawing her upright.

Her heavy lids closed and she gave a dreamy sigh, savouring the tensile strength in his lean body, conscious of the febrile shudders that intermittently shimmied through the length of his body.

'Are you all right?'

'I'm amazing,' she said, tucking her head into the angle

between his chin and shoulder. She had never imagined that weak and helpless could feel so liberating.

She felt the soundless growl of laughter vibrate in his chest. 'Well, amazing Rose, I think we should take this discussion into the bedroom.' His urgency intensified, as did the ache in his groin as he anticipated the touch of her bare skin against his. His urgency deepened as he imagined her body closing tight around him. 'Right now,' he added, bringing his other arm around her waist and hauling her higher and closer against him.

Feeling the pressure of his erection against the softness of her belly, she gave a startled, '*Oh*,' and her eyes flew open. As she gasped for breath her eyes connected with the heat in his and she melted some more. '*You're* incredible.'

Rose had never in her life felt the primal drive, the need to be possessed by a man. But she had been fantasising about being possessed by Mathieu Demetrios from the first moment she had set eyes on him. Maybe he was right, maybe it was about something programmed into her genes, but frankly she didn't care.

It didn't matter, she realised with a sense of relief—she had moved beyond the guilt, the tortuous heart-searching and trying to make sense of it.

Even if this was the worst decision of her life she was going to make it happen... Even if she spent the rest of her life regretting it, she wanted Mathieu so much it was more important than breathing and just as essential for her continued survival.

For the first time ever she understood the real meaning of all-consuming passion. She had met the love of her life and she might not be destined to spend the rest of her life with him, but she was going to savour every moment that she did have.

'How can you be surprised? You must know how much I want you.'

'Tell me,' she whispered in a husky voice he had to strain to hear. He expelled a long deep breath and said, 'I'll show you.'

She let out a small shriek as he cupped her bottom and lifted her upwards. As he swung her around and began to stride towards the bedroom door she wrapped her legs around his waist and, pressing her breasts against his chest, linked her arms around his neck.

She fitted her mouth to his and kissed him hungrily, opening her mouth in response to his probing tongue, and groaned into his mouth as the kiss deepened. When she came up for air her fingers still curled into the hair on the nape of his neck.

They were both breathing hard as they stared into each other's eyes.

'You're staring,' he said thickly.

She nodded. 'At your mouth. I think,' she mused, 'that it is one of my most favourite things in the world.' It was strange not to be censoring her words, strange in a good way.

'Your mouth is in my top ten,' he admitted, 'and, while kissing it is even higher, you do realise that if you carry on doing that we're never going to make it to the bedroom.'

'Beds are good, but the floor is fine.' Did I really just say that?

'True, but the thing is I've been imagining you naked with your hair spread out over silk sheets since the moment I met you.'

He'd been imagining her, imagining her being some red-hot lover… Rose's insecurities came crowding in. She really ought to tell him up front there was every possibility she would be rubbish…enthusiastic but rubbish.

'What's wrong?'

For once she wasn't dismayed by his ability to read her thoughts. 'I don't want to make a mess of this.'

She leaned close so that her nose almost grazed his, her nostrils quivering as she inhaled the musky scent of his arousal overlaid by the light citrus tones of the obviously expensive cologne he favoured.

He was so totally delicious, everything about him fascinated and excited her.

'Not possible.'

'You say that now, but—'

'Shut up.'

He was kissing her so she didn't have very much option and, anyway, about two seconds into the kiss she forgot what she wanted to say. A second after that she forgot her own name.

Still kissing her, he carried her across the room to the bed where he laid her down. Then not taking his eyes off her, he began to remove his clothes, the task made more difficult by the fact his hands were shaking so much.

He had fought his way out of his shirt and kicked off his trousers when she sat up and stretched her arms out to him. Not able to resist the invitation in her glorious golden eyes another moment, he knelt beside her on the bed.

Rose struggled to catch her breath, her throat ached…he was so beautiful he made her ache all over. Just looking at him burnt her up from the inside out.

Mathieu took the hands extended to him and turned them over. 'I want your hands on me,' he rasped, his voice as dark as the hot feelings inside her.

A fractured sigh snagged in Rose's throat as he laid her hands palm down on the bare skin of his tautly muscled belly. Breathing shallowly, she raised herself up on her knees and slid her hands up over his hair-roughened chest. Circling his tight male nipples with a finger, she leant forward, repeating the action with her tongue.

His skin tasted salty; he tasted the way he smelt.

'Sweet mother of God,' he groaned, sinking his fingers into her hair and dragging her face up to his. His hands framed her face. 'Look at me,' he said thickly. '*Dieu*, but I want you, Rose.'

Her eyes slid to his mouth. Just looking at the sensual curve made things tighten and shift low inside her. 'What's stopping you?' she asked, thinking, I love you…oh, God, I love you.

They kissed fiercely with a bruising desperation, fighting to deepen the contact. Mathieu's hands fell to her hips and he jerked her hard to him, sealing their bodies at hip level, letting her fully appreciate the urgency of his throbbing arousal.

Rose could feel the tremors running through his greyhound-lean frame. 'I didn't know anything, anyone could feel this way.' Her head fell back as his lips moved down her neck, his tongue flicking across the pulse throbbing at the base of her throat.

She pulled back and looked at him, and he smiled a slow smile that felt like a fist tightening very deep in her belly… Her skin burned in an agony of anticipation as he slid down the zip of her dress and, still holding her eyes, peeled it gently off her shoulders.

When the fabric pooled around her waist revealing her full pink-tipped breasts he sucked in a ragged breath. 'You are beautiful, *mon coeur,*' he rasped, weighing one perfect breast in his hand before bending his head and running his tongue across first one engorged peak and then the other.

Desire like a flame licked through her body as her back arched. She found the sight of his dark head against her pale skin incredibly, mind-blowingly erotic.

He was speaking in French, the hot, impassioned words spilling from his lips as he pushed her back against the pillows and spread her hair like a golden curtain around her flushed face. He then curved her arms above her head, his eyes darkening as he watched her breasts quiver, the peaks hardening as they lifted.

'Is this the way I looked in your fantasy?' she whispered, forcing the husky words past the aching emotional thickness in her throat.

He smiled, a fierce smile that thrilled her to the core. 'You are my fantasy, *ma petite.*' One hand gently splayed across her abdomen, he pulled her dress down over her hips until she lay there in a pair of lacy pants. He ran a finger along the pale smooth flesh of her inner thigh and she trembled, gasping his name as his fingers continued to stroke and tease, releasing a flood of heat that washed over her heated skin tingeing it with a faint rosy blush.

'Don't stop,' she pleaded when his fingers lifted from her skin.

She felt rather than heard the deep laughter vibrate in his chest, but when he bent over her and locked his eyes onto hers there was no laughter in his face. There was strain evident in the sharp-drawn lines that drew the skin tight over his incredible bones and a hungry, almost febrile glitter in his deep-set eyes.

'There is no possibility of that happening,' he promised huskily. Then, turning away briefly, he divested himself of his boxers. She watched him through half-closed eyes, one arm thrown above her head in an attitude of wanton abandon.

When he turned back her eyes dropped. A stab of sexual heat shot through her body all the way to her curling toes.

'Oh, my,' she breathed shakily.

She wanted him so much her skin crackled with it, her blood hummed with it. She couldn't put the depth of her longing into words, but she tried, and she wasn't even embarrassed by the inarticulate babble that came from her lips as he moved over her, parting her thighs and trailing a finger along the silky soft skin of her inner thigh, drawing sharp gasps and moans of pleasure from her throat before moving higher and deeper into her moistness.

A keening moan stayed locked in her throat as she moved against his hand.

Nothing, she thought, could be better than this.

She was wrong.

Her body arched as he thrust into her and a wild cry of startled delight left her lips.

Above her Mathieu froze and, between rasping gasps, growled, 'Look at me.'

Rose's mind, every part of her, was so totally concentrated on the incredible sensation of being filled and stretched by him, the heat of him, the smooth thickness of him, that there was a time lag before she responded.

Eyes glazed, the amber colour of the iris reduced to a thin

strip, the pupils were so dilated, she blinked up at him, momentarily blinded by the luminous glow in his.

He stared down at her, his golden skin coated by a glistening coat of sweat, the sinews in his clenched jaw and neck standing out as he struggled to hold himself in check.

'You're…you're…'

I'm dying, she thought as her head began to thrash from side to side on the pillow. Unable to bear the pressure building up inside her—there was nowhere for it to go—she pleaded, 'Please, Mathieu, please…'

Then as she felt him pull back she tried to lift her head and cried out in alarm. 'No…no, I need…'

She grabbed for his shoulders, her fingers sliding over his sweat-slick skin, then her nails sinking in to hold him.

She breathed a fervent sigh of relief as he slid back into her, not deeply enough to satisfy the hunger inside her, but enough to send shafts of shimmering sensation coursing through her body.

He repeated the sequence again and again, pulling back with agonising slowness, then sinking in each time a little deeper until she could feel the rhythm in her head, in her blood, in her bones—she couldn't separate herself from it.

When it got too much to bear she prized her eyes open. 'Mathieu, I can't, this is…I need—oh, God, I can't bear it,' she moaned.

He looked into her passion-glazed eyes and a groan was dragged from deep inside him. 'Neither, *mon coeur*, can I,' he groaned, thrusting deep into her, giving her all of himself.

She responded with a wild cry, wrapping her legs tight around his waist and pushing up to deepen the glorious penetration and the intense nerve-stretching pleasure. Her breath grew shallow and fast as she felt the pressure build, then as the light exploded behind her eyelids she went limp and let the shattering climax claim her.

Mathieu felt her pulse tightly around his length and with a groan let go, and with one final thrust a feral moan was ripped from his throat as, gasping for breath, he collapsed on top of her.

CHAPTER FIFTEEN

As THEY lay there intimately entwined, in a tangle of sweat-slick limbs, Rose smiled and ran her hand down the damp curve of Mathieu's back.

'I am the first man you have been with.' Rolling off, Mathieu lay on his back, one hand curved over his head. The knowledge lay like a stone behind his breastbone. He stared at the ceiling as he added hoarsely, 'How is this possible?' The question seemed addressed more to himself than to her.

Rose, still floating on a cloud of languid contentment, felt the first stirrings of unease filter into her bliss. She opened her eyes to look at him through the damp screen of her lashes.

Back-lit by the shaft of light from the half-open curtain, his tautly muscled torso gleamed like oiled silk and Rose was overwhelmed afresh by the spectacular beauty of his powerful body. Emotion locked the muscles of her throat tight.

'Speak to me, Rose…'

She lifted a hand to her cheek and felt the salty wetness of her tears. She had not been conscious of crying. 'So you're my first—does it actually matter?'

Mathieu looked at her in astonishment. 'Does it matter?' he echoed in outrage. 'You were an innocent.' He swallowed, causing the muscles in his brown throat to ripple visibly as he fought to contain his feelings, unable to believe she could not understand how this altered everything.

'A damn virgin…*Dieu*…' He lifted a hand to his head and fell backwards onto the mattress.

'You were the one who said I'd never had a lover.' Her attempt to draw a smile failed miserably. When his head turned on the pillow towards her she could almost physically see the waves of tension rolling off him.

'I was being ironic and you knew it,' he bit back before he closed his eyes once more.

He had done everything right up to this point. So why did he have to spoil everything now? 'I really think you're in danger of blowing this way out of proportion.'

'Every word you say,' he told her through gritted teeth, 'is making this worse.'

'Fine, I won't say anything.' She felt his rejection like a physical pain in her tight chest. Face white, she rolled onto her stomach, dragging the sheet up to cover her nakedness, nakedness she had just minutes earlier taken voluptuous pleasure in. Now it was all ruined, her hot skin began to cool and she shivered.

She had found their love-making so incredible, more mind-blowingly perfect than she could have imagined possible, that it had not occurred to her until he had begun to speak that he had found the experience less satisfactory. Which, when she thought about it, was not so surprising as she had not known what she was doing, but it had felt pretty good at the time.

He dragged a hand across his eyes. '*Dieu*, what have I done?' he groaned.

'You want me to explain? I thought I was the innocent?'

He turned his head, the anger in his eyes smouldering. He looked as angry as she had ever seen him. 'I hardly think that this is the moment to be flippant.'

The dry laugh locked in her emotionally constricted throat.

'Believe me, I do not feel flippant. If you expect me to apologise for being pretty amateur, forget it.'

'You have some explaining to do,' he told her heavily.

'No,' she said, pulling herself upright. The sheet still gathered around her, she swung her legs over the side of the bed, presenting her stiff, straight back to him.

'The woman I found in my bed in Monaco was not a virgin.' His thoughts flicked back to the aborted seduction scene, his dark brows drawing into a frowning straight line as he shook his head positively. 'Definitely not!'

'How would you know? I thought you threw her out of your bed.'

Rose let out a squeal of protest when with no warning a brown arm snaked around her middle. Clutching tight to the sheet, she fell back across his lap. Lying there, looking up into his lean face, she felt the hunger so recently sated stir.

'A man knows these things.'

'You didn't know these things about me,' she reminded him.

A nerve clenched along his jaw. 'I'm waiting, Rose.'

'I don't owe you anything, least of all an explanation,' she husked, her chest rising in tune to the rapid gusty breaths that escaped her parted lips.

Her angry contention made him stare. 'You were a virgin,' he said rawly.

'Will you stop saying that? It's not like I planned to be a virgin at twenty-six. I just wanted to be sure…' She stopped, aware of the implication of her words, and retrieved the situation by adding with a laugh, 'And then I suppose I just gave up waiting.'

'And I happened along. You know how to make a man feel special, *mon coeur*.'

'Stop calling me that,' she snapped angrily. 'You've got a cheek acting as if I've tried to pass myself off as something I'm not.' It was painfully obvious that he would have preferred the sexy siren she had turned out *not* to be. He would have preferred Rebecca, which made him no different from every other man. 'I never said I was that woman—in fact I've never stopped saying that I wasn't her.'

'But you knew that I thought…'

The condemnation in his manner struck Rose as wildly irrational and it frustrated the hell out of her that he couldn't recognise the fact. 'And I thought enthusiasm would make up for lack of experience. It looks like we were both wrong,' she countered. 'For goodness' sake, it's bad enough you're making me feel like a cheap one-night stand, but do you have to rub salt in the wound by making me feel like a cheap one-night stand who is useless at sex? If I'd known that you only sleep with women with a diploma in fornication I would have—'

'This is not about you being inexperienced in bed.' He looked at her with total incredulity. The women he had relationships with were as selfish as him; with them he knew where he stood. It infuriated him that she could act as though what she had given him was inconsequential.

Rose struggled upright and sat there on the edge of the bed with her back to him. 'Not much,' she grumbled, trying to imply with her small laugh that she found his reaction faintly amusing. The last thing she wanted was him even starting to suspect that she was totally devastated.

'Oh, for goodness' sake, can we just drop the subject and agree it—' she gestured without looking at the tumbled bedclothes '—was a mistake.' And what a mistake! Her soft lips twisted into a wry bitter smile as she added, 'I'm not the woman you wanted. I'm not the woman from your hotel room.'

'I did not want her, desire her…you…' His glance slid down the curve of her rigid spine. His brow furrowed as he tried to tackle the conundrum presented to him. 'You are identical… Even your voices…' One he desired, the other left him cold. He stopped dead, a spark of startled comprehension appearing in his eyes. 'There are two of you...*twins*...?'

Rose dodged his now-angry gaze and began to pleat the sheet between her fingers.

Mathieu muttered something in French under his breath, pulling her around towards him with one hand, and pushing back the locks of hair that concealed her face with the other. His hand stayed there framing her face. 'Look at me,' he commanded, tilting her chin up to him. 'That woman in Monaco, she was your sister, your twin, wasn't she, Rose?'

Rose nodded. There seemed little point in denying it.

He expelled his breath on one long, sibilant sigh.

'And she is the one who was jilted at the altar.' His eyes swept her face and Rose gave a tiny nod. 'The one who went off the rails,' he added, his voice and manner getting angrier with each additional suggestion.

'She's married now to an absolutely lovely man.'

'And do you know this from personal experience too?'

Rose shook her head in bewilderment. 'I don't understand.'

'Well, you seem to share most things.'

A wave of angry colour washed over her skin as the implication sank in. 'You have a really nasty mind—you know that, don't you?'

His hands fell away. His head sank forward onto his chest as the layers of implication hit him. 'I know nothing about you,' he said, lifting his head and looking at her blankly. 'You are not the person I thought you were.'

'The person you thought I was?' she repeated, the bubble of anger inside her bursting. This was meant to be a memory, a perfect moment for her to recall in years to come, and he had spoilt it with his interrogation. 'How can you be so hypocritical?' she asked him.

'You deceived me and it is *my* fault?'

'I haven't deceived anyone,' she yelled. 'I told you until I was hoarse that we'd never met before. And I don't see the problem. Do you normally want to know a girl's history before you have sex? You're a total hypocrite. Five minutes ago you weren't even vaguely interested in the person I am beyond my bra size.' From the direction of his gaze the same thing was still true.

With an angry snort of disgust she brought her hands up to cover her heaving breasts. 'Oh, I'm not criticising you for being shallow, I knew that you didn't care about me, but to turn around and act as though I have somehow cheated you, well...' She shook her head energetically enough to send strands of caramel hair whipping around her face.

'You are calling me shallow?'

On another occasion Rose might have been amused by the expression of stark incredulity written on his lean face.

'I can see why you're so upset. You must have thought I was ideal for your purposes. A woman traumatised by a painful romantic experience.'

Teeth clenched, he ground out, 'You are suggesting that my *modus operandi* involves taking advantage of vulnerable women?'

Rose was not deceived by his soft tone. She doubted she had ever seen anyone as angry as he was right now. On another occasion she might have been cautious about her response, but she felt strangely disconnected from what was happening as she stared at the nerve clenching and unclenching in his hollow cheek.

'I'm saying a woman who was just dipping her toe back in the water after getting burnt.' Even as she said it she recognised that you could drive a cart and horses through the analogy. Any woman who thought Mathieu was a little light relief, a safe place to get back into the dating game, would be seriously unbalanced.

'And you were—just dipping your toe in the water?'

He waited for her response, glaring at her as though this was all some part of her fiendish master plan.

'I suppose I got tired of waiting for Mr Perfect. You see, I thought I was in love, but he was married and I thought honourable, but he was just using me. I found out the day you offered me this opportunity…' She gave a shaky laugh as her gaze slid across the tumbled, still-warm bedclothes. 'I really don't think this is what the graduate career service had in mind when they talked about opportunity.

'I had this mad idea that it would be a good idea to find out about sex with someone I didn't care about.'

'So you approached this like a scientific experiment?'

'For God's sake,' she exclaimed. 'It lasted for about two minutes before I wised up. I admit I was curious what everyone was going on about. What I'm trying to say is I'm not really in a position to judge your motives.' He obviously did not feel similarly restrained.

'You are not the person I thought you were.'

'Can you hear yourself? I'm not the person you thought I was. As if you'd know.' She released a hard little laugh. 'You didn't know the person I was; you didn't know anything about me. What could you know about the person I am?' she asked him. 'The person I *really* am,' she added, pressing her hand to her heaving bosom.

'You didn't sleep with me, Mathieu, because you liked who I am or even who you thought I was, because I am the person you have been looking for all your life. You slept with me because I'm here and available and you thought I'd be low maintenance. Well you can relax.'

Her advice did not seem to have any immediate soothing effect. He looked about ready to implode.

'I'm out of here as soon as I can thumb a lift.' The trouble about an island was a grand sweeping exit was hard to achieve.

Dragging the sheet from the bed, envying him his total obliviousness to his nakedness, she stood up and walked towards her bathroom.

Inside she lasted until she had locked the door, where she slid down the wall to the cold marble floor. Where in a foetal huddle she cried until there were no tears left.

She didn't know if she would have opened the door if he had asked, but her resolve was never tested because Mathieu didn't knock and when she crept out in the early hours the suite was empty.

'You might as well unpack,' Mathieu said, entering the room and glancing down at the suitcase she had left by the door. 'Nobody is leaving this island today.' Did it make him insane that he would lie just to have her the other side of a wall, soft and lovely and hating him?

'Then why is that helicopter out there?'

His eyes slid from hers. 'You may think I have delusions of grandeur, but even I can't control the weather.'

'Or me,' she told him, registering for the first time the wetness that had his clothes clinging wetly to his body and his hair slicked back and drenched. 'Helicopters don't stop flying because of a bit of rain.' She picked up her case and willed him to say something to stop her. But of course he didn't because basically he couldn't wait to see the back of her.

'The ring is on the dressing table. Oh, and don't be surprised if your father looks smug when you see him.'

'Oh?' he said, studying her expression with a frown.

'We had a breakfast meeting. And I've made him really happy.'

'He has clearly not done the same for you.' The clenched teeth and flashing eyes were the clue.

'He offered me money to leave you. You don't look surprised that your father tried to buy me off,' she accused, studying his expression. 'Does he do this often?'

'It was not something I had anticipated, but I should have. If he is happy, I'm assuming that you said yes?'

'Not immediately. I negotiated. After all, you are a very rich prize for a dedicated gold-digger like me.' Her teeth ached as she held the fixed white smile in place.

'Would it be indelicate to ask how much I'm worth?'

'I wouldn't give a brass farthing for you.'

'No, you did make clear to me last night that your only interest in me was…' he swallowed, struggling to keep a lid on his anger '…scientific.'

'I never was very good at chemistry.' But he was—her eyes dropped—very good. 'Actually I can't remember how much we settled on. I was angry,' she admitted with admirable understatement. 'Here,' she said, taking it out of her pocket with a shaking hand and shoving it at Mathieu.

Mathieu smoothed the scrunched paper. His brows lifted as he read the figure above his father's distinctive scrawl. 'You are a good negotiator,' he said, handing it back to her.

'You think I want that?' she said, looking from the cheque to him. 'You're as bad as he is.'

'You might as well keep it. The money means nothing to him and you have earned it.'

Rose felt strangely removed from what was happening as her hand began to move in an arc. It wasn't until it met his cheek with a resounding smack that sent his head sideways that she registered what she had done.

'This time I'm not sorry,' she said. 'And if you're ever in town be sure not to get in touch, because I promise you there is more where that came from.'

She swept out, the image of his grey furious eyes imprinted on her retina.

The helicopter was over the grey stormy Aegean before the first sobs were torn from her chest and she doubled over in pain.

CHAPTER SIXTEEN

'THIS is your first scan?'

Rose, feeling a light-headed mixture of trepidation and excitement, nodded as she lowered herself on the high bed. Maybe some of the former showed because the woman in the white coat explained in a soothing manner, 'We've had a cancellation, the appointment following yours. I could wait for Dad to arrive if you like?'

Rose swallowed as weak tears rushed to her eyes. With a tight little smile she struggled to regain her composure. 'No, he won't be coming. He's—'

'Right here.'

Rose's head turned; her expression went totally blank. Shock froze her mental faculties as she stared in disbelief at the tall figure framed in the doorway.

Had she finally lost it totally? Was she hallucinating?

Her eyes locked on platinum-silver and the colour rushed back to her face the same moment her brain began to function. This was no hallucination; this was something much more dangerous—the real thing. A hundred questions swirling in her head, she chose the cautious option and asked suspiciously, 'What are you doing here, Mathieu?'

Mathieu's brows lifted. 'Where else would a man be when the mother of his child is having her first scan?'

'America?'

Escorting long-stemmed American beauties who did not present him with the tedious burden of their virginity she tacked on silently.

She had read the story of his proposed trip in the financial pages. For a supposedly serious journalist, the woman who had written it had been almost gushing in her praise of the man she said would bear watching.

But then who was she to talk about lack of objectivity? she thought. She was the idiotic woman who had cut out the article and kept it.

She sucked in a deep sustaining breath, telling herself she could do this. Actually she could do little else but stare at him as though she was afraid if she blinked he might vanish.

'America? No, as you see, no…I am here.'

At that moment the shrill sound of a bleeper broke the expectant silence in the room.

The radiologist reached into the pocket of her white coat and shared her apologetic smile equally between the two prospective parents. 'I'm sorry. I'll have to take this…I won't be long.'

Rose, who had levered herself up into a sitting position, watched the woman go and barely restrained the impulse to beg her to stay.

She cleared her throat. 'I really don't think you being here is such a good idea, Mathieu. Not really…appropriate.' She gave a weak smile and touched her stomach. 'I'm pregnant, you know. It was quite a surprise.'

He gave a dry laugh and dragged a not quite steady hand through his dark hair. 'For me too, Rose. You do know that you can't do this alone…?'

His woman giving birth alone, having his baby alone… His chest swelled as he fought to contain his emotions. This was just not going to happen, not while there was breath in his body. If she didn't love him he would make her…if necessary he would change.

'God, no, I'm pretty clueless, but the staff here are absolutely terrific and I'll see the same midwife all the way through to the birth, build up a relationship…'

Listening to her, Mathieu bit back a frustrated groan. Spitting hostility, he reflected, would have been easier to deal with than being treated with this stilted politeness. 'I think it's our relationship we should be concentrating on. Don't you, Rose?'

She still wasn't totally sure that he wasn't a figment of her imagination, but when he bent forward there was nothing imaginary about the lips that brushed her forehead before claiming her mouth, or the warm, clean scent of his male body.

The light kiss left her breathing hard and aching.

'We don't have a relationship, Mathieu.'

He stood, his hands resting either side of her. 'But we have a baby.' He cupped her chin in his hand and tilted her face up to him.

'How do you know the baby is even yours?' It was a ridiculous thing to say, but she felt pushed into a corner.

'Are you saying it is not?'

'No, I'm not saying that,' she admitted reluctantly.

'Good call. It is always good to keep deceit within shouting distance of the truth.' Something he had not been doing when he had told himself that he could function perfectly well without one Rose Hall.

'Is it so impossible that I might have had sex with a man other than you?'

'Frankly, yes.'

'Well, you didn't find me so repulsive once,' she retorted, stung.

Amusement flared and died in his eyes to be replaced by a simmering heat. His eyes darkened with desire as they swept over her face. 'You are the most desirable woman I have ever seen in my life, Rose.'

Her head spinning dizzily, Rose's eyes fell from the warmth in his. 'If you had found me repulsive I suppose we wouldn't be here now,' she conceded shakily. 'Not,' she added hastily, 'that I'm blaming you.'

His mouth curled into a grimace of self-recrimination. 'Who else would you blame?' he wanted to know.

'Well, you hardly had to beat me into submission with a stick, did you? And we…you were careful.'

'But accidents happen,' he added on quietly. 'I'm not angry about this, Rose, if that's what you think.'

'No, you're resigned,' she accused in a quivering voice. Resigned enough to ask her to marry him? And if he did would she have the strength to say no?

'The reason, Rose, I know you haven't slept with another man, leaving aside the lack-of-opportunity factor, is firstly because it is not in your nature to have casual sex—it is not a mechanical act for you, you make *love*—and secondly you do not want another man…just me.'

This display of male arrogance drew a dry laugh from her aching throat. 'Do you know how that sounds?'

'It sounds true.'

Rose glared up at him. 'I suppose you think you've spoilt me for any other man…that I'll spend my life comparing all other men to you…' Well, if he hadn't thought it before he was in no doubt now—way to go, Rose.

'You won't have to. I'll be right here for you.' He ran a finger down her cheek and Rose, her skin tingling and her heart aching, jerked away.

'Of course you will.'

And they both knew why, she thought dully. She had always known this was going to happen when Mathieu found out about the baby.

Which made her prepared…or *should* have, because he was reacting exactly as she had anticipated. He was doing everything in his power to prevent his child growing up without a father as he had.

And he was obviously willing to do whatever it took to bring that about.

He was even prepared to pretend to love her. A flicker of raw anguish crossed her face at the thought.

The awful part was she was tempted—tempted to take what he was saying at face value and not question it. It would be easy to rationalise, there were a lot of pluses, the baby would be secure and loved…Mathieu would be a great father. She would wear his ring, share his bed, and wait for the day he came home and admitted he had fallen in love for real.

She firmed her jaw and took a deep sustaining breath. Her baby deserved better. A lot better than a mother so pathetically desperate for the love of a man who didn't return her feelings that she was willing to live a lie.

'I can't wait to see you grow even more lusciously lovely carrying our child.' He ran his hands down her bare arms and she shivered. 'We will do this thing together, *ma belle.*'

He knows what you want to hear, she reminded herself, and he's saying it. She attempted a laugh. It wasn't her most convincing effort, but it did bring a flash of baffled frustration to his face.

'How did you even know there was a baby?' Her brow furrowed. This ought to have been her first question.

'You mean it was a secret?'

His brows lifted in mock incredulity, but behind the cynical mocking smile that curved his lips Rose saw anger lurking.

'And here was I thinking I was the only one not in the loop.' Mathieu was unable to keep the bitterness from his voice.

'I haven't told anyone. I've barely got used to the idea myself.' Rose was annoyed to hear the note of apology in her voice.

'You've known long enough, according to your sister, to decide that you don't want me in your life full stop. I think,' he mused, 'that was roughly what she said, give or take the odd assorted insult concerning my birth.'

Rose's jaw dropped. '*Rebecca* came to see you…but she and Nick are living in New York.'

'I've been in New York for the past couple of months, Rose.'

Rose buried her hands in her face and groaned. 'Oh, my God, I'll kill her. She promised me.'

'She did mention something along those lines, but she felt, and I have to say that under the circumstances she was right, that the situation warranted a little deceit. When exactly did you intend to let me in on your little secret…or did you not plan to?' His jaw clenched, he struggled to contain his anger. He wasn't the injured party here, he reminded himself grimly.

'Look, I would have told you first, but Rebecca is my twin and…she just knew.' The twin thing was a bit hard to explain to someone who didn't have firsthand experience. 'It must have been a bit of a shock.'

'I didn't get the news directly from your sister. She was still crossing town when Andreos rang to tell me you were pregnant.'

The moment his words registered, the colour fled her face. 'Your father?' Rose, her eyes wide with horror, lifted a hand to her mouth.

He nodded. 'Rebecca had apparently turned up at his hotel looking for a Demetrios to castigate and got the wrong one… She arrived at the right hotel just as I was leaving to catch the flight here. It's possible that I might have upset her.'

Rose responded to this admission with a grim smile. 'Good.' Why did her twin, who was barely five minutes older than her, think she had the right to interfere in her life as and when she deemed necessary? She slanted a curious look at him and wondered, 'How did you upset her?'

'I had a plane to catch and time was running along; your sister is quite fond of the sound of her own voice. So there came a point when I had to bring the conversation to a close.'

'You're not saying you threw her out…*again*?' Despite everything, Rose's lips twitched at the mental image.

'I showed her the door.' And it had barely closed when Andreos had banged on it. It had felt to him at the time that fate was conspiring to make him miss his flight, though thanks to the skill of a cab driver who gave a new meaning to fearless he had caught it. 'I was polite…well, *fairly* polite,' he amended. 'It was not easy.'

'Why?'

'Your sister kept telling me that I slept with you because I thought you were her…'

'You did think I was her.'

A spasm of exasperation flickered across his lean face as he framed her face with his big hands and left her little choice but to look at him. 'Well, that is one thing that you have in common: you are both stupid.' And the most stupid thing he had done in his life was letting Rose walk out of it. Well, that wasn't going to happen again.

Before Rose could object to this scathing observation he added, 'I told your sister that if I had wanted to sleep with her I would have when she offered.'

A minute before Rose had been thinking some pretty unkind things about her sister, but it didn't stop the reflex to fly to Rebecca's defence kicking in at the first hint of criticism from someone else.

'Don't run away with the idea that Rebecca was behaving normally when she—' She broke off, shifting uncomfortably in her chair under his sardonic scrutiny.

He arched a dark brow. 'When she what?'

The flush on Rose's cheeks deepened as she glared at him resentfully.

'Propositioned is, I think, the word you are searching for,' he inserted helpfully. 'The polite one, anyway. But don't worry— Rebecca was anxious to put the record straight on the subject. Apparently she couldn't have been in her right mind at the time because I am not her type.'

Rose stopped short of calling her twin a liar, but she couldn't prevent the sceptical snort escaping her throat before her teeth clenched. In her opinion Mathieu was every woman's type.

'I assured her that this was mutual and the reason I didn't take what she offered was because I *was* not and *am* not attracted to her.' His lips twitched slightly as he confided, 'She was not inclined to believe me.'

Neither was Rose. She could not imagine why he would not be attracted to Rebecca. Despite his protests, she knew that Mathieu had been enchanted by Rebecca. All men were.

'That,' he mused half to himself, 'is something you do not share...'

He was running the tip of his forefinger very gently across the curve of her upper lip and it was actually quite hard to respond at all, but she managed a husky, 'What is?' before her eyes closed, and a deep sigh shuddered through her body.

But pretending that she wasn't wildly attracted in a fatal moth-to-a-flame sort of way had never been a serious option. And Mathieu knew exactly what effect he had on her. But had he realised yet that she was in love with him?

She gave a fatalistic sigh. If he hadn't it was only a matter of time.

'An ego.'

'What?' she asked, confused.

'Your sister appears to think that she is irresistible to men.'

It was news to Rose that she wasn't.

'You, on the other hand...' He shook his head slowly, his voice fading as he continued to study her face with an intensity that bordered on compulsion.

Slowly a smile so incredibly tender that it made her heart skip several beats spread across his face, softening the hard contours and bringing a glowing warmth Rose had never seen before to the mirrored surface of his spectacular eyes.

'What about me?' she whispered. It could do no harm to listen if she didn't lose sight of the fact none of this was true. Mathieu's objective was laying claim to his child and making sure history did not repeat itself.

'You, *mon coeur*,' he observed with a husky catch in his voice, 'appear not to have the faintest idea of the effect you have on men.'

It wasn't the effect she had on men that Rose was concerned about—just one man. As her eyes lingered with a mixture of fascination and longing on the familiar stark purity of a face that would have made a sculptor's fingers tingle a tiny sigh bubbled past her clenched teeth—he was nothing less than beautiful. The sort of beauty that made a person's heart ache.

Her hand went to her stomach. Would their baby inherit his stunning looks?

'Look, you don't have to say these things.' She actually didn't need to be reminded of what she was missing. 'I'm fine with the fact that Rebecca is the sexy one and, for the record and just to save time, energy and your inventive powers, I wouldn't dream of trying to cut you out of the baby's life.'

The corners of his mouth lifted in a smile that left his grey eyes hard. 'I'd like to see you try.'

Rose flung up her hands and, grabbing hold of the billowing skirt of her gown, stood up. 'Oh, for pity's sake, I try to be nice. Offer you an olive branch and what do I get? Bloody-minded macho belligerence. Why does everything always have to be a fight with you?' she asked wearily.

'You expect me not to challenge you when you say stupid things?'

'I mean it,' she protested as he dragged a frustrated hand through his hair. 'I'm not trying to cut you out. You can be as much a part of—'

'Who told you that Rebecca is the sexy one?'

'I thought you were here because of the baby. You seem more interested in Rebecca.'

'I am here because of the baby…but mostly I'm here because I can't…' He stopped dead and searched her face. 'My God, you're jealous.'

'It's your fault,' she wailed. 'I never have been jealous of Rebecca before and, God knows, I've had enough cause. I've been fine with it, her being the sexy one.'

'You're talking rubbish and you know it.'

Rose's jaw tightened. 'What would you know? You're not a twin. You think because we're identical, give or take the odd fifteen pounds, that if one is sexy so is the other. Sexiness isn't just about looks…though it doesn't do any harm if you are a size eight.' In another century her curves might have given her the edge, but not in an era when you were judged on the smallness of your jean size.

He heard her out but his impatience was obvious. 'Have you finished? Is this the end of the lecture? You think I don't know these things are more than skin-deep?'

Rose swallowed. She had asked for honesty so it wasn't really logical to feel hurt when she got it.

'I'm sure your sister is a perfectly nice woman, but even if she put on enough flesh to lose that androgynous look the entire mood of my day would not be changed for the better by hearing her voice.'

Rose's jaw dropped. 'But Rebecca has the perfect figure.'

'No,' he contradicted firmly, 'you have the perfect figure.' His lips lifted into a smile of satisfaction as his eyes slid over her voluptuous curves. 'But we have a good deal of time to address your body issues.'

'I don't have body issues.' Her protest was automatic but not firm as she read the need in his taut expression. 'I'm just realistic.' If only that were true, she thought sombrely. She only had to catch a glimpse of him looking like all her romantic fantasies made flesh, and pretty perfect flesh too, and realism and practicality flew out the window.

He gave an expressive and very Gallic shrug. 'What reason would I have to lie, Rose? You have already said you will give me what you think I am here to claim.'

'Are you're saying you're *not* here because of the baby?' She was unable to keep the quavering note of hurt out of her voice as she added, 'If that were so, Mathieu, why did you wait ten weeks?' Ten weeks when she had waited and hoped, then finally faced reality. He wasn't coming.

'The baby is part of the reason I came, certainly,' he agreed quietly. 'But not the whole.' He passed a hand across his eyes and sighed, knowing too well how it looked. 'And I had every intention of following you the very next day, but...'

Her face stiffened as his eyes slid from hers. Clearly he couldn't look her in the eyes when he lied. 'Something else came up?' she suggested.

'In a manner of speaking, yes, it did. About eight years ago I had an accident.' His head lifted and he smiled bleakly. 'An occupational hazard.'

Rose did not smile back. The idea of Mathieu risking his life on a race track was not one that made her feel like smiling. It made her sensitive stomach muscles clench.

'I came out of it fairly unscathed. Abrasions, a few cracked ribs and—' he gestured vaguely towards his back '—a compression fracture of my thoracic spine.' He saw her eyes fly wide in alarm and added quickly, 'It was asymptomatic, no treatment required, it healed, was considered stable, and that was that.'

Rose, her heart thudding with dread, swallowed. 'And something changed?'

'I had some pain.' A man expected pain when he had slammed his fist repeatedly into a stone wall to vent his frustration because he'd let the woman he loved leave without a fight. 'I didn't think much of it, then, when I was on the helicopter the next day following you—'

'You followed me?' she said wonderingly.

'I'm stupid enough to let you go, but not *that* stupid. Of course I followed you, *mon coeur*. Only problem was by the time I reached Athens I had a slight numbness in my hand.'

She watched, horror spreading over her like an invisible freezing veil as he flexed his right hand.

'It actually got worse, quite quickly.' Nothing in his tone hinted at the terror and revulsion he had felt when the healthy body he took for granted had failed him and he had been forced to recognise the possibility it would remain that way. 'It turned out that the fracture had moved and was compressing some nerves.'

When he had told the doctors he couldn't have surgery yet because he had things to do they had informed him bluntly that delay could result in the damage being permanent.

'The best surgeon and rehabilitation was in New York, and I'm a Demetrios,' he reminded her with a self-disparaging grin. 'We always have the best.'

'You were in hospital?' How could he sound so casual? Rose felt emotionally numb as she struggled to get her head around what he was saying. As she stared she began to notice for the first time details that she had missed in the initial shock of seeing him.

Mathieu had always come across as a man with limitless reserves of energy; his dynamism was one of the things she had first noticed about him. Once she had moved beyond the sinfully sexy body and fallen angel face. The vitality he projected was almost combustible and if asked before that moment she would have confidently predicted that his reserves were limitless.

Looking at him now suggested her confidence had been misplaced; if he had been anyone else she would have said he was surviving on caffeine and adrenaline.

Normally immaculately groomed, he looked as if he hadn't shaved in a couple of days and there were crescent-moon-shaped shadows she had never seen before under his deep-set eyes that emphasised their extraordinary colour and made them look, if it were possible, even more striking

The strong, elegantly sculpted bones of his narrow oval face had acquired a sharper edge, giving his cheekbones a knifelike prominence. Her concern grew as she saw that the skin stretched over the dramatic dips and hollows had a greyish tinge normally associated with extreme exhaustion and stress or illness.

He'd been ill, seriously ill, and she hadn't been there for him.

'For a while,' he agreed, nodding. 'I was honoured Andreos came to visit, though he spent most of the time telling me that it is my fault that Sacha has accepted a place at the Sorbonne because I broke her heart.' At least one thing he had done had gone according to plan.

She hardly heard him, her head was buzzing. 'You were in hospital and I didn't know? You didn't tell me?' Her voice rose a shrill decibel with each disbelieving addition before falling to a husky sob as she added, 'And you have the nerve to say I mean something to you.'

'Tell you?' He pushed a hand through his dark hair. 'How could I tell you? So the guy does the operation a dozen times a week, it's a walk in the park for him. There was still no guarantee it would work, I could have been left a cripple.' His lean face spasmed as his molten-silver gaze raked her face. 'How could I ask you to take me like that, Rose?'

'How can you say that? I wouldn't…how can you think for a second it would make any difference to how I feel?' she protested furiously.

His chin lifted. 'I did not want your pity.'

Rose snorted. 'Pity,' she echoed. 'I could kill you for doing that alone.' A deep sob suddenly welled up from deep inside her and emerged as a shocking whimper of distress. 'How could you think it would matter to me, Mathieu?'

'It would matter to me. I want to be a whole man for you.' With a groan Mathieu took her face between his hands. 'Please don't cry,' he begged. 'Smile. I've been dreaming about your smile all these weeks. A day that passes not seeing you smile makes me feel cheated, Rose.'

Her cheeks wet with tears, her heart so full she could hardly breathe Rose reached out blindly to steady herself before she found support. His warm fingers closed over hers and she found her hand placed and held firm against his chest.

Outside the door there was the noise of a bleeper shrilling and the sound of running feet, but the din did not register with Rose. 'You like my smile?'

'Like is not quite the right word…'

She swallowed, still not quite daring to believe what she was seeing stamped into those sternly beautiful features, but wanting more than anything to allow herself to.

'I used to think my life was stimulating and productive.' A fleeting self-derisive smile tugged at the corners of his lips as he contemplated his naïvety. 'I used to think that needing someone was a weakness, now I realise that the reverse is true. It requires strength, and also admittedly a little insanity, to care for someone, to put into their hands the power to hurt or heal.' While he spoke he took Rose's hand in his and unfurled each finger like the petals of a flower. 'Such a pretty hand too,' he murmured, lifting her hand to his mouth and brushing her palm with his lips, all the time holding her eyes with his.

Rose's eyes filled with emotional tears as she blinked up at him. 'Needing someone…*me*…?'

'You are infuriating and ridiculously stubborn and also totally adorable. I have known I loved you almost from the start. I was just too afraid to admit it to myself.'

Mathieu was saying things she had never expected to hear him say outside her dreams, but she felt strangely dispassionate. Her clinical detachment wavered under the hungry, searching scrutiny of his narrowed eyes.

'You are still wary of my motives.'

'I don't want to be,' she admitted.

He ran a finger down the furrow between her feathery brows and nodded. 'Before I met you I was arrogant enough to imagine that a man had a choice about who he loved.'

'So you love me against your better judgement?' More than you expected, Rose, she reminded herself, but not enough even had she been inclined to take what he said at face value. 'Because I don't fit into your life.'

The conclusion drew a strange laugh from him. He shook his head and drew his hand heavily across his stubble-covered jaw. 'You *are* my life. Surely you know this?'

His incredulous eyes swept across her face.

'You have to know this, Rose.'

'I have to know…' she echoed, giving an odd little laugh. 'I don't think I know anything any more except that you look terrible,' she husked. 'I know you don't want my advice, but shouldn't you still be in hospital?'

'You have no idea what I want,' he retorted, covering her hand with his.

'I know you didn't want me to be a virgin.'

'*Dieu*, I know I acted like a total fool,' he groaned, lifting her hand to his lips. 'You don't know how often I wished I had not said the things I did.

'I was totally irrational, but you have no idea what a shock it was to discover…' Visibly shaken by the memory, he closed his eyes, his fingers tightening around Rose's until she winced and, mumbling an apology, he let them go.

'The truth is, Rose, that I had been rationalising my feelings for you, telling myself that it was just physical and you felt the same way, then when I discovered what a precious gift you had given me the pretence was ripped away and I had to face the reality of my feelings for you.'

Rose's heart lurched. There was no mistaking the sincerity glowing in his luminous eyes. 'Keep talking, Mathieu,' she encouraged.

'I love you, Rose…marry me…' Mathieu said, watching her face.

With a cry she was in his arms and he was holding her and kissing her with a tenderness and passion that drove her last lingering doubts away.

'You know,' she said when they broke apart, 'it's going to take a lot of those…' her eyes darkened as she followed the sensual curve of his mouth with a finger '…an awful lot,' she warned him huskily, 'to drive away the memory of these last weeks.'

His smoky gaze slid over her face. 'I will do my best,' he promised, taking her hand and, before she realised his intention, sliding the big emerald back in place. 'Now that,' he said with satisfaction, 'is where it belongs.'

'And where do I belong?'

'You have to ask? In my arms, of course.' As he pulled her to him she gave a sudden laugh.

'I've just thought—what will your father say when he finds out we're back together?'

'Does it matter? And, besides, miles may have separated us, but you were never for a moment out of my heart or thoughts.'

Enchanted by this romantic confession, she wound her arms around his neck and froze, her anxious eyes seeking his. 'The operation…I don't want to hurt you…'

'I have a scar, which I will show you later,' he promised with a look that made the heat bloom in her cheeks. 'But,' he added firmly, 'I am not fragile or breakable. I will cause metal detectors in airports some stress…' he shrugged '…but the surgery was a total success.'

Rose sighed as she felt the last cloud vanish from her emotional horizon. She struggled to stay sensible and focused even though his lips were tantalisingly close. 'About your father, though, Mat—'

His mouth a few inches from hers, Mathieu groaned.

'I really didn't mean to make things worse between you with the things I said to him.'

'My father and I are fine—well, for us fine at least.'

'Seriously?'

He nodded. 'I'll tell you about it later.' With a wave of his hand he brushed aside the subject. 'But not now.' Now there were other things he needed to tell her. He curved his hand around her face. 'You know, for a split second when Rebecca walked in through the door I thought it was you.' The joy he had felt had sprung from the depths of his soul. The bitter disappointment and sense of loss when he had realised his error had been equally profound. 'Then I saw it wasn't and it was like having heaven snatched away. I am incomplete without you, Rose.'

Rose covered her mouth with her hand as tears sprang to her eyes. 'Please don't say that if you don't mean it, Mathieu.'

'I have never meant anything more in my life.' There was no mistaking the total sincerity ringing in his statement. 'In my life I have loved people…' His eyes slid from hers as he said huskily, 'My mother…'

She watched the muscles in his brown throat work as he swallowed, clearly fighting to contain strong emotions. Heart aching with empathy, she reached out and caught his hand.

As he raised her hand to his lips his eyes lifted and connected with her wide-eyed, sympathetic gaze. His eyes not leaving hers for a moment, he opened her fingers one by one and pressed his lips to her palm. The tenderness in his expression and the gesture made her throat constrict with emotion.

When he lowered her hand he didn't release it, but kept it tightly enfolded between his big hands.

'You remind me of her sometimes.'

'I do?'

He nodded, one corner of his mouth lifting in a lopsided smile that squeezed her heart. 'Not in looks. She was very dark.' His eyes brushed her fair hair, letting the silky strands fall through his fingers. 'But she was a fighter like you and stubborn too. And her pride sometimes…' he reflected, a shadow crossing his face '…made her suffer more than was necessary, but she was never bitter, you know, or angry. I had enough anger for us both,' he admitted, dragging a hand through his dark hair.

'What I am trying to say is, Rose, that I have loved people…my mother, then my stepmother and my brother. I lost them all.

'It hurt so much that I think to avoid ever feeling that way again I sealed away my emotions and nailed down the lid.' His brooding gaze rested on her face and the grimness lifted. 'Then you came along and I no longer had any control over my feelings…' Unable to resist the temptation of her lush lips another second, he closed his mouth over hers with a hunger that drove the breath from Rose's body.

When they broke apart Rose's head was spinning and she was smiling with dreamy content.

'What I felt for you, *ma petite*, could never be confined within any box. Somehow, I knew that to lose you,' he rasped in a voice that throbbed with raw emotion, 'would be unbearable, and it was.' Eyes bleak, he drew a hand across his face as if to extinguish the memory of the last ten weeks. 'For delivering me from my private hell a day early, I will always be grateful to your sister.'

'Me too,' Rose admitted. 'I can't imagine what your father made of her.'

'He did mention the fact that it could be worse—she might be the one I had to marry.'

'*Had* to marry? Nice to know he approves,' she teased, running a loving hand down his lean cheek.

'Approves might be a little strong,' he admitted, turning his face into her hand and pressing a warm kiss into the small palm.

When accused of turning his back on his parental responsibilities, Mathieu—already shaken to the core by the news he was about to be a father—had retorted without his usual self-restraint that this comment was nothing short of breathtaking hypocrisy.

In the following bitter exchange the simmering resentment of years had spilled out. Even that eavesdropped conversation from years before had been dredged up and in his turn Andreos had accused Mathieu of being a thankless wretch incapable of showing affection and always looking for an opportunity to throw his generosity back in his face.

In the end Mathieu had turned his back with every intention of walking away for good, and he would have except he had happened to look back to deliver one final comment.

It was a comment that he had never voiced, nor had he walked out of the door. Andreos Demetrios, the man who could make other strong men wilt with a look, had been standing, his face contorted with grief, as tears ran unchecked down his cheeks.

Mathieu had only paused for a moment before he had moved to comfort him. He had listened while his father had told him that if he had stayed outside that door a little longer he would have heard the rest of the conversation.

A conversation in which Andreos had admitted to his wife that he knew it was irrational to blame a child for his own sins, even if it was guilt that made him unable to show affection to his older son—that and the belief that the boy hated him.

It would have been an overstatement to say that the past had been washed away, but it was a beginning, which was just as well because he suspected that Rose would not rest until she had seen everyone kiss and make up.

'So you're marrying me because your father tells you to...?' She laughed.

His eyes darkened as he caught her passionately to him and growled, 'I'm marrying you because I adore every hair on your glorious head. I've just made a very interesting discovery.'

'You have?' she asked, letting her head fall back as he kissed the base of her throat.

'There is no back in this thing.' He laid his hand on the smooth curve of her bottom that was exposed to the elements and the gaze of anyone who happened to look through the glass panel in the door.

With a shriek of protest Rose backed away, holding the sides of her gaping gown together. 'Stay away from me. This is a hospital and the radiologist could come back any moment.' Conscious this was a very real possibility, Rose retook her place on the couch and rearranged the blanket primly over her legs. 'You,' she warned, 'keep your distance.'

Mathieu looked at her, a wicked glint glittering in his eyes. 'You don't get turned on by the idea of being caught in the act, then?' He watched her blush... *Dieu*, but he loved that blush.

'No, I do not...' She slid him a curious look. 'Do you?'

Mathieu threw back his head and roared with laughter. 'Oh, I'm dark and twisted—ask anyone.'

'I like to form my own opinion,' she told him, dimpling prettily.

He folded his arms across his chest and strolled over to her side. 'And what's your opinion of me?'

He recognised the irony. He'd spent his entire adult life not giving a damn what anyone thought of him and now there was someone who he desperately wanted to think well of him. The most surprising thing was recognising the new vulnerability did not appall him as it once might.

'Too soon to tell. Ask me again in twenty years or so.'

'I will,' he promised thickly.

Rose's eyes filled as he laid a warm hand over her abdomen. 'This baby, *mon coeur*, you're happy about it...?'

'More,' she promised with a palpable sincerity that drove the last trace of lingering uncertainty from his face, 'than you can imagine.'

'So tell me,' he said, dragging a chair and placing it beside her. 'About this scan? Is the image 3D? Do we get a DVD? Are—?'

She held up her hand, laughing. 'Oh, no, you're going to be one of those men who cut the cord, aren't you?'

'Hell, no,' he drawled, giving a visible shudder. 'I'll stick to moral support.' He caught her small hand to his lips. 'It is my job to keep you safe, *ma petite*, and I will,' he swore solemnly, 'do that with the last breath in my body. I will do that.'

'Oh, Mathieu.'

The radiologist returned a few minutes later. She paused, shocked, on the threshold for a moment before silently retracing her steps.

She waited a tactful space of time before returning, making sure that a tone-deaf wall could have heard her approach.

The pink-cheeked and tousle-haired mother-to-be with the just-kissed look smiled as she walked in and said brightly, 'We were just wondering what had happened to you.'

Her partner grinned. 'That was not what you said you were wondering about to me, *mon ange*.'

The technician cast him a reproachful look, but thawed towards him when she saw the tears in his eyes as he looked at the first images of his unborn child.

A man who looked like him, and he was in touch with his emotions—now that, in her experience, was rare. But not perhaps as rare as the look the couple exchanged as they linked hands.

'We did this?' Mathieu breathed as he stared with sparkling eyes at the tiny image magnified on the screen. 'You are brilliant!'

Rose smiled at his enthusiasm and awe. 'I can't take all the credit. This was a joint effort.'

'We're a team.'

Rose gave a sigh of content. 'Totally,' she agreed, seeing no limits to what they could achieve together. She was the luckiest woman alive.

THE MAGNATE'S INDECENT PROPOSAL

Ally Blake

When **Ally Blake** was a little girl, she made a wish that when she turned twenty-six she would marry an Italian two years older than her. After it actually came true, she realised she was on to something with these wish things. So next she wished that she could make a living spending her days in her pyjamas, eating M&Ms and drinking scads of coffee while turning her formative experiences of wallowing in teenage crushes and romantic movies into creating love stories of her own. The fact that she is now able to spend her spare time searching the internet for pictures of handsome guys for research purposes is merely a bonus! Come along and visit her website at www. allyblake.com.

To my editor, Bryony Green.
Thank you for discovering me, indulging me with unexpected opportunities, and knowing just how to draw the best writing out of me. None of this would have been possible without you.

CHAPTER ONE

CHELSEA flicked a stray streak of wet mud off the nose of the beagle motif on her old umbrella as she ducked under the silver and black striped awning of Amelie's, a newly opened Melbourne restaurant a stone's throw from the Yarra River at South Bank.

She peered through the floor-to-ceiling windows to see the place was peppered with bright and shiny types decked out in designer gear. While the chocolate-brown knee-length skirt she'd found in the back of her closet sat at a slightly askew angle to hide a fresh doggie shampoo stain.

'In a couple of hours I'll be out of these high-heeled boots and back into sneakers,' she said aloud. 'While you'll all have bunions before you're forty.'

As some kind of perverse justice, her boots teetered beneath her as she twirled out of the way of a rushing pair of suits barging out of the restaurant barking into their mobile phones rather than looking out for stray women on the pavement.

Not wanting to push her luck, she slipped inside the glass doors and patted the criss-cross of bobby pins holding back her too-long fringe to make sure they were still in place and not dangling from the end of her hair like some odd mobile.

'Do you have a reservation?' the skinny, bald *maître d'* in head-to-toe black asked.

'I'm Chelsea London,' she said, leaning back slightly to make sure he wouldn't get a waft of the mothball scent of her recently de-cupboarded fancy clothes. 'Meeting Kensington Hurley. She's always madly early. I'd be happy to sneak through and find her myself—'

'Not necessary.' He gave her a cool smile.

Phoney schmuck, she thought as she gave him a weak smile in return.

He ran a bony finger down the pale pink diary page and nodded. Then said, 'Your phone, please.'

'Excuse me, my what?' said Chelsea.

'Your…mobile…phone,' he repeated, more slowly this time. 'They are a nuisance to other customers thus we don't allow them in the restaurant. You would have been told at the time of reservation.'

'My sister chose this place,' she explained through gritted teeth.

'Nevertheless, you need to check it into the cloakroom.'

She bit her lip while she made up her mind about what to do. Her whole life was in her phone. Her address book, her appointments calendar, her grocery list, her emails, the profit and loss statements to take to the bank later that morning now that she'd finally made an appointment with a loan officer to see about expanding Pride & Groom, her pet-grooming business, from one salon to three. He might as well have asked for her future firstborn child for all it meant to her.

She sank her hand into her oversized handbag and held it tight as she asked, 'What if I don't have a phone?'

He kept his hand outstretched, palm up.

'Okay, fine,' she said, doing a quick, obsessive-compulsive

message check before handing it over. 'But couldn't you just ask everyone to turn their phone to silent? And confiscate those who don't comply?'

'This isn't high school, Ms London. We believe mobile phones are antisocial. And haven't you come here today to be social?'

High school is for ever, she thought. *Those in new uniforms compared with those in hand-me-downs, all living out the failures or successes of their parents like some great evolutionary joke.*

She kept her theory to herself and instead muttered, 'I came here today because my sister has the kind of big brown cow eyes you can't say no to.'

He gave her a pink ticket with a smudged black number written upon it in return, then she pressed on into the restaurant.

Weaving her way through the tightly packed tables past a plethora of 'new school uniform' types with money and time and an apparent desire to be social on a Tuesday morning, she made a determined beeline for Kensey's curly brown 'do. Thus she didn't notice a gentleman prepare to slide back his chair until it was too late.

She put on the brakes but her inexperience in her high-heeled boots meant she lost her grip upon the swanky silk carpet. Her momentum pitched her forward and everything from that point on seemed to happen in slow motion.

The man turned, alerted by either the whoosh of air she displaced before her, or perhaps the frantic oath she'd emitted a second before that. As she fell she found herself amidst one of those time-stood-still-while-my-life-flashed-before-my-eyes moments as she made eye contact with her attacker, whose features burned onto her brain one after the other.

A toothpick between perfect white front teeth. Smooth dark

hair so neat it looked as if it had been cut that morning. A jaw line so defined it made a girl want to reach out and run the back of her finger along it. Dark glinting eyes the colour of the Pacific just before dusk.

Even that tremendous collection of visual stimuli wasn't enough to stop the laws of physics. Chelsea had no choice but to reach out and grab him by two handfuls of his suit jacket to stop herself from going completely head over heels.

He instinctively slid both arms around her middle, slowing her momentum until she came to a complete stop. Upright, or almost, considering her legs were twisted, she clung. Bodily against him. Her breasts pressed into his chest. Her stomach hard against the zipper of his trousers. Her shaky right knee clamped snug between both of his. She knew enough about the shape of him that in some cultures they'd be considered betrothed.

She curled her fingers gently beneath a lapel or two. His suit felt *really* nice. Expensive. The fabric was soft and warm. And it smelled so good. Like falling leaves and crisp fresh air. At least she assumed it was the suit. Maybe it was just him.

When time finally caught up with her, the surrounds of the restaurant swarmed in. Clinking cutlery. Tinkling laughter. Steam from the kitchen. The feel of his long thin wallet beneath her knuckles and next to his heart. And the intermingling whisper of the pair of them breathing heavily.

'Are you okay?' he asked. His voice was husky. Deep. It rumbled through her hands and into her chest until it found a home deep within her stomach. She gave into the need to lick suddenly bone-dry lips.

'Hey,' he rumbled again, and tucked a finger beneath her chin, lifting her gaze to his face as he repeated, 'Are you okay?'

His skin was unblemished and evenly tanned, his eyes so

blue it hurt, and he truly smelled beautiful, like the rainy autumn day she'd left outside. All that glowing, carefree perfection made him as tempting as the yummiest forbidden fruit. But this gal had already eaten away her lip-gloss, her clothes were a decade old, and she smelled like wet dog and mothballs. Thus forbidden fruit would never be hers to have.

She slowly let her grip abate.

'I'm fine,' Chelsea said. 'Dandy, in fact. Embarrassed, but there seems to be no permanent damage to the patch of carpet my boots did their best to take on. It could have been worse.'

'True,' he said. 'If there'd been a dessert cart in the vicinity we would very quickly have become a scene out of a Pink Panther film.'

Her cheeks twitched in amusement. 'Can't you imagine a barrage of chocolate cream pies flying through the air and landing on *that* table of coiffed princesses until they are dripping in pearls *and* chocolate sauce?'

The man's eyes darted sideways to the table of women who had been eyeing Chelsea as she had walked in. And he said, 'It would certainly have added a dash of sunshine to such a drab morning.'

As he smiled at her some more, his eyes now twinkling, his toothpick twirling as though behind his teeth his tongue was hard at work, Chelsea's stomach felt unnaturally hollow. And she didn't think it had all that much to do with hunger for food.

She smiled back, all lips, no teeth, and then proceeded to disentangle herself as elegantly as she could manage. But once she'd let go she discovered she'd scrunched up his lovely suit lapels something awful. She spent a good ten seconds flattening them out, running her hands along the soft wool, which did little to hide the hard body beneath.

'Though I'm not sure I could handle any more sunshine

than I have right now,' he said, his voice ever deeper, and so close she could feel the air of every word brush against her fast-warming cheek.

She bit. 'And why's that?'

'I've never before had a woman fall for me quite so quickly. Usually I count on an introduction and a little flirtation before the sunshine part.'

She glanced up into his eyes again. Deep. Absorbing. Blue as the heavens. He was pure charm. And she had the distinct feeling he knew it. Which meant he also knew she was no longer hanging onto him for balance.

She stopped her fussing and said, 'One little hint? Next time you're looking to land yourself a girl, don't bother with the chair. Props are for amateurs.'

His playful smile faded until it was no more than a glimmer in his eyes. He breathed in through his nose, she felt it in the swell of his chest, and then realised that to all intents and purposes she was still feeling the guy up. She gave his lapels one last tug, then said, 'Now nobody will know I was ever here.'

He removed the toothpick and with his deep voice so low only a person a mere breath away would be able to hear him he said, 'I'll know.'

His words slid through her, hot, liquid, and unimpeded by any kind of sense or self-defence. In a stab of unadulterated desire it occurred to her that if she slanted her head an inch, two at the most, she could find out if his smiling lips tasted anywhere near as good as they looked.

She took an abrupt step back and bumped his table hard enough his full latte glass rocked mercilessly and sloshed a gulp or two over the edge. Mr Suit and Tie leapt for the glass and caught it just before it tilted all the way over.

Free of his autumnal scent, his magnetic gaze, and the

pleasure of luxurious wool, Chelsea slid out of his gravitational pull. 'That's my cue to leave before I accidentally set you on fire.'

'No, wait,' he said, putting the glass back on the table, and patting down the polished wood with a napkin.

But she hitched her handbag higher onto her shoulder, and then eased around him and hurried to join her sister on the other side of the restaurant.

Kensey stood, kissed her cheek. 'Tell me you got his phone number,' were the first words out of her mouth.

Chelsea dumped her bag beneath the table, sat, then threw her hands over her face, cooling her hot cheeks with her freezing palms. 'And when was I meant to have done that in between throwing myself in his arms and knocking over his drink?'

'What's your number, honey?' Kensey said. 'You can find time between anything for four such important words. Especially for such a specimen as that one.'

Chelsea came out from behind her hands to glare at her sister. 'And this from a married woman.'

'You're comparing Greg to *that?*'

Chelsea glared some more. 'Don't you dare intimate Greg isn't the best thing that ever happened to you.'

Greg with his thinning hair and thickening middle wasn't Chelsea's type, but every time she saw the two of them together it only reminded her she shouldn't be so picky. Kensey and Greg were mad for one another while she didn't have any man who'd take her hand as they walked down the street, whose shoulder she could lean on at the movies, to hold her when she fell asleep.

'How do you think a girl gets herself married these days?' Kensey asked. 'It takes putting herself on the shop shelf to begin with.'

'I like dating,' Chelsea said. 'Especially men with muscles and dark eyes and all their teeth. I'm *on* the shelf.'

'Right. With a big Do Not Feed the Animal sign slung around your neck. One sideways glance at another woman, one bounced cheque, one hint he might have feet of clay and you bite the hand that fondles you. Whereas that creature over there is so-o-o on the shelf fluorescent lights aim towards him wherever he goes.'

Chelsea scoffed, then twisted to sling her cropped jacket over the back of her chair and spared a glance back through the restaurant to the man in question. He was standing talking to another guy in a suit. One hand was pushing his jacket back as he searched his trouser pocket, revealing an expanse of neat white business shirt stretched just tight enough across a broad chest to make it difficult to look away.

Like the first wisp of smoke heralding a coming fire, a thread of longing curled through her stomach. Her fingernails dug patterns into her palms as she imagined tearing open that flawless expensive starched white shirt until the buttons popped off.

She blinked hard at the ferocity of her reaction. It wasn't as though she didn't come in contact with any number of good-looking men every day of her life. Her job gave her a veritable platter to choose from. Nice men, responsible men, men who loved dogs, men who were well and truly within her comfort zone.

In the past couple of months there had been an Alsatian owner who was also a plumber. Cute. Brawny. He'd unblocked her pipes in the shop but not in any other way worth mentioning. She'd let him go when he'd let on he loved betting on the greyhounds. Then there'd been the Bijon Frise owner, a single dad who only had the dog as he'd inherited it in his divorce along with the kids every second weekend. She'd let him go when he'd cried watching a long-distance phone ad. And the consultant with the matching set of fox terriers called Mitsy and Bitsy. She'd turned him down after one dinner for obvious reasons.

But comparing those dating experiences with three minutes spent looking into a pair of Pacific blue eyes made her wonder briefly if responsibility, sense, and comfort were all they were cracked up to be. Mr Suit and Tie and Flirty Look in the Eye made her hanker for fire, flash, flare, electricity, excitement, heat, danger, no care for the consequences...

Right then a dark, glossy brunette in a tight black skirt suit and heels so high Chelsea felt dizzy just looking at them walked by, landed a flat hand upon Mr Suit and Tie's chest and leaned in to whisper something in his ear. Mr Suit and Tie laughed, said something that made the brunette flutter a hand across her face before sauntering away swinging her hips like a pro. He paid attention for a few moments, and then pulled a flat black wallet from the inner pocket of his jacket before letting it swing back into place.

Chelsea came to as if fairy dust had suddenly cleared from before her eyes. She turned back to Kensey, who was watching her with a knowing smile on her face.

'He's a man. He's moved onto the next sure thing,' Chelsea insisted with a scowl. 'Big surprise there.'

'Fine,' Kensey said with a dramatic sigh. 'So how's work?'

'Great. Fun. Hard. Wouldn't trade it for anything. The kids?'

'Great. Fun. Hard. Wouldn't trade 'em for anything. So are you coming to the Yarra Valley with us this weekend? It's Lucy's birthday, remember.'

'Of course. Wouldn't miss it for the world.'

'You know you don't have to come alone. If you ever wanted to bring someone...'

'How about I bring Phyllis? She loves country air,' Chelsea said, referring to her longest-serving employee, a six-foot-tall woman with short grey hair and a booming voice who terrified the bejeezers out of Kensey.

'I meant a man.'

'If it's that important to you I'll see if I can pick one up on the road along the way. Tell Greg he'll have the darts partner he's always wanted, though I can't promise the guy will have bathed in some time.'

Kensey's gaze slid down to the tabletop where Chelsea was wringing her hands. 'Relax. Please. This is meant to be a celebration breakfast.'

'I haven't got the loan yet.'

'You will. Pride & Groom is just the kind of thing banks want to get their claws into.'

'You've been working on that line for days, haven't you?'

'The whole month,' Kensey said. 'But I'm serious. You own your shop outright. You've been on the telly. You're a woman. You are quite simply dripping in reasons for them to invest in you.'

Chelsea had a sudden image of the brunette in the black suit *dripping* in chocolate-cream pie, which made her smile. But when it rather quickly morphed into a certain dark-haired man *sans* suit and tie dripping in chocolate sauce her mouth began to water.

He's a prince of the 'new school uniform' set, she yelled inside her head. *You're the leftovers of a hand-me-down youth. And never the twain shall successfully mate.*

Along those lines Chelsea reminded her sister, 'You know how much trouble Dad got himself into over the years, borrowing against each new get-rich-quick scheme while the bastards just let him. Keeping Pride & Groom as a one-off, boutique, secure investment wouldn't be a silly idea.'

And it would remain all hers. Something nobody could take away from her. Even though she had to turn away more clients every time she appeared on TV, or had her salon highlighted in a magazine, making her think Pride & Groom could be really beyond-her-wildest-dreams successful. The problem with that was she'd learnt young just how crushing wild dreams could be if they didn't come true.

'Honey,' Kensey said, 'you want to update this outfit of yours to something of this century, you're gonna need more money. You wanna find yourself with more opportunities to go chest to chest with the likes of Hunka Hunka Burning Love over there, you're gonna need more money. If they offer the loan, take it.'

Chelsea leaned forward and whispered conspiratorially, 'Why? You think he's a male escort? What is the going rate these days?'

Kensey's eyes narrowed. 'No idea. But I do know you're a fool not to have given him your phone number. Or at least an accidental grope of that fantastic backside.'

Chelsea leaned back and picked up the menu. 'Maybe next time,' she said, then did her best to keep her eyes in her head when she caught a load of the prices. Nearly thirty dollars for a poached egg on toast? Seriously. What *did* these people have to promise the gods to be able to afford to eat like this on a daily basis?

'He watched you walk the whole way over here, you know,' Kensey said.

Rather than answer, Chelsea stole Kensey's iced water and took a sip.

'Top to bottom,' Kensey said, 'with a nice lingering moment spent on your behind.'

'He was probably trying to see where I was hiding it. If the bank was giving away curvier curves and charging interest then I'd be first in line.'

Boobs that could fill a bra without padding, hips that swung as she walked without the chance of pulling a muscle, the kind of figure that would garner the attention of a man like Mr Suit and Tie without having to literally throw herself at him. Though what she'd do with the likes of such an alien creature if she ever caught him, she had no idea.

'Truthfully, he was probably making sure I didn't knock over any other poor unsuspecting patrons,' she said. 'Most men like to think themselves knights in shining armour.'

'Maybe that one really is.'

'Well, then, he's the last thing I need. I rescued myself a long time ago.'

'Then how about a bit of rough and tumble? How long has it been since you indulged in a scintillating affair? No plans. No future. No "what kind of dog does he own and what does it mean in terms of his level of responsibleness?" but just hot, sweaty nakedness—'

'Okay, I get it!'

Kensey motioned over Chelsea's shoulder. Chelsea glanced back to find the gentleman making his way towards the front door looking unfrazzled by a single thing in his perfect world, and completely untouched by the eyes of a dozen women burning into his back. He really was so beautiful, so tempting, it physically hurt. But if he took responsibility for another creature more animated than a pet rock, she'd be very much surprised.

'One night,' Kensey said. 'With that. Satisfaction guaranteed.'

Chelsea gave into a few last moments gazing over gorgeous tailoring, dark neat hair, broad shoulders and lithe movement

born of pure male confidence before turning back to her sister
with a blank face.

'I told you I didn't even get a name. And I don't think sky-
writing "Trying to track down tall dark handsome man in suit"
over the city is going to help. Hot, sweaty nakedness will
simply have to wait.'

Kensey raised both eyebrows, sucked in her cheeks and
picked up her menu and Chelsea hoped that would be the end
of it. Until her sister said, 'We can switch seats so you can make
final eyes at him, if you'd like.'

'I'm fine. Thanks anyway.'

Besides, the mirrored wall behind Kensey showed him patting his Suit and Tie friend on the back as together they weaved
through the tightly cramped tables and headed back to Stock
Market Land or wherever it was they stored such glorious, untouchable, never-had-to-work-up-a-sweat-to-get-everything-
they-ever-wanted creatures once they'd drifted happily through
high school and beyond.

Chelsea harnessed her concentration, whipped it back into
line and focussed fully on her sister. 'Now, enough about me
and my behind—what's been happening in your world?'

CHAPTER TWO

'YOUR tickets, sir?'

Damien reached into his jacket pocket and pulled out the pink stub for his phone and the grey one for his coat. He handed them over to the skinny blonde *femme fatale* who'd taken over from the snappish guy as *maître d'*.

Ticket stub in hand, she bent to the locked boxes at the bottom of the closet, showcasing the edge of a black lace G-string atop her tight denim.

'Nice,' Caleb said from behind him.

'All yours,' Damien murmured back.

'Sure she's no Bonnie…'

'I thought we'd agreed that name was banned for the meantime.'

'You agreed. I never did. She was smashing. Never in my life seen cleavage to rival hers. She passed your parents' stringent tests for what a future Halliburton bride ought to be. She looked great in tennis whites and was a far better sailor than you can hope to be. But, for the record, I was the one who told you not to move in with her.'

Damien bowed to his friend in agreement.

'Now,' Caleb said, 'it's been a good month since you moved

out of her place and back into the land of the sane. Time to get back on the horse.'

'Caleb, I was with Bonnie for two and a half years, while you've never dated anyone for more than a month. You're no better than a horse.'

Caleb threw his hands in the air. 'Fine. All I'm saying is, if you stop practising, one day you might wake up and realise you've forgotten how to use it.'

'Is this where I pipe in and say it's like riding a bike?'

'If you think that, then I fear Bonnie did a worse number on you than I imagined.'

Damien turned away. Bonnie hadn't done anything wrong. She'd taken their relationship at face value and assumed he was committed to the long haul. He was the bad guy. He'd been the one to walk out on her when he'd realised in playing house he'd only been kidding them both.

'But this one is fantastic,' Caleb said, all but salivating over Ms G-string.

'She's a teenager.'

'You're a killjoy.'

'You're a pig.' Damien glanced back at the wiggling backside. As far as invitations went, it was pretty clear. Caleb couldn't be entirely held to blame. So he added, 'Of course, if the G-string had been hot-pink…'

She stood and held out his goods. 'This is them?'

He glanced at the long black coat and wide, flat, silver and black mobile phone. 'That's them.'

She cocked her hip against the desk, and glanced at Caleb. 'How about you, honey? Anything here for you?'

Damien laughed out loud, before grabbing his friend by the jacket sleeve and dragging him from the restaurant and into the fresh air.

'You're not just a killjoy, you're also plain mean,' Caleb said.

'You work for me. And despite your darker predilections, you are this town's greatest shark when it comes to attracting new clients, therefore you make me lots of money, thus keeping me in the manner to which I've become accustomed. So think of me as the guy keeping you out of jail and in gainful employ.'

'Whatever.' Caleb cricked his neck, and stretched out his shoulders before heading street side to hail a cab.

Damien slid his arms into his coat and in the same move glanced back through the windows hoping to get one last look at the one woman who had created a stir within what he'd thought had been a pretty impenetrable fortress of anti-female sentiment he'd managed to cling to since leaving Bonnie high and dry.

After a few seconds he found her. Dark skirt, pale knit top, the dangerous-looking heel of her right boot bobbing up and down rhythmically. Long, silky, caramel-blonde hair cascading down her back in soft waves.

While the whole room reeked of clashing perfume and aftershave and money, she smelled like... Something soft and homey. Talcum powder? And when he'd talked to her of sunshine the word had just appeared from some deep, dark, murky, poetic place inside him he wasn't sure he needed to know existed. But the second she'd landed in his arms it had been as though a ray of light had shone through the window of the city restaurant and brightened the dank autumn day.

For a guy who'd only recently managed to extricate himself from the claws of a woman he'd thought perfectly amiable and in tune with his own life timetable, but who'd turned out to have a ticking internal clock the size of a three-bedroom suburban house, he was pretty captivated by this woman.

That alone should have made him run a mile. His conscience

still smarted at the way he'd led Bonnie on, even if it had been unintentional. But he didn't run. Instead he watched Little Miss Sunshine lift a forkful of strawberry pancakes to her lips.

It had been a month, longer really, since he'd been that physically close to a woman. All that purely feminine warmth wrapped in a package tall enough to look him in the eye in her high heels. And she had looked him in the eye. Dead on. Direct. With the golden eyes of a lioness.

He turned around to see Caleb waving his arm like a maniac as he unsuccessfully tried to hail a cab. So he went back to watching the caramel-blonde fingering a double string of tiny gold beads around her neck.

He let himself wonder if *she* owned a hot-pink lace G-string. He imagined what it would look like wrapped around her slight curves like a picture frame, no stockings, leaving the lean length from her hips to the tops of those sexy boots naked so that a man could slide his hand beneath her skirt and touch warm, bare skin…

'You coming?' Caleb called.

Damien blinked and turned from the restaurant window to find Caleb halfway into a yellow cab. He cleared his throat when he realised he wasn't in the frame of mind to sit. 'You take it. I'll walk. I have a new client near Flinders I hoped to see in person today anyway.'

'Fine. Whatever.' And Caleb was gone in a screech of burning rubber.

Damien glanced back into the restaurant one more time, but his view was obstructed by a table of newcomers, more clones in black skirt suits and glossy hair and no doubt lashings of perfume, hugging and kissing cheeks and discussing how to lock unsuspecting men into matrimony.

The lure of the female abruptly and thankfully negated, he

drew his coat tight about his neck, looked upward to find the earlier rain had already stopped and stepped out into the teeming morning city foot traffic.

'Are you going to finish those pancakes?' Kensey asked after the 'who's the hottest guy on *Grey's Anatomy*' argument had hit a lull. 'I'm starving. Probably because I'm pregnant.'

Chelsea let her fork drop to her plate. 'Did you just say that you're—?'

'Up the duff,' Kensey said. 'With child. Bun in the oven. I did. I am.'

Chelsea's gaze slid across the table to Kensey's large water glass, not the usual fancy-looking cocktail heavy with tiny paper umbrellas or pink plastic flamingos she ordered any time she had an adult meal without her kids in tow.

'Wow. But didn't Greg just have the…?' Chelsea mimed a pair of scissors.

'They did tell us it doesn't work right away, takes a few weeks to be sure. But it was our anniversary, and we were both in the mood, and the kids were all asleep by nine.'

Well what do you know? Kensey was pregnant with her *fourth*. The crazy number that meant she needed a people mover and extensions to the holiday hut in the Yarra Valley they could barely afford. It meant chaos. Yet Kensey looked so sublimely happy. Chelsea felt an unexpected surge of bitter-sweet envy form in her veins.

'How far along are you?' she asked.

'Eight weeks, give or take.' Kensey let out a long shaky breath and Chelsea realised this was half the reason behind the big fancy breakfast and she'd been so tunnel-visioned about her own issues. She was a bad sister. 'I have no idea how we are going to do this.'

'You'll be fine. You guys are always fine.'

Kensey grabbed Chelsea by both hands. 'If you believe in my judgment so much, then let me find you a man of your own so we can have babies together. Imagine a brood with dark hair and blue eyes like that Mr Handsome burning love from earlier.'

'Whoa there, partner. You're the one who ended up with the white-picket-fence gene while I got the modicum-of-business-sense gene. Both miracles considering our parentage. Besides, can you imagine that guy coming anywhere near the Pride & Groom? He'd be covered in white dog hair the minute the door let in the slightest gust of wind. Karma would crucify me for daring to mar such perfection.'

'Well, so long as it's something of great magnitude keeping you from grabbing such a man with both hands. What was wrong with the last guy again?'

'Gay,' Chelsea shot back.

'Okay, so maybe your reasons for sending your menagerie of admirers on their merry way are becoming more sensible over time. Less like purposeful sabotage. By the time you're in your fifties you'll give some poor guy a break when you finally realise they are not all deadbeats like Dad.'

Chelsea glared at her sister as she grabbed her plate back. 'Maybe I will finish those pancakes after all. And I sincerely hope you're having triplets.'

Damien's mobile phone chirped melodiously.

He vaguely recognised the ring tone as the theme song from some girly TV show. *The Gilmore Girls? Laverne and Shirley?* Bloody Caleb must have been mucking around with it at some stage that morning.

'Halliburton,' he answered in a clipped tone as he checked

the street for traffic before jogging across in front of a slow-moving taxi.

'Ah, hi,' a hesitant female voice said. 'Is this the Pride & Groom salon?'

'Nope. Sorry. Wrong number.' He snapped the phone shut. And moved into the stream of pedestrian traffic heading uptown.

The phone rang again. This time he recognised it instantly as the theme from *The Mary Tyler Moore Show*. Bloody *bloody* Caleb. In a fit of guilt he'd let Bonnie keep the lease on his old apartment and been living with his best friend ever since. He really would have to get off his friend's couch very soon.

'Halliburton,' he answered.

This time there was a pause. 'I am calling for Letitia Forbes from the special features desk of *Chic* magazine,' the hesitant female voice said once more. 'Is Chelsea London nearby?'

Damien pulled up short. He turned to look over his shoulder to see if perhaps this was some kind of joke and Caleb was following at an indiscreet distance. But all he saw was a wall of people looking as drab as the grey sky above. He slipped out of the stream and ensconced himself against the window of a comic-book shop.

'I'm in Melbourne, Ms Forbes. London is on the other side of the planet.'

'I know where Chelsea, the place, is. I'm looking for Chelsea London, the proprietor of the Pride & Groom salon. This was the phone number I was supplied.'

'Apologies. Still can't help. I am the proprietor of a day trading institution, Keppler Jones and Morganstern, this is my number and all I know of *Chic* is that my little sister used to hide it from my mum when she was fourteen.'

Letitia Forbes' assistant laughed a pretty tinkly laugh that was all flirtation and no substance. Damien appreciated it for what it was, but it did nothing to move him. Not like when the caramel-blonde had blinked up at him with her golden eyes and made him give in and slide his hands that much further around her waist, lean in that much closer to capture the scent of her hair…

He closed his eyes to squeeze out the unwelcome wave of pure lust swarming over him.

'So what do you know of animal-print dog collars?' Letitia Forbes' assistant asked.

His eyes flew back open. 'Because…?'

'That's why I'm trying to track down Chelsea London. For her professional opinion. But I'm now wondering if your opinion might be just as valid.'

He checked his watch. This day was fast slipping away from him. 'Unfortunately my only experience with animal-print anything has been with the underwear variety.'

'Yours?' she asked.

'That I cannot say for fear I might incriminate myself.'

She paused, and he sensed she was searching for a way to keep him on the line. With a sigh she said, 'Alas I have other phone calls to make, hopefully with as much fun but more success. Good day to you, Mr Halliburton.'

'Same to you.' He snapped the phone shut and stared at it for a few seconds as the world continued to walk on by.

Right. So in the past hour he'd had a woman fall into his arms, one flash her G-string at him, another whisper a suggestion in his ear that would have been more fitting for a key party, and yet another flirt him into intimating he was wearing zebra-print undies beneath his trousers.

For all the female attention he was getting today it was as if the women around him had some kind of radar. The only time in his thirty-two years on this planet he *wasn't* seeking out any kind of co-ed companionship, it took no kind of effort on his part to have it rolling towards him in waves.

Women… he thought. *Can't live with them…*

He glanced up, caught the eye of an elderly lady with tight purple ringlets. She smiled, and blushed. He wondered if he ought to head straight back to Amelie's and ask exactly what they'd put into his hollandaise sauce.

But even as he thought it he knew it wasn't the sauce. Sure, he was easy enough on the eye, had means, skills and other intangible assets that seemed to appeal to more women than not, but what was happening to him today was something other. Something primal. And it had begun the moment the woman of all things warm and sunny had fallen into his arms and set his pheromones alight.

Since then he'd been on some sort of constant sexual high. Walking, talking and acting like a normal person, but only half his mind was on real life. The other half had been replaying the memory of the most subtle scent that somehow took him back to a simpler time when all he'd wanted from life was a hug and a kiss before bedtime. Perhaps if he just stopped thinking about *her* he could get back to work without being mobbed in the street by a hundred ready-dressed brides.

His phone rang again and he flinched like a spooked schoolboy. He took a deep calming breath and this time waited to see if his address book recognised the phone number. It did. 'Letitia @ Chic Mag,' it read.

Sure, it was one of those computer/organiser/mobile whizbang things that cost a small fortune, but as far as he knew it didn't have any kind of cognitive memory. Unless he'd saved those details they shouldn't be there.

He continued staring at his phone as it played out *The Mary*

Tyler Moore Show theme. Once it rang out, he flipped it open and found himself staring at the large inner screen, which instead of a plain font espousing the name of his mobile phone company had an animated picture of a pink paw-print.

The truth finally dawned.

It was not his phone.

Damien slowly flipped the phone closed and breathed deep through his nose, gaining a lungful of car exhaust and day-old garbage for his effort.

How could he not have known it wasn't his phone? Real men loved their electronic toys more than life itself. Hell, every other guy he knew surrounded themselves with 5.1 surround sound, sub-woofers, and fancy walkmans with earplugs and wireless remote who knew what.

When he'd been talked into trading in his trusty five-year-old Nokia with its comforting scratches and dents for some top of the range gadget, he'd been told it would change his life. And now it had. Right now he had no idea of the address or phone number for the new clients he was hoping to meet, and he had a ring tone that made him seem far from manly.

'Dammit!' he said loud enough several people took a wider berth around him.

He reached into his trouser pocket and there was the hot-pink ticket for *his* phone, meaning the one he'd found on the floor behind his chair just as he'd left Amelie's hadn't been his.

The phone was thankfully unlocked, so he dialled his old friend Directory Assistance. 'Amelie's Brasserie, Melbourne,' he requested when a voice with a light foreign accent answered.

He saw a gap in the traffic between a tram and oncoming cars and jogged back across the wide street where he found a cab, slipped inside and gave directions back to his Collins Street office.

Amelie's answered.

'Damien Halliburton here. I breakfasted with you guys today and managed to pick up the wrong phone.' He pulled the phone away from his ear for a second to get the attention of the cab driver. 'Left onto Russell will be quicker this time of day.'

He waited for the grovelling and simpering on the other end of the phone to die down before interjecting, 'Can you check box J? It's empty? Right.'

Plan B. Which was…

Perhaps he ought to get the cabbie to make a sharp turn and get him back there a.s.a.p. so that he could search for it himself. And if the caramel-blonde happened to still be there he could also…what?

He glanced at his watch. No time. And the gent on the other end of the phone was talking again.

'Don't bother,' Damien said. 'I'll sort it out myself.'

He snapped the phone shut tight. It made a softer, more worn-in sound than his did, meaning it belonged to someone who would be missing it. Christy something or other. No, Chelsea. Chelsea London. An apparent expert on zebra-print dog collars. He couldn't have had the same type of phone as another executive type with big muscles and an even bigger stock portfolio, could he? No, it had to be some broad with parents who should be shot for giving her such an unforgivable name.

The cab pulled up outside the imposing thirty-storey building that housed the Keppler Jones and Morganstern Trading Company. He tossed the driver a twenty and hit the ground running.

Chelsea kissed Kensey goodbye at the cloakroom at Amelie's and stood watching her sister walk away with a lightness in her step.

Kensey's news was lovely. Despite their erratic and fly-by-night childhood her sister had made good and then some. They both had. There was really nothing for Chelsea to be feeling this edgy about.

'Your ticket, ma'am,' a girl behind the counter said.

'Right.' Chelsea searched her handbag. The pockets of her jacket. Down her bra where she often slipped notes to herself when she didn't have her phone or pockets to hand. She glanced up to find the blonde watching her blankly.

'I seem to have misplaced it.'

'It'll be hot-pink. Hard to miss.'

'Yet visualising it still hasn't helped it appear.'

The blonde raised an eyebrow. Chelsea took a deep breath and managed to count to seven before she leant over the counter and said, 'It's black. With a silver spine, off-white buttons, and if you flip it open it will have this picture upon the screen.'

She slipped the blonde a Pride & Groom business card with the hot-pink dog-print logo upon it. The blonde took the card and then her right eyebrow joined her left.

'Cool. You work for those guys?'

'I am those guys.'

'Ri-i-ight. Weren't you on the telly a few months back? On that celebrity pet show? You're the one who clipped that rock star's poodle and he freaked out that you'd swapped his dog, and sued you.'

The rock star had threatened to sue, had been appeased by the show's producers that the dog was his just with a haircut, and by the next day couldn't even remember a word of it. Pride & Groom's business had doubled overnight, making Chelsea believe whoever said all publicity was good publicity deserved a cookie. 'I am the very one,' she agreed.

The blonde tipped her chin and looked up at Chelsea from

beneath clumpy eyelashes. 'I have a Basenji. Any chance you could swing me some freebies?'

Chelsea blinked back. 'Any chance you could find my phone? Black, silver, off-white keys…'

The blonde smirked and ran a finger along the wooden boxes until she found the only one that was locked. She pulled out Chelsea's black and silver friend. 'This it?'

Chelsea slid it out of the girl's hand and wrapped her fingers around the familiar length, comfort seeping into her joints at having her life somewhat back under her control. 'This is it.'

'Any time you need a table at short notice, just ask for Carrie. That's me.'

'Thanks, Carrie. I'll keep it in mind.'

The give and take of commerce, Chelsea thought as she snuck a knee-length wool scarf from her handbag and wrapped it twice around her neck and headed outside into the crisp, but at least now dry, Melbourne autumn morning. *Luck out with the right product and today you were on everybody's speed dial. Dream too big in the slight wrong direction and tomorrow you're toast.*

She pulled her hair out from under her tight scarf as she headed down the street towards the underground car park where she'd left the Pride & Groom van.

And promptly began dreaming big in the exact wrong direction. Each footstep heralded the memory of another delicious moment locked in the arms of a tall dark handsome stranger from so far on the other side of the tracks he was in a different postcode.

And Kensey had made a point that had hit deep.

She was twenty-seven years old. Self-sufficient. Post puppy fat and pre middle-aged spread. She could still touch her toes and her hair had yet to turn mousy. These were meant to be her golden years, yet the only man she'd purposely dressed up for in weeks was the bank manager.

She felt a sudden desire to turn on her high heels, march back into the restaurant and ask the blonde if she could find out the booking name and phone number of Mr Suit and Tie. Even though he'd been too beautiful for her, too beautiful for anyone bar maybe three or four of the world's top supermodels, he'd looked at her as if…as if he'd wanted to see more of her.

The way his arms had tightened around her, the way his gorgeous blue eyes had darkened, made her feel that having a man like him hold her, touch her, bury himself in her, call out her name, even just the once, would be some kind of validation that she was young and single and would be perfectly fine if life deemed she remain that way evermore.

But then again, if she ever had the chance to experience such a dreamy specimen, would she, being of London genes, find it impossible to appreciate ordinary pleasures ever again?

CHAPTER THREE

DAMIEN burst into Caleb's office without knocking. 'Don't laugh or I *will* hit you.'

Caleb didn't laugh. He was too busy running a lazy hand through his short hair while a tall lean blonde straightened her skirt. She gave Damien a quick smile before sliding out the office door and shutting it behind her.

'Do I know her?' Damien drawled.

'Zelda's from the typing pool. She was replacing my printer cartridge.'

Damien nodded. 'That was nice of her. But how about you stick to looking after your own printer cartridges while in the workplace? My workplace. For which I am legally liable. Now, I need your help.'

Caleb sat back in his chair and leant his chin on steepled fingers. 'What's up, boss?'

'You know how I suggested we try Amelie's because they don't let anyone use their mobile phones? How I railed that it might well become the one place in this city where a man could eat in relative peace?'

Caleb nodded, feigning deep understanding, though when he leaned forward and started fiddling with the mouse on his desk Damien knew he had to be quick.

'In some kind of karmic response to my admittedly anti-technology sentiments, when I picked up my phone from the cloakroom, they gave me the wrong one.'

Caleb glanced up at the phone Damien held by his finger-tips. 'Looks like yours.'

'But it ain't.'

'But it looks like it…'

Just then the offending machine began to ring. The two men stared at it as it blared out its powder-puff tune.

'That's not your phone,' Caleb said, deadpan. 'Give it to me.'

Damien pulled it out of Caleb's reach. 'Every time you go anywhere near my computer I end up with porn pop-ups I have to call on others to delete. Now every Friday for the past two months Jimmy the IT guy has asked me if I want to join him and the other techies at the Men's Gallery.'

'I can't put porn on this phone by simply answering it.' Caleb clicked his fingers, and, half believing him, Damien handed over the offending instrument.

'This is Caleb,' he said after answering the phone, leaning back in his chair, and proceeding to ask sensible questions. When Caleb's voice dropped and he began to have a chat, Damien kicked hard against the side of his desk.

'Right, nice talking to you, Susan,' Caleb said, then hung up. 'She was returning a missed call herself. Didn't know whose phone it was. If you'd let me talk for a few more minutes we might have figured it out between us.'

'Nevertheless.'

'I think it's a chick's phone,' Caleb said.

'I do believe it is. Someone rang earlier looking for a Chelsea London.'

'Now why do I know that name?'

'You don't,' Damien said, knowing that Caleb wouldn't spot the obvious.

Caleb grinned. 'You bought a chick's phone.'

'On your recommendation.'

'That was a month ago. Times change. I can't see the future.'

'I wonder what they did with my old one. Do you think it's too late to get it back?'

'Far too late. If they haven't melted it down they've donated it to a museum.' Caleb's thumb began zooming over the keys at lightning speed.

'You're going through her personal files?' Damien asked.

'That I am.'

'Good idea.' He moved behind Caleb and looked over his shoulder at the bright flashing screens.

'No photos of herself or her friends. Means she has no friends or isn't the cutest thing on her block. But we do have photos of…'

Damien's eyebrows lifted and he was sure Caleb's did the same. The first photo they came upon was of a black studded dog collar. He should have guessed.

'Kinky,' Caleb said.

'Just your type,' Damien said.

'Ha. Ha. Okay, moving on, in her diary we have "breakfast @ Amelie's with Kensey". Kensey. Sounds like the name of a fortune-teller. Ooh, maybe this Kensey knows what they've done with your old phone.'

Damien closed his eyes for a moment. 'So now what?'

Caleb held up the phone to the light pouring through the office window as though that could make it magically ring again. 'What happened when you called your phone number to see if this Chelsea chick has your phone?'

Damien squeezed his eyes shut all the tighter as he mentally berated himself. The caramel-blonde had done more than awoken his dormant hungers; it seemed she'd also dulled his brain cells in the process. That had never happened to him after *not* having seen a woman he was keen on naked. In fact, he couldn't remember feeling such debilitating mind fuzz upon actually seeing a woman he was keen on naked.

It occurred to him in some kind of cruel flash of remembrance that he'd even remained focussed in every which way during the worst of the fights leading to the eventual Break Up. Bonnie had declared him a dyed-in-the-wool Halliburton incapable of a committed relationship other than with his work. And he hadn't even thought to argue.

Damien looked at his watch. The markets had been open almost an hour and he'd not placed one trade for a client. So much for his impassioned commitment to his work. He clicked his fingers, and Caleb handed over the phone.

He pressed it to his ear and paced to the window, looking out over the Melbourne city skyline. The now bright blue skies streaked with perfect fluffy white clouds mocked him as the phone buzzed ominously in his ear.

Just as Chelsea pulled into a parking garage beneath the imposing Brunswick Street building, the phone on the passenger seat began to vibrate so vigorously it almost fell off the seat.

She jumped in fright. She never used vibrate. Her phone was far too important for all that silent-mode nonsense. She made a mental note to write to the restaurant and let them know their cloakroom staff had been mucking about with her ring tone.

She grabbed it, and her bag, and leapt out of the van. She screened the call. Her right foot slid to a stop in a pile of white gravel when her own mobile number looked back at her.

She glanced about her. Hippies, Goths, punks and innumerable other marginal folk who gravitated to the funky urban *je ne sais quoi* of inner city Brunswick Street brushed past her on the pavement, but she saw nothing in any of their faces to help her make sense of her current situation.

Her tone was more than a mite cautious when she flipped the phone open and said, 'Chelsea London speaking.'

After a pause, a deep male voice said, 'Chelsea London, am I glad to have found you.'

She began walking again, this time more slowly. 'Who is this?'

'My name is Damien Halliburton. I'm a day trader with Keppler Jones and Morganstern.'

A day trader, she computed. Was that some kind of market research thing? Ooh, she hated those guys! Phone calls just as she'd settled down to lasagne, red wine and *House.* Though at least this one's voice was something out of the ordinary. Booming deep, slow and easy, like really good pillow talk.

God! Was her mind now permanently switched to hot, naked, sweaty mode?

She shook her head and pressed the phone tighter to her ear so Mr Pillow Talk could feel the full force of her disappointment that a man with a voice like his had taken on such a job.

'Mr Keppler-Jones or Morganwhoever, I never answer surveys, never tick the "please send me more information" boxes on forms. Didn't you know that Australia's privacy laws actually refer to you as well as the rest of the population?'

After a distinct pause, which she saw as something of a victory, especially since he was likely being graded and recorded by a boss with a clipboard, he said, 'I think you may have me mistaken for somebody else, Ms London.'

Ms London? That settled it. This guy didn't know her from Eve. She stopped atop the front porch of the large white build ing and crossed her spare arm over her stomach. 'Right. So how the hell do you have my phone number?'

'I have more than that,' the deep voice said. 'I have your phone.'

She pulled the phone out from its nook between her shoulder and her chin as though it had emitted an electrical charge. She stared at it. Black. Silver spine. Glowing off-white buttons.

She ducked inside. Only when she glanced through the glass door at the street outside did she tuck the phone back beneath her chin. She picked up only what must have been the end of his next sentence.

'…Amelie's today?'

Amelie's? Was he some kind of crazy stalker?

'Whoever you are, call me again and I will be onto the police before you can take your next heavy breath.'

With that she hung up, and threw the phone into her handbag. Then she took a deep breath and marched up to the service desk at the local bank. 'I'm Chelsea London. I have an appointment to see your manager about a business loan.'

Damien held the phone away from his ear and stared at it for several blank seconds.

'All sorted?' Caleb asked.

'Well, no. Not exactly. I think she may in fact be a crazy lady.'

'The dog-collar photo didn't ring those bells for ya? Maybe she stole your phone on purpose,' Caleb said. 'Maybe this is something she does to get her kicks.'

Damien redialled. After several rings it went through to his voicemail. 'She's not answering.'

'Maybe she's on the phone again. Maybe she's calling her

crazy relatives overseas. On your dime. That's her con! So who do you know overseas we could call at this time of day?'

Damien didn't wait to hear the end of it. He simply upped and left Caleb's office and walked down the hall to his own, wondering whom he'd hurt in a previous existence in order to have so very many women adding unnecessary pressures to what, until a month ago, had been the kind of easy, breezy, fortunate life most men would give their right arm for.

An hour and a bit later, Chelsea trudged inside the converted house in which the first Pride & Groom salon had grown from a one-woman, one-van operation into a brand-recognised, seven-staff, three-van endeavour with room for up to half a dozen domestic animals to be washed, clipped, perfumed, primped, preened and pampered at once.

She threw her handbag onto the white cane tub chair in the corner of her tiny office, her muscles aching as if she'd carried her own body weight from the car. Though all she'd done was carry a couple of dozen pieces of paper, which basically said if she signed them she'd owe the bank somewhere in the region of a million dollars.

She kicked off her boots, then licked her finger and rubbed it hard over a spot of strawberry sauce on her top, which had thankfully been hidden beneath her jacket.

She then changed into her more comfortable 'uniform' of faded jeans, long-sleeved white T-shirt with a big hot-pink paw print splodged dead centre, and thick socks to stave off blisters associated with being on her feet all day.

As she sat to tie up the laces on her sneakers the office door burst open and Phyllis stuck her head in. 'Well, now, where the heck you been? I must have tried to call you a good half-dozen times. Kept getting your voicemail.'

'Sorry. Phone was on silent.' For once. The last thing she'd needed was crazy stalker telemarketer man bombarding her whilst she and the bank manager had been chatting.

Phyllis leaned her heavy form against the door frame. 'So how did we go?'

'It's all ours if we want it. Enough money to buy and fit out another two salons.'

Phyllis let out a resounding whoop. 'I knew it. You clever *clever* girl. Now, just a quick warning. The Joneses brought Pumpkin in this morning and she seems to have a slight, okay not so slight, tummy upset. She has had it all over the green room, in fact. Lily's on lunch. Josie gags every time she walks past the room. And I would clean up but I have Agatha's Burmese and if I leave her alone for another two minutes you know she'll turn feral.'

Chelsea let her sneaker-clad foot drop to the floor with a thud. It seemed her pretend life as a sophisticated city gal with a million dollars to spend and sexy city-banker types drooling over her was well and truly over. 'Call the Joneses. Ask if they'd like us to take Pumpkin to Dr Campbell. Then give me a few minutes and I'll clean it up.'

Phyllis left. Chelsea pushed up her sleeves and tied her hair back into a pony-tail. She fished her mobile out of her bag and placed it on a spare corner of her desk, which was overflowing with trays filled with 'to do' lists, samples of dog-grooming products that arrived in the mail every day, and a just-short-of-stale half-packet of shortbread that would be morning tea.

She stared out the small window into the rose garden next door, her eyes fuzzing over as she watched a bee flit from flower to flower. And her thoughts once again turned to Mr Suit and Tie.

She wondered if he wasn't what he'd seemed at first glance

either. Perhaps right now he was pulling on a pair of overalls, or pulling off his shirt and tie to reveal superhero Lycra beneath. Or maybe he was still dressed in glorious top-to-toe suiting, leaning back in a thousand-dollar chair, counting his money and laughing maniacally at the little men pedalling hard to make his privileged world go round.

Damien sat forward in his chair, the soft swish and swing of German engineering making him bob comfortably behind his oak and leather desk.

Far more comfortably than he deserved, as his day was still occurring in slow motion since his hormones had mutinously overtaken his higher brain function. All because of a willowy body so light in his arms he could have swung her around and not done his back in, golden-brown eyes, pale warm skin, tumbling waves he'd never had the chance to touch.

He needed to give himself a break. A man and a woman taking pleasure in one another and leaving it at that wasn't unheard of in this day and age. And if it couldn't be her it would have to be someone else and soon. If only he had her number.

His gaze slid to the mobile phone on his desk, which had not stopped singing about Mary Bloody Tyler Moore all bloody morning.

He rubbed his eyes again, shook his head until his brain rattled inside his skull, then placed his fingers over the keys and clicked on the next email.

Then Caleb sauntered into his office and Damien wondered then and there if the time had come to simply call it quits and go find a nice warm bar somewhere to hole up for the duration.

'So, at the bank today…' Kensey's voice crackled through the landline phone tucked between Chelsea's ear and shoulder.

'I'm approved. Though I haven't signed the papers.'

'Chels!'

'I know. I know. It's a great opportunity. But it's such a huge gamble.'

Kensey paused, making sure she was listening. 'This isn't some pie-in-the-sky get-rich-quick fantasy like Dad would have taken on.'

'You're right,' Chelsea said. 'I'll sign them. I'll probably sign them. Later.'

She flipped open her mobile with one hand and stared at the screen as she had been incessantly for the past minute. There was still no Pride & Groom logo where a logo should be. 'Now as I was saying, this isn't my mobile.'

'So whose is it?'

'If I knew that I'd be talking to them right now and not you.'

The phone suddenly began vibrating in her hand. She whispered, 'It's ringing.'

Kensey finished chewing what sounded like dry biscuits, then said, 'I can hold.'

'No, not this phone, the other phone. The evil impostor phone.' She screened the call, to find her own number looking back at her again. 'Hang on, I'll put you on speaker in case it's the market research guy and he threatens me again.'

She hurriedly put down the landline, tentatively picked up the mobile, and answered. 'Hello?'

'Chelsea London?' the same clear, deep masculine voice from earlier asked.

'This is she.'

'This is Damien Halliburton again. Don't hang up. Please.'

'I'm listening.'

'Did you dine at Amelie's earlier today?'

'I did.'

'Well, then, Chelsea, I do believe there was some kind of mix-up in the cloakroom. I've been forced to relive *The Mary Tyler Moore Show* more times today than I thought I would have to during the rest of my life. Sound familiar?'

'It does.' It also made more sense than the stalker alternative. Chelsea blushed furiously as Kensey's laughter trickled through her speaker phone.

'Then the mystery is solved. We have one another's phones. So how about you give me your address and I can send a cab—'

'Lord no!' Chelsea shot back. 'I'm not sure how close you are to your phone, but mine contains my whole life. Sticking it in a dark pigeon-hole in that rotten restaurant was bad enough. I don't want it out of safe hands again.'

'Okay,' he said. 'So I guess we meet. Swap. Go our merry ways.'

'Much better.' Chelsea remembered the Joneses' dog with the tummy bug. 'I'm afraid I'm stuck at work. Can you come to me? I'm in Fitzroy.'

'I'm in the city. And considering I've spent the past hour trying to figure out what happened I'm more than a tad behind on my work for the day.'

'Right. So when could we make this happen?'

'How about we meet at seven back at Amelie's?'

Her lip curled at the thought of returning to the place. But it made sense. 'How will we find one another?'

'It's typical for the man to wear a rose in his lapel.'

Her right eyebrow shot skyward even though he wasn't there to see it. 'This is a business transaction, Mr Halliburton. Not a blind date.'

He cleared his throat. 'So it is.'

'Hey, Chels,' Kensey's voice blurted from the speaker phone.

'Hang on a sec,' Chelsea said to the guy. And then to Kensey, 'What?'

'Send each other a picture.'

'What?'

'On your phones.'

Brilliant! She knew she had a sister for a reason.

'Mr Halliburton, did you get that?' Chelsea asked.

A pause. Muffled voices. Was he checking with his own partner in crime at the other end? Could this day get any stranger?

He finally said, 'How does one do that?'

Chelsea blinked. 'My phone is exactly the same as yours.'

'Now might be the time to admit something to you.'

'And that would be…'

'I have no skills in the electronics area. Can't even program a VCR.'

'Lucky nobody makes VCRs any more. It's all about the DVD hard drive.'

'And there I was wondering why my *Rocky* tape wouldn't fit in the slot.'

Chelsea realised she was grinning. Now that she knew he wasn't a stalker, she could appreciate the sense of humour that came with the lovely deep voice. 'How charming. You're a Luddite.'

'Card-carrying,' he said.

'So get Keppler-Jones or Morganwhoever to give you a hand.'

'Two of them are dead, and one's so old he ought to be. And they've left the idiots to run the asylum.'

'You?'

He laughed down the phone, the sound vibrating across radio waves, through metal and down her arm until she gave into the need to scratch her elbow.

'Nice of you to make that leap so fast. But yes. And lucky for me I have hired well and have someone nearby who I'm sure would have used a photo function on a phone more often than entirely necessary.'

'Excellent.'

Chelsea knew she ought to sign off and get to work, but all she had waiting for her was goodness knew what gastronomical disaster in the green room. And besides, this peculiar exchange was turning out to be fun. Risk-free, anonymous fun, which was the kind she was more than happy to indulge in. So instead she asked, 'Um, perhaps we ought to keep note of any phone calls that come through to our respective phones too.'

'Right. Sorry, I should have mentioned you did have a couple of calls from…ah, *Chic* magazine, earlier.'

'*Chic?*' Chelsea clenched a fist in happiness. She had been waiting on confirmation that they wanted her to host a two-page spread on celebrity pet accessories. If she wanted a platform from which to announce a possible expansion… 'I do believe you just made my day.'

'I take it they're not chasing you down to pay up on a new subscription, then.'

'Ah, no.' This time the grin came with an accompanying laugh, which after the uneasiness that marred her morning felt as good as an hour-long Swedish massage followed by a bubble bath.

'And when you get back to *Chic* to explain why I was not you, if they mention anything about my predilection for zebra-print underwear they're making the whole thing up.'

Chelsea slowly leant back in her chair and began to play with her hair. 'I'm not sure *Chic* are in the habit of spreading rumours like that about random guys.'

'It's a scandal. Best kept under wraps for all our sakes.'

He paused again. She took a long breath and let it go, the release flowing from her cheeks all the way to her toes.

'So, any messages for me?' he asked, and his voice dropped lower. She felt it like a hum in her very centre. Like a warm glow building so slowly her fingers and toes felt cold in comparison.

She sat up straight and curled her toes in her shoes until the blood returned.

Bloody Kensey's pregnancy, she thought, *and, worse yet, rotten Mr Suit and Tie.* He was the real reason the voice on the other end of the phone was making her feel warm and fuzzy. She was like a light bulb that couldn't be turned off. Even the married loan manager at the bank had tried to flirt with her.

'Ah, no,' she said, clearing her throat. 'The only phone call I've had was from some guy who claimed to have kidnapped my phone.'

'I hope you told him where to go.'

She laughed again despite herself. 'In no uncertain terms.'

'That's my girl.'

They both paused again, conversation suddenly, sadly, exhausted.

Chelsea sat forward again, and shook her fringe off her cheeks. 'So…we do it now? Send the photos, and see you at seven?'

'Chelsea London,' he said, 'consider it a date.'

And before she had the chance to remind him that it was a five-second phone-swap, and no lapel roses would be necessary, he was gone. She slid the phone shut. Slowly.

'Humona humona,' Kensey said and Chelsea jumped halfway out of her skin, having forgotten her sister was still on speaker phone.

'I'm sorry? *Humona* what?'

'I could feel the sparks from here. I think he likes you. And for this one you don't even need to ask for his number! You know it off by heart.'

'Kensey…' she warned.

'He had a great voice,' Kensey said. 'Like Irish cream liqueur: creamy smooth and, oh, so bad for your balance unless in very small doses. Call him back. Or, better yet, call Amelie's and book a table for seven and casually ask him to stay for dinner when you meet up.'

'I can't! What if he's some kind of crazy? Or if he's eighteen years old? Or married? Or brings his imaginary friend to the table? Or smells like fish? Or hates dogs?'

'Or is tall, dark and handsome and this whole phone-swap deal was a sign from the gods.'

Oh, no. Chelsea was pretty sure she'd been given her fair share of tall, dark and handsome strangers this day.

'So what picture are you going to send?' Kensey asked.

'Oh, um, I guess I'll just snap one off now and—'

'Nuh-uh. Those things are such bad quality. The kids are still in school for another couple of hours. I'm coming over. I'll help you come up with something sweet with just a hint of slutty.'

'Kensey…' Chelsea said, for what must have been the tenth time that day.

'Don't argue. Besides, we haven't finished the bank-loan conversation yet. See you in fifteen minutes,' Kensey said and then was gone.

For a moment Chelsea wished for simpler times when keeping one's front door shut was enough of an excuse not to have to make contact with another soul.

CHAPTER FOUR

AFTER what felt like an age later, a soft tinkling sound like a wind chime shifting in a light breeze heralded the arrival of a picture on the mobile phone in Damien's hand.

'Let me do the honours,' Caleb begged.

'Not on your life.'

'I have to see what the kinky cat lady looks like.'

'Now she's a cat lady?'

'I'm picturing a sari-wearer. Maybe even bald. Hurry up and check. I'm dying here.'

She sure hadn't sounded like a bald cat lady. She'd sounded…lovely. Likely because every woman he'd come in contact with since The Caramel-Blonde had turned into a purring temptress as though he were wearing a sign around his neck saying: *Newly single. On the market. Fresh meat.*

Maybe what he needed was a long holiday. Somewhere warm. And isolated. Palm trees, coconuts, no women, and no mobile-phone coverage. But excellent computer facilities and air-conditioning and twenty-hour working days.

He flipped open the phone, hoping that was all he'd have to do to determine whom he had to find in several hours time. Then he'd get back to work like a good little business owner.

The picture formed on the screen. He blinked. And blinked

again. A swell of heat poured like lava through his midriff as his eyes roved over silky hair the colour of rich caramel, delicate cheekbones, and fine pink lips. And he would have recognised those eyes of gold in a crowd of thousands.

He landed back in his chair and swung it around to face the city beyond the great smoked-glass window in his corner office, and ran a hard hand over his chin.

'Well, what do you know?' Caleb said, breathing over his shoulder. 'The cat lady's a hottie.'

'Of course she is,' Damien spat out. 'It's *her.*'

'Her? Her who?'

'The woman from the restaurant.'

'But she was blonde and—'

'Not the G-stringed teeny bopper. The one who fell into my arms when you were in the loo. I pointed her out to you just before we left.'

Caleb looked closer. 'Bloody hell, you're right. She was hot too.'

Damien turned his chair back to face his office, dropped the phone to the desk and leant his forehead into his open palms. 'Her ticket must have fallen to the floor when she fell. I picked it up. And by all that's holy we have the same phone.'

'You lucky sod,' Caleb said. 'Now what you have to do is ring her again, tell her you have to change your appointment to later in the evening. Book a table. Get there early. Order a bottle of wine…And why aren't you writing any of this down?'

Damien shook his head. 'Because I broke up with Bonnie little more than a month ago. I can't…'

Want some stranger with such all-consuming immediacy, he'd been about to say. Instead he went with the much safer, 'I'm of the thought that it would be better for me to not indulge in such pursuits just yet.'

'I'm not suggesting you marry the girl. Or any girl, for that matter. Dinner. Cocktails. Maybe a grope in the back of the cab on the way home. Sounds like a perfectly fine Tuesday evening, if you ask me.'

Damien did his best not to let Caleb's words infiltrate. When it came to dealing with the fairer sex Caleb was a schmuck. But he certainly painted a nice picture. Her soft, soothing scent still lingered on his jacket even now. Who knew what levels of pleasure more than two minutes in one another's company might bring them? Certainly more pleasure than he'd had in some time.

'So are you going to call Amelie's or should I do it for you?'

Damien glared up at his friend. 'Don't you have work to do?'

'Slave-driver,' Caleb said.

And as soon as Caleb sauntered from Damien's office with a wink and a smile, he was on the phone to Amelie's to insist they give him a last-minute table to make up for the emotional stress they'd put him through.

Caleb wasn't often right, but this time he might have been just on the money. The time to get back on the horse was nigh.

Chelsea came back into her office after cleaning and disinfecting the green room feeling as bad as the poor Joneses' dog had looked. She was wet and bedraggled from top to toe. And she wasn't certain her shoes had managed to avoid every little surprise left on the concrete floor.

The mobile phone on her desk was buzzing and vibrating until she felt it in her fillings.

'It's been doing that for ten minutes,' Kensey said from her position on the soft window-seat in Chelsea's office, her nose buried in a catalogue of doggie accessories.

'So why don't you answer it?' Chelsea asked, pulling off her long-sleeved T-shirt and replacing it with an exact match, though one that was warmer and dryer.

'Fine,' Kensey said with a sigh, then grabbed the phone, flipped it open, and stared for a few moments, her expression so blank Chelsea began to get worried.

'What? Tell me. It's him, isn't it? Is he creepy? Is he famous? Is he my evil twin? What?'

But when Kensey began to laugh, so hard she clutched her belly and drew her knees to her chest for support, Chelsea grabbed the phone.

She stared at the picture. It was slightly askew, cutting off his left ear and showing far too much room atop his head, but the face, *that* face, was unmistakable.

Thick, dark, preppy-perfect hair. A dead straight nose. And permanently smiling blue eyes. Damien Halliburton of the creamy voice, charmingly off-kilter sense of humour, and apparent predilection for zebra-print underwear was the very man into whose arms she had fallen.

Chelsea sank into her chair with a thud. 'It's *him,* isn't it? It's really *him.*'

Kensey nodded.

'And now I have to go back there, tonight, and see *him* again.'

'You sure do.'

She glanced down at the wet patches on her old jeans, and flicked a blob of soapy hair from her cheek. 'He won't remember I'm, you know, the girl with the bad balance, will he?'

'You have been given a second chance to blind the guy with your fabulousness. Does it matter if he remembers you?'

Chelsea bit at her inner lip. In the long-suppressed, non-pragmatic, romantic, dreamy, girly places deep inside her it mattered more than she would ever admit.

'So what does Mr Gorgeous here do again?' Kensey asked.

Chelsea screwed up her nose and squinted at Kensey. 'I think he's some kind of telemarketer. For Keppler Jones and somebody.'

Kensey only laughed all the more. 'Did you pay any attention to how much our breakfast cost us today? He's no telemarketer.'

Kensey stood and bumped Chelsea aside with her hip. She leaned over the computer on the desk and typed his name and Keppler Jones into a search engine then clicked on the top listing. And up came a schmick website with all the latest Flash graphics. All creams and sky-blues and greys. Cool, sophisticated, and intimidating.

'It's a trading firm. Stocks and bonds and the like.' Kensey's nimble fingers skipped over the keys. 'These places always have pictures of their staff. It's a total male vanity, "look at me and just guess how much money I earn" thing. Now here we go. Search for Damien Halliburton.'

His page loaded. And another photograph did indeed accompany a bio short on personal information but long on awards, successes, plaudits from financial magazines, big-name clients and other brokerage houses alike. Both girls sagged a little. He was just the kind of guy who made a woman go weak at the knees.

'He's really dreamy, Chels.'

'Yes, he is,' she admitted.

'Looks fine in a suit.'

'That he does.'

'I'd bet anything he looks just as fine out of it too.'

'And what a pity that you'll never know.'

'So you're meeting at seven o'clock?' Kensey asked.

'That's right,' Chelsea said, biting at a fingernail.

'You'll both be needing dinner about then. How about you casually slip into the conversation something like, "Here's your phone, Damien. And, boy, am I famished? Aren't you famished? Perhaps we could pop inside and unfamish together." Then later, much later, call me. Please. If I don't get a complete rundown on every second I'll never forgive you.'

Kensey kissed her on the cheek, then swanned out of the room. A crash and a bang somewhere else in the building snapped Chelsea completely back to real life. Time she got back to work.

But first… She dialled the number of Amelie's restaurant. It was the kind of place you had to book a month in advance, but she saw no harm in trying. Especially when she had a desk covered in samples of rose-scented doggie shampoos and be-dazzled cat ponchos from which to choose a nice little sweet-ener for her new favourite cloakroom attendant.

Three o'clock came around slowly. Damien knew as he'd checked his watch a dozen times since he'd found out exactly who had his phone.

He'd probably made less money for his clients that day than he had for himself when his father had insisted he get a job flipping burgers to learn the true value of money, and a hard day's work, during the holidays from his private boys' high school.

Because now he'd decided he was ready to handle some pleasure for pleasure's sake he couldn't think past her voice, her fingers running up and down those gold beads, her lips smiling softly, her crossing her legs and rocking her top foot up and down to some slow, seductive inner rhythm. It was as though she was all he had room for in his mind for.

And the bold truth was he couldn't wait until seven to get a fix.

Needing privacy, especially from Caleb who had an even better radar for sexual tension than for making money, he took a walk into the executive bathroom, checked under the stalls, and, finding himself alone, slid Chelsea's phone from his inside jacket pocket.

Chelsea was in the blue room blow-drying a Persian when the mobile rang. She tugged it from her back pocket, flipped it open, shoved it to her ear and said, 'Chelsea London.'

'Hi,' a by now all too familiar deep male voice said, and she almost dropped the hair-dryer.

'Give me two seconds,' she said, before throwing the phone to the metal bench. She turned off the dryer, put an almost dry Snookums back into her cage, washed her hands, straightened her back, looked in the mirrored wall and flicked a fleck of cat hair from her cheek before picking up the phone again.

'Hi,' she said, her voice breathier than usual.

'How's it going?' Damien asked, the face and the voice merging to create a killer combination.

'Fine,' she said.

'So what are you doing?'

Chelsea frowned. Suddenly she felt as if she were in the eighth grade talking to the boy she'd had a crush on who'd ended up only using her so he could copy off her Biology paper. Another dud to add to the list of men who'd left her disenchanted in the gender as a whole. 'Damien?'

'Yes.'

'Was there something in particular you were after?'

Something about his pause had her holding her breath. The sounds of traffic from nearby Brunswick Street permeated the silence. Until he blew out a fast shot of breath and said, 'I was just thinking about you.'

'Oh,' she said, just managing to make it over to the sunny

window-seat to sit with one leg tucked beneath her. Better that than be upstanding when her knees gave way. 'What were you thinking exactly?'

She could have sworn his voice dropped an octave when he said, 'I was wondering what it is you do for a living.'

And just like that her blood returned to her extremities. He wasn't *thinking* about her as she'd been thinking about him. He was bored. She flicked herself in the side of the head.

'My friend Caleb has a theory that you are in fact a vendor of adult products. I just wanted to set him straight. Or not, if that's the case.'

Chelsea blinked. 'Your friend thought…?'

'He did. He has some imagination, my friend.'

Well, what do you know? she thought. Mr Perfect was nothing at all out of the ordinary. He was just a guy after all.

'Is your friend in the room with you?' she asked, her voice now in total control.

'Not at the moment, no.'

'Well, you can tell him that there is a great way to waste your own time rather than other people's. So why don't you go right ahead and search for me on the Internet.'

And at that she hung up. She threw the phone onto the window-seat where it bounced and settled like a glaring shiny beacon of collective disappointment.

She poked her tongue out at the phone and shot to her feet. But it began to vibrate again. She knew it was him. But she wasn't all that sure what to do with him. Beautiful him. Contradictory him. He was either funny or a jerk. And she wasn't sure which she preferred him to be. Which would give her the chance at a better day's work. A better night's sleep.

With a muffled oath she stormed over and snapped it open. 'Would you prefer I told you to bite me? In case you missed the nuances in my voice that's pretty much what I was trying to say.'

'Chelsea, forgive me,' he said, his voice contrite, and, oh, so deep and delicious she wanted to forgive him. 'It was my attempt at finding a believable reason to call.'

'Why?'

And then he said the only words he could have to redeem himself. 'Because you're the girl who fell into my arms, and spilled my coffee, and stole my phone and gatecrashed my thoughts until I had to admit to her that I've been seriously thinking that a two-minute phone swap isn't what we ought to be doing tonight.'

This time her knees really did give way and she sank back to the window-seat and tucked her spare hand between her knees to stop it from trembling. So much for Damien Halliburton being a mere male clone. She'd never had a man tell her she was *the girl* before.

She closed her eyes shut tight as she said, 'You could have knocked me sideways with a feather when I realised it was you who had my phone too.'

The second the words were out of her mouth she wished she could take them back. She suddenly felt as though the walls around her had been stripped away until she was sitting out in the cold alone. Naked. Unprotected.

She pressed her toes into her shoes, and her shoes into the concrete floor, trying to ground herself. Gambling on a successful business she owned lock, stock and barrel was quite different from gambling with her tender emotions. 'Damien, I—'

He cut her off as though he'd sensed her backtracking. 'So have dinner with me tonight. At Amelie's. I've booked us a table. We can swap phones. Eat. And see where the night takes us from there.'

She opened her eyes, was hit with a burst of bright sunshine from outside. Though the sun hit the cold glass so that she could barely feel its warmth.

Dinner. A date. With the most beautiful man she'd ever met. 'Sure,' she said, wondering where the word even came from. 'Why not?'

'Excellent. So long as you don't mind if we make it a little later. How's nine o'clock?'

'Nine would be fine,' she said, infinitely glad she'd have time to change…either her outfit or her mind. 'Better even. I feel like everything has taken twice as long as normal to be achieved today.'

'All because I have your phone, I suppose,' he suggested, though by the smile in his voice she was sure he knew that wasn't even half the reason. He probably ruined women's concentration spans constantly.

'Of course,' she said smoothly. 'It's all about the phone. So don't forget to bring it at nine.'

'Hmm,' he said, his voice a deep hum that tickled across the back of her neck as certainly as if it were his fingers brushing away her hair. She imagined his lips following. The brief brush of his tongue along the delicate patch of skin… 'And there I was thinking you had some kind of love affair going on with that phone of yours and wanted it back yesterday.'

'I do. I did. I…' She flicked herself again. 'I'll see you at nine, Damien.'

'Until then,' he said, and hung up.

Until then, Chelsea thought, slowly shutting the phone.

She stood and found her reflection in the shiny steel industrial-sized sink in which they washed the cats and miniature dogs and pictured Damien standing behind her, all dark good looks and effortless polish.

She sucked in her stomach and pursed her lips. If you could see past the flat chest and boyish hips, and her slightly crossed front teeth, which had never seen the back end of a pair of braces, her hair was long, her nose passable, and her eyelashes incongruously dark and never in need of mascara.

She let her breath go and slumped into a more normal posture, and her dirt-smudged T-shirt, the third of the day, turned wrinkled and sloppy.

She picked up the closest landline to ring and cancel the seven o'clock table she'd booked, and made a mental note to organise another set of samples for skinny Carrie to keep her mouth shut that the booking had ever existed.

CHAPTER FIVE

BY SEVEN, Damien's employees had all gone home to their wives, husbands and assorted pets while Caleb had a date with an apparently very bendy Cirque de Soleil performer, leaving Damien alone in his big office with only the high winds buffeting his double-glazed window to keep him company.

He checked his watch. Two hours until he was due to meet Chelsea.

He flipped open her phone, pressed the exact right buttons to find her picture and stared at it. Her face half in shadow, half in too-bright light. A shy smile curved her mouth, silky hair tumbled over her shoulders, her pale slender neck seemed to go on for ever.

He ran his thumb back and forth over the image.

She seemed the kind of woman who'd enjoy curling up on a soft, cosy couch on a rainy day, legs tucked beneath a blanket, her head resting on a man's lap, half-empty cups of hot chocolate leaving twin mug rings on the coffee-table while they watched a run of old movies.

He flipped the phone shut with a satisfying snap.

That life would never be his. He was a *Halliburton,* which meant working, living and playing hard. He hadn't spent a day of his life curled up anywhere and he'd never craved hot chocolate.

As he'd blithely walked out her door Bonnie had blamed his parents' divorce for making him as commitment-phobic as he was. He thought it more likely his parents' subsequent friendship without the marriage part getting in the way had more to do with his unwillingness to settle down. Though they had agreed that the sooner he was honest about what exactly he *did* want from any woman who came into his midst, the world would be a safer place. So what the hell was he doing asking a woman like that on a date?

Could it be because he hadn't forgotten the chemical reaction that had lit those golden eyes when she'd first looked into his? The instant surge of attraction. And just like that the image of her on the soft homey couch changed to include a shift of her lithe body, a lifting of her chin as she kissed him, and melted against him, as he spent hours so devoured by her he could no longer remember any other woman he'd ever met.

He ran a hand fast over his face, over his tired eyes, and hard through his hair. So what did he want?

For the rest of his life? He wasn't sure he'd ever be able to answer that question.

But for now, for tonight, he wanted Chelsea. More than he remembered wanting anything in a long time. And until he had a bed of his own, he'd settle for having her wherever he could get her.

It was around a quarter past seven by the time Chelsea made it home.

Home was a beautiful art deco apartment smack bang in the middle of the city. It had been bequeathed to both girls by a maiden aunt on her mother's side, a woman they'd never met or even known had existed since their mother had done a runner in the months after Chelsea herself was born and never been heard from again.

She'd agreed to check the place out unwillingly, but the second she'd set foot inside she'd fallen in love. The chintz lounges, cream panelled walls and curling antique furniture created a warmth and a history the likes of which she'd not known growing up in string of small cold apartments.

Kensey, who at that stage had had a husband, two kids, three chickens and a turtle, had had no need for a one-bedroom city apartment with no yard, so Chelsea had offered to buy her out, convincing herself that prime city real estate was never a gamble.

She now felt great peace in watering the flowers outside her windows, in polishing to a gleam the dining table she never used, and in allowing piles of books and magazines to teeter in corners of the room. Clutter meant permanence, just as dog-loving meant responsibility. Life could be just that simple if one let it.

She kicked off her shoes at the door and aimed for the shower to wash off the day's worth of dog spit, cat hair and other unmentionable ooze.

She padded into the large master bedroom, pulled off her jeans and threw them onto the floor. Her decade-old sweater was halfway over her head when the mobile phone vibrated atop her dresser.

Her heart thumped against her ribs as she screened the call but it wasn't her number looking back at her. It was the offices of Keppler Jones and Morgenstern. It could be important. A message to pass onto Damien in two short hours. Something to fill the conversational void they would no doubt encounter within five minutes of seeing one another again.

She flipped it open. 'Damien Halliburton's phone.'

'Are you still at work?'

Her heart leapt to her throat the instant she heard that sinfully delicious voice.

'Home.' She leant back against the end of the bed for leverage as she pulled off her socks one-handed, and so that he didn't guess she'd come home to change for him she added, 'I had to feed my neighbour's cat. She's away.'

He laughed. 'Caleb knew there'd be a cat somewhere in the picture.'

She wiggled her toes in the lamplight to find at least half of them needed to be re-pinked. 'Caleb's the one who thinks I am a kinky sex-toy purveyor, right?'

'Right.'

She pulled the phone away from her ear briefly to tug her long-sleeved T-shirt over her head. 'Are you sure you shouldn't be finding yourself less troublesome friends?'

'I'm certain I should be. But I'm too nice a guy. Without me he'd be lost.'

'You are Sir Galahad himself.'

'I like to think so.'

Who are you trying to kid? she thought. Conversation with this guy wouldn't be hard to come by. Every topic touched upon seemed to open up between them like a minefield of verbal possibilities.

After a pause he added, 'Are you alone?'

Her undressing came to a sudden halt with her T-shirt hanging off her left shoulder. 'Is that imperative?'

'Not entirely. It would just help clarify my mental picture.'

'You've formed a mental picture?' she asked while flicking the shirt from her arm and through the open door onto the *en suite* floor with the rest of her dirty clothes.

'Haven't you?' he asked.

'Not so much,' she lied.

'Well, just in case you're waiting for me to go first, here's mine.'

He paused for effect. And it worked. Chelsea stood in the centre of her large carpeted bedroom now naked bar a pink lace bra that had seen better days and white cotton knickers, and she held her breath.

'I see an apartment,' he said. 'Lamps everywhere, high ceilings, soft couches a person just sinks into until they never want to get up again. And not an animal print in sight. How am I doing so far?'

Chelsea wrapped an arm around her stomach. 'So far…kind of scary close.'

'Mmm. I'm moving through now, deeper. An ajar door catches my eye. I press it open to find myself in a bedroom. Your bedroom.'

'Just like that? With no invitation? That's pretty forward.'

'Not only am I forward, I'm also not alone.'

'If you tell me there's some snaggle-toothed madman under my bed—'

'Chelsea,' he said with enough force to shut her up.

'Yes, Damien.'

'Did I say you get to talk in my imaginings?'

She shook her head no.

'That's better. Now, I'm not alone in your bedroom because you are there with me. Happy?'

She nodded. And imagined he had just entered, fully dressed in his beautiful suit, one hand in his trouser pocket, pulling his white shirt across his broad chest. His dreamy blue eyes dark in the low light of her muted art deco lamp. She placed the back of her spare hand to her suddenly hot cheek.

'Now, to tell you the truth,' he said, 'I have not one clue what your bedroom looks like. It could be wall-to-wall shag-pile carpeting. It could have bunk beds and beanbags. It could have a disco ball and mirrored ceilings.'

'How disappointing your imagination only stretches so far.'

'Don't be disappointed. All I see right now is you.'

She thanked her lucky stars her bed was there to catch her as she swayed. Permanence and responsibility be damned. She *wanted* him. With a power and a need that ought to have had her hanging up the phone and ordering in. Instead she allowed herself to luxuriate in his smooth, rich, decadent voice.

'What am I wearing?' Chelsea asked, this time dead centre in the middle of his imaginings.

She could all but hear the stretching of his cheeks as his face broke into a sexy smile. 'You tell me.'

Her toes dug into the carpet in order to keep the rest of her upright. Because she knew that this was not just another phone call. This time he had a purpose.

Seduction.

The idea seeped beneath her skin and warmed her cold, tired bones better than the best hot shower in town could ever hope to.

She closed her eyes and reached around behind her to unhook her bra. As it slid over her arms, scraping along her highly sensitised skin, she said, 'I'm naked. Well, not quite.'

His voice was almost unrecognisable when he finally came back with, 'How not quite?'

'Underpants.'

'What kind?'

'Bikini brief.'

'Colour?'

White cotton didn't exactly ring exciting, so she took liberties. 'Burgundy with gold lace.'

Her quivering knees belied her true nerves. She finally gave in and sat on the edge of the bed, crossing her legs to quell the heat already slicing through her centre. 'So what are *you* wearing?'

'I'd love to say I was standing outside your apartment right now wearing nothing bar a bunch of roses and a smile, but unfortunately, unlike you, I *am* still at work.'

'Are *you* alone?'

'As far as I know,' he said.

'So-o-o…'

'So?'

'So it's only fair that if I'm freezing my butt off in nothing bar a tiny sliver of rather flimsy translucent lace that barely covers half my butt cheeks that you do some undressing too.'

The pause was significant as he took the time to add her latest descriptions to his vision. 'But I'm imagining you in your natural environment. Snug in your lovely warm home. Curtains drawn. Locks bolted. Alarm system activated. Killer cat next door to protect you from prying eyes.'

She pumped a coin-sized blob of moisturiser from her bedside table into her palm and began running it up and down her legs, ankle to thigh. The stretch felt good. But it did little to nothing to ease the sexual tension radiating through her. Making her feel wanton. Uncharacteristically reckless.

'Damien,' she purred.

'Yes, Chelsea.'

'I don't think we're playing the same game here.'

'We're not?'

She shook her head, the feel of her hair tumbling down her naked back unbelievably erotic. It was as though every nerve ending were suddenly alight. Every sensation heightened.

She turned and lay down on her stomach, her knees bent, feet in the air rubbing one another. 'My hair is down. My bedroom lights are low and I am naked bar tiny triangles of fabric. And the only way I am getting any more of my kit off is if you do too.'

'Is this really how this is going to go?'

'Things have changed somewhat since Dean Martin ran with a pack. We have equality of the sexes. Or at least wherever we can get it. And two places I insist on it are in the workplace and in the bedroom.'

'How convenient.' This time his pause was momentous. 'You really want me to strip?'

'I really do. Perhaps my imagination isn't quite as good as yours.'

Which was rubbish. She was well and truly in the middle of a great big fantasy about finding a man who craved her so deeply he was willing to get naked, physically and emotionally. And who made her able to feel the same way.

But even now as her feet tingled as they rubbed against one another, as her bare breasts pressed into the quilted comforter, as she kept a man of Damien's calibre on tenterhooks with not much more than a few sharp one-liners, that thread of doubt and mistrust that kept her company on countless lonely nights seeped in beneath the pleasure.

If her upbringing had taught her anything it was that big dreams never really came true. They lingered, they tempted, they dangled just out of reach. What if he was merely setting her up for a one-night stand as he did with every girl whose phone he stole? Normally she'd be able to handle it, but this guy felt…different. He made her feel different. She barely knew him and already she wanted more.

But then Damien Halliburton of the broad shoulders and deep bass voice said, 'Fine,' followed by the sound of his phone hitting wood with a thunk.

She pressed her phone to her ear to better hear a rustle of

cotton, the slide of satin lining, and the distinct whir of a zipper, and felt as though everything she'd ever believed about men like Damien, who'd so obviously had advantages and experiences she could never dream of, was slowly but surely turning on its head.

'Right,' he said a few moments later, his voice a tad breathless. 'I'm down to my jocks.'

A bubble of laughter gurgled up into her throat and out her mouth.

'Are you laughing at me now?' he asked.

'No. Not really. I...' By now the bubble had burst and she was really laughing, lying back on her bed with her legs dangling over the side, holding her stomach. 'I'm just picturing you in some great hulking swanky up-town office with the city sprawled out dark and twinkly behind you, and you in Y-fronts, brown socks and black shoes.'

His pause spoke volumes. As did the clunk, clunk, that accompanied his shoes as he kicked them off.

'My socks are black, thank you very much.'

'Well, then, either you have a very involved mother or a woman organises your sock drawer.'

His voice was dry as he said, 'I haven't worn brown socks since grade school.'

'Meaning no interfering mother or girlfriend to speak of?' she asked, then she bit her lip and scrunched up her eyes.

'My mother is too busy interfering in my father's life to worry about mine,' he said. 'And no. No girlfriend.'

She let out a breath she didn't even know she'd been holding.

'You?' he asked.

She shook her head. 'No mother. No girlfriend.'

'Funny. I've found myself a funny girl. Tell me there is no man in your life whose sock drawer you organise on a regular basis.'

His demand was so serious the tension coursing through her slid away until she rolled over and let her spare arm flail sideways. Loose. Warm. Limber.

'No man,' she said. 'Not a single one.'

'Good to know.'

This was getting ridiculous. She was practically naked, and lolling about on her bed as if she were a teenager, hoping the boy she had a crush on might like her back. But this was no boy. This was a grown man with the knowledge and confidence that came with being an honest to goodness walking aphrodisiac.

'So are you wearing Y-fronts?' Her voice was little higher than a vibration.

'Boxers.'

'Cotton?'

'Silk.'

'Colour?'

'Black.' Then after a pause, 'With little pictures of ducks all over them.'

Chelsea laughed again, amazed that he was being truly honest. Amazed and a little taken aback. While she was in the middle of a 'close your eyes and think of goose-down pillows, king-sized sheets, and the first touch of a beautiful stranger' fantasy, everything he had said and done so far pointed to the fact that he was utterly present.

She rolled over and sat up, crossing her legs and biting at her fingernail. Unless…

'Take a photo,' she demanded.

'Excuse me?'

'I don't believe you're not sitting there in your big plush office unzipping pencil cases and tapping pencils on your desk to sound like buttons popping.'

'Now what have I done to make it so hard for you to trust me so quickly?'

'Don't take it personally. I don't trust anybody. I want proof.'

'Fine. Ditto,' he shot back.

Okay, so that had backfired. 'I'm not sending you a picture of me half naked!'

'No trust. So sad. Yet you desperately want a naked picture of me. Interesting.'

'Not *interesting*, I just don't want a photo of me to end up on some Internet porn site where my sister's kids can find it.'

'They are allowed to browse porn sites? That's some forward-thinking sister you have there. Maybe I want her phone number instead.'

'Don't be ridiculous,' she said. 'And she's married. Happily. And pregnant.'

And would die laughing if she knew her intractable little sister was on the verge of engaging in phone sex with the hottest man on the planet, yet finding myriad modes of sabotaging it every step of the way.

'But you know how kids are.'

'Actually, I don't.'

'No nieces or nephews?'

'Nope. One sister, Ava. Perennial student. Studying at Harvard this year. Not the lay-down-your-hat kind at all. Therefore no kids.'

'That's a pity. They're a riot.'

'And sneaky, so it seems.'

It hit her then that somehow she'd found out more about this guy in one phone call than she had about her last three dates collectively. She wondered just how much she'd inadvertently given away in turn.

'Now, tell me,' he said, 'did you turn the conversation

because you are trying to avoid me seeing you half naked? Or is there something else you're trying to avoid?'

How did he know? 'Maybe I'm just not in the mood any more.'

'Meaning you were?'

'Meaning…I'm not sure.'

'About what exactly?'

'This.'

'And what is this?'

'I don't know. You rang me. You tell me what this is.'

Again the pause. Which was the one thing she hated about having spent so much time on the phone with the guy while she found herself getting deeper and deeper into some potent, totally crazy, out-of-control attraction towards him: she never got to see his expression, the look in his eyes, to know the nuances of his voice. If she'd read him wrong from the beginning…

But then he once again pulled the perfect words from thin air, saying, 'This was meant to be me finding a way to be with you again as soon as I possibly could.'

'You'll see me in two hours.'

'I couldn't wait two hours.'

That one deserved a gulp. If he was straining that badly at the bit she was kind of terrified about what might happen when they did meet; terrified that the sparks would make them both combust on the spot and equally afraid they wouldn't.

She'd never been this messed up about seeing a man before. But he made her feel as if the world were rushing so fast beneath her feet it was passing by in a blur. She needed to get her feet on solid ground again.

'Damien—' she began.

'Chelsea,' he warned, cutting her off. 'I want you to know

that I'm normally extremely content with the headlong daily routine that makes up my life. But from the moment you landed in my arms…' He took a breath that could have come from her own over-taut lungs. 'Let's say I've ended up standing still in my office in my boxer shorts and I'm beginning to notice there is a draught.'

'So get dressed,' was the only thing she could think to say.

'I plan to. But I also need for you to make me one small promise.'

She dug her hand into a fist, biting into the back of her thigh. 'Okay…'

'I'll get dressed if you promise me you won't.'

'Ever?'

He laughed. She liquefied.

'Not for the next hour,' he said.

'So your imagination doesn't stretch as far as you thought it did.'

'My imagination stretches plenty far, and I want you to slide off that bikini brief, throw it over your shoulder with no care as to where it lands, then I want you to lie back on that large soft bed of yours and let me show you just how far my imagination can take you.'

CHAPTER SIX

'LIE back,' Damien insisted.

'Come over,' Chelsea said, rashness searing her veins and making all sense flee. 'Let's forget Amelie's.'

'Ain't gonna happen.'

Hot, then cold. He was driving her crazy. Making her reckless. Making her want to try harder, gamble more, do whatever it took to get what she wanted, which was to release this agonising pressure that had her pinned, half naked, to her bed.

'Now do as you're told, and lie back. Make yourself comfortable.'

She wanted to. More than almost anything she could remember wanting in her life she wanted to give in to the firmness in his deep voice. But the yearning to have him there beside her, to watch his eyes turn dark with pleasure, pulsed through her like a drug. An addiction. 'You are driving me crazy, Damien.'

'Welcome to the club.'

'So why won't you come over here and do something about it that will satisfy the both of us?'

If it's to be a one-night stand, she thought, *then let it be that.*

'Because that's not *all* I want from you.'

It wasn't?

'What else can you possibly want?' she asked, her voice weak as a kitten.

'I want dinner. I want conversation. I want to watch you over the top of a stubby candle, a couple of wineglasses and a half-finished steak.'

'Can't you use that renowned imagination of yours to imagine that part instead?'

He laughed, the sound warming the various minuscule bits of her that weren't already burning hot. 'Are you trying to make my unusually gentlemanly behaviour even more difficult?'

'Well, yes, actually.'

He laughed again. And since her skin was saturated with sensation, this time she felt it deeper inside. Just behind her ribs and a little to the left. She pressed her hand to the spot as though needing to check it was really real.

'You, Chelsea London, are some woman.'

'I've always thought so.'

'Which is why I am putting my clothes back on right now, and hanging up and not calling you again before nine regardless of how much I might want to. Unless…'

'Unless I let you seduce me over the phone line.'

'Mmm.'

His murmur was almost enough to put her over the edge into acquiescence. But not quite. She knew in her heart of hearts it would be far more sensible to talk to him face to face over the top of a stubby candle before she let him into her bed, or any deeper under her skin.

Chelsea grabbed an angora throw rug from the end of the bed and wrapped it around herself as though it would somehow make her seem more demure, less like the raging sexpot she had been a minute before. 'So nine o'clock?'

'Outside Amelie's,' he said. 'I'll be the one with the rose in my lapel.'

'I thought we'd already agreed that was the mark of a date.'

'So we did.'

'So this is a date?'

Again the pause, and again she wished she could see the look in his eyes to know what it meant.

'So it seems,' he finally said. 'See you soon, Chelsea.'

'Bye.' She hung up. Slowly. And let the warm phone rest against her lips for a few moments as her heart rate slowed, and her nerve endings stopped overreacting to every sound, thought and movement.

She glanced at the other side of the bed. Empty, pillow long since undisturbed by a friendly head. And her heart twisted.

'Careful,' she warned herself out loud.

Damien hung up the mobile phone and slowly pulled his clothes back on realising he had actually turned Chelsea down.

The second she'd offered he should have been over there in a flash. God knew he'd be kicking himself ten ways from Sunday as he railed against peak-hour traffic while driving back to Caleb's.

He'd convinced himself it was all he wanted. But as it turned out he could wait. He was a sophisticated man, not some creature controlled by nothing but his basest needs. He wasn't Caleb.

As he fixed the knot of his tie he stared at the sleek black and silver contraption lying, oh, so innocently on his large desk. 'Hold me. Use me,' it called to his subconscious.

But some other part of him spoke louder. His instincts told him that ravaging Chelsea senseless might well give him some relief, but he had no idea how it would affect her. And after how effortlessly he'd hurt Bonnie he had to keep that in mind if he was ever to look himself in the mirror again.

He could back up a step. He could sit down to dinner with Chelsea. And in doing so he could test the waters more thoroughly to see if a wild night wrapped in her lean limbs was still on the cards.

The very thought had him jerk his tie knot until it almost strangled him. He eased it back, then shut down his computer and, seeing his reflection in the dark blank screen, said, 'Just be careful.'

At nine that evening Chelsea stood outside Amelie's, her gloved hands holding her old pink tartan coat tighter about her body.

The footpath was bustling as the weather was as good as could be expected for a Melbourne autumn night: breezy cool, starlit, yet giving people ideas about getting indoors and getting warm however they could.

An extra several layers beneath instead of her chocolate crossover wool dress would have been more sensible. But at least it didn't smell of mothballs, and it was the most date-worthy thing she owned.

She rubbed her arms as she scoured the crowd while trying not to look as eager as she felt.

Damien stood at the end of the block, hands deep in his trouser pockets. His eyes were zeroed in on the slender caramel-blonde struggling with her coat, her fly-away hair, and the jostling crowd outside Amelie's.

Again she was like a burst of sunshine amidst the river of Melbourne black. And again she infused him with as much energy as though she'd hit him with a stun gun.

A gust of wind whipped down the street, ruffling his hair. It whipped her glittery gold scarf from around her neck, sending it fluttering to the ground with the grace of an autumn leaf. She forgot her coat, which split open as she leant over to pick up her scarf revealing a glimpse of lean honey-golden leg curving in and out in all the right places and feminine curves poured into some stretchy brown fabric that hid just enough and hinted at everything.

Her dress tipped forward and Damien saw a hint of bra. Pale pink. Half cup. He could barely suppress his groan.

She stood, wrapped herself up tight and looked at her watch and he took it as a sign that he'd better get a move on. He cleared his throat, ran a quick hand through his hair, checked his breath on his palm and headed down the street towards the hopeful release of a month's worth of holding back from what no man should rightfully have to forfeit if he could possibly help it.

Chelsea watched as the fiftieth dark suit in eight minutes rounded the corner.

But this one was a half-head taller. A couple of inches broader. Dark hair gleamed under the lamplight. And the length of his strides meant that people simply got out of his way. She wasn't sure it was Damien, but at the same time she just knew that it was.

He neared. He was even more beautiful than she remembered. More blessed by the gods of all things extraordinary. Through the noisy crowd their eyes caught and held. *Pacific-blue,* she thought with an internal sigh, *like the ocean at night.*

'Hi, Damien,' she said.

'Chelsea,' he said as he stopped in front of her.

She must have swayed towards him, or maybe it was an optical illusion, but he suddenly felt closer. And then he was leaning in towards her. She instinctively lifted her cheek for a friendly peck, but instead his lips landed square upon hers. She blinked in shock for a good second or two before his mouth began to move over hers.

As her eyes flittered closed her hand fluttered up to land gently upon his chest. His arm slunk around her back to pull her closer. And right there, in front of a street full of bustling pedestrians, everything floated away, leaving only the taste of him, the scent of him, the feel of his heavenly lips. Her hand curled into his shirt, and she hoped against hope that would be enough to keep her from collapsing in a puddle at his feet.

When the kiss broke her eyes opened. A small smile lit his, creases fanning out from the edges.

'Well, what do you know?' he said, his voice low, rumbling, pure sensuality.

Needing to catch her breath and regather her scattered senses, she slid her hand away and put a metre of space between them. Then she pulled his phone out of her clutch purse and held it out for him on an upturned palm.

'Right,' he said, closing his eyes and shaking his head as though he'd completely forgotten why they were really there. He opened his jacket, once again revealing a broad mass of starched white shirt and enveloping her in a wave of his light but wholly masculine scent. She breathed deep.

He found her phone and held it out to her. Her left palm tickled as he slid his gently from her grasp, while her right hand immediately soaked in the warmth still remaining in the phone she now had back.

'So,' Damien said. 'Now that the formalities are out of the way, shall we?'

Formalities? Kissing her to the point of melting her knees from the inside out was to him a *formality?* Boy, oh, boy. What was she letting herself in for?

He held out an elbow. She tugged her hand into a tight ball to get the feeling back before placing it in the crook of his arm. He tucked her tight against him, drawing her close enough so that the heavy pedestrian traffic could not break their hold, and so that she could again smell the scent of autumn clinging to his clothes.

During the day the restaurant had been bright and bustling, all flashy money and flashier people checking to see who was walking through the front doors.

But at night it was as if they had walked into a cave. It was warm and dark, the ceiling lights recessed so that the whole place seemed lit only by discreetly scattered candles bathing it in a dark red light. It was so romantic. More than romantic. Decadent. As if an orgy could break out at any second.

Damien pressed a gentle hand to Chelsea's back and she jumped. She could feel the heat of his palm searing through the heavy coat and straight to her skin. He leaned forward to whisper against her ear. 'I think she wants our phones.'

Her gaze shot to the hostess. Tall, skinny, brunette hair to her waist and staring at Damien with a small smile and her hand outstretched as though she'd take from him whatever he chose to give her.

Chelsea glanced back at Damien to find herself so close to him she could see just how close he'd shaved before coming to meet her tonight. It somehow gave her a jolt of confidence.

'Do you think we should revolt?' she asked as she slid her coat and scarf from her back.

'I haven't eaten since lunch,' he growled. 'I'm starving.'

She glanced back again to find his gaze had been inexorably drawn to the neckline of her dress. To the barely there hint of cleavage deep within the V. His eyes slid up to hers, connected. Actually, it was more as if they clashed, sending little sparks of heat all over her body.

Chelsea handed over her phone and coat and said, 'I give in.'

'That's my girl,' Damien said, and handed his phone to the hostess. 'In the same compartment, if you please. These two have a way of causing trouble if left on their own.'

The woman's smile faltered as she realised she was beaten before she'd even had the chance to play.

And while Chelsea watched the phones with an eagle eye, she sensed that Damien didn't once take his eyes off her as he waited for the numbered ticket to be placed into his outstretched hand. He slid the ticket inside his jacket pocket, and she realised that she wouldn't be leaving the restaurant without him unless she wanted to leave her phone behind too.

'Where would you be comfortable sitting?' the waitress asked as she picked up a couple of menus.

'I think it's far too late for all that,' Damien said beneath his breath, but Chelsea heard him loud and clear.

She'd had crushes before, but for the first time in her whole life she was absolutely in lust. He created in her urgency that beat down every other wholly sensible qualm. She hung on to her clutch purse with both hands to stop herself from taking him by the hand and dragging him to the nearest dark alley. Hard bodies, slick, sweaty limbs, and nothing left the next morning bar the lingering scent of day-old aftershave.

Damien breathed out hard before turning back to the brunette and Chelsea thankfully felt the hook through her chest melt away.

'A nice private corner would suit us well,' Damien said. He smiled, the low light doing things to his eyes that made her stomach turn to liquid.

'No problem,' the hostess said. 'Follow me.'

Damien held out an arm to encourage Chelsea to go first. What he really wanted to do was continue where they'd left off outside, to lean in, slide his hand around her waist, and kiss the point where her neck met her shoulder, but instead he placed a gentlemanly hand in the small of her back and followed.

Beneath the soft fabric of her dress her skin was warm. Tugging left then right with each swaying step. He closed his eyes for a second and begged heaven to help him make it through dinner without giving in to the desire swarming over him.

They reached the private booth in a far dark corner of the room. Before the hostess had the chance he pulled the table away from the wall so that Chelsea had to slide past him to get to her seat.

He was breathing perfectly normally up until that point. Until he swallowed a mouthful of her scent. Sweet, airy, gentle; the complete antithesis of the sensual vision before him.

The woman was a walking dichotomy. It only made him want her more yet in the same breath made him fear she was exactly the wrong girl for the job.

'Much appreciated,' Chelsea said, smiling up at him from beneath her lashes.

Damien slid behind the table at a right angle to her, and allowed the hostess to lock them into place, glad to have a table hiding his lap.

'Any drinks for starters?' the brunette asked.

'God, yes,' Chelsea shot out at the same time that Damien said,

'I asked for a bottle of Mount Mary Pinot Noir 1993 to be placed on hold under Halliburton.'

'Oh,' the brunette said, her eyes widening. Then she collected herself, nodded, and sent Damien one last lingering look that should have made him puff out his chest even though he was in the company of another woman. But she left him completely unaffected.

Then he and Chelsea were alone, hidden from view of the rest of the restaurant by the angle of their table, a large potted Ficus and the clever lighting. Their booth was cramped. But intimate. Low candlelight flickering from an alcove on the rendered wall above shot waves of gold through Chelsea's hair, and created shadows beneath her lashes, her nose, and full lower lip.

Simply looking at her, he felt anything but unaffected.

A waiter with an eyebrow ring and three more through his nose came back with their wine. Damien did the whole sniff, sip, thumbs up before they were each poured a healthy glass and the bottle was left in an icebox nearby.

Chelsea fussed with her dress, her hair, the placement of the napkin in front of her and said, 'There is something I've been meaning to ask you.'

Damien leant his elbow on the table and his chin on his palm. 'This should be good.'

Her hands fluttered to her lap, but she gave him direct eye contact. All golden light and sunshine and radiant energy. He could have snuffed out the candle and his senses would have told him exactly where she sat.

She asked, 'Whatever did happen to Keppler-Jones and Whosiwhatsit?'

The laughter that burst from Damien's chest was so sudden he almost pulled a muscle. He leant back in his chair and rubbed the strange spot of discomfort beneath his left pec. 'Meaning did I knock them off in order to get a corner office?'

She took a sip of her wine, smiling at him from over the glass. 'Your words, not mine.'

He leaned forward again. 'You have to promise me that this will go no further.'

'Cross my heart,' she said, and the action tugged his gaze to her chest where the stretch fabric clung to her curves.

He licked his lips before dragging his eyes north and saying, 'It was a dark and stormy night.'

Her eyes gleamed. 'Isn't it always?'

'The company had been around since long before the heydays of the eighties. Jones was a family friend of my god-father and I worked for them part-time while studying business/law at university and stayed on afterward. Once I'd risen as far in the firm as a non-partner could I made them an offer they couldn't refuse.'

'And the dark and stormy night?'

'Was the retirement party. One to go down in the history books. I'm certain it took five years off each of their lives. That's my story and I'm sticking to it. Now tell me about the animal-print dog-collar connection before I go any further into imagining what kind of job would make you some kind of expert fit for *Chic* magazine.'

She grinned up at him. He could practically feel the blood in his veins revving itself up to explode through his system the second talking finally turned to touching. And before the end of this night there *would* be touching.

'I own and run a pet-grooming salon in Fitzroy. Disappointed?'

'Infinitely,' he said with an answering smile. 'So what was it about clipping dog toenails that drew you to the cause?'

She shook her hair off her shoulders and sat back in her chair, into deeper shadow, her face in richer relief. 'There's a tad more to what I do than clipping dog toenails.'

'Surprise me.'

'We see up to sixty clients a day. Their treatments can include brushing, dematting, therapeutic baths, fluff or towel dry, nail-clipping, haircuts and shave-downs. They leave us looking brand-new. *Feeling* brand-new.'

'And don't we all need to feel that way every now and then?' he said.

Her glorious eyes shone with a fire that was pure dynamite. He couldn't remember feeling lit by such an inner blaze. It had him wondering if his life was far too comfortable. Maybe it could do with a little spicing up.

'Come on down one day,' she said, 'and I'll give you the works. I'll guarantee you'd leave the place unrecognisable. And flea-free.'

Damien laughed, though truth be told his mind hadn't gone much further than *the works*. Imagining those small hands giving him a therapeutic bath and a towel dry was almost his undoing.

'It's some kind of thrill, don't you think?' he asked.

Her right eyebrow rose in question.

'Working for oneself. Balancing the kind of satisfaction, control and wealth you can only gain if you own the business against the daily possibility of losing everything. I like to think of it as a masochistic gamble rather than anything as mundane as a job.'

She again reached for her wine. 'Unless you never gamble more than you can afford to lose.'

'Never?'

She shook her head.

'Then that's not really a gamble at all, is it?'

She shook her head again, a small smile lifting the corners of her mouth as though she knew some great secret he and the rest of the world had yet to catch onto.

'That said,' she added, 'I had a meeting with the bank today and they have approved a loan for me to expand out to three salons.'

'Good for you. It seems this is a celebratory dinner as well.' He topped her up wine.

She watched as the dark liquid poured into her deep glass.

then said, 'But I'm not sure if I want to sign.' She added a little
shrug, then sank further away from him again as though she'd
said more than she'd meant to.

'Why not?' he asked, adding a dash to his own mostly full
glass. 'If they think you warrant such an investment, they have
faith in your product.'

'I guess. But I'm not sure that I'm willing to put all my faith
in someone else's judgment.'

For the first time Damien *saw* the genuine vulnerability he'd
sensed all along in the lift of her cheek, the blush across her
neck, the shy tilt of her head.

He shifted in his seat, mighty glad he hadn't zoomed over
to her place as she'd begged him to do. Right about now he'd
be dealing with the fallout. With those great golden eyes boring
holes in his back as he walked out of her life as he was wont
to do. He thanked his lucky stars he hadn't gone so far he didn't
still have time to pull out graciously without hurting her
feelings.

'Am I being ridiculous?' she asked.

It took him a moment to remember what they were talking
about. He gulped down half his wine before saying, 'If your
bank works anything like my team do, they keep their ears to
the ground. We watch the news, read the papers, I even have a
team on gossip magazines, as you never know where new
market patterns will emerge.'

'But once you see something worth your attention you know
it? It's that simple for you?'

'It really is. And then I gamble everything at my disposal on
that instinct.'

'What if your instincts are wrong?'

'What if they're not?'

She looked up at him from beneath the shadow of her long

lashes. Her lower lip disappeared between her teeth. And he knew there was far more going on behind the golden depths of her eyes than the conversation at hand. It seemed he wasn't the only one ignoring the elephant in the room—an attraction so intense he wasn't sure just how long he and his chivalry could hold out.

'So now that I've given you some free financial advice,' he said, 'you owe me.' He turned over his palm and pulled a pretend pen from behind his ear. 'Give me the address of your business. It's time I had a haircut.'

At that she laughed, as he'd hoped she might; only the foot loose sound stirred all sorts of shackled feelings deep inside him, enough for him to keep on pouring until his wineglass was full all the way to the top.

CHAPTER SEVEN

CHELSEA kicked off her shoes beneath the table and rubbed life back into the balls of her feet.

She wanted nothing more than to run her bare foot up the inside of Damien's trousers. To scrape her toenails along a length of manly leg hair and just forget all about dinner. He was so utterly and totally beyond the realms of gorgeous that her nerve endings felt as if they were on constant red alert.

Added to that she was beginning to *like* him. To really, actually like the guy. Beneath the suit and tie he was nice. Funny. Sharp. Thoughtful. And he kept looking at her as if he wanted nothing more than to continue the kiss he'd started outside.

But, and it was a huge but, it seemed he was that mythical creature that she had spent her whole life both desperately wishing to know really existed, while at the same time despising to the depths of her soul.

He was a gambler. Who won. And again and again by the looks of him. By the loose way he sat in the chair. The ease with which he wore his immaculate clothes. The way he rattled off the name of some no doubt ridiculously expensive bottle of wine.

And for him to always win meant guys like her dad had to always lose.

She grabbed the leftover cork from the wine bottle and spun it over her knuckles, from one end of her hand to the other with ever increasing speed.

There was only one way to settle this. The clincher that she had always known since she was a little girl must determine the worthwhile men from the jerks.

'Do you have a dog?' she asked.

He looked up from his perusal of the dinner menu. 'Ah, no.'

There is no point in liking him. Unless, perhaps, the question merely needs one more qualifier. 'Do you *like* dogs?'

'I love dogs. I had a golden lab when I was a kid. Buster. He had an inner-ear problem and ran into walls all the time.'

'He did no such thing.'

'You have no idea. He was the best sounding-board a boy could have. Helped me get over my father's wrath when I got a C in history. He helped me get over being dumped by Casey Campanalli in the eight grade. Helped me survive my parents' trigger-happy divorce. To this day he's still the best hug I've ever had.'

Chelsea bit her cheek to stop from sighing. He was born to wear a suit. He was born to eat in expensive restaurants day in and day out. He had a natural reserve about him that had her instincts screaming at her to back away fast. But Damien Halliburton was a *true* dog lover.

The plumber had wanted a dog for company. The single dad had been landed with his in the divorce. The consultant had treated his dogs as if they were his children. But this guy…he had understood the importance of having love in your life that was not for sale.

She *liked* the guy. She *wanted* him. And now he'd accidentally made contact with the deepest personal touchstone she had in her arsenal. She was in trouble.

She flicked the cork into her palm, then onto the back of her hand, then continued twirling it over her knuckles. 'So yours wasn't an idyllic childhood, then?'

'I have no complaints. Both parents are still well and truly around and I do believe, on their diet of matching dirty martinis and tennis three times a week, they will live for ever. They divorced when I was eleven, which is likely why they are on such good terms and are now the poster children for contented singledom.'

He smiled, as much as spelling out to her that he was happy being single too. Which was great. So was she. Single and in charge of her own destiny. So why did it feel as if her stomach had sunk like a stone?

Damien took a sip of wine and watched her over the top of the glass, his deep blue eyes smiling, seeing. His mouth stretched into a smile that was built to make a woman just want to give in and surrender. 'You like me more now, don't you?'

She leant her chin on her upturned palm, stared right on back and called his bluff. 'Infinitely.'

His eyes narrowed as he watched her for several more seconds before shifting in his chair, stretching out his legs. The air around her knees wafted and her skirt blew up before settling back against her suddenly sensitive skin.

'So do you have a dog?' he asked.

'I live in an apartment. I'm out a lot. It wouldn't be fair.'

He nodded. And she restlessly spun the rounded end of the cork on the end of her pointer finger before it landed on the back of her hand again.

'Okay, I bite,' Damien said, his dark gaze dropping to her hands. 'Either you were once a croupier in some dive in Vegas or…nope, that's the only thing I can come up with for a girl with that kind of hand-eye coordination. Give me a go.'

She tossed it in the air so it spun, and by the time he'd caught it she sat back swirling his wineglass in her left hand and hers in her right.

His eyes grew wide. And impressed. They slid up her chest, past her neck, warming every inch of exposed skin along the way until they landed with a heated thud on her eyes. 'You're some kind of witch, aren't you?'

Laughter tickled her throat. 'And I'd gone to so much trouble to hide my broomstick out of sight in an alley down the street.'

Only after taking a decided sip from his glass did she give him back his wine.

'Thank you,' he said with a new kind of smile in his eyes that did violent things to her heart rate.

'My pleasure.'

He threw the cork in the air, then spent a good thirty seconds trying to flip it across his knuckles but he only succeeded in dropping it again and again. 'Where *did* you learn to do that?'

She grabbed the linen napkin and began folding it into smaller and smaller triangles, using it as an excuse to break eye contact. She thought about lying. She'd certainly done it before: hidden her own inadequacies while frenetically determining those of any otherwise likeable man in her midst.

She sat back in her chair and pretended to be on the lookout for a waiter. 'Why is it always the posh places that give such slow service?'

'Chelsea, spill. Or I'll find a way to make you.'

She blinked back at him. This guy… Something made her want to tell the truth. Hoping it would bring them closer, or push him further away?

'My father was a grifter.'

'Like a conman?'

She tucked a strand of hair behind her ear. 'Every once in a while. But more consistently a gambler, always following the next big dream, looking for the next sure thing which would make us rich. And when that failed, as it inevitably did, he would turn to stealing wallets, identities, candy from babies as he moved us from pillar to post and back again.'

She glanced at Damien and away again to give herself enough time to see if he was looking for the nearest exit. If she were in his shoes that was what she would have been doing. But if anything he was sitting further forward, intrigue adding a further glint to his eyes. No matter which way she thought he'd spin he continued to surprise her.

She took a much needed deep breath and crossed her feet at the ankles, accidentally brushing the side of her bare foot against his calf. She stilled, wondering if he'd even noticed. When his eyes grew a shade darker and he took his own deep breath she knew he'd noticed all right. Noticed and reacted instantly.

He lounged a tad more, shifting until his knees came so close to hers she could feel his warmth against her bare skin. And that time she just knew it wasn't in the least bit accidental.

'So could you steal my wallet?' he asked.

Chelsea glanced at the region of his heart where by habit she'd felt the consistency of a flat leather wallet that first day. 'What makes you think I haven't already?'

His eyes grew wide as his hand flew to the spot. He slid his long black leather wallet from its home and let out a long slow breath. Then his eyes shot to hers. Flickered left to right. Dark, searching, mesmerised.

He slid his wallet back into place, his eyes not leaving hers. Their depths glinted as though reflecting the last gasp of sunlight of the day.

Her teeth scraped against the edge of her glass. The zing she felt through her jaw at the clash of hard substances was nothing compared with the zing singing through her stomach, ricocheting from surface to surface until she felt as if a truckload of fireworks had gone off inside her belly.

'I'm not sure whether to find you a complete delight or to fear what each encounter with you will bring, Miss London.'

He reached for his own glass of wine, but merely swirled it beneath his chin as his gaze roamed lazily over her face, her hair, and her breasts, which strained against the tight fabric of her dress as though he'd actually reached out and grazed them with his touch.

Finally he looked back into her eyes. A smile warming them. Warming her. Challenging her.

He said, 'Right now I'm leaning heavily towards delight.'

Chelsea pressed her knees together. She was the one who ought to be feeling fearful of what each meeting with this man might bring. She who was usually so untouchable was becoming very very touched. And the need to touch and be touched as long as she could handle it was overwhelming. She fought to find a way to relieve the pressure inside her before it exploded into something terribly messy like genuine affection.

'Your turn,' she said.

'For?'

'A party trick. It's another family tradition of mine. On the rare occasions we ate out anywhere fancy Kensey and I would always end up trying to outdo one another by performing the strangest acts we could while not drawing attention to ourselves. For example...' She crossed her eyes and curled her tongue into a tube.

Sabotage, her sister would have called it. Chelsea liked to think it was better to know the measure of a man as soon as possible. When she uncrossed them Damien was still watching her with such a look of honest fascination she had to scrape her tongue back through her teeth to stop the tingling.

'I have something you might like.' His voice had dropped low and deep. Enough for the sound to create skitters of awareness across her arms. 'We have to go uncaught? That's the rule?'

Chelsea's feet and hands cooled as all the blood inside her seemed to rush to her cheeks. To the vertical dip between her breasts. And lower.

She nodded.

'Right. Then I'm going to need a drink.' He turned his wineglass so that the exact spot from which she had earlier drunk was facing him. He brought it to his lips and took a sip, letting his mouth rest around the lip of the glass a mite longer than entirely necessary.

Her lips tingled as though his were pressed just as surely and closely against her own. His breath tickling her tongue rather than creating minuscule waves in his glass.

The upholstered booth seat beneath her suddenly felt as though it were tipping. And when he unbuttoned his jacket, and loosened his tie, then dropped his hands beneath the table and leant forward so that she could see the splash of navy surrounding each of his ocean-blue eyes she clung onto the edge of the table to stop herself from swaying under his gaze.

'Ready?' he asked.

'Am I meant to be involved in this somehow?'

'Mmm, that's the general plan.'

'What do I need to do?'

'Keep very very still. And if you give us away then you lose, and I win, right?'

She nodded.

And in the next instant the back of his knuckles grazed gently across her knees.

Chelsea's bare toes dug into the carpeted floor. Her fingers gripped the table so hard her knuckles were turning white. 'What is it exactly that you are thinking of doing?'

'Believe me when I say this game will be that much more fun if we left that a surprise.'

When she didn't flinch, or protest, the knuckles made a return journey, this time brushing across her knees and around the outside until his thumbs ran over the top of her kneecaps and just beneath the hem of her skirt. And she kept her mouth shut tight.

When he touched her for a third time Chelsea glanced quickly around the restaurant, but it was dark, and the table positioned just so. Unless someone came leaping out from behind the Ficus…

Damien's thumb ran back and forth beneath her skirt and she drew in a shuddering breath. And when his hands wrapped around the outside of her thighs and began sliding up her legs, she wasn't sure when she ever might find the chance to breathe again.

He smiled. Though it was more of a tilt of the lips, a deepening of the creases below his cheeks, and a change in the colour of his eyes. But in that smile she saw arrogance, confidence, and purpose. Damien Halliburton knew just what kind of power he had over her.

Her head protested. But it was too late. Nothing could have prepared her for the mass of sensation that spread like wildfire through her whole body when his hands slid over the tops of her thighs, his thumbs delved into the gap between and gently, but insistently, pressed her legs apart.

She let her eyes flutter closed. He was so supremely sure of his effect on her, while the only times in recent history she'd had a male get this close was when she'd had to straddle the Kellets' Great Dane to hold it in place while Phyllis clipped its nails.

She squeezed her eyes tighter. *That's it, you idiot,* she said to herself. *You are in the middle of the sexiest moment of your entire life and you are doing your best to diminish it. To distance yourself. Well, not this time.*

This time it felt too good. This time it had been building and building and unless she let it come to its natural conclusion she knew she would never forgive herself. This time she slowly uncrossed her ankles, released her death grip on the table and let the pressure of his thumbs guide her knees inches apart.

Her pulse pounded beneath her skin, which felt so hot it almost hurt to move. Her head suddenly felt loose upon her neck. And a trickle of perspiration made a slow, hot trail down her spine.

Ambient sounds of the restaurant served as a cushion to her senses: the soft murmur of voices, the whisper of footsteps on expensive carpet, the chime of cutlery against dinner plates. And above it all, like a pulse throbbing across her skin, were Damien's deep intakes and slow releases of breath, evidence that beneath his self-assurance he was as affected as she was.

He twisted his hands until his fingers were splayed atop her thighs. He tightened his grip, digging into the tense muscle for a brief second before his left hand disappeared. She almost cried out for the sudden erasure of half her pleasure.

Until his right hand continued its journey, circling her thigh until it dived between the two. Her legs spasmed. Clutching at his hand. But it wasn't to be deterred. The backs of his knuckles grazed one inner thigh, while the pads of his fingers dug into the soft flesh of the other. Then slowed imperceptibly until he came to a stop at the edge of her cotton briefs.

'Chelsea,' he said, his deep voice seeming to come to her from a mile away.

'Yes,' she managed to breathe out. *Yes, yes, yes!*

'Is this the kind of thing you had in mind?' His fingers teased at the edge of her panties, brushing ever so lightly around the hem.

Since the moment I laid eyes on you, she thought.

She began to tremble. Her hands shot to grip onto the padded bench. Her toes dug harder into the soft carpet. Her tongue darted out to wet her lips, which felt as if they were burning up. 'So far so good.'

He laughed, the sound vibrating through his arm and into his hand. Until her legs eased further apart. Just enough to give him all the access he desired.

Then, with no more finessing, one finger slipped behind the cotton barrier, then two. And her whole body shook with such a tremendous release of tension; hours' worth, weeks, years, a lifetime worth of holding everything close to her chest lest someone take what little she had away from her.

This trick, this *game,* was no longer anything of the sort. As with her eyes closed tight, her knees shoulder-width apart, and her usual abundance of common sense having taken leave on another planet, she put every ounce of faith she had in her body not to let them get caught. And to let this man continue bestowing gift upon gift upon her every second his desire for her grew.

He touched her gently, deftly, as if he *knew* her. As if he knew exactly how far to go. When to apply pressure and when to pull away. A warm, melting weight made her body feel heavy. Pulling everything inwards towards his barely there contact.

Her breaths began to hitch in her throat. Her surroundings swarmed in on her. 'I can't,' she said, her voice a desperate plea.

'Yes, you bloody well can.' His voice became little more than a growl, and it only made her hotter still. 'You have no idea how much I want shove this table aside and lunge at you and sink my teeth into that spot where your neck meets your shoulder. I have truly never seen anything so gorgeous in my entire life. The only way to stop that kind of racket from happening is to give in and let me do this instead.'

With that he pushed her panties aside so that his whole hand could cup her, his every finger could move with her as she moved with him. As she tried so hard to keep still while instinct took over and she gave into it as he'd told her to do. She slid forward, let her head press against the back of the seat, and trusted him.

And in that moment she knew that even if she lost this round, she won.

It was enough for the last shreds of her self-control to fade away like a mirage in the far distance of her subconscious. She bit her lip to stop from making any sound as every warm, delicate sensation built to a tremendous crescendo before everything turned a blinding white and she dissolved into a million tiny little pieces.

It felt like hours later when his hand tidied her panties before sliding away. When her breathing returned to normal. When she could see more than a swirl of colours behind her eyelids.

'Are you ready to choose your orders, sir?' a male voice called from somewhere to Chelsea's left.

Her eyes flung open to find Damien leaning back in his chair, cool as you please. 'Are you ready, Chels?' he asked.

He smiled at her then, a smile that would have seemed to any onlooker as though he was politeness himself. But she saw the pulse in his neck throb and his fingers clench the menu.

She pressed her knees back together and brought herself fully upright. It took for her to lick her lips and blink about a dozen times to collect herself into a position where she could find a word to say, but she got there in the end.

'Steak,' she said, ignoring her menu. 'I was promised steak.'

'Twice over,' Damien said, closing the menu and passing it to the waiter. 'I'll have mine rare.'

'How would you like yours cooked, ma'am?'

'Well done for me. To the point of being dangerously dark. Tell the chef to take all the time he needs to cook it.'

The waiter glanced up at her, then at Damien, the slightest of frowns as he tried to decipher what he was missing in the conversation. But when they continued making eyes at one another across the table he figured it was better left unknown. 'Very good,' he said, then walked away.

Chelsea tugged her skirt back into place with one hand and reached for a glass of water with the other. She took a long sip, not quite knowing where to look. But when her eyes eventually found Damien's, what she saw there eased her mind.

His eyes were the colour of a starless midnight sky. His hair ruffled as though he'd just run frustrated fingers through it. He wanted her even more. And she had the distinct impression this wasn't even close to being as good as it was going to get.

She had to take a deep breath before throwing him a quick, 'So what's the party trick? I'm still waiting.'

And with that he burst into laughter. Loud, rolling waves that took the slow burn lingering in her limbs and blew them into the beginnings of a wildfire.

'I'm going to freshen up,' he said, sliding out from behind the table. But before he left he leaned down to kiss her. Holding her chin with enough force that as his mouth moved over hers she melted in his hold. Their tongues slid past one another. Their body heat intermingled.

He pulled away looking down into her eyes. 'Delight,' he said. 'An unmitigated delight.'

Then he was gone, easing past the Ficus and through the labyrinthine tables and out of sight.

* * *

By the time dessert was almost over Damien cleared his throat and Chelsea glanced up at him, playing with the last strawberry, pushing it around with her fork and drowning in his dark eyes and chiselled jaw line.

He wiped his mouth with his napkin, then said, 'Well, I for one think this has been a remarkable first date. What do you say to a second?'

His words hit somewhere deep inside her like a flaming arrow shot from point-blank range. It was enough for her to put her fork down, sit back in her chair, and fold her arms.

'I'm undecided,' she said. 'Though they do say it's the last five pages of a book that sell the next one.'

'Talk about putting pressure on a guy,' he joked, but for a moment he seemed genuinely surprised that she was keeping her options open. But he recovered remarkably quickly and said, 'Time to turn the spotlight, I think. I've told you far more about my screwball family than you could ever want to know, so now it's your turn. What's your family like, apart from felonious?'

She coughed out a laugh, her turn to be surprised by him. 'One sister. She was Kensington London to my Chelsea London until she very smartly married a guy called Greg Hurley. I blame my mother, who named us then left. My father died when I was sixteen.'

'I'm sorry.'

'Don't be. Neither of us have followed in either of their footsteps. Though Kensey did sell life insurance for a while. I'm sure there are many who would consider that a scam.'

'One I'm afraid shadows my own family name. My father owns Universal Life,' he said, naming one of the largest insurance companies in Australia.

Chelsea blanched. She'd known Damien was one of the bright and shiny ones, but he was a Halliburton of *those*

Halliburtons? He was beyond a New Uniform type. Half the buildings in his school were likely named after his ancestors while her father had been a scab on the face of existence and she had no clue if her mother was even still alive.

Enough was enough. She put her fingers to her mouth and whistled loud enough to grab the attention of a passing waiter, as well as the five tables in between. 'The bill, please,' she told him, 'and the faster it comes the more my friend here will tip.'

As Damien helped her from her seat he whispered in her ear, 'If you only knew how much that acid tongue of yours turns me on I'm afraid you'd only bite it.'

He was dead right; she didn't say another word, even as she quickly slid a small package from the pocket of her coat and left it with the hostess to give to Carrie.

Once they sorted out whose phone was whose, Damien held open the glass door for her and led her outside. It was dark. Cold. Her breath expelled in short white puffs of air. She stomped her feet against the cold pavement and waited for him to join her.

He walked to her side, rubbing his hands together. 'So,' he said.

'So,' she said back through cold lips. 'This has been some day.'

'One I don't think I'll easily forget.'

She glanced sideways; her gaze caught with his and held. So blue. Her heart did some kind of acrobatics in her chest and, though she knew it was a bad idea, she desperately wanted him to ask her out again. *Again.*

'I bet you didn't picture being here twice in a day when you woke up this morning,' she said, giving him time.

He laughed. 'Ah, no. I think I may have pictured meetings, phone calls, working through lunch, leaving the office way past dark, taking more work home and falling into bed some time after midnight.'

Bed... At the word *bed* his voice dropped, and her nerves danced beneath her skin.

'How about you?' he asked.

'Believe it or not you took the words right out of my mouth.'

Mouth... At the word *mouth* his gaze dropped to hers. It felt dry, in need of a quick lap of her tongue. As though he knew the self-control she was struggling against Damien smiled, abundantly confident in his sexual power.

But it didn't make Chelsea feel like smiling. Her lungs felt tight, her nerve endings on fire, and her heart was beating so fast she thought it might pop fair through her chest.

Was he punishing her? Leaving it up to her to ask him back to her place for coffee and finish what they'd started because she'd been so blasé about the idea earlier? It *was* what her body was aching for her to do. It was practically screaming.

She was beginning to shake with the cold. She should just listen to her head, and kiss him on the cheek, and say goodnight. Or better yet goodbye.

But then she thought about what it would be like to go home to her empty apartment, where she would shiver for a good ten minutes until the central heating kicked in. And even when she was dressed in her comfy flannelette pyjamas and bed socks, she would still be alone.

So without a second thought she followed her instincts and reached out and grabbed two handfuls of glorious soft wool coat, stood on tiptoes, and kissed him full on the mouth. Giving everything she had.

As though he'd merely been waiting for her to make a move, he immediately wrapped his hand behind her neck, pulling her closer still. Her eyes closed, she breathed out through her nose and once again let down her guard and let him in.

He opened his coat and scooped her inside. She slid her arms around his waist and sank against him. And in his hold she felt warm, secure, desired, beautiful, and brimming with power. And maybe, just maybe, this thing that had sprung up so suddenly between them had the potential to be far more than what it seemed.

A wolf-whistle from some young punk in a passing car pulled Chelsea out of her reverie. She slowly ended the kiss and pulled back just far enough to draw breath. Hard breaths, heavy breaths, but not nearly as hard and heavy as those belonging to the man in her arms.

'Come home with me,' she said, her voice husky and soft.

He swallowed and leaned his forehead against hers. For so many seconds they felt like minutes. Until she began to wonder if he'd heard her at all. She prepared herself to ask again when he finally said:

'Not tonight, Chelsea.'

Her blood turned to cold sludge in her veins. Now she just wanted to get out of there and fast. She began by uncurling her fingers from his coat.

'You have no idea how much I want to,' Damien said, not letting her go just yet, pulling her closer until she felt the physical evidence of his words. 'But I have an early meeting. And after spending every spare minute on the phone to you, I have a pile of papers to catch up on at home before then.'

He reached out and tucked a lock of hair behind her ear. 'Any chance I can get your phone number, though?'

Chelsea thought about telling him where he could stick her number. But now more than anything she wanted to walk away feeling sophisticated, or at least hoping he saw her as such. Not used and shattered and weak and self-destructive for trusting him so quickly when he'd given her no real cause to apart from seeming too good to be true.

She reached into her purse, pulled out a pen, grabbed his hand, turned it over and wrote her mobile number on his warm palm and then began backing away.

'So that's goodnight?' he asked, arms outstretched, broad form haloed by the light spilling from inside the restaurant.

She kept backing away, her heels clacking on the concrete beneath her feet, putting more and more distance between them. 'You'd better get home quickly if you don't want my number to rub away.'

His arms dropped to his sides and, the further she went, the darker and more shadowed his face became until she could no longer see the expression in his eyes. And just like that he was no more to her than a beautiful stranger again. She would do well to remember it.

He pushed his coat aside, reached into his jacket pocket and pulled out his phone. Lifting his hand towards the streetlight, he punched in a bunch of numbers.

Her phone vibrated in her pocket and out rang the theme tune from *The Mary Tyler Moore Show*—a show she and Kensey had loved watching the few months growing up they'd had access to a television. Despite the fact that she was doing her best to disentangle herself from him, she answered it.

'Hello?'

'Chelsea, hi. It's Damien.'

'Damien who?' She felt his smile from twenty good metres away. She *didn't* know him, but it sure felt as if she did. Knew him, liked him, and much more… She picked up her pace.

'Ah, the age-old question. Right up there with who am I? Why am I here? What's my favourite colour? Now you have my number in your phone you can call me back some time in order to find out.'

She watched him flip his phone shut, a flat tone buzzed in her ear. She flipped hers shut as well and slid it back into her purse. From halfway down the block he was now half hidden by the light pedestrian traffic.

She saw him raise a hand goodbye, but she just turned and walked away, knowing there was no way on God's green earth she'd be calling him.

His second rebuff in one night well and truly restored the temporary kink in her self-control.

CHAPTER EIGHT

'Sir?'

Damien's vision cleared to find Mindy looking at him expectantly. 'I'm sorry, what?'

'Are you ready for our reports?' she asked.

He glanced at the clock on the wall. It was just after seven a.m. He looked around the oval conference table at his team, who all had mugs of steaming hot coffee in their hands to combat the early hour, and looks of faint concern in their eyes that their intrepid leader obviously wasn't firing on all cylinders.

'Your reports,' he said. 'Of course. Go. Shoot.'

'Right,' Mindy said, then launched into a bullet-point breakdown of every news report of the night before that she thought might be relevant to the upcoming day's trades.

Damien's leg started shaking at the lead story. He'd torn off the ends of his fingernails on one hand by the time they hit the special interest section. He almost made it all the way through the weather, before he scraped his chair back so loud the whole room went quiet.

Caleb mouthed, *What are you doing?*

'I'll be back in a sec. Keep going.'

And then he tore from the room.

'I have an early meeting,' he said aloud, repeating the words that had been thumping in his head the whole night through as he'd lain awake on Caleb's couch, alone, wishing he could turn back the clock and follow Chelsea wherever she led.

He *had* had an early meeting as he did every day of the week and it had never stopped him from indulging in night-time action before.

But when Chelsea had asked him to come home with her, something about her, about the ingenuous intensity of her preceding goodnight kiss, had spooked him enough for him to tell a beautiful and willing woman who'd had him wound up as tight as a new spring, 'Not tonight.'

He'd been, of all things, honourable. And then somewhere in the middle of the night, as he'd tossed and turned on Caleb's couch, he'd decided honour could go jump.

So what if she smelt like sunshine not perfume? So what if she was soft, and vulnerable, and honest and nothing about her screamed one-night stand?

He had to see her again.

He found himself in the lift and pressed the button for the ground floor. He slid his phone from his pocket and keyed in her phone number, which was now already imprinted on his brain like a brand. It rang. And rang. And rang.

The lift binged, he was in the foyer and moving through the revolving glass doors to Collins Street. The autumn chill seeped beneath his shirt, tie and suit trousers in a Melbourne minute.

Damien gripped the phone in preparation of slamming it closed, when the ringing tone stopped and a familiar voice said, 'Good morning, Damien.'

'Chelsea.' He turned down a side alley and out of the way of passers-by and the bluster shooting down the Collins Street wind tunnel. 'Hi. Hi. Good morning yourself.'

He slapped a hand across his eyes. *Okay, so now that you have her what are you going to do with her?*

'You'll have to be quick,' she said, her voice far cooler than his. 'I'm literally on my way out the door. Early meeting.'

Well, he deserved that. 'Of course. No worries. I just… I wanted to call to say hello.'

Smooth. You are truly some kind of Valentino. She'll be quivering at the knees right this second.

'Would have been cheaper to send a text message. Or a postcard. How about next time you get the urge you post me a letter? People don't write nearly enough nowadays.'

'Chelsea—'

'I get it,' she said. 'Truly. You don't have to ease your conscience with some heartfelt rendition of "it's not you it's me". Yesterday was one out of the box. And last night was something else entirely. But all in all it was a story with which to delight your friends come Friday night happy hour. You're not the first, and I'm sure despite my best efforts you won't be the last, man I meet who'll have an early meeting.'

Again he was hit with a wave of absolute vulnerability. Most of the time she came across as so gung-ho. So unruffled. But he could hear, as clear as if she'd said the words out loud, that he'd done it again. He'd hurt her.

But awful as that was, as much as it was exactly what he'd been trying to avoid, the strength of her reaction gave him hope he might convince her to see him again. Once they were within touching distance he'd be in his element again and he'd know just how to make them both feel better.

He stopped pacing and planted his feet on the ground and stared hard at the graffiti-riddled brick wall of the alley. 'I haven't called to tell you I don't want to see you again, Chelsea.'

She remained silent. Her disbelief palpable.

He ran a hand through his hair. 'I don't know what kind of guys you've dated in the past, but for me this whole phone thing we have going on leaves a lot to be desired. Especially now that I find myself missing the Mary Tyler Moore ring tone.'

She laughed through her nose, or at least that was what it sounded like. He clung onto the small noise for dear life.

'Let me prove it to you. Let me take you out again tonight. I'll pick you up, I'll take you somewhere nice where there will be no waiters with nose rings or exposed bra straps, I'll pay and I'll escort you home like a regular old-fashioned date. No funny business.'

He crossed his fingers through the last part. He wanted funny business with her so much he could barely walk straight.

After a long pause she said, 'I don't mind nose rings. What I don't like is bad service. And small portions at exorbitant prices. And snooty uppity sorts who think themselves above other people.'

He had a feeling she was somehow referring to him, which didn't bode well for funny business so he chose to ignore it. 'Fine,' he said. 'I'll do my best to find somewhere suitable. Tattoos all round and at the first sign of snootiness we walk. And afterwards, well, we'll cross that bridge when we come to it. Okay?'

'Fine,' she said. She sounded as though she'd agreed against her will, but he had the feeling this woman didn't do anything against her will. Her will was even stronger than his. And her will said he'd done enough to have her want to see him again.

He punched the air and let out a silent whoop.

'Excellent. Let's say seven o'clock. Text me your address as I'm nowhere near a piece of paper—'

'You do know your phone has a notebook function?'

'That's nice. But I actually know how to retrieve a text message.' He thought he did anyway. He'd better get back to the office just in case.

He looked around and realised he was halfway down a hill heading goodness knew where. He headed up the hill hoping he'd remember which way to turn when he reached civilisation again. 'Does this thing have a Global Positioning System?'

'Of course it does.' She laughed again and this time it was softer, gentler, more forgiving. 'Someone ought to buy you a pocket-sized paper notebook for Christmas.'

'I'll add it to Santa's list,' he said. 'So, I'll see you at seven?'

'You will. Although I could just as easily send you to some deserted block as punishment for how you ended things last night.'

Damien grinned as he hit Collins Street and got his bearings and marched back towards the office. 'No,' he said. 'You like me far too much to do that.'

She didn't deny it. All she said was, 'Then don't be late.'

'I'll be so early I'll be embarrassing.'

'Bye, Damien.'

'See you soon, Chelsea.' Damien hung up only once he was sure the line was dead.

He pushed through the glass doors and jogged across the foyer, a newfound spring in his step. He knew that day he'd work as hard as ten men, to make up for the day before, and so that time would fly until he would be at her door.

And this time nothing, not cold feet, or honour, or guilt would stop him from happily taking from her whatever delights she readily offered.

Chelsea slowly hung up the phone. The only early meeting she had was with a cup of coffee and the newspaper.

She left the remains of both on the table in the kitchen nook at home, finished off the last bite of reheated leftover chicken teriyaki from a couple of nights before, then padded into her bedroom, disrobing as she headed towards the shower, wondering when exactly she'd become a masochist.

She'd gambled big three times in her life. Finishing high school via correspondence while she worked full-time in a pet-grooming business after her father died to help Kensey pay the rent. Taking over the business when her mentor retired. And buying out Kensey for this apartment.

All had given her the beginnings of stomach ulcers at first. But now…

She looked around her at the beautiful bedroom. Sunshine spilled through the small balcony window, a light breeze kissing the gauzy curtains. The opulent furnishings made the large space feel cosy. Her instincts had been dead on.

So what were her instincts telling her about Damien? That he was a creature of comfort who was emotionally unavailable. Not looking to fill any kind of void in his life with one woman.

She padded into the *en suite* and turned on the hot water, waiting until the room filled with heavenly steam before she cooled it down and slid under the invigorating spray.

But he was also a man who made her laugh. A man who made her able to forget her inhibitions and give herself to another person more intimately than she ever had.

Damien Halliburton was a man who just might be worth the gamble, or might yet prove her to be the greatest fool who ever walked the earth.

Right now she felt as if the odds were about even.

Just before seven o'clock that night, Damien walked up Flinders Lane pressing past clumps of scantily clad waifs spilling from funky restaurant doorways. He smiled at those who smiled at him first, but his steps did not falter. He was a man on a mission.

He looked up. Solid black wrought-iron balconies scattered the dark brick façade above. Several had light from inside spilling through translucent curtains, others yet trailed in blood-red bougainvillea. The building was unique and utterly charming. Much like the inhabitant he was here to see.

He straightened his tie, ran a hand over his hair, and paused with his finger over the doorbell of Chelsea's apartment, wondering what on earth this night might bring him. It wasn't as though any of this had gone according to plan so far.

He steeled himself, puffed out his chest, clutched at the bunch of lustrous orange tulips he'd bought for her and poked the button with as much force as his finger could take without breaking a bone.

After a few long seconds, the breathy sound of the intercom broke through the white noise of a city at play, and a husky voice answered, 'Hello?'

He checked he had the right apartment number, then leaned into the speaker. 'Chelsea, it's Damien.'

Another pause. 'Damien? Oh, heck, I'd completely forgotten.' And smoked three packets of cigarettes in a minute flat by the sound of her.

Then the gist of what she'd said sank in. Forgotten? When he'd rushed out of work the minute the markets had closed to make sure he wasn't a second late, she—

'Damien?'

'I'm still here,' he said, not bothering to hide his annoyance. 'Are you going to buzz me in?'

'I can't. I—'

'Don't tell me you're not ready,' he said, feeling more and

more frustrated at having to talk to her through a wall. They might as well have been on the phone. Again.

He didn't want that any more. He wanted to see her. Touch her. Smell her. Kiss her. Slide her clothes from her limbs. And to sink into her, to ease the ache that had built inside him since the first moment he'd looked into those golden brown eyes.

'I'm happy to wait for you to tidy up or pick an outfit or dab on perfume or whatever it is you have yet to do. Just let me in.'

'I…can't. Damien.' She paused. He even heard the sound shut off at the other end for a second before it came back on. 'The truth is I'm sick.'

'Sick,' he repeated, wondering if that was some kind of code, like washing her hair, or paying him back for the early-morning excuse after all.

Frustrated to the point of a painfully clenched jaw, he looked over his shoulder. Melbourne was alive all around him. Music pouring from restaurant speakers. Tables full of young women laughing and young men paying close attention. All he wanted was to be a part of that scene again.

Maybe this thing between them had been all too hard from day dot for a reason. The fates were telling him to leave her well enough alone. To reinvigorate his weary libido in another pair of willing arms.

'Damien?' her reedy voice said again, and he knew, despite what his instincts were blaring at him, something else inside him simply wouldn't let him leave.

'Chelsea,' he said, dropping his voice to its most persuasive level. 'Let. Me. In.'

The smoked-glass door beside him clicked and he grabbed it and yanked it open. He shot through the marble lobby, giving brief nods to the octogenarian couple leaving the lift as he entered it. The art deco lifts took far too long to take him to the third floor. But when he got there her front door was ajar.

He took another deep breath and pushed it open to find Chelsea pacing the floor of a one-bedroom apartment over-stuffed with furniture and books and knick-knacks and floral patterns so rich he practically had to squint to block them out.

She whooshed past him, a blur of tartan flannelette and bare feet. The frivolous hot-pink glitter on her toenails had him rooted to the floor. It took her husky voice to cut through his little daydream.

'I didn't want you to see me like this.'

He dragged his gaze upwards from her sexy toes past her baggy clothes to find her hair sprouted from a messy pony-tail atop her head. She wore not a lick of make-up. Her eyes were huge pools of muted gold, her lips overly pink against her pale skin. She looked warm and ruffled and ready for bed. All over his body his skin tightened until it felt a size too small.

'I'm never sick,' she wailed. 'I'm so careful about everything as I can't afford to be sick. I take multi-vitamins. I drink two litres of water a day. I wash my hands so much I'm in danger of being compulsive. Though when you deal with the kind of stuff I deal with on a daily basis hand-washing is a must. I—' She came to an abrupt halt and began to breathe deep through her nose, her nostrils flaring, her cheeks bright pink.

She looked so wild. He wanted nothing more than to stride over to her and drag her into his arms and kiss her. His hands gripped so hard on the flowers he felt the stems crush.

But then her skin lost all semblance of colour. Her lips turned grey and she bolted. And the wretched sounds coming from her direction left him in no doubt that she was sincerely as sick as she'd said she was.

Still standing in the entrance, he had not one clue as to what to do. Surely he should go. She'd tried to warn him. And it wasn't as though he had any kind of qualifications. Did throwing up call for chicken soup? Or was that lemon and ginger tea?

When after a good three minutes he'd heard nothing of her at all, an overwhelming wave of concern that she'd gone and done something foolish like pass out overrode any kind of squeamishness he might have had. It seemed his gallantry was not yet at an end.

He closed the door behind him with a soft click, placed the flowers on the hall stand, shucked off his jacket, leaving it hanging over the back of an overstuffed couch upholstered in some awful pink-rose fabric, and rolled up his sleeves.

She wouldn't be the first girl whose hair he'd held off her face in a time of need. But she was the first girl he'd ever eaten humble pie for, and he had come all this way to see her so if this was how their second date was meant to play out, so be it.

Chelsea awoke with the thin morning sun teasing pink and pretty through the gauzy curtains of her bedroom window.

Her head felt like a bag of sand—dry, coarse and far too heavy to lift. Her mouth tasted as if she hadn't cleaned her teeth in a week. She put a shaky hand over her eyes and sat up.

When she opened them she saw a folded newspaper on her bedside table. A plate of dry crackers and crumbs proving some of them had been eaten during the night. A single perfect orange tulip in a water-filled spaghetti jar. And just like that her night came swimming back to her.

Damien.

While she'd spent most of the night sleeping on the couch or with her head over the toilet bowl, he'd been there. Not hovering, not mothering, just there. Watching TV. Reading a magazine by the window with the blinds open and the city iew painting its golden light upon his gorgeous profile. And ad he really made her toast with Vegemite, cooked himself dinner from the pathetic contents of her fridge *and* loaded her dishwasher?

She pulled herself from her bed, and realised she had no idea how she'd ended up there and in a frilly sleeveless neck-to-knee white cotton nightie she hadn't worn in years.

She grabbed her plush cream robe from the knob on the side of her cheval mirror, wrapped herself in it, tight, then headed out into the lounge room.

But all was quiet. Her kitchen was clean. And she was most definitely alone.

She poured a large glass of tap water, then headed to the lounge-room balcony. She opened the glass door a smidge, just enough to let in some morning sunshine, air, and comforting noise to drown out the plethora of embarrassing images in her head.

Whatever would she say to the guy when she saw him again? If she ever saw him again.

She dropped her head into her hands with a groan.

Damien stood below Chelsea's apartment building holding a bag filled with croissants, cheese and bacon rolls and three different types of fresh bread as well as two steaming hot black coffees, with his mobile pressed to his ear.

'Yeah, hello,' Caleb said at the other end of the line.

'It's Damien. I need you to do me a favour.'

After a loud long yawn Caleb said, 'Name it, buddy.'

'I need you to take the morning meeting today.'

Silence.

'Caleb?'

'Yeah, I'm still here. Just needed a moment to check the

number on my screen, make sure it was really you. You're going to be late?'

'Yes, I'm going to be late.'

'You realise it's a weekday, right?'

'Caleb—'

'Wow. I feel like I should commemorate this day with some kind of plaque, or parade, or something.'

'Commemorate by holding the morning meeting.'

'So what time will you be in?'

Damien glanced up at the third-storey balcony, which he now knew looked out from Chelsea's small lounge-room. Fine white curtains fluttered in a light breeze, meaning she was up padding about her apartment in just about the sexiest night attire he had ever come across.

'Not sure,' he said. 'Later. Maybe. I'll call you.'

'But, Damien—'

Damien tore his gaze away, used the key he'd pilfered from Chelsea's hall table, and walked into the foyer. 'Let the gang talk. Any info that sounds interesting, use. Check on each trader during the day, touch base with each of the platinum clients in my Rolodex, leave your office door open, and try to refrain from fondling any of the staff. I trust you.'

'I'm not sure you should.'

Damien jabbed the lift button with his elbow.

'Are you in the hospital?' Caleb asked. 'Have you been kidnapped? Does someone have a gun to your head?'

Damien watched his reflection on the inside of the silver panelled lift doors. 'I'm fine. In one piece. I just have something more important I need to do right now.'

'Like what?'

'I'm with Chelsea.'

Caleb paused. 'The hot get-back-on-the-horse cat lady?'

Damien breathed out slowly through his nose. 'If you call her that again I'll slap you silly.'

'Why?'

Why. *Why?* Damien ran a hand over his eyes and counted to ten. 'Because it's rude, that's why.'

'You're playing hookey for her? You met her, what, five minutes ago? And now she's what? Your girlfriend? Did you give her your varsity jacket?'

'Caleb. She's not my girlfriend. She's a girl in need of a helping hand. Nothing more.'

'Right. Though take one piece of advice from a veteran in the ways of the heart, won't you?'

'And that is…?'

'Be careful.'

His own words from the night before came swimming back to him. 'Careful about what, exactly?'

'This girl. You know who you are. Who your parents are. What they expect of you. You know what you have to offer. Just be careful about how and why she's managed to get her claws into you so quick. Be sure about your reasons, and hers.'

'Caleb,' he warned.

'I'm your best mate. Everything I say I say out of love. I've known you for umpteen years. Our parents play gin-soaked tennis together on a weekly basis, and that's a lifestyle I intend to protect so that when I grow in need of my first facelift I can take on the mantle of that fantastic life where they leave off. And I want you there by my side. Well, three or four blondes to my left, but in sight all the same.'

The lift binged. Damien's reflection wavered and split. The cream panelled walls of the hallway leading to Chelsea's apartment appeared before him. Images of sleep-ruffled caramel-blonde hair, wide golden eyes, and slim pale arms lifting trustingly so that he could slide a nightie over her half naked form swarmed over him and he pushed Caleb's words far to the back of his head.

'Gotta go,' he said, then hung up.

Chelsea heard a noise. She spun towards the front door to see the handle moving. She could hear keys jangling. Her heart thundered in her chest as she simply stood there staring at the door waiting for the intruder to enter.

It was Damien. Tall, dark, slick, and tidy in a dark grey pin-striped suit with a white shirt and deep blue, soft patterned tie the exact same colour as his eyes. A bakery bag was clenched between his teeth, and he held a cardboard tray of coffee she could smell from all the way across the room. She tidied her hair as she said, 'You scared the life out of me. How on earth did you get in here?'

Damien threw her keys back onto the hall table and pulled the bag from between his teeth. 'I stole your keys. I thought you might be up for some breakfast.'

She wrapped her arms around her stomach, less from any kind of modesty and more to quell the tumbling sensation rocketing through her at the very sight of him. At the knowledge that he *had* been there the night before. Had come expecting a date he'd had no doubt would this time end up horizontal, had instead found her a sick mess, fed her, undressed her, and stayed.

'Hungry?' he asked.

Her empty stomach rumbled. She took one small step his way. 'What have you got?'

'Just about one of everything from the bakery downstairs.' He dumped the paper bag and coffee tray on the table in the kitchen nook, then headed into her kitchen where he found her dinner plates, first try.

She plopped into a chair and tucked her knees against her chest, wrapping her arms tight around her calves as she watched him pull out cutlery and napkins.

She'd never had a man in her kitchen before. Well, apart from Kensey's Greg, who usually stood there looking lost until one or the other of them sent him scooting into the lounge while they looked after his every need.

But Damien looked so at home. He looked…right. *So* right something shifted behind her ribs with all the force and might and destructive power of a newly unstable tectonic plate until deeply affectionate warmth bled through her body like lava.

'So what happened to you last night?' Damien asked as he joined her at the table.

She pretended to pick at a small stain on the Chantilly lace tablecloth. 'I'm not sure. It could have been a bug from a dog washed up after a couple of days ago. Or maybe it was the leftover chicken teriyaki I had for breakfast yesterday.'

She glanced up and caught him watching her from over the top of his cup of coffee. All beautiful eyes, and expensive clothes and perfect hair. And attraction. Unguarded attraction so palpable it lay upon her shoulders like a warm blanket. She broke eye contact lest he saw a heightened version of the same emotion stampeding through her.

'I…I don't know how to thank you for last night,' she said. 'For the toast. And the tidying. And the company. That was most certainly above and beyond second-date duties.'

He smiled, and the disturbing shift inside her only deepened, making her feel as if her chest were now nothing more than a gaping hole waiting for him to fill it up. 'My pleasure,' he said. 'Now eat up.'

She reached forward and grabbed a croissant, eating a layer at a time. 'No early-morning meeting today then?'

He grabbed a roll and lathered it with butter. Then glanced up, stunning her silly with the cocky smile in his brilliant blue eyes. 'There is,' he said with a smile. 'Only this time I'm not going to be there.'

'Oh. And that's okay? You can do that?'

'As it turns out when you're the boss, you can do whatever you damn well please. And you? Are you going to do the sensible thing and call in sick?'

She hadn't even thought that far. She still felt weak after her night-long purge, but she'd worked through worse. 'I have no idea what kind of day I have today. But Phyllis would have blue-toothed me the appointment list before I left work last night.'

Damien looked at her as if she were speaking Swahili.

'My phone,' she explained. 'Have you seen it?'

'On the coffee-table, I do believe,' he said.

They both stood at the same time and made a move in that direction. Then stopped, staring at one another. He was close enough she could smell the scent of fresh bread on his clothes. She could see the soft haze of dark stubble on his cheeks.

His gaze flickered over her hair, her cheeks, her lips, which felt moist with croissant grease. And he leaned towards her. To kiss her. She could see it in his eyes, the set of his jaw, the tension in his shoulders.

She leaned back and pressed a hand to his chest and said out of the corner of her mouth, 'I have the worst morning breath have ever known.'

His eyes narrowed, as though he was thinking through whether he gave a damn, before he leaned away from her. He hand dropped. And as soon as it did he was there, gathering he close, pressing his lips against hers.

She closed her eyes and let him, her limbs relaxing wit every second he encouraged her to open her mouth to his.

When he pulled back he was smiling down at her with such desire she could have whimpered. 'I've wanted to do that since I first saw you last night.'

'Worth the wait?' she asked.

'You tell me.'

Instead she bit her lips, hiding her fuzzy teeth and just as fuzzy breath as she extricated herself from his divine embrace.

He made his way back to the kitchen table and she stumbled into the lounge, where she grabbed her phone and her thumbs ran purposefully over the keys until she found her appointments list. The day was as full as it ever was.

But with Damien lounging on the other side of her kitchen table, his gaze still lingering on her lips, not looking as if he had any intention of going anywhere this time, she pressed a number on her speed dial and waited for Phyllis to answer.

'You're not in until ten,' Phyllis chastised.

'Actually I'm calling to let you know I won't be in at all.' As she said the words out loud her legs began to shake, as though they could finally give into how weak she truly felt. She sat on the couch.

'You okay?'

'Sick as a dog, actually. But a day ought to do me.'

'Right. Good. Don't worry about a thing. I'll handle everything. Just you wait and see. I can manage this place, no worries. Or a place just like it if there's one on offer. So, you signed the papers for the loan yet?'

'Ah, no. Not yet.

'But you will.'

'I yet may.'

'Hmm. Well, rest up. Take care. Lie down. Eat well. Don't do anything to wear yourself out, okay?'

She glanced at Damien, who had his right leg crossed over

his left as he read the morning paper. His pinstriped trousers strained against the muscle of his thighs. His pale shirt stretched across his broad torso. His tongue darted out to catch a crumb on the edge of his lip. And all Chelsea wanted to do was crawl up onto his lap and wear herself out thoroughly.

'I'll see you tomorrow,' she said, then rang off.

Damien closed the paper before glancing up at her, pinning her to the lounge-chair with his dark gaze. 'Day off?'

She nodded, and turned her phone over and over in her palm.

He glanced at the coffee and bakery feast on the table, then back at her. 'This is a first for me.'

'Me too,' she admitted.

He picked up a piece of hot flaky bread and took a bite. And only after he'd swallowed it down did he break the silence again. Saying, 'Whatever will we do to fill in the time?'

CHAPTER NINE

CHELSEA again woke with light filtering through the backs of her eyelids. Only this time she was curled up on the pink floral couch in the front room wearing velour track pants and a long sleeved T-shirt. She blinked to clear her fuzzy vision and the display on the mobile phone on the coffee-table read 4:15. She could only assume it was in the afternoon.

The TV was on with the sound turned down low, which wasn't all that unusual. She liked having the TV on when home so that she didn't feel as if she was alone.

What was unusual was that her head was resting on a pair of strong male thighs.

She peeked up into Damien's face. He was completely immersed in the action on the TV. She glanced back, and over the half-empty bowl of popcorn realised he was watching Doris Day sling it out with Howard Keel in *Calamity Jane*. She bit back the laughter that bubbled into her throat.

She moved slightly then, trying to extricate herself before he realised she was awake. But when she went to move the arm beneath her head she realised she was trapped. Her hand was tucked neatly between his warm thighs. She sent a quick prayer to the heavens in the hopes that was as far as it had ventured while she slept.

She managed to slide her hand less than an inch before his thighs clamped down. Her gaze shot northward to meet with a pair of smiling blue eyes.

'Good afternoon,' Damien said, his deep sexy voice washing over her like a shower of warm milk.

'Hi,' she said, her voice soft and croaky with sleep.

'Sweet dreams?'

The last hazy remains of what had been a pretty hot and detailed dream still lingered on the edge of her mind. She looked away before he realised he had been the star. 'How long was I out?'

'A couple of hours.'

'Wow. I haven't had a nap during the day since… I can't remember when.'

'You needed it.'

She tried to sit up again, and his thighs only clamped down tighter. 'May I have my hand back?'

'Don't know how I feel about that.'

'Well, I have *no* feeling left from my wrist down, so it won't do you any good to keep it there.'

Damien held eye contact for a few heated seconds longer before slowly releasing his grip. She slid her hand from the space and brought it out into the cold of the open air.

She sat up, rubbing at her fingers, but there was no way she could regather the kind of warmth they'd felt being so near his skin.

He grabbed the remote from the coffee-table to turn off the TV.

'Oh, no,' she said, 'don't stop on my account. You a big Doris Day fan?'

Damien's eyes narrowed, piercing her until her lethargic heartbeat kicked up to a jogging rate. 'I had been watching

Ocean's Eleven, the Rat Pack version. This simply came on afterwards and I knew if I moved to get the remote I'd wake you.'

'How benevolent.'

'Just call me Nurse Halliburton. I seem to have a flare for it. Odd considering the only time anyone in my family has been in need of a hospital has been the rehab kind.' A smile pulled at his cheeks.

She tucked her feet up onto the couch and wrapped her arms around her knees for protection. But nothing could have protected her from the rush of feelings when he reached out and ran a finger down her cheek.

'My trousers have left a crease mark,' he said.

Her hand flew to her face. She could only imagine how she must have looked. Even after her long hot bath, and the three times she'd cleaned her teeth, her hair must by now have again looked a mess. Her eyes puffy. Pink-cheeked with the image of wool trousers branded into her face like some kind of over-familiar tattoo. She let her hair fall forward to act as a curtain.

Damien's hand reached out again, pushing her hair behind her ear.

'Chelsea,' he said, his voice insistent. He looked so deep into her eyes she could scarcely breathe. His hand continued sweeping her hair over her ear, and along her neck. Over and over again. 'There's something I want to say to you, to make clear, before you fall asleep on me again.'

Her hand dropped to her lap. 'Okay.'

'I wanted to tell you, now, while we're here alone, with no distractions, bar Doris Day's finest hour on film, that sitting here, watching you sleep like an angel in my lap, I have come to the conclusion…'

He stopped and took a deep breath. Chelsea held hers until her lungs felt as if they were about to burst.

'I can't go another day without making love to you, Miss London.'

Chelsea's heart thundered in her chest as hard as she'd ever remembered feeling it thunder. The reciprocal words caught in her throat as pride and fear and hope and history egged her to hold her cards close to her chest. She'd never felt like this before in her whole life. Never experienced this kind of euphoria just by looking into another person's eyes. Each moment with him was a gamble with the chances of losing her guarded heart to him becoming greater with every passing moment. Nevertheless she gave into temptation and threw the dice.

'I want nothing more either, Mr Halliburton.'

He cupped her cheek, held her gaze and said, 'Then I also need you to know that I recently came out of my last relationship just shy of bloodshed. I don't plan to bore you with the gory details, but suffice it to say I'm not on the hunt for someone new to fill that place in my life.'

Chelsea swallowed hard, but Damien kept eye contact so she couldn't move.

'But,' he continued, 'I can't get you out of my mind. Your face, your lips, your skin haunts me and I can't deny that I want you.'

Chelsea's instincts screamed at her to listen and listen hard. He was openly admitting he wasn't in the market for permanence or responsibility. It wasn't just all in her head. Now was her chance to pull out, before she became the next in line to bleed for him.

But as she looked into his beautiful eyes she knew it was already too late. The temptation of him was simply too great. She reached out and ran a trembling finger over his lips. Every second seemed to stretch out before her, longer and longer until he leaned slowly in, and placed his lips upon hers.

It was the sweetest kiss of her life. His mouth gently moved against hers, coaxing more and more from her with every touch. And every conscious thought, every warring emotion, slipped away bar the feel of the man at her side.

He tasted of fresh roasted coffee and hazelnuts. Any hint of cologne from the night before had been replaced by the smell of pure warm male skin. The slight stubble on his chin rasped lightly against her chin, so that the goose-bumps trailing every inch of exposed skin did not for one second let up.

As the emotions inside her swelled to breaking-point, she pulled away the tiniest possible amount, and whispered, 'What if I'm contagious?'

His breath whispered against her lips. 'I'm willing to take the chance if you are.'

She looked into his eyes, and knew he was asking more of her than the possibility of sharing germs. He was asking her to take a chance on him, to let this kiss play out to its inevitable conclusion. He was asking her to dream big, damn the consequences.

She took a long slow breath, and nodded.

He blinked, just once and the deal was sealed.

This time when his lips met hers it was with more pressure, more urgency, and she couldn't have pulled away if she'd tried. Not that she wanted to try. All she wanted was to sink into him. To lose herself and find herself all at once.

Her hand moved beneath the hair at the back of his neck, sliding into the soft thick texture the way she'd wanted to ever since she'd first laid eyes on him. And she moved until she was lying on his lap, his strong grip holding her upright.

Then she opened her mouth to him and with it her powerless heart.

The kiss went on for ever, as they got to know one another's

taste, and feel, and the particular things that made each othe
shiver and sigh.

Finally, his hand moved down her back, sliding along he
spine until she curved into him. He reached the top of her trac
pants and didn't stop there. His hand dived beneath the waist
line and managed to find skin on its first try.

His large warm palm cupped her left cheek and lifted he
gently towards him. Deeper into his arms. If he was looking fo
a new way to make her shiver and sigh he'd found it.

She let her own hands drop to blindly find the buttons of hi
shirt. The kiss didn't let up as she undid each one and pushe
the starched cotton off his shoulders, her hands stroking ove
hot, rolling muscles of his arms, which were far more beauti
ful than she'd even imagined.

As her hands moved around to the front, to course over hi
perfect chest, scraping against a smattering of dark, curling hai
until her fingernails reached the fly of his trousers, Damien'
hands slid up to grip hers, pulling everything to a halt.

The kiss broke apart so suddenly the two of them came u
gulping for air.

'What's wrong?' she asked, turning her fingernails into he
palms. If he rejected her for a third time she'd never forgiv
herself for being so consciously imprudent. For trusting a ma
who'd all but told her she shouldn't.

He shook his head, his eyes so dark she couldn't hav
guessed they were blue if she didn't know better.

'No?' she asked, wondering what she could possibly hav
done wrong.

'Yes,' he said. 'God yes. Just. Well. Hell.' With that h
scooped her up in his arms.

She let out a whoop as her legs were flung into the air an
her arms instinctively wrapped tight about his neck. And whe

he began to jog, no, run, into the bedroom she laughed so hard she was sure Mrs Luchek next door would have heard her had she not been away.

Chelsea took about half a second to worry if the bed was made before she landed upon it with a bounce. 'Whoa. I think I felt the earth move.'

Damien said nothing. He just stood at the end of the bed with his white business shirt open and hanging off his shoulders like a pirate on the front of an old romance novel. His breaths rose and fell in great slow moves and her mouth went completely dry. He was, quite simply, the sexiest man to ever walk the face of the earth.

He slid the shirt from his back and let it drop where it fell. If his body had felt beautiful it looked, if at all possible, even more daunting. Tanned, sculpted, mature. This was no teenager with whom she was exploring, no leftover New Uniform high-school fantasy come to life.

Damien Halliburton was all man.

And as he walked towards the bed, popping the button of his trousers, unzipping his fly, she felt a sudden need to scurry to the head of the bed, but instead grabbed a hold of a hunk of her angora throw and hung on tight lest she pass out from pure anticipation.

He stepped out of his trousers and his black silk boxers in one go until he was naked from the top of his dark head to the flats of his large feet. He was ready for her in every way possible. Veins stood out on his arms as though he was straining. His jaw was sharp and his lips tightly clenched. His erection was quite simply glorious. And rather than let her simply admire he just kept on coming.

She tore her T-shirt over her head and the moment his knee hit the bed she was reaching up and wrapping a hand behind his neck and drawing him down to her.

He held himself away, only just, but enough so that he wouldn't crush her with his heavy weight, while his mouth held back nothing, plundering hers with his tongue, until she felt deliciously bruised.

He lowered himself to her side so that he could free his hands. To caress her stomach, which quivered beneath his touch. To brush her hair from her neck before following through with an array of searing kisses. When he gently nudged aside the strap of her bra with the tip of his nose and scraped the very bottom of her neck his tenderness almost broke her.

'So you are a shoulder girl,' he murmured into her neck, before nipping lightly outwards until his teeth sank into the soft flesh just before her shoulder-bone.

Her head dropped back to the bed and she arched into him. 'Who knew?' she managed to say.

'Well, if that works, I wonder…' He reached behind her, unclipped her bra with one hand, slid it away, then threw it to the other side of the room. His eyes turned impossibly dark as they roamed over her breasts, which felt so very heavy against her chest.

'Which one first?' He lowered himself so that she could feel his hot breath whisper across her breasts. Her nipples hardened into tight peaks as she fought against the urge to grab him by the back of the head and pull him down to whichever breast was closest.

He went left, laying a row of kisses beneath until she could have cried out. His tongue darted out, leaving a trail of moisture until his mouth closed over her nipple. A spasm rocketed through her, lifting her hips off the bed.

He lightly grazed her with his teeth before moving over to the right breast and following the same pattern, which only made her ache more, knowing exactly what was coming next.

Once she was sure she could stand it no more, he began kissing down the sensitive inside of her arm. There was little she could do but let her arm hang limply in his care as wave after wave of warmth spilled outward from every touch of his mouth.

His hand trailed a gentle course along the beltline of her track pants, and then he blew across her naked stomach until a wave of agonising goose-bumps sprang up. Her hand flew to rub the skin prickles away but he stopped her.

'Uh-uh. This part is mine now.'

She lifted her head enough to catch his eye. 'Says who?'

'Says the guy who is about to show you why you should stop yabbering and just let him do as he pleases.'

As he spoke his fingers stroked back and forth across her stomach, moving ever lower with each caress, until they began to push her pants lower and lower past her hips.

Her neck muscles gave way, her head collapsed, and her arm flopped over her eyes until all she could see was the backs of her eyelids. All she could hear was the heavy sound of her own breath. And all she could feel was the smooth slide of velour down her thighs, past her calves and off.

The central heating was on low to hold the cold autumn afternoon at bay. But her skin felt as if it were on fire. As if she was blushing from head to foot. Her blood vessels must have been on overload.

The bed shifted as Damien moved. Her imagination went crazy as she tried to foresee what he would do next. And just as she thought she couldn't take the wait another second his hands closed around her feet.

His thumbs rubbed the soles, his fingers sliding against the muscles of her ankles until she sighed with the luscious pleasure of it. They moved up her calves, making her thank her lucky stars she'd shaved that morning. Once they hit her knees she began to shake. Her self-control broke down, inch by beautiful inch.

His caress was so gentle as his hands rounded her thighs, kneading ever so slightly before delving in between and pressing her legs until they fell apart. One hand continued up her side, his thumb brushing into her navel, then up her ribcage as he again rested beside her.

His mouth claimed hers in the very same instant his other hand reached the juncture between her thighs.

Her groan was swallowed by his insistent mouth, his searching tongue. She writhed beneath him, her senses confused as to whether to let her concentrate on the delicious sensation of his lips playing, oh, so gently, and, oh, so tenderly with hers, or to let go and give into the feel of his fingers touching her, stroking her, sliding against her flesh with ever so slightly increasing pressure and pace that her whole body thrummed.

She began to peak all too soon. She tilted her head sideways and begged him, 'Wait.'

'Not going to happen.' His gravelly voice almost sent her over the edge all on its own.

'I don't want this to end,' she said, her voice now a desperate whimper. But it was the truth. In her blissful state she could truly imagine holding back, slowing down, and finding a way to feel like this until the end of time.

'Too bad,' Damien said, then kissed her until she was completely breathless.

With that, she finally allowed herself to feel every ounce of pleasure. The kiss, the caress, the weight of him pressing against her came together as a slow boiling-point vibration coursing from her centre and spreading out through every nerve ending to the tips of her fingers and toes.

The hand over her eyes reached out and clung to his shoulder. Her right knee bent and spilled sideways until she was completely open to him, body and soul.

And the heat, and shakes, and pleasure and lack of control came to a head until her whole body went numb for one brief idyllic second before sensation returned and rolled through her like a tidal wave, destroying every shred of restraint in its wake, leaving her so ragged she had not even enough energy to lift a finger.

'Open your eyes,' Damien said an eon later. She struggled against the heavy weight of her eyelids before she was able to blink into the late afternoon light, which sent the cream walls in her room a bright burnt orange.

He looked deep into her eyes, and she was too shattered to hide what she felt for him. But what she saw in his eyes soon woke her up.

Burgeoning compassion. Genuine, honest to goodness care that he had in no way hurt her. Which meant that he believed he had the power within himself to do so. Which in turn meant that, not only was he arrogant as all get out, he also saw far more in her expression than she cared to reveal.

She broke eye contact, crossed her legs, lifted herself up onto her elbows and leaned up to kiss him, to run her tongue along his bottom lip before taking it between her teeth and tugging him until it must have hurt a little bit.

She reached out until she found the evidence of just how very turned on he still was. She looked up at him from beneath her eyelashes and said, 'Your turn.'

And the look in his eyes changed. Concern transformed into heat. Desire. Self-interest. That she could handle.

'Condom?' he asked, and she pointed to the top bedside drawer. He reached out with one long arm, found what he was looking for, tore the packet open with his teeth and was sheathed and ready to go before she even had the chance to take another breath.

And then he pulled her to him, kissing her with newfound intensity, crushing her against his broad chest, wrapping his leg around her until she felt so small in his arms. If he continued doing this to her, making her feel so powerful and vulnerable all at once, she was terrified she might start to cry.

So she gathered every vestige of strength she had and rolled him over until she was lying on top of him, one leg casually thrown across his.

At first his face registered surprise, but then the gleam in his eyes took on more light as a sinful smile spread across his face. He rolled onto his back until she lay fully atop him.

'Helpful as always,' she said.

He grinned, like the wolf just before he revealed himself as a villain to Little Red Riding Hood. 'Mmm. Though I don't know if there is a scout badge for my brand of helpfulness.'

She pushed herself into a sitting position, nudged herself against him until his eyes closed and his mouth fell open. 'Next time I find myself up close and personal with a scout leader I'll suggest it.'

His eyes flew open and his hands snuck out and grabbed her by the buttocks, stilling her, controlling her still even while he looked beyond ready to lose all control. 'It's not smart to tease me about being up close and personal with another man while I have you like this.'

'You don't have me,' she said. 'Not yet.'

She reached up and held her hot hair off her sweaty neck. Damien's eyes zeroed in on her breasts and glazed over. She lifted onto her knees, and he groaned. Then she sank down over him until her eyes fell closed with bliss.

And he began to rock. The rhythm so easy, so unhurried, she gave in and went along for the ride.

He ran his palm down her front, moulding her left breast, then running lovingly along each rib before landing across her hip, his thumb resting at the juncture of where their bodies met. And there it stayed. Seemingly accidental, but so erotic Chelsea found her desire building with such unexpected and sudden force she fell back and grabbed a hold of his thighs.

The change in position only made the pleasure all the greater. For her and for him. She saw it in the darkening of his eyes. The sweat beads on his brow. The tendons straining in his neck. She felt it in the grip on her hips, in the impossible deepening pressure inside her.

The rocking soon quickened. The heat between them scorching until she too was lathered in a layer of sweat. She could taste it on her upper lip. Feel it cruelly tickling every inch of her hot skin.

'Chelsea,' he called out and it was enough to loosen any last withholding place inside her. She let her head fall back, pressed her hips into his. She left just enough room for his thumb to slide between them and as though he could read her every move he did as he was told.

Her whole body throbbed. Ached. Needle-sharp stings pricked her all over as a draught washed across her damp skin.

Then everything changed as Damien swelled inside her, as his thighs clenched beneath her hands and a primal roar tore through the heated silence.

With that she too let go, every sensation shrinking to the point where their bodies met before exploding in a burst of stars behind her eyes.

And as she finally fell apart in his arms, her cheeks burned hot with sweat and carefully hidden tears.

CHAPTER TEN

DAMIEN lay beside Chelsea as again she slept.

The faded top sheet covered her body, revealing only her smooth creamy neck and her soft jaw hidden partially behind feathers of her caramel-coloured hair. He braced himself on one arm and reached out, brushing her hair from her cheek, letting it slide over his fingers, smooth as silk.

She moved beside him. The sheet over her lithe body slid and shifted and settled until one bare breast was naked to the night air.

He stared at it like a drowning man would stare at a lifebelt, fighting the overwhelming desire to reach out and run a hand down her side. To wake her. To take her again.

Instead he ran a fast hand over his unshaven jaw, abrading the skin on his palm. For as it turned out the events of the evening had done nothing to quell his desire for her. It had only made him want more.

She was on the verge of waking. He should go.

He'd known her, what, two days? Three? They'd crammed a hell of a lot of getting-to-know-you stuff into that time, but it certainly hadn't made him take some dramatic about-turn in his life. He'd been on the market for a fling and he'd found one. It would be cruel to allow Chelsea to hope she was dealing with any other kind of man, especially after what he'd seen in her eyes as she lay sated in his arms.

Gathering his will-power, he slid out of her bed, found his suit trousers draped over an upholstered chair in the corner. He pulled them on for the third day running, zipped up, left his top button undone, then sat in the chair and watched her for who knew how long until she stirred again, this time her eyes flickering open.

'Hi,' she said, her voice husky.

He clenched his hands together to stop himself from bolting back into bed with her and damning the consequences.

She half sat up, demurely taking the sheet with her, her creamy skin lit blue by the moonlight spilling through her gauzy curtains. 'Is everything okay?'

Okay? No, it was not okay. Everything was moving too fast. They were both getting in over their heads. If he saw her again he'd only continue half-heartedly and end up hurting her. Unless…

Unless he was completely honest right now. Unless the boundaries and limits were spelt out in absolute final detail. 'I want to see you again,' he blurted before he could change his mind.

Her eyes softened, darkened. 'So come get me.'

He stuck a fingernail into the palm of the other hand to keep himself grounded. 'Not yet,' he said, and her eyes widened enough that he knew she was now fully awake.

He took a deep breath, filling his lungs to bursting point before he said what he needed to say. 'Chelsea, when I told you earlier that I recently came out of a bad relationship, I should have made myself perfectly clear.'

She blinked up at him, so sweet, so undeserving of what he was about to ask of her.

'The relationship was fine. Bonnie and I dated, exclusively, for two and a half years. We lived together for the past several months. Her parents know my parents. Our work timetables meshed neatly. I thought everything was perfectly comfortable. Until a month ago she gave me an ultimatum. Marry her or leave. It took me less than half a second to decide.'

She watched him carefully for a few moments before saying, 'Please tell me you left.'

He laughed despite himself. She was such a trouper. But she also couldn't hide the deep breaths, which proved she wasn't as ignorant of what he was trying to tell her as she made out.

'I left,' he said. 'So fast she barely had time to call me a heartless bastard more than three times before I was out the door.'

'I don't blame her. Sounds like you acted like a total cad,' she said, flicking her hair over her shoulder in a move that was pure self-defence. 'So why are you telling me this now?'

'Because I came into this with no expectations and now, even if it does indeed make me a heartless bastard, after last night I know I'm not yet ready to walk away from you.'

At that a slight smile tugged at her cheeks, at her soft lips; he did his all to not lose himself there and dragged his eyes upwards.

'But one day I will walk away. It's my *modus operandi*. I'm being utterly honest when I tell you that I'm not built for anything lasting or exclusive. It's not in my genetic make-up. All I have to offer is good company when it suits us both and, I think we can agree, some pretty great sex.'

He let that last word hang on the air, hoping it might be the thing to sway her. It sure swayed him.

She didn't say anything. Didn't agree, or disagree. She didn't cry, or rant, or toss her hair and feign indifference. She just watched him, her eyes steady on his as she let his statement sink in.

'I could be making a total ass of myself,' he said, giving himself and her one last out, 'even bringing this up. You could well have been ready to tell me to sod off and never see you again. And if that's the case, I wouldn't blame you either.'

He felt enormous relief at having set the ground rules before this went any further. Though his lungs felt tighter and tighter with every passing second as he awaited her verdict.

Finally, she shifted, lifting herself upright until the sheet fell away, leaving her naked to the waist. Then she lifted the sheet for him, welcoming him back into her bed.

Weak sunlight tickled the backs of Chelsea's eyelids. A self-indulgent smile made its way across her face before she even opened her eyes.

She stretched her beautifully aching limbs and reached out to find the other side of the bed was empty. Cool. Ruffled to prove she hadn't dreamt the events of the night, but devoid of Damien all the same.

She slid her naked form from the bed and grabbed her gown before heading out of the bedroom only to discover the apartment was silent. There was no gorgeous dark-haired man sitting in the kitchen nook, no newspaper splayed out over her small table, no breakfast waiting for her.

She could picture such a scene so clearly it felt like more than a memory. Or a wish. But the reality she was given was that he wasn't there.

Which was fine. Really. Especially since the tenderness with which he'd made love to her when he'd come back to bed after his little speech had tempered the difficult words, and she'd fallen asleep assured that not kicking him out on his ear had been the right move.

She ignored the nagging, dissenting buzzing in her head as

she shuffled into the kitchen, where a white folded piece of paper lay atop the coffee percolator. He'd left her a note. A smile stretched across her face until she noticed the percolator was cold.

If she was to be consistent and continue with the 'actions speak louder than words' mantra she was clinging to, no matter what the note said the cold percolator told her something far more potent.

Damien had foregone his usual aromatic morning brew as he hadn't wanted to wake her. To face her. To kiss her goodbye.

The buzzing in her ears soon became a twisting in her heart as the enormity of what she'd agreed to bubbled over her.

She closed her eyes and clung to the kitchen bench. 'You daft mug. You know your feelings for the guy are already far too strong to accept something so casual. Of course kicking him out on his ear was what needed to be done. But, no, you just had to have him again.'

Her mobile rang and she was so tense she jumped in fright, the note crumpling in her palm.

She checked the number. It was him. She took a deep breath, put on her smoothest phone voice, and answered. 'Chelsea speaking.'

'Good morning, sunshine,' he said, his voice thick with suggestion.

Her uncooperative knees turned to jelly and she slumped against the kitchen bench, clutching her gown shut over her naked breasts, which were already straining as though they too were wondering why he wasn't still there.

'I'm taking you out tonight,' he said. 'I've seen how you react to a good feed.'

She tried desperately to find a way to give herself more time. Either to come to terms with his terms or to extricate herself from this thing without looking a complete fool. And in the end came up with, 'What if I'm busy? I might have a date with someone else.'

'So you'll cancel,' he insisted.

A shot of searing frustration jolted her upright. He was the one who wasn't making any promises about keeping his goods just for her, for goodness' sake. 'What if I don't want to cancel?'

'I…I don't quite know what to say to that.'

She could feel his own impatience pouring through the phone. And this time when she chose to pay more attention to his actions than to his words all she could see was his level of care, the look in his eye when he was about to kiss her, the fact that he regarded her highly enough to be so honest with her in the first place.

She slapped a hand over her forehead as she said, 'Oh, relax, Damien. I'm coming out with you.'

'Tease,' he said, the lingering hum in his voice telling her he liked it.

'Bossy boots,' she shot back. 'So where are we going?'

'A little Jamaican bar around the corner from my office we often go to after work. How do you like rum?'

She shrugged. 'Don't mind it.'

'And bars full of men in suits?'

'Love them to bits.'

'Mmm, I thought you might. So how about it? You, me, a hundred of my closest friends, a leather couch and a couple of rum toddies to keep us warm this cool autumn evening.'

Right, so he didn't want to be her boyfriend, but he didn't mind introducing her to the people in his life. As what? She ran her hand over her eyes.

'So what does one wear to a Jamaican pub to meet your closest friends?'

'Ah, I'd suggest not a lot of buttons. Or layers.'

Chelsea blinked, having had no idea that this season buttons must have been some kind of fashion *faux pas*.

'So long as it's easy for me to take off,' he clarified, and her tension didn't subside one little bit. It only morphed all too easily into a flurry of imaginings about him sliding a dress over her head versus tugging trousers over her thighs.

I can do this, she thought. *I'm strong. I can put up with a lot to have more of this man.*

'I'll pick you up around eight,' he said.

She nodded.

He laughed. 'Have a good day, Chelsea.' Then he hung up.

Chelsea put the phone down, and realised she still had his note crunched up in her hot palm. She unfurled it.

'Early meeting,' it read. 'Seriously. I'll call you. D.'

With a growl she tossed it into the sink where a few drops of moisture made the blue writing bleed.

That evening Chelsea sat on a backless barstool, trying to keep her back straight, and running her finger back and forth through a drop of condensation that had slithered from the glass of her Jamaican Cobbler to the shiny black bar.

It had been a long day. She'd had to contend with a phone call from Kensey, who'd pressed and pressed until Chelsea had filled her in on as much of her past couple of days as she could while keeping the conversation clean. Another from *Chic* magazine, pushing her interview up a week. And yet another from the bank manager wondering if she'd signed the papers as yet.

All the while she'd managed to find plenty of time in her over-packed day to go over every second of her relationship with Damien all the way up until he'd had to sit her down and give her *the talk*.

She could feel a tension headache coming on.

She glanced over her shoulder to look for Damien, who had disappeared to find a quiet corner amongst the fake palm trees less than five minutes earlier when his mobile had rung.

But all she could see apart from the blinding green black and yellow décor of the up-market city bar was a sea of New Uniform types. All grown up yet no less sure of themselves and their privileged place in the world. She was pretty sure Damien would never have made a speech like the one he had to any one of the glossy nymphettes gyrating on the dance floor. He wouldn't have needed to. As they skimmed their hands over one young guy after another they looked as if they understood the transitory nature of affection.

Thankfully his 'friends' hadn't arrived as yet so she hadn't had to try to be whatever he introduced her to them as being.

'So sorry,' Damien said as he came from nowhere to slide onto the seat beside hers. 'My father after his weekly report.'

Chelsea raised what she hoped might be a sophisticated eyebrow. 'You're a little old for that, don't you think?'

'He's retired. Bored out of his mind. Mum has a bunch of cronies over for drinks every Friday night and I think I'm his way of feeling like he's still out there climbing the corporate ladder rather than spending his days following my mother around like a good little lapdog.'

'Yet they're divorced.'

'That they are. And so much happier that way. No strings. Meaning they can do whatever they please when they please. They just so happen to be pleased with one another at the moment.'

He grinned at the idea. He actually grinned. As though he thought she was so on the same page as him about those nutty types who thought marriage and commitment were something to aim for, she'd feel the overwhelming need to grin back.

She rubbed at her now throbbing temple.

'And speaking of dear old Dad, he has some experience in banking too, you know,' he said. 'I'm sure he'd be prepared to look over your loan papers if you'd like him to. He'd be able to spot any dodgy loopholes in an instant and it would make him feel like he still has his finger on the pulse.'

She continued staring at Damien as though she'd never seen him before. He was willing to introduce her to his friends and his parents even though he wasn't willing to promise he would ever be there when she woke up in the morning. She would never inflict any guy on Kensey and her family unless it was serious.

'I'm not yet sure I'm even going to go that way,' she said.

'Why on earth not?'

She closed her eyes for a second and reminded herself *never* to let Kensey anywhere near him, no matter how long they stayed together. She'd never be allowed to make a decision on her own.

She opened her eyes to be blinded by the kaleidoscope of colour shining from the mirrored wall behind the bar. The drum-heavy music now pulsated inside her head. And she thought, *Well, if you can't beat 'em...*

'Do you want to dance?' she asked.

Damien looked at her as if she'd grown an extra head, but when the dance song eased into a slow and ultra-romantic beat he put his untouched drink down, gave the barman a wink, then took her hand and eased her through the crowd out onto the dance floor.

Half a dozen women gave him the eye before giving her a once-over. In her tight jeans and black off-the-shoulder top she felt as if she ought to have at least looked like she belonged. Still she grabbed his hand tighter.

He spun her out and then into his arms until he held her in the classic ballroom hold. She had to look up to see into his eyes, which were smiling down at her. Pristine pools of blue.

The lights turned low, with only sporadic shafts of disco-ball light flickering over his face, proving his eyes never left hers.

The words of the song permeated. Talking of fear and tears and not knowing whether to hang on tight or go back to being lonely and confused. She leant her head on his shoulder and blocked them out.

As they slowly moved around the hardwood floor she felt their bodies meld closer together of their own accord. She managed to slide inside the soft lining of his suit jacket until her stomach rested flush against his with only two swathes of thin cotton separating her building warmth from his.

There, she thought, her whole body sighing in relief. In his arms everything felt okay. Better. As if she weren't a fool agreeing to his terms even though she knew she was a thousand miles further down the road towards wanting this to last for ever than he was.

Whether he leaned down or she stood on tiptoe first, she had no idea. Their lips met, gentle yet insistent. Her eyes closed and she drank him in.

His kiss was like magic, pouring warmth and unstoppered emotion through her body until she reached up and ran her hands around his neck, clinging to him, impressing herself upon him in every way possible.

His tongue lapped the roof of her mouth, sending her into some kind of free fall. She tipped her head to the side and opened her mouth to him, and with it her whole heart.

He let go of her hand and reached down to cup her buttocks, pushing her against the evidence of just how turned on he was.

'Not here,' she said against his mouth.

His eyes flickered open, dark and heavy with desire. She would have put money on the fact he hadn't even remembered where they were. She was momentarily tormented by the fact at times he was so sure, so clear-headed, and other times keeping his hands off her seemed more than he could bear.

'Where?' he said.

'Let's get out of here.' She dragged him from the dance floor, through the heaving, glittery crowd.

'But we haven't had dinner.'

'I don't need a feed to put me in the right mood.'

'So it would seem.' Damien had found his head after all. He moved in tight behind her as he hastily collected their things from the cloakroom, nodded a quick goodbye to the bouncer and herded her out into the chill evening air. She shivered; he gathered her close.

They scooted around the corner into the car park, and Damien was off driving down the street towards Chelsea's apartment before she'd strapped herself in.

She leaned back against the leather headrest in the passenger seat of Damien's gorgeous primrose-yellow Austin-Healey Sprite. The top was down, her hair was flying, she felt just fabulous, as if every drudging daily concern had been whipped out of her ears to be lost on the wind.

This was the life. The kind of life she could be living hanging with the likes of Damien Halliburton of the Halliburton Halliburtons. This was the fire, electricity, excitement, danger, no care for the consequences she'd *known* he had to offer before she'd even known his name.

'Where can I get me one of these?' she yelled.

'One of what?'

'This car. Tell me they go for a song. Please.'

'More like an opera than a song.'

Damien glanced sideways and offered her a sexy smile. Their eyes locked and held. She couldn't wait to get back to her place and knew he couldn't either.

'Hang on,' he said. Dragging the car down into such a low gear it groaned, he turned off the main road and headed towards the Docklands precinct with its wide open spaces cleared for future high-rise developments and phenomenal view of the Melbourne city skyline.

The second the car pulled to a stop atop a patch of grass hidden behind a billboard they were in one another's arms.

They came together with such force, such unbridled passion, it was as though they'd been away from one another's touch for years, not mere minutes.

Fast and furious, she thought. Then right on top of that… *It can't last for ever.* For Damien the relationship would burn out, or she would from the sheer force of keeping her true feelings from him.

Blocking out her contrary thoughts, Chelsea was in Damien's lap and he'd flipped the seat back as far as it would go. In that moment she regretted wearing jeans. She wanted him so desperately. Needed to lose herself in the sensations he created in her to stop the torrent of rebellious emotion sweeping over her.

He groaned. 'I haven't done this since I was a teenager. I only hope I'm still as flexible.'

'If you're not, I am,' she said, and his next groan was lost in her kiss.

He was right, she thought five minutes later when both of their shirts had been tossed into the back seat. They sure could make some beautiful love together.

So how could he be so wrong about the rest?

Her eyes flew open, and she was momentarily shocked by

the sight of the Melbourne skyline looming huge and glittering before her. The sky was black and clear, the moon large and luminous lighting the glossy dew on the grass around the car. She shivered.

'You can't be cold,' Damien said, wrapping his arms about her and pulling her to him. Her breasts scraped against the hair on his chest as he only added to her physical pleasure by biting into that magical spot where her neck met her shoulder.

But even that wasn't enough to cover up the certainty that none of it was enough. And never would be. She was in love with him. She wanted a future with him. What she didn't want was to see him day in and day out knowing it was only one step closer to the time she'd have to say goodbye.

'Stop,' she whispered, but her throat caught the word before it made it to the outside world. So with greater force she said 'Damien, no more.' And she pushed him away.

'Are you all right?' he asked, his voice barely more than a rumble. 'Did I hurt you?'

She sat up, her eyes frantically searching the back seat for her bra, her top, anything to make her feel less painfully naked. She slid her top over herself, inside out though it was. And had to swipe a tear that she felt sliding from her left eye.

She pulled herself off his lap and he helped her, running his hands down her arms as though checking for broken bones. He glanced up into her eyes and must have seen the anguish therein as he swallowed, and his own eyes were suddenly filled with such care it made her choke.

'Chelsea, what did I do?'

'Nothing,' she blabbed. 'Truly. It's me. All me. I just…' God, how could she say this without sounding ridiculous, and giving herself away completely? 'This affair, or whatever it is we have going on, I don't think I can do it.'

Damien leaned slowly back into his seat and ran a hand through his hair. 'But last night… I thought we'd agreed it was what we both wanted.'

'I know, I did. I thought I did. But as it turns out I can't.'

'So in the past twenty-four hours what's changed?

I've fallen in love with you, you idiot!

'I've changed my mind. It's a woman's prerogative.'

He swore loud enough it seemed to echo across the large empty block of land. He reached into the back seat of the car and grabbed his shirt and jacket, tugging them over his arms as her words sank in. And when he spoke again his voice was deathly quiet. 'I never promised you anything.'

'I know.' Hers was barely above a whisper.

'So this is it. You're breaking up with me?'

God, was she really?

'What difference does it make?' she asked, prolonging the final step. 'You said it yourself, there will be an end point. I just think it would be better to end it now.'

'I don't agree.'

Did he have to make it so hard? Couldn't he see her heart was breaking for him? In that moment she so wanted to reach out and beat her hands on his chest until he could see the truth. Instead her anger turned to words.

Her voice was chilly when she said, 'The last thing I need in my life is another man who is going to let me down.'

His chest swelled as he took the barbs full on. 'And the last thing I need in my life is another woman making demands of me I simply can't fulfil.'

Chelsea crossed her arms over her chest as she realised she had begun to shiver for real. 'Well, then, you should be thanking me for letting you off the hook.'

He ran his hand over his face and with it seemed to wipe

away every ounce of feeling. 'I can't believe I'm saying this, but I should have listened to Caleb.'

'About what? About me?' Her accompanying laughter was shrill. 'Not bright and shiny enough for his tastes? Well, you can tell him I don't think much of him either.'

Finally, he looked at her. His eyes were so dark, so hooded in the moonlight she had no idea what he was thinking. 'You don't even know him.'

'I know enough to guess he wouldn't be thrilled with the idea of you slumming it with someone who clips dogs' toenails for a crust.'

Damien's laughter was tinged with a bitterness she hadn't imagined he might possess. 'God, Chelsea, I have never met a woman with as big a chip on her shoulder as you have.'

His tone only made her more sure. And more angry. With him, and with herself for ever thinking he might be different. He might be worth putting her defenceless heart on the line for.

'Well, don't panic,' she spat out, 'you won't have to worry about your friend's anxiety for your well-being any more. You and he can go off to some other swanky club with your bright and shiny friends and talk money and markets and boating and tennis, because I have a glorious weekend mapped out for me where I belong. In a dilapidated cabin in the Yarra Valley with my sister, her balding husband, their nutty three kids, and goofy dog, eating cheese on toast, crowded around the twelve-inch television, playing Pass the Parcel at a six-year-old's birthday party. Your scene's not my scene and vice versa. And I say thank goodness for that.'

She stopped to take a breath. Her lungs felt tight, her cheeks hot, even in the cold evening air.

'Are you done?' he asked, his voice cool.

She gathered every ounce of self-preservation she had inside

er, turned to him and said, 'Even better. We're done, Damien.
o are you going to take me home now or do I have to hitch-
ike?'

He looked at her for several long seconds. She was close
nough she could see every single hair on his head as the breeze
fted it off his face, see the twitching of a muscle in his left
heek, the rise and fall of his breaths beneath his quickly
uttoned shirt.

And with every passing second she felt him moving further
nd further away, taking with him any warmth and hope she'd
ver felt in her heart.

He licked his lips, shucked his jacket into a more comfort-
ble position, then turned over the engine with a steady hand.

This time as he drove her through the dark city streets he
ept just below the speed limit. Already there was nothing
etween them bar space and time, and the wind whipping about
er face only served to take away her tears.

As he pulled up at the end of Flinders Lane, Chelsea turned
o him to…what? Apologise? Wish him well? Change her
iind? Beg him to love her back?

But he kept his gaze dead ahead, his fingers clenched hard
o the steering wheel, his jaw set like stone.

She slid from the car, grabbed her jacket and bag from the
ack seat, and had barely closed the door when his engine
unned and he was gone down the glistening city street until
he had nothing but the sound of his revving engine to prove
e'd ever even been there.

For a moment she felt a bond with the faceless Bonnie. She
elt the pain that woman must have felt at having to watch this
nan slip through her fingers. Chelsea tried to console herself
vith the fact that she hadn't lost two and a half years of her life
efore coming to the realisation that the man couldn't be tamed.

But she wouldn't worry any more about his past. For her future felt as bright and rosy and full of possibilities as the gutter beneath her feet.

CHAPTER ELEVEN

MID Saturday afternoon Damien was sitting on a large brown leather ottoman at the rear of Caleb's favourite haunt, a dapper mirror-and-wood-infested bar tucked away secretly beneath Russell Street.

He'd been staring blindly at the half-melted ice cubes clinking around the bottom of his untouched Scotch for goodness knew how long when a familiar scent tickled at his nose. Something warm, and soft and homey.

He glanced up, enough of him expecting to find a beautiful caramel-blonde walking towards him that his skin warmed a degree and the hairs on the back of his neck rose.

But instead all he saw was a slick redhead passing for at least the third time that hour. She caught his eye, and he smiled. She was gorgeous, she deserved recognition and that was what he was here to do. To mingle with the plethora of gorgeous young things on offer. To move on from Chelsea London, who herself had been meant to mean no more to him than a scratch for his itch.

The redhead pulled up to supposedly fix her shoe and held eye contact, brazen as you like. He knew all it would take was a tilt of his head, a broadening of his smile, to bring her over, to begin the dance, but at the last second he looked away.

'Since when did you become such a grumpy old man?' Caleb asked as he threw himself onto the ottoman until he wa lazing across it like some modern day Caligula.

Damien sniffed in deep, letting the scents of all the mixe perfumes, wash away all memory of Chelsea's scent for good 'Since the day you came into my life and I realised I was t become an unpaid babysitter until my dying day.'

'Funny. You know that redhead's been giving you eye all af ternoon.'

'So she has.' Damien brought his drink to his lips.

'But she's no hottie dog groomer, is she?'

Damien's hand stilled, the smell of Scotch in his nose, th taste of it still missing from his lips. 'I wouldn't know,' he said 'She may well be.'

'You really like this girl, don't you?'

'I liked her well enough.' Damien didn't even pretend to no know to whom Caleb was referring. He licked his bottom li and nodded, squinting out into the hazy room rather tha looking Caleb in the eye, rather than giving away just ho much he'd liked her.

'Then what the hell are you doing sitting here moping wit me when you could be elbow-deep in all that lovely warm willing female flesh?'

'That particular female flesh is not so willing any more.'

'That was quick. What happened?'

'I was honest with her.'

Caleb sucked a hiss of air through his teeth. 'Bad move What did you say?'

'I told her I couldn't give her any more than what we had.

'And what was that exactly?'

Damien opened his mouth to say fun and games, but he knew that was rubbish. He searched for the words to describ

hat he and Chelsea had found together. To pinpoint what it
as about her that made it so easy for him to reject it out of
and. And he couldn't. His mind felt bruised, making him
nable to think straight about a lot of things.

'I made it clear we ought to keep things casual. Knowing
either of us was in a place to promise more. It's been a month
nce Bonnie, and Chelsea's, well, she's bloody neurotic.'

'And what did she have to say about that?'

'I thought… She thought… She told me where I could stick
y offer.' With that he brought his Scotch to his mouth and let
s watered down bitterness sear his throat.

Then behind the resultant hum in his ears he heard Caleb
ugh. So loud and so hard the ottoman began to shake. He
rned to his friend and glared.

But Caleb just grinned back. 'You poor devil.'

'Excuse me?'

Caleb sat up, rested a hand upon his shoulder, looked him
the eye and said, 'I'm thinking the hot get-back-on-the-horse
t lady has turned out to be the one.'

He waited for the punchline. For the jibe. But it never came.
aleb instead looked, if anything, envious.

'The one what?' Damien asked.

Caleb took a deep breath and seemed to search for patience.
When you left Bonnie, you never sought to drown your
orrows in a glass of Scotch. But since you met this girl, you've
een distracted, you've been moody, you've been a right dullard
ocially. And it's all because you've gone and accidentally
und yourself the one woman in the world who was finally
ole to capture your imagination enough to pull you from the
orld of boring bliss in which we found ourselves born.'

It took about thirty seconds for Caleb's words to stop
choing inside Damien's head. 'You're dead wrong, mate. One

woman, marriage, house and home… I can't. If being Halliburton taught me anything—'

'Don't go holding up your crazy parents as some kind example, my friend. They're madly in love and both ha sloshed before dinner. And if it wasn't for the number the divorce did on the two of you I would have run off with yo sister years ago.'

Damien kept his mouth shut and let Caleb's words sink i Chelsea. The one. His *sister?*

'You and Ava?'

Caleb smiled, though there was no roguish humour in h eyes. 'We're focussing on you right now, my friend.'

'Right. Me. And Chelsea.' *The one.*

He'd told her he didn't want permanence, or exclusivit because he'd thought he couldn't give them. He hadn't want to hurt her because he'd seen the way she was falling for hi But the truth was, he'd pulled back because he'd been falli for her too. And from what he'd learnt about her dating histor and her childhood, he knew she was just as jittery about t prospect of for ever as he was. And having never been in th predicament in his whole life he'd been trying his hardest stop himself from getting hurt too.

When all the while she'd been there, offering herse Offering a whole new world.

'I'm a bloody fool.'

'Nah, you're just a man. But you're also a Halliburton m and Halliburton men have a knack for getting everything th always wanted. So how about you stop cramping my style a get the hell out of here and go find your girl and get down your knees and beg her to forgive you for being such a prat'

Damien's mind swirled so fast he could barely focus. 'Do you need a lift home?'

'Damien. Leave now, before I stick a boot in your butt for making me feel so syrupy sweet I might puke.'

Caleb stood then and reached out to take Damien's hand, helping him stand. At the last moment they hugged, in a manly fashion, thumping fists on one another's backs. But it was enough for Damien to know that Caleb wasn't entirely the blackguard he made himself out to be.

He too was a man content enough on the island to himself, but who would give away every speck of sand if it meant truly finding the woman he could love for ever.

As he pushed blindly past transient, easy men and women that until now he'd always thought just like him to get to the front door, to fresh air and sunshine he so desperately craved, he patted his pockets for his car keys, his mobile phone.

They were all he needed where he was going. That and a whole lot of luck on his side.

Chelsea sat on a swinging love seat on the front porch of the ramshackle wooden house that Kensey and Greg had bought with the money she'd paid them for Kensey's half of the apartment. Kids' bikes lay forgotten on the patchy lawn beside her Pride & Groom van. Hanging plants made a jungle of the roof above her.

She'd rolled her mobile over and over in her hands so many times it was warm to the touch. Not that she wanted to call anyone. It just made her feel connected to the world she'd left behind in the city.

'That's the last thing you need,' she said aloud as she shoved it into the back pocket of her faded jeans.

She'd signed the bank-loan papers and sent them off. She'd put Phyllis completely in charge at the salon for the day. She'd made the beginnings of what would be many changes to her life to give herself the illusion she had it back under her control.

Now what she needed was fresh air, space, new scenery. And this was the place for it. This place that felt more like home than any other she'd ever known. It was true. Real. Messy. Honest. Unpretentious. And the complete opposite of Damien Halliburton's world of fast and furious bright and shiny living. If she had to pick one place in the world to lick her wounds and get over him, and to get over the trust she'd so naively put into the possibility of him, this was it.

Suddenly Hurley kids galore spilled out of every available doorway fracturing the peace. 'Auntie Chelsea!' one said. 'Have you seen my Spiderman pyjamas?'

Another asked, 'Can you give me a piggyback?

'What did you bring me for my birthday?' said the third.

'Ah, no, later and that's a surprise,' she said, giving each of them a quick kiss before they were gone around the side of the house as quickly as they'd arrived.

Kensey came out of the kitchen wiping her hands on a tea towel.

'My sister, the little woman,' Chelsea said, moving over to make space for her.

Kensey sat. 'Are you ever coming inside?'

A gust of wind swirled a pile of autumn leaves down the dirt driveway. 'In a minute.'

'It's getting cool. Dinner will be ready in forty odd minutes And the kids keep asking why you're frowning.'

Knowing she could never fool Kensey as well as she could fool herself, Chelsea dropped her head into her hands and frowned to her heart's content. She revelled in it, feeling as sorry for herself as she wanted. 'I'm frowning because I'm miserable,' she sulked.

'Of course you are. But good riddance to bad rubbish, I say Who needs a handsome, hunky, rich guy who cooks and isn' scared of a little illness lusting after them? You did the right thing cutting him off. Feel better?'

Chelsea lifted her head and somehow managed to laugh. 'Infinitely,' she lied. 'Thanks ever so much for your understanding.'

'He did make you glow, though, pet.'

'Kensey—' she warned.

'Well, he did. Made you glow and glisten and act all gooey and girly and give me hope that one day I'll be able to get you off my hands for good.'

'If you truly do want to get me off your hands for good, then you'd do better than to say things like that while I'm in the process of moving on.'

Kensey drew her in for a hug. 'You're right. Sorry. You will feel better. Eventually. Time wounds all heals and all that. And until then, tonight…there's cake. And vodka. And a Hugh Jackman movie marathon on the telly.'

'Thank goodness for you,' Chelsea said, feeling some small measure of relief that her itinerant father and absentee mother had given her this woman in her life at least. Everything else would come together eventually. Her business, her love life, her broken heart.

Hopefully.

The sudden grumble of a high-octane engine had them facing the road. When Chelsea saw Damien's sports car pull into the driveway she had to blink twice to make sure she hadn't conjured him up from her gloomy imaginings.

'Holy cow,' Chelsea said.

'Lookie here,' Kensey said.

'Nice wheels,' Greg said, coming outside to see what the noise was about. 'Who's that?'

'*That* would be Chelsea's Damien,' Kensey said.

'Ooh,' Greg said. 'He's flash, Chels. Handsome fella too. S‹
why did you dump him again?'

Kensey answered for her. 'I believe the theory on this on‹
was do unto others before they do unto you.'

Chelsea heard their words as though they were coming fron
the other side of the world. Despite having let him go, seein;
him again in the flesh had every part of her straining toward
the car, and the man getting out of it.

The man in the sleek black suit, the crisp baby-blue shir‹
the silk tie that likely cost more than her whole outfit, with th‹
dark preppy hair lifting sexily in the breeze. The man she'‹
watched drive away only the night before, certain she'd neve
see him again. The man who was behind the fact that she nov
sat there with unwashed hair, red-rimmed eyes and an achin;
chest.

'Kensey, do you know anything about this?' she whispere‹
loudly, but Kensey just shrugged, and snuck towards Greg
who put an unconscious arm around her waist. 'Then how o
earth did he find me?'

And more importantly, why?

Damien shut the door, straightened his jacket, then turne‹
and found the three of them watching him. He lifted his han
to give a short wave, then let it drop.

Chelsea motioned with her eyes for Kensey and Greg t‹
make themselves scarce, but Kensey just smiled all the bigge›

Damien slid his keys into his trouser pocket and headed u
the path. He ran a hand through his hair. She'd never seen hir
looking so nervous before. Or so adorable. And completely ou
of place in the rustic setting as she'd known he would be.

But he was there. And that was something.

She suddenly didn't know what to do with her hands. T
wring them, cross her arms, or slide them into the back pocke‹

of her jeans. In the end she let them hang at her sides in loose fists.

Damien stopped at the foot of the steps and looked up at her. His blue eyes so achingly familiar and beautiful they managed to create a new series of cracks in her already fragmented heart.

'What are you doing here, Damien?' She was dead pleased when her voice came out without shaking.

His mouth curved into a half-smile and he said, 'I was passing through. You know there's a wine-tasting festival down the road?'

Well… Her eyebrows shot skyward and she had a whole slew of retorts to shoot back at him despite the audience before he held up a hand, shook his head and pinned her with the most serious gaze she'd ever seen him use.

'Wipe that last statement. Please,' he said. 'I drove up here without really knowing what I would say when I got here. So let me start again.'

She shrugged.

His lungs filled and deflated before he said, 'I'm here to see you.'

Her heart rate kicked up a notch. Her long since empty well of hope filled so fast it threatened to spill over. But she couldn't let him see. He *hadn't* said he felt any differently than he had twenty-four hours before. 'How on earth did you find me?'

'I looked your sister up in the phone directory of a public phone booth in town.' He glanced at Kensey and nodded. 'A paper one. Sometimes technology isn't all it's cracked up to be.'

'You won't find any fancy technology here,' Greg said. 'Damien, right? I'm Greg Hurley and this is my wife Kensey.'

Thus invited, Damien sidled up the stairs, stopping at Chelsea's side.

'Chelsea's told me a lot about both of you,' he said.

She felt his warmth, smelled the faint rays of autumn sunshine clinging to his clothes as though loath to let go. She closed her eyes and leaned as far away from him and his magnetic scent as she could.

Then the Hurleys' collie chose that exact moment to bolt around the side of the house, run straight to the newcomer and leap, his great muddy paws landing smack bang in the centre of Damien's shirt.

'Oh, Lord. Slimer, down!' Kensey cried out.

Chelsea grabbed the dog by the collar, but he lived up to his name and slobbered all over her hand.

'He's fine,' Damien said, rubbing hard hands over the dog's ears and grinning from ear to ear. 'Slimer?' he said to Kensey. '*Ghostbusters* fans?'

Kensey's face broke into a matching grin. 'You bet. The reason I went out with Greg in the first place was because he reminded me of a young Bill Murray. Do you have a dog?'

He laughed. 'What's with you girls and dogs? Chelsea asked me the same thing on our first date.'

Chelsea felt as if she were in the twilight zone. She was so confounded she wasn't quick enough to stop Kensey from telling her tale.

'When we were little we spent a few months living out this way with a friend of our dad's. He was nice. His house was clean. He could cook. Which made me fall in love with him as only a hungry eight-year-old can. But for Chelsea it was all about his dog. A fluffy grey mongrel of a thing that only ate what we ate. That always looked and smelled worse five minutes after a bath. And who slept on the end of Chelsea's bed and followed her around like he was her guardian angel. She's had a thing for dogs, and the people who value them, ever since.'

Damien continued rubbing Slimer behind the ear, but his gaze was all for Chelsea. It was a nice gaze. A warm gaze. A gaze full of promise that he'd assured her again and again was not there. Glutton for punishment that she was, she gazed right on back. She needed her head read.

'But you've never owned a dog yourself?' he asked.

Chelsea shook her head.

'Yet you run a pet-grooming company?'

She narrowed her eyes and nodded, daring him to make something of it. To overstep the mark even slightly so that she could grab him by the scruff of the neck and shove him back into his car and out of her life, before all this niceness and dog-patting made her love him so much more she'd never *ever* get over him.

'When we eventually moved out of the place,' Kensey added to be that much more helpful, 'it was like the world had ended. Having to leave the dog behind broke poor Chelsea's heart. And I don't think she's ever found herself a replacement love who measured up with Rover's level of commitment and adoration.'

'Fascinating,' Damien said, slowly easing Slimer to four feet. He stood, blinked at Chelsea and she could see the wheels turning behind his far too intelligent blue eyes. 'Can we talk?'

Here we go. Without preamble she demanded of Kensey and Greg, 'You guys. Inside now.'

'Right,' Greg said, practically dragging Kensey away. 'Dinner's in half an hour.' Chelsea thanked her lucky stars he was smart enough to know if he'd extended an invitation to Damien she would have killed him.

Feeling far too close to Damien for comfort, Chelsea jogged down the stairs and headed around the side of the house towards the back yard. Damien followed close enough his smooth aftershave curled around her nostrils, blanketing the scent of Italian herbs and lemon cake wafting through the open windows.

'They seem nice,' he said.

'They are. And they mean everything to me. Whatever you reason for coming to find me, choosing to do so while I'm here is playing dirty. So say whatever you've come to say and make it quick. You heard Greg—I have less than half an hour before the macaroni and cheese is on.'

He shot her a quick sideways glance, which still told he nothing of his motives. Or of his opinion of macaroni and cheese He could have been there because she'd left him in such a state the night before he'd come in the hopes for one last booty call to prove to his ego that he could still have her despite her protestations, or for such fantastical reasons she dared not think for all the damage they could do to her determination to stop loving him

She led him out to the back deck and folded her arms across the split-wood banister looking out over rolling hills covered in the spoils of other people's wealth. There were white grapes as far as the eye could see and a lone bright yellow hot-air balloon floated lazily across the sharp blue sky.

About a foot of space lay between her fingers and his. But he might as well have been leaning his might and muscle against her for the way he affected her simply by being near.

'It is beautiful here,' Damien said.

'Too quiet for your tastes, I would have thought.'

'Not at all.' A smile curved Damien's cheek and for a moment Chelsea forgot she was no longer allowed to lean in and kiss the crease at the edge of his mouth. To tuck herself against his side and take his arm and wrap it around her shoulders so that she could lean into all that strength and warmth.

She looked away, and she hoped he had not seen her intimate desires splashed across her face.

'If I wasn't here I'd be back in the city at a bar with Caleb.'

'Very cosmopolitan.'

'It was,' he said. 'A bunch of people I've never met and likely will never meet again, a glass of over-iced Scotch at my fingertips, and shouting at Caleb to be heard over the loud music.'

'Sounds just your kind of place,' she said.

'A week ago I would have said the same.'

She felt his eyes on her still, and she did her very best to hide the quickening inside her as she tried to decipher just what he was trying to say.

He turned to rest the backs of his elbows on the railing and crossed his feet at the ankles. Without the distraction of rolling hills of wheat-yellow grape vines laid out before him, his eyes were all for her.

Her eyes hurt from crying, her hair needed a brush, her nose was pink and her lips were raw from biting at them. While the late-afternoon sun lent his skin a glow that made him look so healthy it just wasn't fair.

But the way he looked at her…it was as if he couldn't even tell she looked a mess.

This time her voice shook like crazy as she asked, 'What are you doing here, Damien?'

CHAPTER TWELVE

DAMIEN reached out and pushed a lock of hair from Chelsea's cheek. The gentle touch did such things to her senses she gripped tighter to the railing to stop from trembling all over.

'I couldn't handle leaving things as we did,' he said.

She swallowed. 'It was pretty awful. But you didn't have to follow me out here to remind me. I think you know my mobile number.'

He smiled but it didn't really reach his eyes. 'Nevertheless I didn't want to tell you the things I have to say over the phone.'

She wished he had. Because then she could have cried silently while he broke things off in a more civilised way. Now she had to see him, smell him, hold herself together within touching distance of him.

'There's nothing more you need to say, Damien. Don't think walking away from this makes you the bad guy again. I understand where you are coming from. I do. But you meant what you said, and I meant what I said. So that's that. It was pretty great while it lasted, but now we *are* done.'

He nodded, though all the while his gaze still roved over her face as if he couldn't believe she was really there in front of him. And then he had to go and say, 'Then why did I miss you so terribly when I fell asleep last night? And when I woke up this morning. And as I drove up here breaking the land-speed record.'

No, no, no! the voices of reason inside her head screamed. *Don't do this to me!*

'When two people agree to stop seeing one another that's one of the down points,' she said.

'If you could tell me any up points to us not seeing one another, I'd like to hear them. Because I've racked my brain and I can't think of one.'

She shook her head. Hard enough to make her brain rattle and crash against the sides of her skull in punishment for momentarily agreeing with him. 'Damien, you were right to put the brakes on, and I was right to end it. Can't we just leave it at that?'

'Remind me why.'

She clenched her fists and dug her toes into the flaky mossy tiles beneath her feet and reminded herself he was smooth and gorgeous and always said the right things and that was why she'd fallen in love with him. But that it didn't mean he would ever love her back.

'Because,' she said, 'ninety per cent of the time you'll find me with limp hair, wet clothes, and head-to-toe sweat. I don't own a suit and you live in a world peopled by them. I eat leftovers for breakfast, not eggs hollandaise. My idea of a fabulous Saturday night is hunkered beneath a mohair blanket watching a movie in the park. I don't know one wine from another, I don't give a hoot about the FTSE or the yen, or bar openings, and when it comes down to it we don't have one single thing in common.'

'I think we've verified that we both love dogs,' he said, his voice so warm, so understanding, so near.

'Not good enough,' she said, squeezing her eyes shut.

'Okay, so I like movies. And mohair. And the idea of you in a wet T-shirt almost short-circuited my brain right now.'

At his words she actually felt her uncooperative breasts straining against the cotton of her long-sleeved T-shirt. 'I have no boobs. Wetting them is not exciting.'

'It's exciting to me.'

Damn him, he knew just how to get beneath her defences. She took a deep breath and mentally brought in reinforcements in the form of her old friends doubt and mistrust.

He reached out again and continued to play with her hair, sliding it over her back, running his fingers along that special place between her neck and shoulder. 'Chelsea, all I see every day are women in suits. Slick and cunning in head-to-toe Melbourne black. While you have been like a breath of fresh air in my life. Since the first moment I laid eyes on you it was like my world view shifted. No woman had ever sassed me like you did. No woman ever continually confounded me as you have. And no woman ever gave into me with as much delight as you did. And I find I can't let that go. I want you to come back to me. I want you to give us another chance.'

There. He'd said it. The words she ached for yet had hoped for the sake of her tender heart he hadn't come here to say.

'I couldn't,' she blurted out before she threw herself into his arms. 'I can't.'

'Why?' He moved nearer, all but blocking out the setting sun with his broad shoulders.

'Because *you* are one of those slick and cunning types in your head-to-toe Melbourne black.'

His languorous, sensual exploration of the skin behind her ear came to an agonising halt. It was obvious that was not the answer Damien had been expecting. 'Meaning?'

She momentarily blinked into his eyes before looking back

to the ramshackle house with its broken roof tiles and faded floral curtains. The real home and family her sister had built for herself from the ashes of a debilitating childhood. A youth peppered by parasitic—

'Men in suits,' she said aloud, 'from my experience, may never think to steal your wallet but would con the contents of your bank account out from under you as soon as look at you if it might make them an extra buck.'

'Is that really who you think I am?' he asked.

No, she thought instantly. But instead out of her mouth came the words, 'I don't know who you are.'

A lock of hair fell across her face. She knew he'd noticed but he didn't make a move to tuck it anywhere, so she was forced to do so herself. But that was nothing compared with the ache that slammed her body when she felt the palpable wall of cool coming from Damien's end of the railing.

His face turned red with rage. Disappointment. Shock. 'No wonder you're hiding me out the back of the house where I can't infect your family with my pestilence. Why did you even bother to go out with me at all if I am just one more example of the kind of filth you wouldn't deign to scrape off your shoe?'

A ray of sunlight suddenly shone from beneath a cloud bringing with it clarity, and renewed optimism. Or at least that was how Chelsea felt.

His words were harsh. The harshest she'd ever heard him utter. But hearing the hurt in his voice only made her realise that he cared more than he'd ever let on.

And to find out just how much he really did care, she was going to have to give up a part of herself without any kind of surety she would ever get it back. She was going to have to gamble more than she could afford to lose.

'Damien, I need you to really hear me. Okay?'

He didn't nod, but at least he didn't turn his back.

'This has all happened so quickly between us. I feel like I've been swept well and truly off my feet. And that could never have happened with someone I didn't trust. Someone I didn't truly believe was different from all the other guys who made me doubt your gender was worth the effort. Why is this so hard?'

She ran a hand over her eyes, trying to subdue the rising panic that it was already too late. And then she found deep within herself a way to make him understand. She lifted her eyes from the relative safety of the ground to his haunting eyes as she said, 'I've always thought that if people were only forced to wear T-shirts with signs on them the world would be a better place. Signs that said who they really were.'

A muscle continued to flicker in his jaw, but his teeth seemed to unclench. The hard line of his mouth softened. He was at least listening.

'Signs like Verbal Abuser with Mother Issues. Self-Obsessive Narcissist. Sweet as Honey All the Way to the Bone. Shark in Goldfish Skin.'

She shook her hair off her face again before asking, 'I'd love to know what your T-shirt would say.'

He blinked slowly. 'I think it's more important right now for you to tell me what *you* think my T-shirt would say.'

The first word that came to mind was *Dreamy*. From the beginning he'd been a six-foot-something, broad-shouldered, delicious dream of a man. But had he, at some stage over the past week, while she had been fluttering and floundering, and finding reasons to keep him at arm's length, actually become real? Was he right alongside her struggling with the enormity of what had *actually* happened between them?

She felt like a butterfly under a magnifying glass as he

pierced her with his unrelenting gaze. And her mouth was so dry she couldn't hope to speak.

'Or do you want to know what I think your T-shirt should say?' he asked.

Yes, she thought. *Desperately. But no. Not while you're looking at me like that. All wounded and gorgeous. Not while our worlds are balancing on a knife's edge.*

She flapped a hand between them as though it didn't matter. He caught it and pulled it to his chest and she stumbled after it until she was bodily against him. Again. Exactly the same way as they had been when they first met. At his nearness, her breath whooshed from her lungs and a pulse began to beat erratically in her throat.

Only this time he wasn't a beautiful stranger; this time he was a man with whom she had shared far more of herself, of her thoughts, her dreams, her past, her body, and her innermost self than she had with any man.

She tried to pull away, but he only tugged her back, sliding one hand around her waist, stopping where the small of her back met the top of her jeans, pressing her against the full length of him while with the other hand he turned her hand in his until he held it over his heart. She could feel the pulse beat strong and fast behind his ribs. And hers soon altered to match his beat for beat.

A shriek of laughter spilled from somewhere inside the cottage. A crash of saucepans was followed by Kensey's raised voice scolding someone. But after about ten words the admonishment turned to laughter too.

'Come on,' Damien said. He held her hand and drew her down the rambling, weed-encrusted back steps to the messy yard below. Feeling like an emotionally overwrought rag doll, she gave in and let him lead her where he may.

When they reached the shade of an old oak tree, Damie
edged her around the side so that they were shielded from
prying eyes by the shade of the large trunk and a curtain o
drooping branches that almost touched the ground.

She leaned back against the tree, the bark digging into he
back in twenty different places. He leant a hand beside her head
so close all she'd have to do was look left and she could nuzzl
against his warm skin.

'I hurt you, didn't I? Trying to squeeze you to fit you into
compartment in my life like I do my job, my friends, m
family?'

Okay, now this was getting really real. There was no artific
between them. No flirtation. No mobile phones to keep ther
at a comfortable distance.

'I'll live,' she said.

'I know you will. And I know I will too. But what I don
see is why either of us should just live. I want more than tha
And I know you do too. I think… I believe that we owe it t
ourselves to see if we might just be able to do it together. Wha
can I do to make you trust me again?'

She shrugged. Tempted by the almost promise behind h
words, but completely unsure it would be possible for her t
trust anyone again, least of all herself.

'Your father really did a number on you, didn't he?'

She blinked up at him, sideswiped by the change of tacl
'Excuse me?'

'I'm not like him. Or the people who let him down. I'
here,' he said, 'even after you brushed me off. And I can te
you that took some kind of leap of faith on my part. Now it
your turn. Chelsea. Tell me about your father. What did he d
to make you so unwilling to take a chance on us?'

The thread of apprehension for ever wrapped aroun

Chelsea's heart tightened, strangling her ability to do as he asked. But the thought of feeling that way, trapped between her desires and her fears for ever, suddenly felt too much. And just not fair.

She breathed in as deeply as she could until she felt the thread snap and her breath shuddered as it released. And she watched the pulse beating in the base of his neck as she said, 'He used to use us in his scams.'

Damien swore beneath his breath. 'Were you ever in any danger?'

'Not in the line of fire as far as I can remember. He was smart enough to move us onto a new place whenever he got close.'

'And when your family stayed out this way with the guy who could cook? The man with the dog?'

'I never knew how they knew one another. But I've always wondered if he was my uncle. My mum's brother. Whoever he was he made us go to school, and kept Dad on the straight and narrow for a full six months before we upped and moved in the middle of the night.'

'And your uncle loved dogs.'

'With all his heart.'

The questions dried up. She wondered if he'd found out what he wanted to know. If he had enough information to slap himself over the back of his head and tell himself to give up on her for good. The backs of her eyes burnt anew as she began to feel the pain that losing him now would cause.

'So you could really steal my wallet easy as you please,' he said. 'No joke.'

A shift in his voice made her look up. There was a glimmer in his eye. The tiniest glimmer, but enough that she knew that he was turned on. By her ability to hoodwink him. Hope sprang through her veins like the elixir of life.

'I might have done it a half dozen times already, and put it back, and you'd never have known.'

He leaned in towards her. If he kissed her now she wouldn't be able to stop him. But at the last second he pulled back. The hand beside her head moved to hover at her cheek, then clenched and tucked into the pocket of his trousers.

He looked past her into the distance. 'I don't chase women, Chelsea. Maybe because I've never had to. It may seem arrogant but it's the truth. I've never begged a woman to be with me. Then when I drove away, believing I might never see you again...' His eyes blazed and when he looked at her it was as if now he wasn't sure whether to kiss her senseless or wring her neck.

But the very fact that he was struggling at all meant the world. It meant her hope, her trust, had never been misplaced. Her instincts were right. He was different. He was worth the fight. And her spirit was not completely downtrodden yet.

'Damien...' she said, reaching out and laying a hand upon his chest. The moment her fingers curled into his cotton shirt his eyes darkened, his breaths grew deeper beneath her hand, and she knew she wasn't ready for him to not be there. Would never be. 'If you'd like to stay that would be okay with me.'

He breathed deep through his nose. All neck-wringing thoughts seemed to have dried up as his gaze dropped to her mouth. 'Never has a man heard happier words.'

'I meant for dinner,' she explained.

His gaze travelled up her warming cheek and back to her eyes. 'Are you sure?'

Sure? Sure that she wanted him back, even though he'd not once told her he loved her, or could promise her more than he already had? She'd never been less sure in her life. But she was willing to take the chance that he cared enough he might yet one day grow to love her.

She swallowed the lump in her throat. This was it. Time to test her newly unfettered heart. 'I'm highly protective of my family. I've never invited a man to eat dinner with them before.'

His left eyebrow rose. 'Yet you chose me. A fully fledged suit-and-tie conman?'

She nodded. 'And if you don't behave there are plenty of places out here in which to hide a dead body.'

And for the first time since he'd arrived, he laughed. The beautiful sound raced through her veins.

'That's my girl,' Damien said, leaning in against her flattened hand until her elbow brushed against the tree and their noses were mere inches apart.

'Will you stay?' she asked.

'I did come all this way,' he murmured.

'Stalker,' she said, biting back a smile.

'Cynic,' he shot back before closing the gap between them and kissing her with such heat she clenched a fist into his shirt.

His tongue swooped into her mouth and took her breath away with such intensity she truly believed he'd wanted to kiss her from the second he got out of the car.

He pulled back and whispered against her swollen lips, 'I knew I missed you for a good reason.'

'If that's the only reason, then I warn you I consider that already misbehaving.'

'If I get my way we'll both be misbehaving a hell of a lot more before this night is done.' He leaned in and kissed her again, with even less restraint than he had before.

And she let herself do the same. She let go. Completely. Allowing her love for him to overflow, to tell him just how much she missed him through *her* actions rather than her words.

He pulled away far too soon. 'I can smell dinner.'

'She's a bad cook. It can wait.'

He smiled. 'The sooner we eat, the sooner we can think about moving onto after-dinner pursuits.' He let her go, easily as you please, and walked past her headed back to the house.

She hugged her arms about herself, amazed anew that he had come. That he was staying. And that she was letting him. But the absolute truth was he wasn't the same man she'd left the night before. There was still something different about him. Some kind of calm resolution she couldn't put her finger on.

She wasn't sure if it was a good or bad thing, just that somehow, after today, things were never going to be the same again.

Her heart ached to know if this weekend would be a bitter-sweet end to the greatest week of her life. If he might stay with her a month. Two. Or if the whole dream really was there for the taking.

He turned to walk backwards, away from her. 'Coming?'

She pushed away from the tree and followed.

'Still want to know what I'd write on your T-shirt?' he asked as she approached.

She nodded.

'You'd need enough cotton to go to the moon and back to fit upon it all the things I think make you you.'

And with that he jogged up the weedy back steps and into the house.

CHAPTER THIRTEEN

CHELSEA followed Damien into the cottage on shaky legs to find the place in uproar. Kensey stood over Slimer with a tipped-over cake-mix pan while Slimer sat on his rug trying to lick the delicious mixed ingredients off his fur.

'Chelsea, thank God,' Kensey said. 'Can you do the honours while I whip up another batch? Lucy, stop crying, honey. There will be birthday cake.'

Chelsea kept on walking into the laundry where she found the Slimer pack: a bucket, soap, a pair of clippers, and a hard bristled brush.

'Slimer, outside,' she called out and turned to run smack bang into a hard wall of Damien.

'I'll give you a hand.'

She glanced at his beautiful suit with the paw-print stains already baked on. Then thought that if she left him inside how quickly the kids would smell fresh blood and climb all over him and what else Kensey would let on if she wasn't there to stop her.

'Are you sure? It's getting cold out and I can do it by myself.'

'Not gonna happen,' he said, shucking off his jacket and laying it casually atop the dryer.

Her certainty there had been some kind of change in him in-

tensified until it actually gave her goose-bumps. 'I class being
bossy as misbehaving.'

'Well, that's just tough. The way I see it I'm going to need
a firm hand if we are going to have any kind of chance at
turning this crazy attraction into what it seems determined to
become. So get over yourself and let me be there for you.'

He reached out and took a hold of the handle of the bucket,
his thumb brushing against hers, sending sparks of electricity
from her hand to his.

'What this seems determined to become?' she repeated,
fixated on the words rather than the dark, dangerous look in his
eye.

His voice dropped as he said, 'I have no intention of having
that conversation in a place that smells like wet dog and detergent.'

She wasn't letting him off the hook that easy. 'If you want
anything to do with me, Slick, you're going to have to get used
to the smell.'

He rolled his eyes to the heavens. 'Hell, Chelsea, I wouldn't
want to do it surrounded by computer terminals and screaming, overworked day traders either.'

It? What it?

'Fine,' she said, letting go and sliding past him, through the
kitchen and outside to the grassy area at the side of the cottage.
'Slimer! Here!'

Slimer came bounding outside, as usual too thick to realise
what the hose in her hand meant until she had him chained to
the clothesline.

Damien followed in his wake, dark and broad and beautiful in his designer threads with muddy dog prints on his chest,
dead leaves attached to the bottoms of his shoes, and a crazed
old bucket in his hand. He still looked out of place, but beautifully so.

She turned on the hose and he kept on coming. Let him get
his perfect clothes all wet and muddy. Then he'd really see how
literally messy her life was.

'Come here, boy,' she called out. Slimer came to her, she
held out the hose and at the last second he darted away. She instinctively tipped the hose in the opposite direction to herd him
back where she wanted him.

The shout that came from Damien's direction swung her
gaze his way to find him standing with his feet shoulder-width
apart, his face dripping with water, a neat spray covering his
shirt and the bottom of his trousers soaked. He looked so
shocked, she had to bite her lips to stop from laughing.

He looked up at her, his eyes blazing. 'You did that on purpose.'

'Did not.'

He took a gigantic step towards her and she squealed. She
held the hose in front of herself as a shield.

He shook the droplets from his hair which left it spiky and
left him looking like something out of a magazine photo spread.
With his dark eyes, stormy expression and clothes clinging
wetly to him he was unbelievably hot.

'Don't you dare tell me you're turned on right now,' he
demanded, and her eyes shot from the fabric stretching across
his thighs to his face and her cheeks turned a degree warmer.

But *his* eyes were now dancing. Bright and beautiful and
laughing.

She cocked her hip and let the water tilt away from him.
'And what if I am? Watcha gonna do about it?'

He took another step her way and she baulked. The hint of
smile quickly turned into a devilish grin. Then he moved with
such speed she brought the hose between them only to have his
hand clasp down on hers. The water shot skyward, showering
them both in a thick spray of water.

Slimer barked and frolicked and generally loved the fact that anyone else was getting wet bar him.

Chelsea screamed, and tried to kick Damien in the shin but he was too quick. He turned the hose on her full blast, her hair flew back from her face and her white long-sleeved T-shirt soon became sodden.

When the water spray disappeared, she spat out a clump of hair and opened her eyes to find Damien standing before her staring hard at her breasts. She looked down to find her T-shirt and beige bra had become completely see-through. Her cold nipples stood out hard and dark through the thin fabric.

He dragged his gaze to her face, and her breath caught in her lungs at the level of desire surging behind his eyes.

Love me, she thought with such desperation he must have heard. Instead she said, 'Don't even think about it. There are kids just inside the house.'

'I know,' he said, his voice a deep growl. 'But if there weren't, I want you to know that your dry-cleaner would be trying to get grass stains from your clothes come Monday.'

'I don't have a dry-cleaner. Like most regular people I wash my own clothes.'

His mouth tilted into a smile. 'You're frozen solid, drenched to the bone, without a weapon, and breathing so hard you look like you are about to pass out from it, yet you still manage to dredge up a way to keep me from getting too big for my boots. I love you.'

His words hung on the air like snowflakes. Delicate, ethereal and in danger of melting away lest she pay close attention. Chelsea licked her suddenly dry lips. 'Did you just say—'

'I did,' Damien said, his own breaths suddenly coming harder. He reached over and turned off the hose at the tap and the world turned silent. Even Slimer chose that moment to have a little lie-down.

Damien let the hose slump at his feet and walked over to where Chelsea stood shivering, much less from the cold than from the events consuming her.

He reached out and ran his hands up and down her arms, warming her, inside and out. And then he closed the gap completely and drew her to him and kissed her. Softly, fully, deeply and full of the feelings he had just admitted.

When he pulled away and looked down into her eyes Chelsea wasn't shaking any more. She wasn't scared, she wasn't unsure, she wasn't even the least bit overwhelmed. She loved him and he…he was real, after all.

'Since I drove away from you last night,' he said, his voice low and intimate and true, 'I have been miserable. Wretched even. But hitting that low was what I needed to realise that you are my high. I drove here planning on whisking you away somewhere beautiful, and most of all somewhere private in order to convince you of what I feel for you.'

'Here's fine,' she said, her voice breathless.

He smiled, crinkles fanning out from the edges of his stunning eyes. 'So it is. Now for this moment to at least end the way I planned for it to end I need you to look me in the eye and know, to the bottom of your heart, that I have gone right ahead and fallen madly in love with you.'

Chelsea did as she was told. She looked into his Pacific-blue eyes, and saw the truth. The whole truth. That was the difference she saw in him. He not only loved her, but he was ready to love her and to keep on loving her.

'I'm in love with you too,' she blurted, the words spilling from her like a rainbow splashed across a rain-cleansed sky. 'From the moment I met you you made me feel like for the first time in my life I could dream as big as I wished. You may own a suit or two, and you may be a touch arrogant, but that's only scratching the surface. You're good and kind and generous and fun and playful and you're hot. Have I even told you how beautiful I think you are? And tall. I lo-o-ove that you're really tall. And when you kiss me…'

Her next words were lost within the warmth of his lips. *Thank God,* she thought, because once she'd opened the flood gates she felt as if she could go on and on for ever telling him how alive he made her feel.

He slid the wet cotton of her T-shirt upwards until his warm hand made direct contact with her waist and before she knew it his thumbs were running along the undersides of her breasts.

'Hey, guys, is Slimer done?' Kensey came round the side of the house and Chelsea hid behind Damien and tugged her shirt back into place.

Kensey placed a hand on her hip and glared at them, though Chelsea caught the delighted twinkle in her eye. 'My dog is now covered in cake mix *and* is muddy and wet. And you lot look just as bad. Can I not leave any of you alone for just one second?'

'We'll wash him now,' Damien said. 'I promise.'

'Mmm. You'd better. Though if you turn out to be a bad influence on my little sister, Damien Halliburton, I may just kiss you myself.' Kensey winked, turned tail and left.

'She means it,' Chelsea warned.

'I don't doubt it.'

Damien grabbed the hose, Chelsea the brush and they had Slimer clean in five minutes flat. She rubbed him down with a towel and sent him running in the direction of the house.

'I'm getting the feeling,' he said, wiping his hands down the only dry patches of his trousers, 'the events of this past week

he loss of my phone, the stalker claims, the animal-print-
nderwear fiasco, the food poisoning, aren't actually anything
nusual for those in the London family. This is what life with
ou is really going to be like from now on, isn't it?'

When she looked back over her shoulder and realised just
ow wet Damien was, wet and still beautiful, while she must
ave looked like a drowned rat, Chelsea burst into laughter.

She padded up to him and threw herself into his arms, snug-
ling up to him, sliding her cold hands beneath his clothes and
p his warm back. 'If I admit it is are you going to leave and
ever come back?'

He nibbled at the soft skin below her ear. 'No. I'm thinking
could get very used to your life. So much so, in fact, it would
ean less nights on Caleb's couch and more at your apartment,
m afraid.'

She shrugged, her breasts rubbing deliciously against his
ont. 'We've proven my bed's big enough for the two of us.
nd I loved how you looked in my kitchen. And my shower.
nd on my couch. I could get very used to that too. Move in
ith me.'

He looked down into her eyes, searching, hoping, dreaming
s big as she'd ever seen any man dream as the idea of moving
with her obviously sat well on his shoulders.

A light sprinkle of autumn rain fluttered against her eyelids.
he blinked them away and held her man tighter still. *Her man.*
he man of her dreams. Whatever she'd done to deserve this,
deserve him, she was planning on doing it a whole lot more.

'It would be my pleasure,' he said. 'Though I do have some
ings in storage I'd like to bring over to make me feel more at
ome. A couch and some bookshelves and a desk and some ap-
iances I'll need if we are going to eat anything more nutri-
ous than leftovers.'

'I like leftovers,' she said as she nipped at his neck.

'I hate chintz,' he warned as he angled his chin to give he better access.

'I hate dark leather and stainless steel.'

'Of course you do. But I washed a dog today.'

'You did.'

'So next week you come to a bar with me.'

It wasn't a question. Chelsea sank further against him. 'I come. I'll even play tennis with your parents. But I won't drir Martinis. I prefer Harvey Wallbangers with my sporting ex deavours.'

'You can play tennis?'

'Surprised?'

Damien grinned down at her as he slid his right thigh gentl between hers. 'Infinitely.'

Chelsea's phone buzzed in her back pocket.

'Leave it,' he said.

'Can't. Might be important. Life-changing even.'

She flipped open to find a message from Kensey:

CHELSEA! DAMIEN! DINNER!

'We have to go in now or we'll be in big trouble,' she sai sliding her phone back away.

Damien growled as he disentangled himself from her. 'Wi I never get past second base with you again?'

'Tonight,' she promised.

'So I'm staying after dinner now, am I?'

'If you don't mind sharing a room with me, which is on different floor from the bathroom, has creaky floorboards ar a lumpy double bed.'

'Well…'

'What if I guarantee you a home run? Or two if you're ve nice to me.'

'That's the best you can offer?'

'Fine,' she said on a sigh. 'I can guarantee the same the next day and the next. If that's what it will take to get you inside now before Kensey blows her lid.'

'Minx,' he said, rubbing her nose with his.

'Hunka Hunka,' she said, kissing him hard, and long, and slow before ducking under his arm and running towards the house.

He caught her in about three steps, grabbed her around the waist and threw her over his shoulder. She kicked but soon dissolved into raucous laughter. 'So this is what life with a Halliburton is going to be like,' she managed to say between giggles.

'Sweetheart, you have no idea what you're in for.'

And while a week ago the thought of having no idea what the days ahead might bring would have frightened her silly, she let herself droop until she could slide her hands into the back pockets of his jeans and she hung on tight. And grinned. From ear to ear. Because she knew the most important thing—he'd be there with her.

Damien slapped her on the butt, shifted her into a more comfy position on his broad shoulder and carried her into the great big beautiful future.

HOT NIGHTS
WITH A PLAYBOY

Nicola Marsh

Nicola Marsh has always had a passion for writing and reading. As a youngster, she devoured books when she should have been sleeping, and later kept a diary whose content could be an epic in itself! These days, when she's not enjoying life with her husband and son in her home city of Melbourne, she's at her computer, creating the romances she loves, in her dream job. Visit Nicola's website at www.nicolamarsh.com for the latest news of her books.

CHAPTER ONE

Style guru Abby Weiss wows the fashion world with her incredible work for Australia's leading chic magazine, Finesse. *The Whitsunday islands proved a spectacular backdrop to showcase Weiss's talents, who, thanks to her stellar work on this shoot, secured the number one stylist job at* Finesse. *Look out for more from this brilliant up-and-comer in the industry.*

ABBY could see the headlines.

She'd visualised nothing else since she'd received the phone call from Mark Pyman, CEO of *Finesse*, saying she'd scored the lucrative gig for the magazine's summer spread, boarded a plane for Sapphire Island and checked into this exclusive resort.

What she'd seen of the place so far had fired her imagination and she knew with a little creativity and a lot of hard work this would be her best shot at the top job ever. Mark had hinted at it and the powerbroker of Australia's fashion magazine industry didn't hint at anything lightly.

Oh, yeah, thanks to a little healthy visualisation, she could see those headlines: in huge Arial font, bold, cut out from *Finesse*'s summer issue and taking pride of place over her desk back home in Sydney.

This was it. Her chance at the big time.

Wandering into the hotel's poolside bar with an extra spring in her step, she marvelled at the staggering array of tropical plants and exotic orchids, her excitement growing as she scoped out yet another great site for a shoot.

Sapphire Island had proven to be a gold mine, providing the perfect backdrop for displaying the fashions of Australia's leading designers. True to form, Mark had organised several top models, which made her job a heck of a lot easier.

Dealing with professionals and seeing the results always made her proud of working in the cutthroat industry of fashion. Though she hadn't sighted the photographer yet, she knew Mark only used the best.

As the topic of photographers drifted through her mind, she wondered which part of the world Judd was currently hiding in. They hadn't spoken for three months, an anomaly in their close relationship. Well, as close as they could get over the phone and Internet.

She hadn't even received one of his infamous one-line postcards and she smiled, wondering what he'd say if he knew she'd kept every single one and made a collage out of them that adorned her study wall. Probably something witty designed to cut her down to size, in typical Judd Calloway fashion.

Some things never change.

And she wouldn't have it any other way.

Luckily they'd got past the little mistake on graduation night and had managed to sustain a strong friendship.

Nothing like denial to get through the last eight years as his best buddy and confidante.

'Well, well. Amazing what the ocean can wash up these days.'

Abby jumped and whirled around, seeing but not quite believing what she'd initially thought her imagination had conjured up.

'No way!'

She reached out and poked Judd in the chest: yep, he was real. Very real, if the rock-hard wall her finger had barely made a dent in was any indication. 'What are you doing here?'

He smiled at her, the same lazy grin that lit up the gold flecks in his hazel eyes and had her instinctively grinning right back at him, despite the fact she hadn't seen him since that fateful night of the grad dance.

'Now, is that any way to greet your new star photographer?'

'*You're* doing this shoot? But we're shooting fashion, not wildlife.'

He slid onto one of the barstools and patted the seat next to him.

'I'm not too sure about that. I've seen the way some of your crowd party and it ain't pretty.'

'They're not my crowd. I just work with them.'

'And you date them,' he teased, reaching for a stray curl and tucking it behind her ear. 'No accounting for taste, is there?'

Abby fought a losing battle with a blush as the heat surged up her neck and settled somewhere in the vicinity where he'd touched her.

He hadn't touched her in a long, long time: those hot dreams on sultry Sydney nights of him touching her as she wanted him to definitely didn't count.

'No, there isn't, seeing as I keep in contact with *you*.'

Judd chuckled, the familiar sound warming her like the hot chocolate sundaes with extra fudge they'd shared as kids.

'So, tell me the whole story. Your last postcard said you were in the wilds of South Africa shooting zebras, and now you're here. What on earth would tempt the world's best wildlife photographer to do a fashion shoot of birds of the non-feathered variety?'

He'd scoffed at what he termed 'the shallow world of fashion' ever since she'd started working in the industry, so she knew something, or *someone*, important had to be behind this.

'All will be revealed in time.' Judd beckoned the waiter. 'Drink?'

'The usual, please.'

He grinned, his eyes crinkling in the corners just as they used to. 'Is this some kind of test?'

'You bet.'

Shaking his head, he chuckled. 'You're still drinking the same poison you used to in high school? How sad is that?'

'Like you'd remember anyway,' she scoffed. She was more than a little impressed when he nodded at the waiter and said, 'Soda and lime for the lady and a beer for me, thanks, mate.

'So, did I pass?'

'You always did have a good memory,' she muttered, seriously thrilled he'd remembered something as innocuous as her favourite drink. 'Now, tell me why you're really here.'

'A friend set this up. She begged me to do it as a favour for a guy she gets a heap of assignments from, some big shot called Mark Pyman, so here I am.'

He signed for the drinks while one word penetrated her brain.

She.

He'd said *she*.

So who was this mystery woman he held in such high esteem that he would leave his much-loved wildlife and return home? Something he'd avoided doing at all costs once he'd finally escaped Pier Point.

Taking a sip of her drink, she aimed for nonchalant.

'Do I know this friend of yours?'

'Probably. Paula does loads of work for *Finesse*.'

'Paula, as in Australia's top supermodel? Yeah, we've worked a few shoots together. She's nice. I didn't know you knew her?'

He continued to swig his beer, oblivious to how green she was at the thought of Paula having such an influence on *her* best friend.

'We met in South America. I was shooting anacondas and took a short break in Rio afterwards where Paula was doing a bikini shoot.'

'You never mentioned it,' she said, aiming for casual yet knowing it sounded lame. Since when did he have to tell her if he met someone new?

He shrugged, drawing her attention to the breadth of his shoulders; yet another thing that hadn't changed much. In fact, all that hefting camera equipment around had broadened his shoulders to spectacular proportions and she briefly wondered if they still felt as firm, as solid, as they had that one night when her hands had gripped onto them for dear life while his lips had wrought havoc on hers.

'Paula's a great girl. We have a lot in common.'

'Oh?'

She barely managed to restrain herself from wrinkling her nose, the stab of jealousy nothing new. She'd been envious of the few lucky girlfriends he'd had, relieved when they hadn't lasted beyond a week or two.

Pitiful, considering she'd dated extensively—in the vain hope of proving to herself and him that she'd got over him—had always confided in him about her dating disasters and they'd spent hours laughing over her exes' bad points.

So why did the thought of Judd hooking up with leggy Paula leave a sour taste in her mouth? Had to be the extra dash of lime in her drink.

Yeah, right.

She knew exactly why. The women he'd dated had meant nothing to him yet he'd left his precious travels to return home for the first time in eight years for Paula? Not good.

'Yeah, we've both travelled the world and love doing it, we both hate being tied down to one place and we share a passion for ice-cream sundaes.'

How sweet. Not.

'Ice cream? You're kidding me? Paula the Pretzel eats ice cream?'

His eyes narrowed as he cast a speculative look her way. 'It's not like you to be bitchy. What gives?'

Abby shook her head, wondering if the heat on the island had melted her brain. Judd was her best friend, she hadn't seen him in eight years and here she was giving him grief over a favour for a friend.

'Nothing. Just tired, I guess.'

His face relaxed, and before she knew what was happening, he placed a finger under her chin and tipped it up.

'Sounds to me like you're jealous.'

'In that case, you need your hearing checked.'

His touch confused her and it shouldn't. She'd been there, done that and had the T-shirt to prove it—before she'd folded it up and stored it along with her giant crush when he'd left town.

More than a little disconcerted by the erratic beat of her pulse, she tried not to react as he leaned towards her, glimpsing tenderness in his eyes before he planted a brief peck on the end of her nose.

'I've missed you, Weiss.'

His aftershave wafted over her, an expensive musk blend that suited him. He'd never worn the stuff in high school yet had smelled just as good.

And she should know. She hadn't washed the top he'd given her the day after the dance for almost a month, preferring to wear it to bed every night and dream of him.

The sad thing was she still had it folded neatly in the back of her underwear drawer, a memento of the one time she'd thought they might have a chance at more than friendship.

She pulled away quickly, annoyed by the flashbacks to a time long-gone, and saw the surprise flicker across his face.

'We talk all the time. How could you miss me?'

'Talking over the phone isn't the same as this, is it?'

He smiled and reached for her hand, the warmth of his

fingers enclosing hers more than welcome despite the hyper reaction her body was having in response to seeing him after all this time. She'd missed their physical contact: the playful pinches, the casual hand-holding, the bear hugs. They'd been inseparable in high school.

Judd was right. Regular phone contact had nothing on this, the shared affection of two close friends chatting as if they'd never been apart.

'It has been a while.'

'Hey, what's eight years between friends?'

'True,' she said, twirling the lime wedge in her glass with the straw, wondering why she felt so edgy around him all of a sudden.

This was Judd.

Her best buddy.

Why the strange feeling that something had shifted between them? After all, she'd handled her crush, relegated it to the backburner, enjoyed their long-distance friendship more than she could've thought possible all these years.

She'd matured, grown up. So what had shifted in the last few minutes to leave her feeling edgy and panicky and much too aware of Judd as a sexy guy?

Eager to change the topic and break the sudden intimacy that had enveloped them, she said, 'How's the job going? Is the wild world of primates and big cats everything it's cracked up to be?'

'It's better. You should try it some time.'

He dropped her hand, turned away and picked up his beer and she wondered why his smile faded as if she'd just put her foot in it.

'Doubt it. Besides, if this shoot is perfect Mark mentioned a major deal for me.'

'So this job is important to you?'

'Of course.'

She didn't add, *It's what drives me these days*.

Though she loved being a fashion stylist it just wasn't enough at times. Her closest friend spent his life travelling the world and she never saw him while the rest of her social circle consisted of work colleagues and acquaintances hell-bent on partying their way through life. And she'd let go of the conga line a long time ago.

Abby didn't understand the emotion that played across his face at her response—it almost bordered on disappointment. His job obviously meant everything to him, too. Why else would he have spent the last eight years leading a nomadic existence?

'Here's to us and doing a good job over the next week.'

He raised his glass towards her, along with her hopes.

A week. A whole week spent in the company of her best friend, the one guy known to bring a smile to her face and whom she'd missed terribly over the years if this strange jittery feeling was anything to go by.

'I'll drink to that.'

As their glasses clinked a tiny crack appeared in hers and she hoped to God a similar thing wouldn't happen to their friendship.

Maybe she'd been pushing herself too hard lately.

Maybe it had been too long between dates.

Maybe she just needed a day or two in Judd's teasing company to put the smile back on her face.

But whatever was causing the tiny trickle of tension between them, she needed to get over it. Judd meant the world to her and there was no way she'd jeopardise their friendship.

For anything.

CHAPTER TWO

JUDD ran a hand over his face and stared at his reflection in the mirror behind the bar.

Yeah, same eyes, same nose, same chin.

Then why had Abby stared at him as if he'd suddenly sprouted horns when he'd surprised her a few minutes ago?

He'd assumed she'd be over the moon to see him and, though she'd seemed happy, he could tell something was bugging her.

It might have been a few months since they'd talked, but he knew her almost better than he knew himself. Their closeness scared him at times—after all, she was a woman and women usually had expectations.

However, Abby was different. She didn't want anything from him. She was happy just being his friend, and if she ever demanded anything more, he'd run, just as he had eight years earlier.

'Preening in front of the mirror, Calloway? Some things never change.'

He swivelled to face Abby as she returned from the Ladies and resumed her seat at the bar, struck all over again by how incredible she looked.

They'd been e-mailing pics to each other over the years so he'd known she hadn't cut her hair and still favoured casual clothes over the designer stuff she worked with, but seeing her in the flesh had him in a spin he hadn't expected.

Those pics didn't do her justice considering her sexy new bod: toned legs, tiny waist, cute butt and great boobs. Her athletic high-school figure had developed curves in all the right places and he'd be blind not to notice, friends or not.

'I never preened back then,' he said, sporting a mock offended expression she didn't buy for a second, considering they'd always sparred like this. If she hadn't bought it back then, there wasn't a hope in Hades she'd buy it now.

She quirked an eyebrow. 'Oh, yeah? I distinctly remember a certain high-school jock flexing his muscles in front of my full-length mirror after he joined a gym. And another time when you bought that atrocious flannel muscle shirt and that time you—'

'Okay, okay. Give a guy a break.'

He held up his hands to ward her off and she swatted them away, her casual touch having a strange effect. Her playful pat seemed to linger, the warmth from her palm tingling against his skin.

He gritted his teeth, hoping the flare of awareness didn't show on his face.

He'd thought he was past all this with her.

He'd thought wrong.

Surely eight years' absence should've dulled the attraction?

'You've got a memory like a damn elephant. I'd hate to think what else you remember.'

'You'd be amazed,' she said, her voice surprisingly low

as she raised her glass in his direction, an enigmatic smile curving her glossed lips.

His beer glass halted halfway to his mouth as he registered with shocking clarity that Abby was flirting with him.

They never flirted.

Teased, ribbed, confided but never, ever flirted.

Friends didn't flirt. At least, they never did. Over the years, it was as if that kiss on grad night had never happened and he wanted to keep it that way.

Then what was with his urge to flirt right back, to see where this new flicker of heat burning between them could lead?

'Well, well, well. Looks as if you're working real hard, boss.'

The booming voice of his assistant, Tom Bradley, rang out a second before he slapped him on the back and he beckoned Tom forward, unsure whether to be relieved or annoyed at the interruption.

'I'm in the middle of a business meeting,' Judd said, sending Abby a wink that said 'right back at you, babe', noting her faint blush with satisfaction. His best friend liked to dish out the flirting stuff, but it looked as if she had a little trouble taking it. 'Meet Abby Weiss, fashion stylist extraordinaire.'

Tom's goofy expression had Judd shifting his barstool closer to Abby's before he realised what he was doing.

'Pleased to meet you,' Tom said, pulling up a stool.

'Likewise.'

Abby shook Tom's hand, a perfectly natural, polite, normal thing to do.

However, there was nothing perfectly normal about the

absurd stab of jealousy burning like acid in his gut as he explained, 'Abby and I went to school together.'

Tom sat bolt upright, sending him a 'what the…?' look. '*The* Abby? Your best mate Abby?'

He nodded. 'The one and only.'

Tom's head swivelled between the two of them, his grin giving way to a knowing smile. 'Isn't this just great? The two of you get to work and play together.'

Abby laughed. 'I'm not sure whether to be flattered Calloway has been talking about me or driven to find out exactly what he's been saying.'

'Oh, it's all good,' Tom said, gesturing to the barman for a beer before turning his attention solely on Abby. 'Though he never told me how gorgeous you are.'

'Why, thank you, kind sir,' she said, batting her eyelashes in an exaggerated display of coquettishness, joining in with Tom's chuckles, while Judd tried to ignore the insane flicker of jealousy that shot through him again.

Damn, he must be more jet-lagged than he thought. He'd heard about Abby's boyfriends before, had poked fun at them, had teased her mercilessly. So why did the thought of Tom lusting after her annoy the hell out of him?

'So you two have been mates for ever?'

'Uh-huh,' Judd said, thankful the big guy had turned off the charm.

He'd seen women flock to Tom, with his Nordic good looks and six-four frame, and he had no idea how Abby would react to his assistant if he set his sights on her.

Why do you care?

A prickle of awareness raised the hair on the back of his neck as he took in her big blue eyes, genuine smile, long brown hair and lush curves, knowing exactly why he cared, but too damned scared to admit it.

'Have you two ever been more than friends?'

Abby made a strange sound somewhere between a snort and a guffaw before quickly hiding a smile behind her glass while motioning for him to answer.

Tom's question instantly resurrected memories of the one time they'd kissed, an event he had no intention of repeating.

It had been far too dangerous the first time around.

He'd felt too much, enjoyed the feeling of her body responding to his far too much. He'd put it down to overactive hormones at the time. What eighteen-year-old wouldn't take the opportunity to kiss the school's resident Miss Personality?

However, he'd been totally unprepared for the depth of feeling that had swamped him after the kiss and the response he'd glimpsed in her eyes had sent him running— and he hadn't stopped running since.

Sending Tom his best 'shut the hell up' glare, he said, 'Listen up, Mr Curiosity. Can the questions and move your ass. We need to be down at the beach in less than an hour for the first shoot, so go grab the equipment and I'll meet you down there.'

'Yes, sir!'

Tom rolled his eyes at Abby before snapping him a mock salute. 'Nice meeting you, Abby. Looking forward to working with you.'

'Same here.'

Judd waited till Tom moved off before leaning across and whispering in her ear, 'So, have we?'

Her baby-blues widened ever so slightly as she registered what he meant, but chose to play dumb. 'Have we what?'

'Been more than friends?'

'You tell me,' she fired straight back at him with a toss of her gorgeous hair.

He laughed and sat back, at ease with the way they slipped into their bantering ways, feeling increasingly stupid about the way he'd reacted to Tom's light flirtation with her.

'I guess you don't ever think about that sensational kiss on grad night, huh?'

'You guessed right,' she said, her fingers plucking at the edge of her skirt before she stilled them when she caught him looking. 'And it wasn't that great.'

'Liar,' he murmured, placing his hand over hers, vindicated by the slight tremor of her hand beneath his, all too aware of her bare leg mere millimetres from his curious fingertips.

Would it feel as smooth as it looked?

Would her skin be warm and soft or cool and firm?

Would touching her leg be a prelude to more?

'Okay, you got me. You're the best damn kisser I've ever had. There. Does that satisfy your humungous ego?'

She squirmed away and he lifted his hand, shaken by how close he'd come to caressing her, by how damn much he wanted to.

'It would if I thought you meant it,' he said, forcing a chuckle as he tried not to stare at her breasts and the evidence of how she'd responded to his touch despite acting immune.

Damn, what was wrong with him?

They'd got past that kiddie kiss, had been best buddies for eight years. Why had he turned into Mr Hormone the minute he'd laid eyes on her?

Draining her drink, she slammed the soda glass a little

too loudly on the bar before sliding off her stool. 'As much as I'd like to stay and flatter you, I've got work to do. See you on the beach shortly.'

'You got it, boss.'

'And don't you forget it,' she said, sending him a saucy wave over her shoulder as she sashayed out of the bar, leaving him with a spectacular view of her lovely legs and the way her short skirt flipped around her thighs, as if teasing the observer to discover the hidden delights beneath.

And, boy, did he have a sudden hankering to go exploring…

Swiping a hand across his eyes in the futile effort to wipe her sexy image from his mind, he picked up his camera bag and headed out the door.

He didn't need this.

He didn't need any complications in his life.

Was that what this new, flirtatious Abby was, a complication?

Damned if he knew.

Abby sorted through several bikinis and sarongs, matching style and colour with efficiency. The latest animal prints, from leopard spots to zebra stripes, were everywhere following the catwalk craze in Paris and Milan a few months earlier and personally she loved the funky twists on an old favourite.

Holding up a flirty bra with matching boy-leg knickers bathing combo, she smiled. She thrived on this, the freedom to combine her artistic eye with practical savvy on what looked good for each season. And if the feedback from *Finesse*'s readers was any indication, they appreciated her keen eye for fashion as much as Mark did. Why else would he hint at some major deal?

She wondered what Judd would think about how far she'd come. He'd always teased her about her interest in clothes, calling her Barbie just to get a reaction, and she'd obliged every time, their arguments as much a part of their friendship as sharing their hopes and dreams.

Thoughts of Judd conjured up his image and how surprised she'd been to see him earlier. He looked good! He'd acquired a bronze tan that accentuated the gold and green flecks in his hazel eyes and the brightness of his smile, and he'd let his hair grow, the thick dark waves curling at his collar. He could turn heads, all right, not that she'd ever let the big oaf know.

'Which bikini is mine? And please don't say it's the thong.'

Tara Lindman grabbed the tiger-print two-piece Abby handed her and held it up for inspection. 'Ugh! I knew it. Time to head back to the gym for another hundred lunges.'

Abby smiled at the model, leaned back and raised an eyebrow as she stared pointedly at her rear.

'Oh, yeah. The butt that inspires a nation needs to be more toned. Give me a break. If those buns were any firmer you could bounce a dollar coin off them.'

Tara wiggled the piece of anatomy under scrutiny. 'Hey, it's not *you* that has to expose herself all in the name of work.'

'Amen to that,' Abby said, joining in Tara's laughter.

She'd worked with the model on and off for the last year and admired her professionalism mixed with a good dose of reality. Most models she knew strutted around with their noses ten feet in the air, but not Tara. In fact, they'd bonded over the many shoots they'd done together, a fact that surprised Abby. After all, what did she have in common with the lithe goddess who had men falling at her feet without trying?

'Have you seen that new photographer?' Tara continued sorting through the bikinis, her eyes lighting up at a sleek black one-piece cut daringly low in front. 'He's absolutely scrumptious.'

Abby smiled and agreed to the understatement of the year. 'Yeah, he's cute.'

'*Cute?*' Tara screeched. '*Cute?* Are you blind? He's drop-dead gorgeous.' She wiggled her ring finger under Abby's nose. 'And, if I'm not mistaken, doesn't seem to have a marital noose around his neck.'

'You're right about his looks, but how can I confess that a guy I've known since second grade is gorgeous? If he ever found out, it'd go straight to his head.'

'You *know* him?'

Tara's voice raised several octaves, if that were possible after her last screech, as she grabbed Abby's arm. 'Ooh, tell me more. How well do you know him? Do you know him or do you *know* him?'

'We're friends. Good friends. And I'd like to keep it that way, so stop with the inferences.'

'Hey, who's inferring anything? I simply put two and two together.'

Abby picked up a magenta sarong and draped it against Tara's fair skin. 'What's that supposed to mean?'

Tara grabbed the sarong and twirled it around her head, leaving her twinkling green eyes peering out of a gap in the material like a gypsy.

'It means that I can tell the future and yours is looking up, sweetie. You got this strange kind of glow when you mentioned your friendship with Captain Australia.'

'That's because he's my best friend and I love him. As a *friend*.'

Abby made a grab for the sarong and Tara dodged, her chuckles doing little for Abby's peace of mind.

'Yeah, well, don't look now but your friend is heading this way. Phew, is he hot or what?'

Abby chuckled as Tara fanned her face, her gaze following the model's line of vision.

Sure enough Judd was heading their way and in his navy shorts, white T-shirt and crumpled, just-out-of-bed hair courtesy of the stiff ocean breeze, with resident killer smile in place, he did look pretty hot.

From a friend's purely objective viewpoint, of course.

'Here I am, reporting for duty, Weiss.'

Abby smiled and returned his half-salute. 'It's going to be more fun than I thought ordering you around. Now, how about you set up over there near that palm tree?'

'Great,' he said, his answering grin telling her he'd give as good as he got over the next week. 'Don't let the power trip go to your head or anything. Otherwise I might just have to take you down.'

'Is that right?'

She raised an eyebrow, loving how quickly they'd slipped back into familiar teasing mode, knowing this job would be a blast courtesy of his quirky sense of humour.

'Ahem.' Tara gave a loud cough. 'I think introductions are in order?' She thrust her hand out. 'Hi, I'm Tara Lindman.'

Judd's grin widened and Abby rolled her eyes. She'd

seen this same reaction from every red-blooded male who came within two feet of Tara.

'I know. I'm Judd Calloway, photographer extraordinaire, at your service.'

'Don't you shoot wildlife?'

'I need a change and this is it.'

He waved in the general direction of the bikinis and sarongs Abby had sorted. 'Of course, it has other advantages. Did Abby tell you we're old friends?'

Tara smiled and slipped her arm around Abby's shoulders. 'She certainly did. Lucky Abby.'

Thankfully, a loud, tuneless whistle of an old Beach Boys hit drifted towards them from behind a pile of windsurfers and saved Abby from giving Tara a swift elbow in the solar plexus as they all turned to see the new arrival.

Tara dropped her arm and straightened, her hands smoothing back her glorious auburn hair in a practised motion.

'Speaking of friends, who is *that*?'

'That's Tom, my assistant. Might be wise to stay away from him—he's a lady-killer.'

Judd stared directly at her and Abby wondered why the pointed glare when a moment ago they'd been trading banter.

Tom strolled up to them, laden like a pack donkey with camera equipment.

'Hello, lovely ladies.' He placed his load gently on the sand like a mother placing her newborn in its crib. 'Hey, Abby. And you, beautiful, need no introduction.' He took Tara's hand, kissed it and bowed. 'I am truly honoured.'

Judd rolled his eyes. 'Don't say I didn't warn you.'

Tara chuckled, obviously loving every minute of the attention. 'I can handle him. You're just a giant pussycat, aren't you, Tom?'

Tom growled in response. 'Does that mean I get my tummy rubbed?'

Abby joined in Tara's laughter—coming from any other guy she would've taken the line as offensive but there was something endearing about the big man.

'Okay, folks. Though I'd love to stand around and chat, we have a shoot to do. So let's get started.'

As she turned away and picked up her clipboard, Judd tapped her on the shoulder. 'Watch out for Tom.'

'What?'

Judd's serious expression had her biting the inside of her cheek to stop laughing. 'I meant it when I said he was a lady-killer. And I wouldn't want you getting hurt or anything.'

Abby smiled, confused by Judd's warning; he'd never done this before, gone all big-brother on her. He'd usually wait till she fell for the wrong guy, then tease her about it later with the usual 'I told you so'.

Reaching up, she tapped him on the cheek lightly. 'Thanks for the warning, but I'm a big girl now. I think I can take care of myself, especially with the Toms of this world.'

'Yeah, well, I'm just looking out for you, one buddy to another,' he muttered, checking out the camera in his hand, a vertical crease between his brows.

'You're gorgeous,' she said, standing on tiptoe and planting a quick peck on his cheek, unprepared for the swift, powerful urge to linger a tad longer than necessary as the scent of his faint musk aftershave enveloped her.

Boy, this island heat was definitely getting to her.

'Right back at you.'

Judd's gaze locked onto hers as she pulled away and for one, long, crazy, loaded moment she wondered if there was more behind his casual comment, if he remembered her using the same phrase on that fateful night, a moment before he kissed her...

Rattled by the electricity buzzing between them, she said, 'Speaking of looking out for friends, why don't you tell me about you and Paula? Is it serious?' Abby fiddled with the sarong in her hands, unable to keep the growing grin from her face. 'You know, seeing as you're sharing sundaes and all.'

'We're friends. That's it.'

He paused, and the second she glimpsed the familiar twinkle in his eyes, she knew he was about to fire a broadside back. 'Besides, models aren't my thing. Perhaps I'm more into fashion stylists?'

To her annoyance, she blushed, heat rising up her neck to stain her cheeks. Damn it, she'd never blushed in her life, his constant teasing eliciting fiery verbal responses rather than embarrassment.

'Isn't it lucky that fashion stylists aren't into you? At least, not this one, anyway.'

She sent him a scathing glance, which would've carried more punch if she'd managed to keep a straight face and not stuck her tongue out at him like an adolescent, swept up an armful of colourful sarongs and turned towards the beach.

'I think you're fibbing,' he called out at her retreating back, his laughter taunting her every step.

'And I think you're delusional.'

Judd grinned as he swung his camera bag over his shoulder and followed Abby down the beach.

God, he missed this: the constant sparring, the teasing, the matching of wills. No one had ever understood him like Abby. No one probably ever would.

She was the family he'd never had, the one bright spark in his life during the miserable years growing up after his mum had died and he'd been shackled to Pier Point courtesy of his father.

She'd always been there for him. So what would she make of his latest plan?

It was too soon to tell her everything, for he had no idea how she'd react.

Would she be happy?

Would she think he was nuts?

Only time would tell as he planned to wait till the job neared completion before divulging the truth.

After all, who needed a week of nagging, which was exactly what dear Abby would do, when he could spend that time teasing her, laughing with her, flirting with her instead?

Yeah, he'd tell her at the end of the week.

In the meantime they had some serious catching up to do.

CHAPTER THREE

ABBY lay back in the bath, closed her eyes and moaned, the jasmine-scented steam surrounding her in a fragrant cloud.

What a day.

Working with Judd had been a pleasure, his professionalism and skill far surpassing that of any other photographers she'd worked with. Having him in such close proximity, smiling at her, taunting her, had been fun, just like old times.

Well, not exactly like old times.

Back then they'd been two kids against the world, teenage rebels who couldn't wait to escape the confines of Pier Point and the memories the place held.

Then again, if they hadn't had such lousy parents, such a strong common bond, maybe their friendship wouldn't have stood the test of time.

Perhaps I'm more into fashion stylists?

She smiled at the memory of his teasing jibe. Their easygoing relationship had never been any different, giving as good as they got, each of them ready with a cutting comeback for every teasing comment fired at the other. And though Judd could turn her winning retorts to losers in the blink of an eye, she could handle it. In fact, she thrived on it and could hardly wait to match wits with him on this trip.

As for the unexpected heat that had flared between them, first when he'd laid his hand on her leg in the bar and later with that loaded moment at the beach, she wouldn't read anything into it.

Probably a perfectly natural reaction of two adults who were the best of friends and hadn't seen each other since their teens getting reacquainted. Either that or she still harboured her pathetic teenage crush, no matter how many times she'd told herself over the years she'd grown up.

The phone jangled and she glared at it. Beautiful black marble bathrooms with exquisite bubble-bath gels and Jacuzzis this size were meant for relaxation and the brainiac who had installed a gold phone on the wall should be shot.

Sighing, she reached for the phone. Unless there was a problem with the location for tomorrow's shoot or one of the models had binged on chocolate and couldn't fit into any of the outfits, she didn't want to know about it.

'Hello?'

'Where are you, Weiss? Hiding in the closet?'

Abby grinned, and stuck her big toe in the bath spout. 'Hey, I'm not the one who has a whole host of skeletons in there.'

Judd chuckled. 'Hey, remind me to stop telling you all my dirty little secrets.'

'And where would the fun be in that?'

Abby stretched an arm and blew gently on the bubbles clinging to her skin. When was the last time she'd taken a bath, taken time out to relax at the end of a busy day? Le

lone have more than a rushed five-minute phone call with
er best friend calling from the remotest regions of the
arth on a crackling line punctuated with static?

'So what are you up to?'

'Taking a bath,' she said, examining her wrinkled fin-
ertips, savouring the luxury of a long soak.

'With bubbles?'

'You bet.'

'Mmm…kinky.'

Rolling her eyes at Judd's *faux* growl, Abby sank further
nto the suds.

'You're depraved. Now, was there a point to this phone
all or do you just like bugging me for the hell of it?'

His familiar laughter rippled over her and she hoped the
nexpected goose bumps skittering along her arm had
nore to do with the only part of her skin not submerged
nd less to do with an uncharacteristic reaction to her best
riend's intimate chuckle.

'I could make a national pastime out of bugging you,
ut actually I was wondering what you're doing for dinner?
Do we eat with the work crowd or can we sneak off and
lay hookey?'

'I'm all for hookey,' she said, eager for some one-on-
ne time with Judd. If they only had a week together, she'd
nake the most of it, every precious second.

'Great. I'll meet you at the Ocean Breeze restaurant
a an hour?'

'Sounds like a plan.'

'And Weiss?'

'Yeah?'

'Wear something sexy.'

The dial tone hummed in her ear and Abby glared at th phone.

She should know him by now. Judd always got the las word in, always, and it was usually designed to drive her mad

Well, he might've got the last word in but he'd asked fo it, and if there was one thing she liked more than ribbin her best friend it was getting the upper hand.

Something sexy, huh?

Shaking her head and sending water droplets flyin everywhere, she reached for a towel.

Her best buddy was about to get a lesson in being careft what he wished for.

Judd had never been a party guy.

Give him the plains of Africa or the jungles of Sout America any day. Saharan winds, Amazonian deluge Asian typhoons…he loved the elements, loved the free dom, always had. He never felt whole unless he had camera in his hand, capturing the animals that had held hir enthralled since he'd opened his first textbook at schoc and seen a huge, scary gorilla with bared teeth staring bac at him from the page.

It had been his dream from that day on.

A dream that had evolved, developed, and landed hir here, smack bang in babe heaven.

Taking a seat at a table near the bar, he watched som of the models boogying on the dance floor and knew tha partying definitely had something going for it. The exclu sive resort was a walking advertisement for the hotte women on the planet and he wouldn't be male if he didn notice and appreciate the luscious scenery.

As if on cue, Abby walked into the room and his mouth went dry.

In a flash he was transported back to the night of the high-school dance and the precise moment he'd laid eyes on her in her first formal dress, a blue satin number with the tiniest of straps and outlandish puffy skirt, tottering down her porch steps towards him in ridiculous heels. She'd taken his breath away, the vision imprinted on his brain for ever.

Friends weren't meant to look like that!

With the dress outlining her body, glossy brown hair piled high with a few curling tendrils framing her face... that face, her blue eyes shining at him with pleasure and more than a hint of mystery in their depths.

And what had he done?

Fired the usual barbs her way, teased her mercilessly, while she'd stared at him with her beautiful eyes, sucking him in deeper and deeper till he hadn't been able to think straight let alone be responsible for his actions. So he'd done the only thing any normal, eighteen-year-old guy would have done.

He'd kissed her.

Correction, he'd pounced on her, half expecting her to slap him silly. Instead she'd responded like a tigress, fuelling his passion till his hormones had warred with his common sense in a raging battle. Fortunately, his common sense had won and he'd played the whole incident down, laughing it off as an experiment between two friends trying to prove they'd just entered the world of grown-ups.

Now, staring at Abby in a fitted black halter dress outlining her curvy body to perfection, with her hair piled in a similar arrangement to that fateful night, he wondered if he'd been so fortunate after all.

He stood up and waved her over, drawing a chair out as she neared the table, unable to tear his eyes away from her.

'Not bad,' he murmured in her ear as she sat down, her light floral fragrance beckoning him closer, and he pulled back with effort, resisting an irrational urge to place a kiss behind her ear.

Jasmine.

She'd always loved it and the scent had haunted him over the years, a poignant reminder of her.

'Is that a compliment, Calloway?'

She'd used a minimum of make-up, just enough to highlight her eyes, which shone luminous in the reflected glow of the torches around the perimeter of the room. He wondered if her eyes had always been that blue, that incandescent.

'Call me Judd,' he said, unable to quell the urge to flirt, hoping she'd join in the swing of things.

She batted her eyelashes, designed to tease. 'In that case you can call me Abby.'

Judd smiled and reached out to run his hand slowly down her arm in a gesture that was part friendly, part daring, enjoying the flare of awareness in her eyes.

Maybe it was the balmy breeze, maybe it was the illusion of being secluded on a tropical island and far enough away from reality, maybe it was the newfound heat sizzling between them. Whatever it was, he wanted to push the boundaries of their friendship and see what happened.

'Abby. What a beautiful name. Conjures up all sorts of images like ancient stone churches surrounded by overgrown cottage gardens with oak trees reaching up to the endless blue sky the same colour as your eyes…'

Abby snorted and rolled her eyes. 'Hey! I'm not one of your bimbos. You don't have to lay it on that thick!'

Judd laughed and shrugged. 'Can't blame a guy for trying. So, what does the name Judd conjure up for you?'

He wondered if she'd take the bait and remember what she'd once told him all those years ago. By the glint in her eyes she wouldn't disappoint.

'That's easy, Judd *Kane* Calloway. A long, thin reed used to put cheeky boys like you back in their place.'

She reached over and tweaked his nose as she used to, resurrecting instant memories of their childhood years and reminding him of how long they'd been friends.

'Now, what does a girl have to do to get a drink in this place?'

'Let me guess—the usual?'

Her blue eyes sparkled with characteristic cheek while her lips curved in a coy smile he'd never seen before.

'Nah…I'm feeling reckless tonight. Surprise me.'

As if noticing how stunning she looked wasn't enough torture, she had to go and throw him a curve ball like that. If he didn't know better, he'd say she was definitely flirting with him again.

But that couldn't be right. Abby teased him, riled him and jibed at him, but flirt?

No way.

This tropical air was definitely getting to him.

He called a waiter over, placed their orders, including a cocktail for her guaranteed to regain the upper hand, and leaned back in his chair.

'Nice outfit, by the way. Glad to know you take my advice so seriously.'

His greedy gaze skimmed the black silk clinging to her curves, ending just above her knees, accentuating her tiny waist, outlining her breasts…

He sat up and sent a frantic glance in the waiter's direction, wishing their drinks would arrive a.s.a.p.

He needed cooling down, badly.

'You think I wore this for you?' If her smile had been coy before, it turned positively smug now. 'Still delusional from all that African heat, huh?'

He couldn't back down from the challenge in her eyes even though continuing this conversation would only make it harder for him to view her as 'just friends' material.

He'd never backed down from one of her challenges and he'd be damned if he would now. Besides, he liked a hint of danger. Kept things interesting.

Reaching out to smooth an imaginary crease from the silk draped like liquid lava across her lower thigh, he said, 'Well, I did say wear something sexy and, boy, does this dress deliver.'

'Clothes maketh the woman and all that?'

She had him there.

If he agreed, she'd know he thought she was sexy. If he disagreed, he'd look like a heel.

Thankfully, the waiter arrived as he racked his brain for a quick response and deposited an icy beer in front of him and a wicked concoction of Cointreau, Galliano, pineapple juice and cream in a champagne glass for Abby.

'What's this?'

She took a sip, her eyes widening imperceptibly as a

faint pink stained her cheeks. 'On second thoughts, don't answer that. It's got a kick like a mule and perhaps it's better I don't know. What my liver doesn't know won't hurt it.'

Struggling to keep a triumphant smile off his face, he said, 'A Hot Dream.'

To his immense satisfaction, the pink in her cheeks deepened to crimson.

'Mmm…nice,' she murmured, her gaze firmly focused on the cherry stuck on the end of a paper umbrella wedged precariously on the edge of her glass.

Her noncommittal answer only spurred him on and he chugged on his beer before taking his stirring one step further.

'So, you like hot dreams, huh?'

Her blue-eyed gaze flew to his and for a split second he could've sworn he glimpsed a flicker of desire there before she quickly masked it with her telltale sass.

Raising her glass in his direction, she said, 'The drink's great. As for the rest, you'll never know.'

'Is that right?'

'Uh-huh.'

She nodded, swirling the cocktail in slow, rhythmic circles as she stared into the drink as if hypnotised.

'Where's Tom, by the way?'

Startled by the swift change of topic, and more disgruntled at her mention of the big guy than he'd like to be, he said, 'Probably terrorising some poor single woman somewhere. Why?'

She sipped her cocktail and looked up at him from beneath her lashes.

'Oh, I was hoping to run into him tonight. I need a big, strong man to help me move some stuff for tomorrow's shoot.'

'And what am I? Chopped liver?'

Her blue eyes gleamed, mischief etched across her face. 'Think you can handle it, huh?'

She reached over and squeezed his biceps as if testing his strength. 'Mmm…not bad.'

And just like that, his libido shifted into overdrive. He tried not to react, wondering what had got into him.

She was his best friend, had been for ever, the one constant in his life when the rest of it had threatened to spiral out of control. She knew about his dad, the lack of money growing up, the way he'd had to fight for his education, accepting scholarships when he hated taking charity from anyone.

Yet here he was, reacting to her simple touch, which left him with a burning desire to push their friendship to the outer limit.

What the hell was he thinking?

Instilling the right amount of casualness into his voice, he said, 'Lady, I can handle anything you care to dish out.'

'Really?'

She let her hand drop, though he was sure she'd let it linger longer than necessary. Or was that a figment of his overheated imagination? The way it had gone haywire since he'd set foot on this damn island and seen her again he wouldn't be surprised if smoke started pouring out of his ears like some crazy cartoon character.

'Really.'

He folded his arms to stop reaching out and doing something even more disastrous, like hauling her onto his lap.

Damn, this wasn't working out as he'd planned. He'd wanted to flirt a little, make *her* squirm, and suddenly his body was way out of control. What was with this insane impulse to throw caution to the wind and get physical with the one woman he should leave alone?

'In that case, follow me.'

She stood and smoothed her skirt down, the action drawing his attention to her long legs that were bare beneath the silky fabric of her dress. 'Oh, and bring those biceps.'

She winked as she cast a knowing glance over her shoulder and caught him staring at her legs. Stifling a groan, he followed her, suspecting, the mood they were both in, she would probably lead him directly into trouble.

Abby had no idea what demon had lodged itself in her brain tonight.

Okay, so that was a lie.

The minute Mr 'I always want the upper hand' Calloway had told her to dress sexy before hanging up on her earlier, she'd known she'd give as good as she got.

So she'd gone the whole nine yards, wearing a new killer LBD, taking extra care with her make-up, piling her hair up in a glam do she'd learned from the hairstylist earlier that day.

She'd always done the opposite of what he challenged growing up so the goofball had probably expected her to wear trendily torn jeans and a crop top to dinner.

Well, she'd shown him.

However, things hadn't gone quite to plan.

She hadn't banked on her bizarre reaction to Judd the moment she walked into the bar area and he saw her dressed up. Then as she'd walked towards him on uncharacteristically wobbly legs and seen that funny look in his

eyes, she'd silently recited the mantra *he's just a friend...
he's just a friend* when the intense way he studied her said
anything but.

So what had she done? She'd flirted with him. Worse,
she'd touched him, adding to her confusion.

She didn't get it.

They'd always traded light-hearted banter like this over
the phone and via e-mails, so what was so different about
this place, about tonight?

'Where are we going?'

Judd caught up to her and she wondered if he'd drunk
his fill. She'd caught him ogling her legs and, despite the
confusion ricocheting through her body, hoped he liked
what he saw.

She'd never seen that look before, the one that said
he'd noticed her desirability as a woman, and it thrilled her
more than it should.

'Trust me,' she said, changing her course at the last minute.

She'd had every intention of asking him to help move
several racks of clothes from her room to the magnificent
waterfall that cascaded through the resort's lobby, but she
wasn't completely stupid. If she led him to her room, there
was no telling what the impish devil newly residing in her
brain might urge her to do.

'Isn't that supposed to be my line?'

'That's just it. When guys say "trust me" it *is* a line.'

'And when a woman says it, I should believe you?'

He ran his hand through his hair, leaving it endearingly
tousled as it had been back in high school.

'Of course. Have I ever lied to you?'

As soon as the words left her mouth, she inwardly cringed.

She'd lived a lie for the first week after the night of the grad dance and their unexpected kiss, hiding her feelings from him like a magician with nothing up his sleeves. And if she wasn't careful—hey presto—her soul would be laid bare all over again quicker than she could pull a sarong out of a sunhat.

He stopped, took hold of her arms and turned her to face him. 'I don't know. Have you?'

She held her breath, unsure what to make of his question or the intensity behind his stare.

Great—just thinking about the past probably conjured up some goofy expression on her face, and if she wasn't careful, he'd get the wrong idea.

'Damn it, Abby, stop looking at me like that.'

Before she could react, he pulled her into his arms and kissed her. Just as swiftly, just as unexpectedly as the first time all those years ago.

However, this time was different, way different, as every nerve ending in her adult body came to life.

This wasn't the abrupt, nervous, fumbling kiss of a couple of kids experimenting.

This was a delicious, spine-tingling melding of mouths, of two people desperately eager to taste each other, an explosion of hot mouths and hotter bodies.

He snaked an arm around her back, his fingers skimming her bare skin, while the other cupped her head, angling for greater access to her mouth and she gave it to him, yearning to feel the first tantalising sweep of his tongue in her mouth, relishing the low, deep groan coming from his chest.

She should've pushed him away, told him she'd been mentally reminiscing about old times and he'd obviously got the wrong message by the expression on her face.

Instead, she complied without logic, amazed she'd been deprived of this incredible sensation for so long and knowing this one delicious, forbidden taste of a guy she'd been platonic with for most of her life would leave her desperate for a lifetime more of his kisses.

No, no! He's your friend. This is a mistake! her voice of reason screamed, which her body happily ignored and did its own thing.

He groaned again as she leaned flush against him, the kiss deepening as his tongue flicked to meet hers, taunting, teasing, just as his words usually did.

However, his words had never elicited this response, this wanton urge to drag him back to her room and lose herself in this moment for ever.

She wrapped her arms around him, wishing she could feel more of him, skin to skin, as he kissed his way across her jaw and down her neck.

Heat exploded between them, searing a burning path through her body and straight to her core.

Just friends, huh?

Suddenly, they'd got a whole lot friendlier and she didn't have a clue how to react. With one kiss he threatened to consume every last shred of common sense she possessed. Not that she cared…she'd passed that point about a minute earlier, the moment his lips had touched hers and sent her straight to heaven.

When he stilled and pulled away, staring into her eyes for a long moment, she met his gaze unflinchingly, trying to read his expression in the twilight, wanting him to be first to break the tense silence.

'Take one sexy dress, a wicked cocktail, island heat,

noonlight, a healthy amount of stirring and what do you
get? Madness.'

Without another word, he shook his head, turned and
walked away.

CHAPTER FOUR

'GOOD morning.'

Abby slid into the seat opposite Judd and plonked an armful of paperwork on the table, raising an eyebrow as she sent a pointed look at the three empty coffee mugs in front of him.

He cradled a fourth and shrugged, sending her a rueful smile. 'What can I say? I'm lousy in the mornings without a caffeine hit.'

What could he say? He could start by explaining what that kiss last night was about.

However, rather than broach the subject that had kept her awake for most of the night—*sans* caffeine—she passed a folder across to him.

'Here's today's schedule.'

She watched him sip his strong black coffee, savouring every mouthful with a low, satisfied 'mmm'. 'Perhaps you should try a healthy breakfast to kick-start your day rather than all that coffee? The last thing I need is my photographer bouncing off the walls.'

'Did you always nag me like this or is it a new endearing trait you've picked up?'

He smiled, the laugh lines crinkling at the outer corners of his eyes as he raised his mug at her in a 'cheers'.

Though it had only been six months since she'd last seen a picture of him, he looked different: older, weary, like a guy in desperate need of time-out.

It wasn't just the deep creases around his eyes but the odd expression she glimpsed there at times, almost as if he had some major stuff going on. She wondered if she should pry as she usually did or wait till he told her in his own sweet time.

'So you think I'm a nag, huh? Tell me again why you're my best friend?'

She tried a mock frown and failed as they smiled across the table at one another like two people in perfect sync. As they usually were and, apart from that little lapse last night, would remain if she had any say in it.

The grin faded from his face as he placed his mug on the table.

'Speaking of friends, I need to apologise for last night. That kiss was way out of line.'

'You bet your sweet butt it was, mister. Been spending too much time in the Sahara and I just happened to be the first woman who came along?'

'Well, I wouldn't put it exactly like that…'

He trailed off as she burst out laughing, an answering smile tugging at the corners of his mouth. 'Well, okay, you could be right. It's been a while between drinks, you looked incredible last night and I sort of lost my head. How does that sound?'

Quite plausible and probably what that kiss had been about, but she wouldn't let him off that easily.

'Pretty pathetic actually, but then I'd expect nothing less from you.'

He clutched his heart as if she'd wounded him. 'Ouch! That hurts.'

'You ain't seen nothing yet. Now, let's talk business. We've got a tonne of work to do.'

Thankful they'd put any potential awkwardness behind them, though she wasn't entirely convinced by his reasoning about the kiss, she flipped open the folder for the day's schedule.

However, before she could hand him a copy her mobile rang and a quick glance at the caller ID told her she had to take the call.

'It's Mark Pyman. I'll only be a few secs,' she said, hitting the answer button as an odd expression she couldn't fathom flashed across Judd's face as he returned to drinking his coffee.

'Hi, Mark. What can I do for you?'

'We've got a problem, Abby. A big one.'

Abby stifled a sigh. It must be big for the scrupulously polite executive to forgo his usual greeting.

'What's up?'

'Bassel Designs wants an urgent wedding-dress shot added to the spread.'

'So what's the problem? Courier it over and we'll slot it in.'

Mark paused, as if searching for the right words, and a ripple of unease slid over her. 'The dress won't fit any of the models on your shoot. Apparently they want a more realistic look for the shot.'

'Uh-huh,' she said, racking her brain for a lightning-fast solution.

It wasn't the first time the biggest designer in Australia had made an odd last-minute request and she'd always come through for them before.

'How about I find a couple holidaying on the island and—'

'Time frame's tight. The dress is on its way over. I need the shot back to me by tomorrow.'

'You're kidding?'

Realising she was fiddling with the leather binding of her notebook in front of her, Abby dropped her hand off the table only to pleat the tablecloth instead. 'That's a pretty steep demand.'

'It's doable, right?'

Mark's abrupt question told her exactly how stressed he was, and she sighed, knowing she'd do whatever it took to make this happen.

'Shouldn't be a problem.' *Yeah, sure thing.* 'I'll get right on it.'

'Thanks, Abby. You come through for me on this, that major deal we talked about is a foregone conclusion.'

'Great,' she said, trying to inject enough enthusiasm into her voice while her mind raced a million miles an hour to come up with solutions for Mark's request. 'What size is the dress, by the way? I can make a start on scouring the guests and have the shot location scouted by the time it arrives.'

'A twelve. And the tux is a hundred and two.'

'Got it.' She jotted down the figures while her gaze quickly scanned the few hotel guests relaxing around them.

'Thanks, Abby. Looking forward to seeing what you

come up with. E-mail me the shots last thing tonight or first thing tomorrow at the latest, okay?'

'Shall do. Bye, Mark.'

The CEO had already rung off and she flung her mobile back into her bag, wrinkling her nose as she stared at the figures she'd jotted down, wondering what were the odds of her finding a couple to match the size requirements among the few guests currently staying at Sapphire Island's one and only exclusive resort, coercing them into modelling and actually having the whole thing go smoothly.

By the end of today!

'The wind will change and your face will stay like that.'

She looked up at Judd to find him smiling at her without a care in the world. Half his luck.

'We've got a problem.'

'We?'

He sat back and clasped his hands behind his head, his infuriating smile widening. 'From where I'm sitting looks as if you're the one with a bit of rearranging to do.'

'Rearranging?'

She lowered her voice when she realised an older couple nearby, wearing the ugliest matching floral shirts she'd ever seen, was staring at her. 'This isn't about rearranging, my friend. It's about jumping through hoops so Mark's biggest customer doesn't throw a hissy fit and ditch the whole shoot.'

'Sounds serious. Anything I can do to help?'

'Not unless you're a size one hundred and two,' she muttered, circling the size twelve on her notepad in vicious circles till the page tore.

'Actually, I am.'

Her pen slowed as a glimmer of an idea flickered through her mind.

No way…she couldn't…could she?

Trying to keep the edge of excitement out of her voice, she said, 'How good is Tom at taking photos?'

'He's fully qualified. Wanted to work with me for a while before branching out on his own. Why?'

'And you're definitely a size hundred and two?'

He sent her an 'are you for real' look. 'I think I'd know my own clothes size.'

He paused as she gnawed on the inside of her cheek to stop a satisfied smile blooming across her face. It couldn't be this easy, surely?

'Come on, Weiss. Spill it. What's this all about? And why are you looking at me like a cut of prime fillet?'

'Am I?'

She batted her eyelashes, knowing Judd would come through for her. He always had before.

He laughed and shook his head. 'Your poker face hasn't changed a bit over the years. It's still useless, so why don't you tell me what this is all about?'

'Fine. I need a model for some fancy tux *today*. The shots need to be done and e-mailed back to Mark tonight, tomorrow morning at the latest.'

He grimaced and held up the schedule in front of his face as if anticipating some missile she would lob his way.

'Uh-uh. No way. I'm not a model.'

'I don't need a model. I need someone real-looking, apparently. And the tux will fit you, which will save me wasted hours scouring the guests in this place to find someone suitable. So you'll do it, right?'

She tried her best smile, somewhat relieved at how he was taking the news. At least he hadn't thrown anything yet, which was what he'd done in the eighth grade when she hadn't picked him to be on her volleyball team.

His eyes narrowed. 'There's more, isn't there?'

'Well, yeah. It's a wedding shot, so there'll be a bride and you'll probably have to look all lovey-dovey but, hey, you can do it.'

He stared at her for a whole five seconds before cracking up.

'You're crazy,' he managed to spit out amidst his chuckles.

She folded her arms and tried a glare. 'Glad my predicament can provide you with a morning's entertainment. And here I was, hoping for a little support.'

His laughter died as he studied her, obviously sensing her discomfort.

'You're in a jam, aren't you?'

'You could say that. Rather than cackling like a hyena you could come up with some helpful suggestions.'

'Seems pretty simple to me. Find some other crazy guy to pose for these shots, let me take them and all's well with the world.'

She snapped her fingers, as if the thought had never occurred to her. 'Brilliant! Now, where do you suppose I find someone like that on such short notice? And find a bride? And have a fitting for them? And scout the perfect location? And reorganise the day's schedule? And organise the make-up artist, the hairdresser, not to mention sorting through the shots after they're taken, choosing the best and getting them to Mark all in one day?'

Her sarcasm fell on deaf ears if his serene expression

was any indication and she knew she had to take a different tack.

Mustering every ounce of persuasive charm she possessed, she leaned forward and fixed him with the same coy smile she'd used to great effect last night, knowing the exact moment when comprehension struck as he frowned.

'I've already said no.' He held up both hands and shook his head vigorously.

'Come on, you wouldn't need to be crazy, just slightly unbalanced enough to donate a few hours of your time to help out an old friend.'

'Don't even think about it, *old friend.*'

She reached across the table and captured one of his hands. 'Come on, Calloway. At least consider it.'

He stared at her as if she'd just asked him to walk on water to reach the mainland. 'I have and the answer is still no.'

'In all the years we've known each other, haven't I been the perfect friend? Haven't I supported you, helped you with your homework and protected you from the bimbos that wanted to date you? Remember all that?'

His frown deepened. 'That was years ago.'

'Yeah, but remember what you said to me?'

His lips thinned as he glared at her in mutinous silence, which lasted all of two seconds. 'That's low.'

'You said that if you could ever do anything for me, your best friend in the whole world, in return all I had to do was ask.'

He yanked his hand out of her grasp and folded his arms. 'You sure know how to turn the screws, don't you?'

'Call it gentle persuasion.'

'I'd rather call it emotional blackmail.'

'Are you pouting?'

His lips twitched and she grinned.

'Damn you, Weiss.'

She let out a loud whoop, which had nearby guests craning their heads to stare in disapproval. 'It's only a few hours. It'll be quick and painless, you'll see.'

'Yeah, right.'

Abby stifled her first impulse to fling herself into his arms. After that kiss last night any physical contact beyond the odd hand-holding or arm around the shoulder probably wouldn't be a good idea. Not with the memory still fresh, still vivid and making her wonder what it would be like to do a whole lot more than kiss her best friend.

'Thanks, Calloway. You're a real pal.'

'Yeah, that's me, a regular run-of-the-mill friend who has just agreed to the most outlandish scheme he's ever heard of. I must have rocks in my head.'

'No, you've got a warm heart.'

His expression softened, a second before his lips curved into a wicked smile.

'You know this is going to cost you big time, right?'

'No problems,' she said, her pulse picking up tempo at the calculated gleam in his eyes.

Whatever he had in mind, it had naughty written all over it.

'It's going to be fun having you in my debt. You owe me and you never know when I'll ask you to pay up.'

She fiddled with the sugar bowl, her fingers twirling the spoon around and around as she wondered if his lowered husky tone was a figment of her imagination or not.

'Like I said, I can handle it. Now, if you don't mind,

have a bride to find, a location to scout and a day's worth of work to rearrange.'

'Need a hand?'

She shook her head, her mind already racing ahead as she multitasked what she needed to do over the next few hours.

'Thanks, but I'll let you know as soon as the tux arrives. If you can word Tom up, maybe check out a few locations, that would help.'

'Shall do.'

He sent her a brief salute before pointing to the note-pad she'd left on the table. 'I take it the bride has to be a size twelve?'

'Uh-huh.'

'Why waste more time searching for a model, then?'

'What?'

Abby picked up her notepad and pen, shoved it into her bag and gulped down the mango juice she'd become addicted to on the island, only half listening to him.

'You're about that size, aren't you?'

She almost choked on the last sip of juice, clearing her throat several times, while his speculative gaze roamed her body with ease.

'So what if I am?'

She didn't like the cunning gleam in his eyes.

Worse, she didn't like the way she'd cottoned on to what he was implying straight away.

He chuckled and squeezed her upper arm. 'Come on, don't play dumb with me. You'd be a perfect fit for the dress. Why waste time trying to find someone else? After all, isn't that the lame-assed argument you used on me?'

She shook her head, hating that he was right. 'I can't

coordinate the shoot and model at the same time. Wouldn't work.'

Her pathetic protest fell on deaf ears as his grin widened. 'You're a professional. What's to coordinate? Tom will take the shots, you just stand there and look like a blushing bride. Easy. And just think of all the time you'll save not messing around trying to find a good-looking couple the right size to wear the clothes.'

He laid his hands out as if his suggested plan was fool-proof. 'Looks like an easy solution all round. Unless you think you couldn't pull it off—'

'Don't try your twelfth-grade reverse psychology on me. I'm not stupid. I can see it makes sense.'

'Then what are we waiting for? Let's get moving. We've got a lot of work to do before our big event.'

Her eyes narrowed as she took in his cocky expression, his smug grin.

'You're loving this, aren't you?'

'Hey, I'm not the one who was cruelly coerced into helping his best friend by some lame-duck act.'

'Lame duck? Why, you—'

'Uh-uh. Is that any way to talk to your model groom?'

His words didn't shut her up as much as the finger he'd placed against her lips. The same finger she had an instant urge to nibble on.

'I haven't got time for this,' she muttered, swinging her bag over her shoulder and grabbing her room key-card off the table.

'Before you go, there's just one more thing.'

'What's that?'

'How about a kiss to celebrate our engagement?'

She couldn't help but laugh, whacking him on the arm. 'You wish.'

When, in reality, it was her who wished for another scintillating kiss exactly like the one they'd shared last night, before she gave herself a resounding mental slap to stay with the programme, considering her promotion was on the line here.

'Come on, we haven't got all day,' she muttered, annoyed by how many times she'd replayed that kiss, by how much she wanted an action replay in slow, sensual detail.

Draping an arm around her shoulders as they headed for the foyer, he said, 'Now is that any way to treat your pretend husband?'

CHAPTER FIVE

ABBY squinted at the schedule, her insides tied in knots. It was one thing to agree to this crazy modelling gig, it was another to sit here and calmly do a final read-through of the plans for this afternoon's shoot.

'Are you going to eat anything?'

Judd pointed to the untouched seafood on her plate with a hopeful look on his face.

'It's all yours, garbage guts.' She pushed the plate across the table and smiled as he speared a scallop and several shrimps before the plate reached him. 'Were you always this much of a pig?'

Her smile turned to laughter as he looked up, mouth full, and pushed his nose up into a distinct porcine shape.

'Gross! If I'd known I would never have agreed to marry you. At this rate you'll be eating us out of house and home in the first month.'

They'd been like this all morning, teasing each other about their 'commitment'. He'd helped her plan everything from finding the best location to shutting Tom up when he gave them a hard time, turning a potentially nightmarish situation into fun, and they hadn't stopped laughing since.

Now, if only she could blink away the image of him in that wedding tux, standing next to *her* in the most exquisite wedding gown she'd ever seen, she'd be a lot happier.

Having a wedding shoot when she'd secretly fantasised about the real thing with her pretend groom was a little too close to home—and had her pondering 'what if?', especially with the groom flirting with her 24/7 like a pro.

Judd finished the mouthful before responding. 'Sorry, it's been ages since I've had decent food. Being stuck in the desert for six months at a stretch will do that to a guy with a healthy appetite.'

Her smile didn't falter though her stomach did a strange little flip-flop at the mention of his appetite as she wondered if that philosophy extended to all his appetites.

Don't go there...

'Speaking of food, do we get to have an intimate little dinner for two after the "ceremony"? After all, it is our wedding night tonight.'

His voice dropped seductively low and Abby took a sip of water to ease the sudden dryness in her throat.

She should be used to his teasing by now but somehow his use of the word *intimate* conjured up a host of images she'd rather not contemplate.

Tossing her hair in a 'dream on' gesture, she said, 'Just because we're doing the whole dress and flowers bit doesn't mean you can go getting any ideas.'

'Who, me?'

Mischief gleamed in his eyes the instant before he ducked his head and continued devouring the rest of her meal. 'If we're going to do this, I think we should do it right.'

'Uh-huh. Next you'll be suggesting a honeymoon, I suppose?'

His gaze snapped up to lock on hers, humour replaced by something darker, deeper, more sensual.

'Now you're talking.'

Abby tried to tear her gaze away, she really did, but she'd never seen him look like this and it had her hypnotised.

'You're such a flirt,' she finally managed to spit out, gulping the rest of her icy water in three swallows and wishing she could run the frosted glass over her heated brow. 'Though you know it's wasted on me, right?'

'Flirting is never a waste.'

He dabbed at his mouth with a crisp linen napkin, drawing her attention to his lips, those same lips that had kissed her last night, the same lips that had demonstrated in startling clarity how much better things could get between them if they moved past the flirting stage.

'Just think, once this shoot is over, we're bound for life. I can leave my clothes on the floor, my towels draped over the furniture, the cap off the toothpaste, the toilet seat up, and you have to put up with me for better or worse.'

She chuckled at his cheeky grin, enjoying their banter now he'd stopped looking at her as if she were dessert.

'Sure. Go ahead, knock yourself out, seeing as all that will be happening in *your* room.'

'What if I sneak into yours and put frogs in your bed? Or, better yet, itching powder?'

He rubbed his hands together in anticipation and suddenly the thought of him sneaking into her room wasn't so bad after all.

She smiled and reached across the table to slap his

ands. 'I'd be forced to retaliate and you don't want to try
ae, you really don't.'

'Oh, yeah?'

'Yeah.'

'What are you going to do? Duck my head underwater
ke you did on sixth-grade camp at Manly beach?'

'Maybe I'll flush it down the toilet next time.'

'Bully.'

She tried a mock frown and failed, dissolving into hopeless
iggles. 'You should be afraid, my friend. Very afraid.'

Judd sat back and folded his arms. 'Bring it on, tough girl.'

She grinned as a waitress placed dessert in front of him,
vatching him eye the huge chunk of chocolate mud cake
s if he hadn't eaten in a month. 'I think I'm pretty safe. If
ou keep eating like that, you won't be able to move let
lone catch me.'

'A moot point if you ask me.' He forked a large piece
f cake in one mouthful. 'I've already caught you.'

'You wish.'

He chuckled. 'I agreed to help your poor snivelling
ide. The least you can do is humour me.'

She rolled her eyes. 'Whatever. Now, if you've finished
tuffing your face, want to move? I should just do a last-
ninute check on the location.'

'Yeah, no problems.'

'By the look of your expanding waistline, you need a
valk.' Grinning, she thrust the schedule into her bag, slung
over her shoulder and aimed a pinch at his waist. 'Make
lat a marathon. Let's go'

'Thanks for the ego-boost.'

He sidestepped her pinch, shrugged into his jacket and

guided her to the door, his light touch in the small of her
back, making her all too aware of how things had shifted
between them.

It wasn't the wordplay, far from it. They'd done that a
million times before, their barbs getting more outrageous
till one of them usually called truce.

She'd changed.

No matter how many times she tried to dismiss that kiss
last night or the way it made her feel—wanton, desired,
special—she couldn't, and with Judd playing up to her in
his usual teasing fashion she needed to keep a lid on her
wildly swinging hormones.

'Any time. Come on, we've got work to do.'

'Don't you ever lighten up?'

She sent him a withering glare. 'You play your part in
this shoot today and I'll lighten up later.'

'Sounds promising.'

She sent him a coy glance from beneath her lashes and
he laughed as she'd expected.

'You're hopeless, Weiss. Trying to act the big, tough boss
just isn't you. You forget I've seen you in your underwear.'

'I was seven years old at the time and the whole class
had to strip off to check for leeches down at the creek.'

He shrugged, draping a friendly arm across her shoulders as they strolled along the deserted beach.

'Minor detail.'

Abby tried not to stiffen at his casual touch. However, her
darn hormones were coming out to play in a big way and
no matter how many times she told herself this was Judd, her
best buddy, slinging his arm across her shoulders in a way
he'd done many times before, her body wouldn't listen.

Instead, her shoulder muscles twinged, bunched and ached with tension while she silently hoped he wouldn't notice a thing.

'What's up?'

He stopped at the exact spot they'd chosen for the shoot, a small secluded cove with the whitest sand, bluest sea and fringed with lush green palm trees, and turned her to face him, searching her face for answers to questions she couldn't contemplate, let alone respond to.

The beauty of the location faded into oblivion under the intensity of his stare and she swallowed, knowing things would get a lot more complicated if she told the truth, yet unable to give this man anything but.

They'd always been honest with each other. It was one of the many strengths of their friendship and, no matter how much she wanted to deny it, her crazy behaviour around him would only get worse over the next week.

For she had no doubt the longer she spent with Judd, trading quips, swapping banter, doing the casual touchy-feely thing, the harder it would be to pretend she only considered him as friend material.

Why not bite the bullet and go for broke now? He'd probably see through any pathetic excuse she came up with anyway.

'Why don't we sit down?'

She sank onto the sand and patted the space next to her, all too conscious of his strong, muscular thigh inches away from her own as she tried to organise her thoughts and string together words that would make some sense.

'I thought you said I needed to walk. A marathon, no less?'

'If you're fishing for a compliment, fine. Your wash-board abs are to die for and you're okay just the way you are. There. Satisfied?'

He chuckled and reached over to tweak her nose. 'I knew it. You want my body.'

Got it in one, sport.

She rubbed her nose before wrinkling it at him. 'I'm merely using my professional skills at observation. I study bodies on a daily basis, in case you've forgotten.'

She let her gaze drift down his body, from his broad shoulders to his sculpted chest, along his long legs to his feet and everything in between, enjoying the opportunity for such a blatant appraisal.

This was Judd's body, the same body she'd seen many times before, but never had her pulse raced or her heart pounded at what she'd seen and suddenly she didn't want to look anymore.

She wanted to touch, to caress, to taste every inch of his tanned skin, to trace the contours she now viewed as sexy, to learn every angle of his lean body.

'Yep, everything's in the right place. Not bad.'

She patted his collar down in a motherly gesture when she would've preferred to grab it and drag him towards her so their lips could meet.

'You're confusing the hell out of me, Weiss.'

Judd reached for Abby's hand before thinking better of it

He had no idea what was going on, why she was acting so weird. As for the scorching look she'd just sent him after checking him out, it had shot straight to his groin, an area he had no right acknowledging when it came to his best friend.

He'd thought they'd move past that kiss last night. Looked as if he was wrong.

No matter how much they'd joked around all day or how hard he tried to concentrate on business, she was in his face, smiling at him, laughing at his jokes, her stunning blue eyes radiating more warmth than the tropical sun blazing down upon them.

Realistically, there was only so much a guy could take and, what with his libido waking up to the fact that his best friend was actually the sexiest thing he'd ever seen in a long, long while, and Abby doing her best to confuse him with mixed messages, he had no idea whether to make an utter fool of himself and kiss her again or trash his whole plan and head back to the desert.

'You're confused!' she muttered, pushing a strand of silky brown hair behind one ear, the gesture heart-endingly familiar.

He'd seen her do it during exams.

He'd seen her do it when she'd been dumped by her first boyfriend.

Everything about her was so familiar yet something had shifted between them and blood pounded through his body at the absurd rush of it.

'Why don't you tell me what's going on? You know I'm a good listener.'

He kept his voice light, trying to reassure her with his tone if he couldn't reach out and touch her.

Damn, did he want to touch her.

'You may not want to hear this,' she said, dropping her hand to her side where she drew lazy circles in the sand.

Okay, so now he was worried.

For one crazy moment he'd hoped she felt the sam
spark he did, the sudden attraction that had flared to lif
between them.

However, her grim expression was miles away from he
usual happy-go-lucky one and he knew that no matter ho
he felt, how tempted he was to push the boundaries be
tween them, he couldn't do it. He would never hurt her. Sh
meant too much to him, their friendship priceless.

He'd always known it, from the first moment she'd tak
en pity on the embarrassed, sniffling seven-year-old he'
been when he'd bowled her over while trying to escape hi
father's loud curses as he'd woken following anothe
drunken binge.

She'd always been there for him so what was he tryin
to do—mess with the most important thing in his life?

'Try me.'

'It's not important,' she said, her voice barely above
whisper as he leaned towards her to catch the words.

'You always were a lousy liar.'

He stared at her, willing her to look up at him, but sh
kept her gaze firmly fixed on her fingers tracing idle pa
terns in the sand.

'And you could always read me like a book.'

She sighed, a small sound that shot straight to his hear
Tread carefully, his conscience warned. *She's worth i*

'That's what you think. Besides, you've changed from
action adventure to mystery genre and I've always bee
lousy at solving mysteries.'

She finally looked up, a glimmer of a smile playin
about her mouth. The same mouth he'd been having illic
fantasies about all night since she'd kissed him back.

'That's got to be a first, you not being able to read my thoughts, finish my sentences. You know, all that general annoying stuff that makes you the great guy you are.'

'Maybe I'm not as great as you think.'

He reached for her hand, shaken by the doubts her faith in him raised. A great guy? How could he be when he couldn't stop thinking about moving their platonic friendship into another stratosphere? One where there were no regrets, no time to think, but plenty of one-on-one action with the two of them naked and sweaty and so turned on they couldn't stand it.

'You are.' She squeezed his hand, twining her fingers through his. 'This may sound nuts but do you ever feel as if things are moving beyond your control? Shifting or changing without you knowing or understanding why?'

He nodded, buoyed by a surge of hope that maybe, just maybe, they were on the same wavelength after all.

'Honestly? I'm caught up in some weird helpless thing lately as if I have no control over my life anymore.'

'You, helpless? Like a lion about to pounce on a zebra, you mean?'

'I always did fancy you in stripes.' He grinned, wondering what she'd say if she knew the truth: that he fancied her, period.

'Do you fancy me? For real, I mean.'

Her blunt reply stunned him though he should've expected it. He'd always been lousy at hiding anything from her and she'd probably picked up on his weird vibes.

This was his big opportunity.

Come clean, see if there was the remotest chance they shared more than a lifelong friendship.

Instead, he ignored what his body urged him to do and settled for the common-sense response: light, playful, designed not to let things get too deep between them.

'What man wouldn't? You're one hell of a woman, Weiss.'

'I'm serious. I need to know.'

Hell.

'You're my best friend in the world and the most important woman in my life.'

She fixed him with a scornful glare. 'That's not answering my question.'

Damn right.

'Our friendship means everything to me.'

Her hand slipped out of his and he immediately felt the loss.

'Just answer the question, Calloway.'

Her blue eyes glittered with intent as she jabbed at his chest and something inside him snapped.

'Do I fancy you for real? Hell yeah.'

Driven by pure need and madness, he reached for her, winding his fingers through her hair, drawing her close until their faces were millimetres apart.

Her careless curls cascaded like the softest silk through his fingertips and he imagined her shiny tresses sliding all over his body, setting it alight with the sensual touch of silk on skin.

'This isn't a good idea,' she murmured, though she didn't pull away. Instead, her hands bunched the cotton of his T-shirt as if she never wanted to let go.

'No, it's not a good idea. It's a great one.'

He brushed a light kiss across her lips, a tentative, testing kiss, giving her the option to stop this madness right here and now.

She sighed—whether in resignation or pleasure he didn't know—and leaned into him, the feel of her curves moulding to him firing his libido in a second and giving him all the encouragement he needed.

He deepened the kiss, nudging her lips apart with his tongue before sweeping into her mouth, exploring the delicious warmth. She met him halfway, angling her head for better access, and it took all his willpower not to drag her down onto the sand and devour her on the spot.

He hungered for her, his hands taking on a life of their own as they skimmed her back, her butt and everywhere in between.

'You feel amazing,' he whispered against the corner of her mouth before nibbling his way across her jaw towards her ear.

She trembled as he licked the delicate skin behind the lobe and blew on it, her soft cry of pleasure shooting straight to his groin.

'This doesn't have to affect our friendship,' he said, trailing a line of kisses down her throat to her collarbone. 'We're both too smart for that.'

'I hope you're right.'

She pulled away, the tip of her tongue flicking out to trail over her lips as if testing to see if they'd actually been attached to his less than a second ago, leaving him burning for her and cursing himself for opening his big mouth and ruining the moment.

'I guess we've established where we both stand on the fancying-each-other issue,' he said, thrusting his hands in his pockets to stop reaching out and hauling her right back into his arms where she belonged.

'Uh-huh.'

She turned away, but not before he'd glimpsed the hea
shimmering in her eyes turning them to liquid sapphire an
he itched for his camera, wishing he could capture he
exact expression at that moment: passionate, glowing ye
strangely shy.

'So you feel this, too?'

Her tentative question slammed into him, making him fee
like a caveman for taking what he could get out of that kis
without getting to the bottom of what was bugging her earlie

'That's what you wanted to talk about? You're a
tracted to me?'

She rolled her eyes, some of her telltale sass evident i
the slight twitching of her lips.

'What do you think?'

'I think we're both crazy for interfering in somethin
this good. But I can't stop thinking about you since la
night, can't stop thinking about how great we could be
we lost our minds totally and go for it.'

There, he'd said it.

Let it all hang out in the hope she'd be sensible enoug
for the both of them.

He read the doubt in her eyes, sure it was a reflectic
of his own. But it was too late for doubts.

This was it, crunch time.

Friends or lovers?

Hopefully both if he had any say in it.

'We've been friends for *years*,' she said, her finge
gripping his for dear life. 'Why now? Why this? It's crazy

He couldn't agree more. 'Crazy.'

'And you know we can't let this thing affect our frien
ship, right?'

'Right,' he said, hope building with every word she uttered.

Suddenly, her lips curved upwards in a blinding smile that took his breath away.

'I guess there's no harm in trying. You'll be travelling the world again by the end of the week, we'll revert to our old friendship as if nothing happened. Whatever we do on the island stays on the island, right?'

He hesitated, hating the tiny white lie he'd have to tell in order to satisfy his unquenchable thirst for this woman.

'Right,' he said, wondering how she'd feel if she knew of his plans to stay in Sydney and his desperate need to find out if there was more to life than the constant buzz of travel, photography and money.

'In that case, let's go crazy.'

Pulling him up from the sand, she laughed at his stunned expression. 'Don't look so scared, Calloway. I promise I'll be gentle.'

'That's not what I'm afraid of,' he muttered, holding her hand tightly as he fell into step beside her as they strolled back towards the hotel.

CHAPTER SIX

'I MUST be crazy,' Abby muttered, stabbing a spray of fran-
gipani into the French roll despite her shaking hands. The
hairdresser and make-up artist had done a great job but her
hair had needed a finishing touch and she adored the beautiful fragrant flower growing wild all over the island.

'Told you this modelling stuff is hard work,' Tara replied, fussing around her like a mother hen as she tugged
and primped at the tea-rose silk-chiffon gown that fitted
Abby like a glove, much to her disgust.

What was with Bassel Designs anyway? Since when did
they go for a realistic look for their clothes as opposed to
the usual 'emaciated waif' fad?

'There. Perfect.'

Abby screwed up her face, reluctant to admit the hairdresser and make-up artist had done a fabulous job. She
could barely recognise herself, which was just as well considering she needed a confidence mask when she faced
Judd so soon after their revealing conversation earlier.

'I look like Island Barbie gone wrong.'

Tara shook her head, her trademark red locks flowing
around her shoulders in blow-dried perfection. 'You look

like Bridal Barbie. With the hots for Ken,' she added, with a cheeky grin.

Having the hots for Judd was an understatement—not that she'd let Tara in on the fact.

'How did I get myself into this?'

'Simple. You took one look into those dreamy hazel eyes and melted like any red-blooded woman would.'

'I don't melt. And for your information, I talked him into helping me out.'

'Yeah? So you're telling me you agreed to wear that dress out of the goodness of your heart?' Tara snorted and rolled her eyes. 'As if. I bet the dreamboat suggested you model alongside him and you fell in a simpering leap at his feet.'

'Not bloody likely,' Abby muttered. She'd never fall at any guy's feet, friend or otherwise. 'This job needs to get done a.s.a.p. and, courtesy of my curves, I'm the only poor sucker who could fit into this darn thing.'

Abby patted her hips, knowing she would never have contemplated modelling unless Judd had suggested it. So the guy had a point? She'd saved hours in not scouring the exclusive resort for a possible model but that didn't make this any easier.

She was about to pose for wedding shots, where she'd have to act all lovey-dovey with the guy she'd just agreed to have a fling with.

The guy she'd secretly never got over.

The guy she'd daydreamed about doing this very thing with, for real.

How much more complicated could this situation get?

Being attracted to Judd as a teenager had nothing on the

buzz between them now. Everything seemed more intense more out of control, just…more.

She wanted him, big time, but could she go through with this? He'd seen her at her best; he'd seen her at her worst. They'd swapped footy cards as kids, she'd ridden pillion on his pushbike to school and he'd held her close when her first boyfriend had broken her heart. He knew everything about her.

Except for one tiny fact: when he'd left Pier Point, she'd had to deal with the devastation of being rejected by someone she loved all over her again.

First her parents, then Judd. Somehow his defection had hurt a heck of a lot more than her parents' had when she'd been barely out of her toddler years.

What if having a fling with her best friend was addictive?

What if she went through the same rejection drama when he jetted off at the end of this job?

Or, worse, what if she fell in love with him all over again?

'Honey, you make that dress look exquisite. Bet you a hundred bucks the dreamboat's eyes fall out of his head?'

'No bet.'

She avoided looking at Tara, not willing to reveal the tiny surge of excitement she felt in the hope her appearance might do exactly that to Judd.

Tara chuckled. 'Okay, I'll quit joking around. Now, remember, head up, shoulders back, boobs out and work it girl. Work it!'

Turning her back on the mirror and poking her tongue out at Tara, Abby said, 'That's what I intend to do. Get this job done a.s.a.p. so I can concentrate on working you into the ground for the rest of the week. Come on, let's go.'

'Honey, I wouldn't miss this for the world.' Tara held out her elbow and tucked Abby's hand under it. 'I can see the headlines now: Abby Weiss, ace fashion stylist, turns model. And turns dreamboat photographer on his ear in the process.'

'Don't hold your breath.'

Though a small part of her couldn't wait to play make-believe with Judd and to see how he acted following their revealing discussion. Would he tease her in his usual way? Or would the thought of getting up close and personal with each other in the not too distant future cramp his style?

Up close and personal... Heat flooded her cheeks at the thought of being in bed with Judd, if his magical kisses were any indication.

'Looks as if the blushing bride is dreaming about the honeymoon.'

'Come on,' Abby snapped, stalking in front of Tara and cursing her own stupidity for landing in this predicament in the first place.

Judd paced the sand, wondering how Abby would act after their cosy chat earlier.

When they'd parted company at the hotel, she'd looked pale and it had taken all his willpower not to reach out and envelop her in his arms. Apart from her pallor he'd also noted her fidgeting and the fake, bright smile she always used when she was nervous as hell.

He'd seen that same smile before final exams at high school, before the inter-school netball championships and the night of the graduation dance.

The first night you kissed her.

He'd made a mess of things that night, too, acting like

a jerk who didn't give a damn, teasing her about her dress, which had secretly driven him mad with its hint of cleavage, and implying that he wasn't interested in her as a woman

If she only knew…

Ironic, as here he was all these years later about to get it on with his best friend and still acting as if he was ready to bolt.

'Chill out, dude. Looks as if you're about to have a coronary.' Tom finished his soda in three gulps and toasted him with the empty bottle.

'I'm fine,' he bit out, wishing he could have a fortifying pint—or ten—to calm his nerves. He should be behind the camera where he belonged, not trussed up in some monkey suit, playing at being a groom.

'Have you rechecked the equipment? The girls will be here any second.'

'No worries. Relax, I'm a professional. Everything's under control.'

Judd grinned. 'Yeah, that's what you said a second before that elephant charged us in Thailand.'

Tom tapped the side of his nose. 'Were you trampled to death?'

'No.'

'Well, quit your whining, then.'

Judd shook his head and glanced at his watch for the hundredth time in the last few minutes, wishing he could get this over and done with. 'Where's Abby? She's taking for ever.'

'She'll show, don't worry. Personally, I can't wait to see her all dressed up.' Tom wiped his brow. 'Is that woman hot!'

Tom watched him closely for a reaction and he deliberately kept his voice cool. 'Too right.'

Tom guffawed loudly. 'Quit acting like you don't care. You want her.'

Was it that obvious?

If Tom could see through him, little wonder Abby had picked up on his sudden interest. What he still couldn't get his head around was the fact she returned it.

What had happened to them? Was it the old 'absence makes the heart grow fonder' tune? How could two perfectly sane people who'd been friends for so long suddenly want to get down and dirty?

It just didn't make any sense. Then again, nothing he'd been doing lately had made much sense, hence his planned change of career, change of location and lifestyle.

'We're good friends, which is why I'm helping her out of a tight spot and why you need to keep your mind focused on the job at hand and not spouting drivel like you usually do.'

Tom's raucous laugh bounced off the palm trees surrounding them. 'Keep on kidding yourself, man. And when you have your first baby, don't forget to name old Tommy as the godfather.'

'Work!'

Judd pointed at the stack of cameras lined up on a nearby trestle and scanned the beach for Abby, wishing they could get this over and done with.

The sooner this shoot was complete and the pictures e-mailed to Mark, the sooner they could continue their interesting discussion earlier, with fewer words—and fewer clothes—if he had anything to do with it.

'Wow-ee! Feast your eyes on that.'

Judd turned and time stood still.

He couldn't move, couldn't breathe as he watched

Abby walk towards him, a simple strapless dress outlining every curve of her tempting body, her hair twisted into an elegant roll that drew attention to her high cheekbone and expressive eyes.

Those eyes…

She fixed them on him, steady, unwavering, and for long, loaded second, he swore he could read raw, hones passion in their glittering depths.

I want you, too, he wanted to scream, his churning gu making him shift his weight from foot to foot.

She took his breath away and if he'd had any doubt about his intentions to keep his hands off her, the kick i the guts at the sight of her floating across the sand toward him with desire in her eyes dispelled them in a second.

He wanted her.

More than he'd wanted anything or anyone in hi entire life.

She stopped in front of him and her coy smile clutche at his heart.

'Don't pass out on me now,' she said, the slight tremo in her voice belying the twinkle in her eyes as she reache out and smoothed the lapels of his tux.

He took a deep breath, placed a hand over hers and winke 'Not a chance. You're stuck with me now for better or worse

'In your dreams.'

His smile widened as his gaze drifted slowly down he body before returning to focus on her face.

'Oh, yeah, in my dreams,' he murmured, delighte when a faint pink matching her dress stained her cheek as she rolled her eyes in familiar fashion and snatche her hand away.

'You'll keep,' she muttered, sending him a mock frown at total odds with the cheeky curve of her lips. 'Now, less talk, more work from you, please.'

'As long as we get to play later.'

A thrill of anticipation shot through Abby at Judd's whispered words in her ear and she determinedly ignored her pounding pulse as she turned to smile at Tom, whom she'd finally noticed.

The minute she'd laid eyes on Judd standing on the beach in his tux, everything and everyone had faded into the background till all she could see was the guy about to turn her world upside down.

For she had little doubt that, once this shoot was over and a hard day's work done, they'd move on to the next step of their friendship, one from which there was no turning back.

'Hey, Tom. Judd assures me you're almost as good as he thinks he is so you can pull this off, right?'

Tom squared his shoulders and gave her a thumbs-up sign of encouragement. 'All systems go here. By the way, you look fantastic. If you ever tire of playing with the clothes, you should consider modelling. You'd make a squillion.'

'Aren't you a sweetie?' she said, wiggling her fingers at Tom in a flirty wave, eliciting a low growl from Judd's direction.

'Go easy on the big guy. You're breaking his heart.'

She laughed, her nerves taking a back seat as Judd slipped his hand into hers and squeezed. 'Yeah, that's me, all right. A real heart-breaker. Not.'

She glanced at their clasped hands and quirked an eyebrow, grateful for the reassuring contact yet wishing her pulse weren't doing crazy things like slamming through her veins at a breakneck speed.

'Just in case you feel like bolting.' He smiled, holding on a little bit tighter, and her breath hitched as the full force of his smile hit her, packing a powerful punch that almost floored her in its intensity.

When he smiled like that, she felt as if she were the only woman in the world and she was all his.

Considering what they were about to do come nightfall, it wasn't far off the mark. He'd always held a special place in her heart as her best friend and he'd soon be her lover. Would they be as good in the bedroom as they were out of it? The way her body was responding to his slightest touches the last few days she'd shoot straight to the stars and back.

Friends. Think friends for the moment, she mentally chastised, knowing she'd have to repeat it constantly over the next few hours. This shoot had to be a success, the photos stunning, and only then could she unwind as she deserved. As they both deserved.

Despite her qualms a small part of her had been looking forward to this shoot, curious as to how the 'other half lived' so to speak. She already knew being a model was hard work, and what better way to make her work come alive than a bit of firsthand experience?

In reality, she should be nervous as all get out, but with Judd standing by her side, reassuring her with his familiar smiles, she felt nothing but confident she could pull this off and look great in the process.

However, as she glanced at Tom standing poised with camera in hand and Tara holding up a huge light reflector a zoo's worth of butterflies took flight in her belly and she pulled away from him, smoothing the front of her dress in a purely nervous reaction.

It was one thing to feel confident, another to actually go through with this modelling gig when she'd never done anything remotely like it before.

'Go easy on the nerves. This'll be a cinch,' he said, picking up on her mood in the same way he'd always done, a way too calm smile crinkling the laugh lines adorably around his gold-flecked eyes.

'Uh-huh.'

She nodded mechanically, casting a frantic glance around for a last-minute reprieve from prancing in front of the cameras like some of her charges. However, the beach was deserted, as she'd requested, and logically she knew there was no way out.

'Wish Tom would hurry up,' she muttered, fiddling with a crystal on the bodice before stilling her fingers with effort. That was all she needed—for the expensive dress to fall apart before they'd done the required shots.

'Hey, chill out. Consider this a game, a bit of a laugh.'

She raised a cynical eyebrow Judd's way. 'Ha-bloody-ha.'

Though he was right. She needed to lighten up otherwise she'd look uptight and constipated in the shots rather than a blushing bride.

'Nice monkey suit,' she said, making an effort to alleviate the tension twisting her body into knots as she pointed at the exquisitely tailored tux that looked as if it had been made for him.

'Thanks,' he said, teasing grin firmly back in place as he cast a pointed glance at her chest. 'And nice to see you're still using tissues.'

'I am not!'

She thrust out her breasts to make a point, unprepared for the swift rush of longing his triumphant gaze evoked and the accompanying heat that sizzled through her body.

'You're too easy, Weiss,' he murmured, his eyes darkening with desire, intensifying the moment tenfold.

'I hope you mean that in the nicest possible way.'

She folded her arms over her chest, knowing it would push her breasts together and upward, hopefully driving him wild in the process, and as he tore his gaze away to shake his head, a dazed expression quickly followed by a rueful smile, she had her revenge.

'Being friends with you is hard enough. I have a feeling whatever we get up to for the rest of the week is going to drive me over the edge.'

'That's the whole point, isn't it?'

She ran a finger slowly down his chest, revelling in her newfound power to make him drool for her.

'Work first, remember?' he whispered in her ear before planting a feather-light kiss on the lobe, setting her nerve endings alight.

'Work? What work?'

She swayed towards him, her legs turning to jelly at his barest touch, knowing she'd lose it completely when they finally got around to doing loads of touching on hot, bare skin.

Placing a finger under her chin, he tipped it up. 'You know what work is. That thing that comes before play,' he said, caressing her bottom lip with his thumb and short-circuiting her synapses in the process as they fired mixed messages between her brain and her body till she couldn't think straight, let alone resist him.

'Save it for the honeymoon, you two. We've got a job to do.'

She leapt away like a teenager found necking with the high-school jock as Tom and Tara's laughter filtered over her. Since when did she get so caught up in swapping quips and flirting with Judd that she forgot the task at hand, let alone they were in the company of two of the biggest jokers around?

She was losing the plot, no two ways about it, and if she wanted to keep her job beyond this…this…fling or whatever the two of them were crazy enough to embark on, she needed to keep focused on something other than the sexy man grinning at her like a goofball.

'Okay, folks. Enough of the funny stuff. Let's get to work.'

Tom saluted and picked up his camera, Tara snapped her hands together in a producer's sign for action and Judd switched into work mode, helping Tom sort out the best lighting spots before being put in his place by the lead photographer on this shoot.

'Listen up, buddy. You can't be model and photographer. Just relax and do as you're told,' Tom said, positioning them beneath a towering palm for the first shot. 'I'm a professional, remember?'

'Famous last words,' Judd muttered, doing as he was told, though Abby could see the strain on his face.

She laid a comforting hand on his sleeve. 'It's hard not being in control, huh?'

'You said it.'

Their gazes locked and for a brief second, she wondered if he was looking forward to losing control as much as she was.

Thankfully, the moment passed and for the next two hours, they posed, preened and acted like the happiest couple on earth as Tom barked directions, ably supported by a smug Tara who took to her photographer's assistant role with glee.

Abby's cheeks ached from smiling, her neck ached from posing and deep down she ached for Judd, who'd taken every chance he got over the last few hours to touch her.

'This should be the final few shots,' Tom said, pointing towards the trunk of a bent palm tree. 'Judd, why don't you take a seat and settle Abby on your lap? I'll do a few close-ups with the two of your faces leaning towards each other to capture the detail on the dress's bodice.'

'You heard what the man said.' Judd sat down and patted his lap while Abby's heart stalled before kick-starting with a *ka-thump*.

Brushing up against him, having his hand in the small of her back and standing squashed to his side had been torment enough; sitting on his lap would notch up the sensual torture to unbearable.

'You're enjoying this way too much,' she muttered, perching on his knees as if poised for flight, trying to ignore the way her pulse pounded and her skin prickled at the contact.

'What's not to enjoy?'

He slid his hand up her back ever so slowly and she stiffened when his palm left the silk of the dress and skidded onto her bare skin.

Her belly dropped away as he inched higher, caressing the nape of her neck, his fingers skimming her rigid muscles in the softest massage, his touch far from therapeutic.

'You're so tense,' he murmured, sliding his free hand around her waist as if he sensed her instinct to bolt.

Not that she could've moved if she'd wanted to, considering her legs had turned to jelly the second he'd touched her.

'We're nearly done and the shoot's gone great. No need to worry.'

'Do I look worried?'

She bit down on her lower lip to keep from crying out as his fingers slid into the base of her hair, gently massaging her scalp in slow, erotic micro-circles.

'You look ravishing.' He wriggled forward a fraction while strengthening the grip on her waist. 'Now relax into me. Tom won't call it quits until we nail these final shots and I know how much you want to get to the good part.'

'The good part?'

It came out a squeak as she wriggled back far enough to encounter evidence of a very good part indeed.

'The honeymoon.' His teasing laugh was as soft and seductive as his touch. 'Don't forget you're in my debt. You never know what I may ask you to do.'

Her breath caught as he shifted beneath her, while she struggled to concentrate on what he was saying, more turned on than she'd ever been in her life.

'Ask away, Calloway. Doesn't mean I'll do it.'

'Oh, you'll do it, all right.'

As if to prove his point, his fingers disentangled from her hair, sliding down to join his other hand around her waist and not-so-accidentally brushing the sensitive underside of her breast on the way.

She gasped as shock waves of pleasure flowed through

her body, the anticipation of the night ahead heightened by his innuendo, by his seductive touch.

'Okay, just a couple more, folks, and we're done.'

Tom's voice wrenched her out of the sensual spell that had enveloped her and she forced herself to concentrate for the next ten minutes, grateful Judd stopped teasing her with words, secretly elated he still touched her at every opportunity.

As the late afternoon sun dipped towards the horizon, sending a dazzling display of magenta, ochre and deep purple shimmering across the endless blue ocean, Tom finally called it a day.

'Nice going, you two.'

Tom rummaged around the cooler that he'd thoughtfully had stocked with water for the afternoon, and held aloft a bottle of champagne in triumph before popping it loudly, filling glasses and handing around flutes filled with the welcome bubbly.

'Here's to a job well done. You two are naturals. Wait till you see the shots.' Tom raised his glass in a toast, linking arms with Tara before guzzling the lot in one go.

Abby laughed, her breath catching as Judd placed a hand in the small of her back, a barely there gesture that burned through the silk all the same.

'Happy?'

'Relieved,' she said, trapped by his potent stare, eager to gulp her champagne but knowing she was light-headed enough without it. 'Thanks for doing this. You really helped me out of a tight spot.'

He inclined his head, the casual smile playing about his mouth at total odds with the intent in his eyes. 'An

time, though our working day isn't over yet. We've got
to sort through the shots, choose the best ones and e-mail
them to Mark.'

'Uh-huh.'

Abby nodded mechanically, her mind already skipping to
the later part, the part after they'd finished work and moved
on to… Blinking, she immediately erased the erotic images
that filtered before her eyes as to what would come later.

'Here's to finishing our work real fast,' Judd said, his hand
slipping from the small of her back around her waist, drawing
her closer, heat radiating off him like a smouldering blaze.

'I'll drink to that.'

However, as Abby clinked glasses with Judd and gazed
into his fathomless eyes she couldn't help but wonder if
their friendship had taken a turn for the better.

Or worse.

CHAPTER SEVEN

ABBY stretched out on the sand, her eyelids drooping as she watched the waves break on the shore, incandescent in the moonlight.

After the bizarre day she'd had, relaxing in the isolated cabana on the perfect stretch of private beach still roped off from this afternoon's shoot was heavenly. Surrounded by flickering fire torchlights, the sound of chirping crickets and the lulling sound of the ocean, she finally felt the tension draining out of her body.

Thankfully, the shoot had worked better than she'd hoped. Tom had done a great job, Judd had helped choose the best shots and they'd e-mailed the lot off to Mark after a snatched dinner of room-service hamburgers, fries and shakes.

They'd shot for two and a half gruelling hours that afternoon, the hectic pace almost making her forget their revelations earlier that day and the fact she was ready to have a fling with her best friend.

Almost, but not quite.

Every time she'd looked at Judd, smiling at the camera, holding a pose, handling her with the skill of a surgeon performing the most intricate of operations, it had struck her anew that she'd agreed to go the whole way with the one guy in this world who meant everything to her.

As for what had happened when she'd sat on his lap… her skin burned just thinking about it.

Darn it, she hoped she was doing the right thing.

Their friendship was so important, always had been from the first minute they'd met. He'd bolted out of his front gate and barrelled into her while his drunken father stood on the porch step shouting abuse. She'd been rooted to the spot, her seven-year-old brain trying to comprehend why the nasty man was shouting at the little boy. As for Judd, he'd glared at her in defiance, swiping at the tears that poured down his dirty cheeks, leaving streaks.

'What are you looking at?' he snarled, picking himself up from the footpath and thrusting his hands into torn pockets, glaring at her with fire in his eyes.

She stood up and dusted herself off before answering. 'Wanna come and play at my place? I've got a cubby house.'

Interest flared in his eyes before he hung his head and muttered, 'Whatever,' and followed her home.

And just like that, their lifelong friendship had been born. Looking back, she would've done anything to protect the fierce little boy that day, though she'd been in shock herself. She'd never seen anything like Judd's father swaying on the front step, with his face a mottled red, shouting rude words at his son.

Even at that age her maternal instincts had rushed to the fore and thankfully the little boy with an unruly mop of dark curls had let her into his life and they'd forged a bond that nobody could breach since.

'Great spot for a rendezvous.'

Abby sat up abruptly, almost banging her head on the cabana's low-lying roof. 'Hey, I was just thinking about you.'

'Good things, I hope.'

Judd stooped and entered the cabana, his large frame filling the small thatched room and making her all too aware of its seclusion.

She'd told him where she would be, needing some time to unwind before facing the reality of what they were about to do, a small part of her counting on the splendid isolation of this beautiful stretch of beach as an enticing prelude of things to come for the rest of the night.

However, now he'd arrived and filled the small space with his potent presence, her heart thumped and her belly flip-flopped with nervous anticipation.

Forcing a smile, she patted the sand next to her, trying to act as normal as possible considering they were about to take an irreversible step down the pathway to carnal bliss.

'Just thinking about how the shoot went,' she said, resisting the urge to tug at her bikini top, hoping it hadn't ridden up while she'd been lying down.

Though he'd seen her in stuff as skimpy as her new swimsuit before, this felt weirder now that her body tingled every time he so much as glanced her way. And right now, he was gobbling her up with his eyes and coming back for seconds.

'You were great this afternoon.'

He sat on the sand, stretching his long legs out in front of him, drawing her attention to them. He looked fabulous in funky black board shorts, a fact that had first registered all those years ago when he'd captained the school football team.

'I'm a professional—what can I say?'

She struck an exaggerated pose and they laughed, the taut tension between them easing a tad.

However, as his gaze slowly travelled the length of her body and back, she stiffened, unable to stay relaxed when every cell in her body was on high alert, desperate for his touch.

The gold flecks in his eyes glittered in the reflected moonlight off the ocean and she swallowed, swamped by a sudden helpless feeling.

She was no good at this.

Should she throw herself at him? Tease him a little and hope he'd make the first move? Judd the joking friend she could handle. This new, intensely sexy Judd was throwing her way off balance and she had no idea how to recover her equilibrium.

'Speaking about being professional, why didn't you tell me about how far you've come in your career? We talk so often on the phone, not to mention our almost-novel-length e-mails, and you didn't mention it.'

'Because we had more important things to talk about besides me blowing my own trumpet.'

'Like what? My latest triumph? My latest trip?'

'Hey, I liked hearing about all that exciting stuff. Don't worry about it. We're here now and you get to see firsthand what a marvel I've become in the fashion world.'

He snapped his fingers. 'From modesty to big head in under a minute. That's my girl.'

Her smile waned a little as she decided now was as good a time as any to broach the subject of their impending shift in relationship.

'Seeing as you mentioned being your girl, are we really serious about changing the status quo?'

He leaned back on his arms, his T-shirt stretched taut across his broad chest, and she gulped. She'd been immune to him physically for years—of course, it had helped no seeing him in the flesh, so to speak. She really didn't stand a chance considering she'd been hot for him as a teenager and absence in this case really had made her heart—and other parts—fonder.

'I'm deadly serious. How about you?'

She sat up, her heart turning over at the serious implication of what they were about to do. 'I'm in.'

'Great,' he said, tracing circles in the sand with one hand while sending her a slow, lazy smile. 'So who gets to make the first move? After all, no time like the present.'

Abby swallowed, her heart pounding in anticipation while her skin tingled with his proximity. 'Now, huh? I'm still trying to get used to the idea.'

'It is a bit much to take in, isn't it? Come here.'

He opened his arms and, bracing herself for the first scintillating physical contact, she leaned over and hugged him. As his arms slid around her torso and she yielded to the pressure of his embrace and the reassuring warmth, she wondered for the hundredth time over the last twenty-four hours what on earth she was doing.

His friendship meant the world to her. Was it worth potentially sabotaging for a quick fling?

'Weiss—' he sighed, his warm breath fanning her cheek as he held her tightly '—you're the best friend a guy could ever wish for. That's not going to change.'

Her eyes closed as she leaned into him, savouring the

hysical contact, trying to keep her hands from wandering
ll over his body.

Damn, they'd done this countless times before at
chool yet it felt so different now. Having the hots for
omeone did that to a person, sending them crazy with
he barest touch.

'It better not.' He stroked her hair, the rhythmic move-
nent soothing her as it always did. 'You sure we're not
otally crazy?'

'That I'm not so sure about.'

She pulled away and stared into his eyes, the adorable
augh lines adding character to an already striking face.

'Promise me that whatever happens, our friendship
von't change. *Promise me.*'

He nodded, his laughter fading as his fingertips
rushed her cheek in a tender gesture that almost brought
ears to her eyes.

'You got it. And don't worry—nothing's going to affect
ur friendship. Consider the rest of our time together as a
lumber party.'

His suggestive wink had her whacking him playfully on
he arm in a familiar reflex gesture.

However, her pulse picked up tempo as the full impli-
ation of what she was about to do hit her. They were going
o sleep together; though sleep would be the furthest thing
rom their minds when they finally got naked together.

'Don't you think we're a bit old for sleepovers?'

He dropped a quick peck on her nose before grabbing
between his thumb and forefinger and twisting lightly.
We're never too old for anything. It'll be fun, you'll see.'

'In that case, your place or mine?'

He grinned, the wicked gleam in his eyes eliciting a jittery response deep in her gut. 'Now you're talking.'

She rolled her eyes and stood up, brushing sand from her butt. 'Flirt.'

'Flirting is good.' He stood up and handed her the sarong she'd been lying on. 'Here, cover yourself up before I get carried away.'

Her mischievous side took over in a second. 'Why, don't you like this?'

She twirled around and struck a model-like pose, enjoying the tortured look that flitted across his face. He wanted to flirt? No problem.

For there was nothing surer than that this time their flirting would lead somewhere: her plush king-size bed covered in Egyptian cotton sheets with a sky-high thread count, with the two of them getting friendlier than they ever had before.

Judd tried not to stare, he really did, but it was like telling a hungry lion not to stalk its prey: his reaction to his beautiful Abby was instinctive and watching her parade around in the skimpy purple bikini had the blood draining from his head and heading south.

He'd done his damnedest not to ogle her while they'd been talking, but now that she was flaunting herself, taunting him to look, he drank his fill, taking in her smooth, lightly tanned skin, her long legs, small waist and full breasts that threatened to spill out of her bra at any second.

She laughed at his reaction and he joined in, trying to make light of the situation when all he wanted to do was lose himself in her right here, right now.

He shrugged and turned away, doing his best to appear nonchalant. 'The bikini's not bad, though I think blue is more your colour.'

He heard her splutter of outrage and laughed, unprepared for the 'straw bag to the back of the head' trick.

'Ouch!'

He swivelled around, ready to do battle, which in the past had involved tickling her till she cried truce. However, she knew him too well and must've anticipated his move for she darted past him and out the entrance of the cabana, yelling, 'You'll have to catch me first!'

'You little minx,' he muttered, giving chase, secure in the knowledge that she didn't stand a chance of getting away.

And though she was quick, he caught her at the ocean's edge, taking her down with a rugby-style tackle that sent them tumbling into the foam washing up on the beach.

'Let go of me, you big brute,' she spluttered, wriggling in his arms like a fish out of water.

'Not till you say truce.'

Water streamed out of his eyes as another wave broke over them, but not before he glimpsed the flash of fire in her eyes, the sexy smile curving her lips.

'Come on, Weiss, you know you want to.'

He released his grip around her waist slightly, enough to tickle the skin there, relishing how incredible she felt, her skin slick and smooth under his palms.

She clamped her lips together and shook her head in response, wriggling even harder to escape.

'Okay, you asked for it.'

He pulled her on top of him and kissed her with every ounce of pent-up need coursing through his body, brushing his hands over every inch of bare skin, hot and wet and oh-so-tempting.

It took all of five seconds for her to capitulate.

'Truce,' she whispered against the side of his mouth, raising her head to stare down at him, her gaze slightly unfocused, her tempting lips parted.

His hands stilled though he didn't let go, relishing the weight of her lying on top of him, soft and wet and compliant in his arms.

'Smart girl.' He brushed away her damp ponytail as it flopped onto her cheek, rubbing the strands between his fingertips, honey brown turned golden treacle. 'Now, about that debt you owe me…'

She smiled, a slow, smouldering smile designed to shoot what little control he had in not ravishing her on the spot down in flames. 'Fine. I'll pay up. What do you want?'

'What do you have to offer?'

He waited for her answer, knowing what he wanted her to say, wondering if this was finally it, having trouble breathing and knowing it had as much to do with anticipation as having Abby lying on top of him wet and semi-naked, her blue eyes luminous in the moonlight.

His concentration had been shot to pieces the minute he'd first stepped into the cabana, the sight of her luscious body clad in that skimpy purple bikini driving all rational thought from his brain. It had taken every bit of willpower to act cool in the face of temptation, to not give in to the wild, driving need pulsing through his body.

'What do I have to offer?' She cupped his face, stared him straight in the eye and said, 'Me.'

Judd groaned and covered her mouth with his, the last

f his self-control shredding as she pressed down on him, issing him as if she couldn't get enough, her tongue delv-ng into his mouth, entwining with his, while waves rashed around them, refreshingly cool against his in-lamed skin where she lay along the length of him.

'I've waited so long to do this,' he murmured, breaking ne kiss to slide her upwards, giving him easy access to asten his mouth over her nipple, filling his hands with her reasts, savouring their weight, anticipating the exact noment he could whip off her skimpy top and have them are and luscious in his hands.

'Ooh…please…'

Abby's whole body quivered as Judd used his teeth to ase her nipple through the Lycra, nipping, biting, mov-ng to her other breast and back, shards of sensation ex-loding beneath his mouth and shooting outwards through er body, washing away any last lingering doubts she might ave had about taking the next step along with the tide.

How could something that felt so good, so right, be nything other than destiny?

His tongue delved in the valley between her breasts, laving er skin as if he couldn't get enough before slowly trailing pwards to kiss her, the taste of salt and sin on his lips.

'You're delicious,' he murmured, his mouth repeatedly razing hers, teasing her, pleasing her, making her shiver vith pure hunger for him as he reached between their odies, toying with the elastic of her bikini bottoms before liding one finger, then another, into her moist heat.

'Cabana. Now,' she ground out as he circled her clitoris epeatedly, massaging her with an expertise that made her asp out loud, 'Oh, yeah, just like that.'

As her climax built, she writhed on top of him, her bod
a mass of coiled nerve endings ready to unravel with th
next flick of his finger.

'That's it, sweetheart,' he murmured as she stiffened
second before falling apart all around him, her orgasr
rocketing through her as she cried out his name, her lov
moan instantly lost in the crash of the breakers on the san
bar just offshore.

Abby had no idea how long they lay there; her limb
had turned as limp as seaweed, her body overloade
with sensation.

Rolling her gently onto her side, Judd brushed the dam
hair off her face, the banked heat in his eyes lighting a fir
within her all over again.

'We didn't make it to the cabana, huh?'

He smiled, tracing the outline of her face with the gentl
precision of a blind man trying to read Braille.

'Considering I don't carry protection around in m
board shorts, I didn't want to tempt fate.'

'Huh?'

His hand left her face to skim over her shoulder, alon
her collarbone and across the top of her breast before h
palmed her breast completely, increasing the unfulfille
ache between her legs only he could satisfy.

'I'm so turned on I can hardly see straight, let alon
hold back if I'd got you naked and all to myself in th:
cosy cabana.'

'Oh, I see,' she said, arching into his hand as a torture
expression flickered across his face, secretly revelling i
the fact she could make him want her this much.

'Actually, I don't think you do.'

He kissed her, a hot, deep, open-mouthed kiss that left her panting and eager and desperate to have him inside her, a kiss that proved they had no business being on a beach when they could be taking this all the way in the privacy of a room.

As his hand slid off her breast and headed lower she braced her palms against his chest and pushed off him slightly.

'You know how I'm in your debt?'

'Yeah?'

Reaching down to his board shorts, she brushed her hand lightly across his erection, his sharp intake of breath turning into a hiss as she stroked along his length.

'How about we head to my room and work out a payment system?'

'I like the way you think,' he said, grabbing her hand and surging to his feet so fast her head spun.

Laughing, they ran across the sand like a couple of teenagers, the moonlight casting seductive shadows while Abby wondered how she'd ever kidded herself she was over this incredible guy.

And wondering how she would survive once this wickedly delicious taste of island magic turned into a healthy serve of indigestible reality.

CHAPTER EIGHT

THEY didn't make it to the front door of her room. In
stead, they stumbled onto the balcony, shoved open the
sliding door and tangled in the sheer curtains before
tumbling into the room.

Abby padded through the darkness and flicked on a
bedside lamp, surprised Judd hadn't followed her in.

'Forget something?'

Turning, she saw him leaning against the door frame,
arms folded, clutching his sodden T-shirt, looking super
sexy with water dripping down his bare chest, pecs well
defined, biceps flexed. Her gaze dipped lower, drawn to the
bulge in his shorts, and he straightened, proud and confi
dent.

By the size of that bulge he had every right to be.

'Um…let me see…I forgot to clean up?'

She darted a quick glance around the room, wishing
she'd had the foresight to tidy up a bit. Not that she'
expected them to sprint into her room via the open balcon
door—she'd assumed he'd take charge and make the firs
move and they'd use his room for their 'honeymoon
night—but now they were here, she couldn't help but wis

he piles of clothes draped over chairs, not to mention her
underwear hanging on a string to dry in the bathroom,
would disappear.

'Unless you're an ultra-modern girl and have a stash of
condoms here I'm going to have to make a quick detour to
my room and meet you back here?'

She muttered a curse that had him grinning.

'Give me two minutes.'

He held up two fingers and she crossed the room in a
second, pushing down one of his fingers.

'Make it one,' she said, slanting her lips across his in a
blistering kiss designed to make him hurry back.

'Thirty seconds,' he said, gently pushing her away before vanishing through the curtains, leaving her touching
her mouth in awe of the havoc one simple touch of his lips
could wreak.

As Abby raced around the room shoving clothes into the
wardrobe and kicking shoes under the bed she expected the
doubt demons to start giving her grief.

Instead, all she felt was wild elation at the thought of
picking up where they'd left off on the beach though this
time she had every intention of satisfying him before she
lost it completely again.

'Made it with a second to spare. Miss me?'

Abby swivelled in the bathroom door, her arms filled
with bras and knickers, and she quickly dropped the lot onto
the nearest chair, her mind blank as Judd advanced towards
her, fire in his eyes, a wicked smile playing about his lips.

'Well?' he asked softly, stopping less than a foot in front
of her, the heat radiating off his body beckoning her to
close the short gap between them and lose her mind.

For the life of her she couldn't remember the question as the green flecks in his hazel eyes glowed like sparkling emeralds in the dim light cast by the single lamp.

'What would you do if I had a first-floor room rather than a ground floor-bungalow?'

She almost smacked herself for saying the first thing that popped into her head and sounding ridiculous in the process.

He smiled. 'Simple. I'd climb the trellis like Romeo.'

'How very apt. Ill-fated lovers and all that…' She trailed off as he leaned towards her, powerless to stop the incoming sensual onslaught, knowing she didn't want to.

'We're not ill-fated and as for the lovers part…' he brushed a kiss across her lips before she could move, a soft sensual touch that left her desperate for more '…I aim to remedy that starting right now.'

His lips slid across hers again, much firmer this time but still not enough considering how passionate they'd been on the beach, how much she craved him, all of him.

'After all, this is our wedding night considering we did the bride and groom thing today, pretend or otherwise.'

Wedding night. The words echoed in her mind, a reminder of all that had happened today. Sure, they'd play acted a wedding for the camera, but no matter how much she tried to ignore it, she couldn't forget how good it had felt having Judd by her side, holding her close, staring at her like a beloved bride.

It had felt way too good, which was why she had to forget about the day completely and immerse herself in this moment, with this man, and focus on the night ahead no matter what the morning might bring.

'Wedding night, huh? Well, then, let's make it memorable.'

She sent him a teasing smile and he responded with a groan, covering her mouth with his and pulling her into his arms, effectively wiping all thought from her mind.

Perfect. Abby didn't want to think anymore.

She didn't want to rationalise or contemplate or wonder how right or wrong this was.

For now, she wanted to feel, to explode, to create magic with the one guy who made her melt just by smiling at her.

Threading her arms around his neck, she arched towards him, inviting closer contact. Judd moaned deep in his throat, accepting her invitation with the consummate skill she'd come to expect from their kisses, from the explosive passion on the beach.

His tongue eased into her mouth, slow and languorous, urging her to join him in its exploration. She met him halfway, eager to sample what he had to offer, playfully nipping at his bottom lip between her teeth and sucking lightly.

He tightened his grip in response and broke the kiss, his mouth roving over her face with precision, scattering light kisses over her skin, notching up her craving for him to unbearable.

'Judd?'

'Hmm?'

His mouth nibbled its way down her neck, leaving a scorching trail to her breasts, which threatened to spill out of her bikini top the longer she pressed against him.

Not that she cared. In fact, she wished he'd speed up the process by untying the strings around her neck and relieve the deep-seated ache that had started the moment he'd first kissed her.

'This is the best,' she whispered as his hands slid around her back, found the first string and tugged on it hard before untying the knot at the base of her neck in record time.

'And it's about to get a whole lot better, sweetheart.'

She didn't doubt it for a second, ripples of longing shooting through her body as the bikini top slithered down her torso and plopped in a wet heap at her feet, bringing her breasts in exquisite contact with his bare chest.

'You feel incredible,' he murmured, his fingertips grazing the undersides of her breasts as he cupped them, weighed them, before skimming his palms across her erect nipples.

'Jeez.'

Her head fell back as an electrifying sensation like a lightning bolt shot from his sure hands to the deepest part of her, now throbbing with need.

She was burning up, heat streaking through her veins, and as Judd's mouth enclosed a nipple and he flicked her with his tongue once, twice, she melted on the spot.

'Wobbly knees, huh?'

'Wobbly everything,' she murmured as he kissed his way across to her other breast, repeating the delightful torture of licking and sucking her other nipple as he eased her back gently onto the bed.

He propped on his side, his fingertips skimming her body, skirting around her breasts, tickling her, teasing her until she could've begged for more while his steamy gaze followed the slow, lazy movement of his hand.

'You're so beautiful.'

She smiled and reached up to trail a finger down his cheek. 'Guess you've never seen me like this, huh?'

Raw, powerful passion flickered in his eyes, turning them from familiar hazel to molten caramel in a heartbeat.

'You've always been beautiful to me, Abby,' he said, lowering his lips to hers, kissing her slower and deeper this time, a soul-drugging kiss that had her wishing to prolong this perfect moment for ever.

The kiss was stupendous.

The kiss was beyond her wildest dreams.

But it didn't affect her half as much as the way he'd said her first name, with tenderness shining like a beacon from his eyes.

'I want you,' she murmured, breaking the kiss to cradle his face and stare into his eyes, hoping he could read how important this was to her, how big a deal.

There was no turning back now.

He scanned her face as if seeking reassurance, and she smiled as she slid her hands into his hair, tugging him towards her.

'Now.'

His answering grin lit up his face, making her heart flip-flop more than ever. 'Well, how can I refuse an order like that?'

'You can't,' she said, surging upwards to plaster herself against his body, her hands sliding down his torso, frantically tearing at his shorts, desperate to feel all of him.

'Let me help you with that.'

He slipped the shorts down his legs and tossed them over his shoulder, where they landed on the fancy chrome lamp by the bedside.

They laughed and, suddenly, Abby was struck by how special this was.

Sure, she'd had sex with her previous boyfriends and it had been fun, but nothing like this extraordinary feeling of being totally in sync with someone, totally at ease despite the enormity of what they were about to do.

Sex could be fun but it could also be awkward and stilted and all about a purely physical act, yet here she was sharing a laugh with her best friend who was about to rock her world.

'Better take that off before it burns,' she said, itching to close the short gap between them and rub her breasts against his chest.

He grinned and slipped a finger under the elastic of her bikini bottoms. 'You talking about this?'

'The shorts off the lamp, wise guy.'

She rolled her eyes, her laughter dying away as he slid his finger along her belly before withdrawing, her breath catching as he moved away from her to grab the board shorts, giving her ample opportunity to study the breadth of his shoulders, the smooth, tanned expanse of skin and the shift of muscles beneath the surface.

Judd was gorgeous, she'd always known it, but having his body to explore, to caress, was something she'd never dreamed possible.

Until now.

'Right. All fire hazards taken care of. Now, where were we?'

'Right about here,' she said, taking hold of his hand and guiding him back to her bikini bottoms while leaning forward and brushing her breasts across his chest. 'As for fire hazards, don't know about you but I'm burning up all over.'

'Same here,' he murmured, ripping the bottoms down

one smooth movement, his hand grazing her mound and
ending her into meltdown as she arched towards him.

'Oh, wow.'

His reverent whisper thrilled her as he stared at her, his
ngers trailing up her thighs with torturous patience, inch-
ig higher and higher at a snail's pace, making her grit her
eth with the sheer erotic torment of it.

And as he shifted his gaze upwards, lingering on her
are breasts before shifting to her mouth, she tingled all
ver as if he'd touched her on each and every one of those
nsitive spots.

They locked gazes and her breath caught at the depth
f desire in his eyes. She wanted him so badly and it looked
s if the feeling was entirely mutual.

'Judd?'

His penetrating stare hadn't flickered, hadn't moved,
nd she hoped he wasn't having second thoughts. She'd
oved way past that stage, around the time he'd first
uched her bare skin with reverence.

'Just admiring the view. It's the photographer in me.'

She smiled and crooked her finger at him. 'This model
ppreciates the sentiment but she's done working for the
ay. It's playtime now.'

Judd didn't need to be asked twice.

He'd wanted to devour Abby ever since their little im-
romptu roll in the surf. He'd been so close to losing it,
o damn horny he couldn't think straight, let alone hold
ack, and now, with her lying naked in front of him, re-
ponding to him, touching him, he could hardly believe
his was happening.

'I'm all for play,' he said, his fingers continuing the lei-

surely exploration of her thighs, stilling when he hit th
edge of her damp curls, toying with her, loving how h
blue eyes turned midnight with need as he eased a fing
inside to touch her damp, wet flesh.

'Good,' she gasped, arching towards him as he circle
her clitoris with his fingertip, soft, rhythmic movemen
that had her moaning his name until he could barely r
strain himself.

He maintained the rhythm while slipping another fing
inside her wet warmth, feeling her clench around him a
she thrashed, arched and stiffened in his arms before me
ing on a long, low moan.

She'd always been fantastic at making him feel goo
about himself but nothing came close to this moment whe
the woman who meant the world to him smiled, a sh
tender smile that made him feel ten feet tall.

'That was great,' she murmured, placing her pal
against his heart, her touch hot against his skin as her han
slid lower. 'And I want more.'

'Greedy.'

He didn't stop her hand as it slid under the waistban
of his jocks.

He didn't stop her hand when she fondled his erectio

And he sure as hell didn't stop her when she surged u
wards, whipped off his jocks in record time and focuse
her gaze on his penis standing to attention.

'This is going to be great,' she said, wrapping her han
around his shaft, an almost reverent look on her face as sh
stroked him.

He groaned, a low guttural sound ripped from the back
his throat as unbearable pleasure streaked through his bod

He wanted to take this slow.

He wanted to make this last.

But right now, watching Abby touching him so intimately, so thoroughly, he couldn't breathe let alone hang nto his fragile self-control.

'Stop.'

His hand shot out and gripped her wrist while he imrinted this unforgettable image on his brain: Abby, with er hair tumbling like dark silk around her shoulders, her yes wide and glittering, her lips parted and swollen from is kisses, straddling him, holding him as if she never anted to let go.

He closed his eyes for a second, capturing the precious napshot, storing it in his memory banks, wondering how e'd got so damn lucky.

'Okay, your call.'

She shrugged and rolled off him, her mouth pursed in *faux* moue as she faked a huff.

He nuzzled her neck till she laughed, the pure, joyous ound wrapping him in its warmth. 'If you hadn't stopped e mightn't have got to the good stuff.'

'You mean, there's more?'

She widened her eyes, her feigned innocence in stark ontrast to the devilish smile playing about her lips.

'Oh, yeah, a whole lot more.'

He kissed her, deeply, thoroughly, before reaching for his iscarded shorts, taking care of protection and rolling back owards her only to discover she'd parted her legs, giving im a shockingly intimate view of her, wet and wanting.

'Hell.'

'Or heaven, depending on your definition,' she said,

closing the short distance between them as he reached fo
her, driven by blind need, filled with a burning desperatio
he'd never imagined.

His hands covered her everywhere, exploring every di
every curve and coming back for more. He couldn't ge
enough of her bare skin, the silky smoothness like a ball
for his work-hardened hands.

'You're so soft,' he said, caressing her butt, bringing he
closer to his erection, which nudged between her legs, an
she sighed, hooking her leg over his and giving him acces
to all of her.

'And you're so hard.'

She squeezed her hand between them, gently guidin
his erection to her slick entrance, rubbing it along he
swollen flesh on the way.

'You feel so good,' she said, sliding both hands up h
chest to rest on his shoulders as he rolled over and into he
in one, fluid movement.

'So do you, sweetheart. So do you.'

Her eyes fluttered shut as he withdrew slowly befor
plunging into her again, harder, deeper, and she clutche
at his shoulders, her fingernails digging into him, spur
ring him on.

With every thrust, he watched her beautiful face conto
with ecstasy.

With every plunge, he watched her mouth part and he
tongue flicker out to moisten her lips, mimicking the in
credible sex they were having.

Watching Abby in the throes of passion fuelled h
libido beyond belief and he picked up the pace, thrustin
harder and faster as she gripped his shoulders, raised he

legs and wrapped around him, sending him spiralling out of control in a frenzied burst.

As his release swamped him, she cried out his name and he collapsed on top of her in a daze, his lungs bereft of oxygen, his mind a complete blank.

Abby, his best friend, was beautiful.

Abby, his lover, was phenomenal.

And he couldn't think of one, damn thing to say as he withdrew and rolled onto his side, cradling her close.

His usual wise-ass remarks wouldn't cut it now. She deserved more than that. Hell, after that performance, she deserved the world and for a guy who didn't know what the future held he was the last person to give it to her.

'That was something else,' she said, her hand fluttering like a butterfly between them, skimming his chest, his arm, as if she didn't know whether he wanted to be touched or not.

'*You* were something else.'

He captured her hand and held it to his heart as it pounded and thudded and slammed against his chest like a wild beast eager to be freed. Ironic, considering after what they'd just shared, the already strong bond between them had strengthened considerably and he didn't feel free.

Instead, he felt inexorably drawn to Abby, tied to her in a way he never had before, and he had no idea if he was ready for it yet.

His entire life had been based on freedom. He hadn't been able to get away from Pier Point quick enough when his dad died, despite the strength of his friendship with Abby. And he sure as hell hadn't stuck around when he'd glimpsed the expectation in her eyes after their first kiss.

So what now?

He was returning to Sydney, but Abby had made it more than clear that an island fling was all this would be.

What if the unthinkable had happened and the ultimate freedom fighter wanted more?

'You're thinking too much.'

She reached up with her free hand and smoothed the frown lines from his brow and he forced a smile, the same carefree smile he'd given her countless times before.

'Thinking is highly overrated. I'd much rather be feeling,' he said, capturing her mouth in a swift kiss, the fire simmering between them needing little to rekindle.

'I knew I liked you for a reason,' she whispered against the side of his mouth as she rolled on top of him, pinning him down and effectively wiping any thoughts of the future out of his mind.

CHAPTER NINE

ABBY rearranged the clothes for the umpteenth time in the last ten minutes, knowing she couldn't concentrate after what had happened last night.

She should be sorting the bikinis and wraps into sequential order. Instead, all she could think about was how having sex with Judd made her feel.

Amazing?

Cherished?

Satisfied?

Definitely the latter as heat sizzled through her body at the memories of every delightful way Judd had satisfied her. The guy might be a world-class photographer and a great friend, but his talents as a lover far surpassed all her expectations and personal experience.

Quite simply, Judd was a master. And she'd just become a very willing pupil.

Trying to play it cool while her body burned up at the erotic memories flitting across her mind, she picked up her clipboard and went over the list of shots for today, the figures dancing before her eyes.

'You're hopeless,' she muttered, flinging the list down

and picking up a bundle of silky slip dresses, dumping them on a nearby table and reaching for hangers. Anything to keep her hands busy and her mind focused on a task other than pondering the fact she'd been avoiding all morning: labelling what she'd shared with Judd as sex.

It hadn't been just sex and she knew it.

She'd made love with Judd.

Love being the operative word.

She did love Judd, always had, as evidenced by the telltale twitch in the vicinity of her heart whenever she so much as thought of him over the years.

But was she in love with him? No way.

She wasn't that silly. Judd was a free spirit and there was no way she'd be foolish enough to fall for a guy like that.

Besides, it would ruin their friendship if he got wind of the slightest emotional entanglement between them as a result of their fling and she'd never jeopardise their relationship like that. He meant too much to her. He always had, always would.

'Friends, schmiends.' Stabbing a hanger through an armhole with particular viciousness, she knew it was time for a little honesty.

After all, look at what had happened when she'd been honest enough to tell Judd how much she wanted him. It might have been in-your-face I've-got-the-hots-for-you-bad type of honesty, but it had worked and if last night's spectacular explosion of passion had been any indication honesty was definitely the best policy.

Now, if only she could summon up the courage to come clean about the rest to him, their friendship might actually have a chance of surviving beyond this week.

Muttering unladylike curses under her breath, she swept the bikinis into a carry bag and stuffed the clipboard on top.

Screw the list. Right now, she needed an extra large lunchtime Mojito.

Followed by a reality-check chaser.

Judd studied the last few shots, pleased with the results of the day's shoot. Though he loved photographing wildlife in their natural habitat, there was something equally satisfying in working with humans. In fact, if he was totally honest, he'd missed the contact with other people during his travels.

Particularly one person.

He grinned as Abby packed up the last of the clothes, sent him a saucy wave and sauntered around the pool's edge, sending one last sexy little shimmy his way before disappearing from view.

He hadn't slept a wink last night—or in the early hours of this morning, more to the point—when he'd finally made it back to his room. Images of Abby—her seductive smile, the noises she made as he thrust inside her, how soft and pliant and welcoming she'd been in his arms—had replayed across his mind over and over again.

She'd made him feel incredible. Then the guilt had set in. He wasn't playing fair. He hadn't told her the whole truth. Would she forgive him once she knew everything?

Closing the shutter over the camera lens, he wondered if she'd do the same once he told her the truth: effectively blot out their friendship despite the many years they'd shared together, despite everything they'd been through.

He should never have taken the risk. He should've told her everything before they'd got physical. However, he'd lost his mind once his libido had gone into overdrive and started doing all his thinking for him.

He wanted her with a fierceness that scared him and, now that he'd had her, he couldn't get enough. He'd barely been able to concentrate on work today, what with her flirty floral skirt swishing about her thighs every time she moved, her white camisole top outlining her breasts to perfection, resurrecting recent memories of how they'd felt, how they'd tasted…

No woman had got under his skin like this, ever. Sure, he'd had a few liaisons over the years, but those women had known the score; he rarely settled in a country for longer than a few months before moving on to the next job and it had suited him down to the ground.

But Abby was different and despite every intention to keep this thing between them light-hearted, he knew that by sticking around in Sydney, he'd changed the rules of the game.

'Your cheerfulness is disgusting.' Tom hoisted most of the equipment onto his broad shoulders and held out his free hand for more.

'Tough.'

Judd grinned and handed over a camera while zipping up the last bag.

'I liked it better when you were a grumpy workaholic.'

'Why?'

'Because then I could lord it over you about all the fun I was having. It's hell when you're strutting around with a smug grin.'

Judd hoisted the last bag onto his shoulders, wondering when he'd last felt this carefree. Tom was right. He was usually so focused on his work, so cut off from people, that he probably never appeared genuinely happy. Which explained why he couldn't keep a goofy grin off his face today considering *happy* didn't come close to describing how Abby made him feel.

'Yeah, well, I can't help it if I'm a chick magnet.'

Tom guffawed and hoisted a few bags, as if the heavy camera equipment draped over his shoulders weighed less than a kilo. 'If I hadn't helped you with women problems before you'd have no clues with Abby now.'

'Helped me?' He chuckled, remembering the few times Tom had *helped* him. 'Let's see. The first time you helped me in Venezuela I ended up with the village chief chasing me through the jungle. The second time in Botswana I almost ended up being a tribe's main course and the third time the mayor of Little Rock wanted a public hanging for "ruining his daughter's reputation", end of quote. So, pardon me if I don't give you any credit.'

Tom grinned. 'Okay, so maybe those other times didn't quite work out as I planned. But look at you now. From where I'm standing, looks like things are hotting up between you two, you lucky dog.'

So the big guy had a point.

All he could think about was getting Abby alone…and naked…all the time…

Tom snorted. 'By that dummy look on your face, I rest my case. These tropical breezes have sent you troppo. Not that I blame you. Abby's quite a girl.'

'You said it.'

He fell into step beside Tom, his mind already on the remainder of the day and the many ways he'd like to spend it with Abby.

'So, you ever thought of doing the wedding thing for real one day?'

Judd's heart stuttered for a split second, filling with fear. He wasn't a marriage type of guy and he had a feeling Abby would love to do the whole 'white dress and flowers' thing for real one day. And now they'd moved from friendship to—what?—it nagged at him that she might expect more from this thing they shared than he was willing to give.

'Butt out. And stop being so damn nosy. You're really starting to pee me off.'

Tom chuckled as he walked away.

So the big guy liked to ask the hard questions? Didn' mean he had to answer them. Besides, he had better things to do with his time starting with finding his best buddy and coercing her into spending some quality *one-on-one* time with him.

Abby accepted the mango daiquiri from Judd, raised it in his direction, sat back and propped her feet on the banana lounge.

'Sure you wouldn't like me to rub some of that suntan lotion on you?'

Abby raised an eyebrow and sent him her best 'not on your life, mister' look. 'Let's just relax and soak up a bit of sun, okay?'

He grinned and shrugged. 'Hey, can't blame a guy for trying.'

Abby lifted her hair off her neck in a purely feminine gesture designed to drive him wild, enjoying flirting with him when she could see how much he wanted her.

She'd never felt this empowered before, this aware of

her allure as a woman and if she'd enjoyed teasing him
when they'd been just friends, it had nothing on the fun she
was having taunting him now they were lovers.

'You've spent too much time with primates, that's
your problem.'

'How so?'

'All you've got on your mind is monkey business,' she
said, taking a healthy slurp of her cocktail as he rolled his
eyes at her lame joke.

'In that case, care to keep me as a pet? I play the organ real
well.' He wiggled his eyebrows suggestively and she burst out
laughing, knowing he always had to have the last word.

'Don't you mean organ-grinder?'

'That, too.' He clinked glasses with her. 'Here's to us,
sweetheart.'

She batted her eyelashes at him. 'Us? My, my, and here
I thought this was just casual sex.'

He leaned forward and ran a fingertip down her bare
arm, setting her skin alight.

'How about some not-so-casual sex? Like all night's
worth?'

A shiver of anticipation slid down her spine and she ran
the icy glass along her forehead. 'A nice thought…'

'Just nice?'

Placing her frosted glass on the table next to her, she
folded her arms and glared, quickly dropping her arms
when she saw his heated gaze focus on her chest.

'Fine.' She shrugged, toying with the bikini string behind her neck, enjoying the beads of perspiration popping
out on his forehead as he tried to refocus on her face. 'It's
a great thought but unless we get plans for this sorted out

now, we might be hashing out solutions all night and that might put a dent in your romantic aspirations?'

He held up his hands in surrender. 'Okay, okay, so what's the plan?'

Abby laughed at his resigned expression. 'I don't know yet, but we've got to do something special for Tom and Tara. They've definitely gone above and beyond the call of duty on this shoot.'

'Yeah, the big guy came through on the wedding shoot. And Tara helped out, too.'

Abby squinted her eyes and tapped her bottom lip with a finger, deep in thought. 'You know, I've seen a few covert glances between the two of them. Maybe if we give them a gentle push in the right direction nature will take its course?'

'Gentle push? More like a hard shove. I haven't noticed Tara reacting much to Tom's incessant flirting.' Judd stilled her tapping finger, drawing it to his mouth to kiss it, effectively wiping all thought from her mind. 'Besides, we're not here to play matchmaker, we're here to figure out a way to thank them, remember?'

'You're right.'

Abby picked up her glass and took a sip before snapping her fingers. 'Maybe the four of us get together for a drink? Shout them a meal, or is that too informal? Not enough? What do you think?'

'I think you're the most incredible woman I've ever met.'

Her breath hitched as he leaned forward, tipped her chin up and slanted his lips across hers, a slow, sensual assault that left her senses reeling.

'Where did that come from?'

Her hand shook as she placed her cocktail on the table, but not half as much as her heart. In fact, *shaken* wouldn't come close to describing the cataclysmic realisation that had hit her a split second before his lips had touched hers.

She didn't just love Judd.

She was *in* love with him.

Heart and soul.

Oh, boy.

Reaching out, he captured her hand in his, steadying her, infusing her cold hand with his warmth.

'You really need to ask that?'

'Uh-huh.'

Damn it, she needed to know if he stood by their initial plan for a fling or if last night had changed everything for him, too.

She needed to know if feeling this way about a guy she'd known for so long was crazy.

But most of all she needed to know if the heat, the passion and the tenderness blazing from his eyes every time he looked at her were real or just part of some role he was playing.

She'd seen him do it before. He'd played roles his entire life: the devil-may-care kid who didn't give a hoot what people thought about him, the rebel teen who pushed away anyone who tried to get close, the adventurous warrior hell-bent on travelling the world and never having ties to one place.

She'd seen it all, had loved him through all of his stages, yet now, what if his role-playing affected her?

'We're good together. So good,' he said, holding her hand as if he'd never let go. 'You *are* incredible. You're the most important person in my life and my head's still spinning from what's happened over the last few days. Surely you know that?'

Abby blinked several times, annoyed by the sudden tears burning the backs of her eyes.

She could've asked him how he really felt.

She could've asked him if this was all a game, a new role he was trying on for size.

Instead, she did what she always did with Judd: kept things light.

'All I know is you're a great friend…and an even better lover.'

Leaning forward, she kissed him, swift and hard, demanding an instant response, needing to obliterate her doubts and questions with the consuming heat blazing between them.

The kiss could've lasted a second, a minute, an hour, she had no idea, and when they finally came up for air, both breathing heavily with stunned expressions, she knew this wasn't the time for thinking or admitting anything.

'Come with me.'

She held her hand out to him and he took it, all but leaping off his banana lounge.

'Should I trust you?'

His sinful smile sent heat rushing through her and she tugged on his hand.

'Oh, yeah.'

'So the Tom and Tara thing is taken care of?'

'Totally,' she said, laughing as they picked up the pace, their feet flying across the sand towards her room. 'Now it's time I take care of something else.'

'A woman who likes to take charge. What a turn-on.'

'Less talking, more running,' she said, laughing as he
tipped over his feet in his haste to keep up.

She had to do this right now. To lose herself in his arms,
in his kisses, in the sheer mind-blowing pleasure of sex,
anything to reassure herself that maybe she'd made a mistake and she wasn't in love with him.

It had to be just physical.

Contemplating the complications if she'd been stupid
enough to fall for Judd didn't bear thinking about. She
couldn't think, didn't want to think about anything other
than how incredible he made her feel.

'Here, let me,' he said, reaching out and taking control
of the key-card to her room as she fumbled with it several
times, cursing softly as the door light repeatedly lit red.

'So much for my *femme fatale* impersonation.'

He smiled and caught her as they tumbled into her room,
the door swinging open first go under his expert touch.

'I'm not into impersonations but I'm sure into you,
Abby Weiss,' he said, nuzzling her neck and sending fire
streaking through her body as his lips brushed the sensitive skin at the nape.

'Prove it.'

She pulled back slightly, staring straight into his expressive hazel eyes and sending him a scorching look
designed to entice.

'My pleasure.'

His elaborate bow made her giggle, but before she could
move, he swept her up in his arms and headed for the bed,
his intent expression leaving her in little doubt that he was
a man of his word.

Laying her gently on the bed, he propped himself ne to her, tracing idle circles on her bare arms as shivers excitement skittered through her before he leaned forwar and grazed her lips with an exhilarating kiss that promise more, so much more and, boy, was she ready for it.

However, just as his hands left her arms and move across to her breasts, his mobile rang.

'Damn it,' he muttered, fumbling in his back pocket. 'I turn it off.'

'Might be important?'

Though at that precise moment what could be more in portant than assuaging her raging desire for him?

Shaking his head, he flipped it open, stared at the scree and her heart sank as the passion faded from his eyes.

'It's about work so I really should take it.'

'Go ahead.'

She fixed a smile on her face and gave him a gent shove, hating that even at a time like this his job came fir Not that it was any surprise. His work had always been th number-one priority in his life ever since he'd fled Pi Point for bigger and better things all those years ago. Ba then it had hurt but she hadn't begrudged him his ambitio After all, she hadn't lost her best friend, merely resorte to non-physical means of contact.

Yet now, hot on the heels of the stunning realisation sh felt more for him than she'd ever thought possible, the fa he could relegate her to second best in the blink of an e hurt. A whole damn lot.

The caller had hung up by the time he answered but sh watched a shadow flicker over his face as he listened to th message. When he snapped the phone shut, he didn't ha

say anything. She could read his up-coming message
ud and clear.

Capturing her chin, he dropped a quick kiss on her lips.
'm sorry, sweetheart. I really have to sort out some issues
ith this guy. Can we take a rain check?'

Hating the disappointment welling in her chest, she
odded. 'Yeah, I really should do some planning for the
ial shoot tomorrow anyway.'

'So a rain check's okay?'

Rolling into a sitting position, she forced a laugh. 'Only
you're lucky. I've heard the rainy season ended around
ere months ago.'

'Tonight,' he murmured, taking her by surprise with a
ift, scorching kiss that made her toes curl. 'Take it from
e it's going to pour cats and dogs.'

She laughed despite her disappointment, watching the
iy she'd been stupid enough to fall in love with walk out
e door, taking a huge piece of her heart with him without
iowing it.

dd strode away from Abby's room, oblivious to the
iarkling turquoise ocean, the lush tropical foliage and
e endless stretch of pure white sand. An anomaly in itself
insidering he couldn't go anywhere without switching off
s powers of observation, the photographer in him always
i the lookout for the next perfect shot.

However, ever since he'd listened to that damn message
: couldn't focus on anything until he found out what
ark Pyman wanted with him.

If it was the phone call he'd been expecting and hop-
g for…

Closing his eyes, he tried and failed to block out the loc of acute disappointment on Abby's face when he'd said h had to take the call.

Her reaction had hit him like a knockout punch and this phone call didn't have the potential to affect h future—*their* future—he would've quite happily throw the phone against the wall and ignored it.

Taking a deep breath, he opened his eyes and stabbe at the redial button on his mobile, forcing his pace to slo when he realised he'd made it halfway up the beach whi waiting for the CEO to answer.

'Mark Pyman.'

'Mark, Judd Calloway returning your call.'

He heard a quick murmur of voices as Mark dismisse his secretary. 'Thanks for calling me back so quickl Judd. I was going to wait till you got back to Sydney have a chat about your future, but after seeing the sho you e-mailed me for the job so far I think we can do bett than that.'

'What did you have in mind?'

Judd kept his response ultra-cool, deliberately dampe ing the surge of excitement that this was it.

'When Paula recommended you and said you were th best, she wasn't kidding. I'm offering you the job as hea photographer at *Finesse*. Your work is brilliant and I wa you leading all our big jobs. I'm open to negotiating sala and benefits when you get back, but I really wanted to l you know the offer's on the table and I'd appreciate an i dication of interest from you.'

'I'm interested.' He clenched his fist in a victory salut 'I'll look forward to working out job conditions when I g

ack to Sydney, but in the meantime, rest assured I'm look-
ng forward to the challenge in working for *Finesse*.'

'Great. Ring my secretary when you get back and tee
p a time for us to meet. Glad to have you on board.'

Realising he was scuffing sand like a three-year-old
ith a big grin on his face, he said, 'Thanks for the offer.
ee you in a few days.'

Mark had already rung off by the time he'd flipped his
obile shut and he stared out over the ocean, dazzled by
e deepest indigos blending with cerulean greens, wanting
run screaming into the water and splash around like a
isterous kid without a care in the world.

All his plans were coming to fruition.

He'd already decided to stick around Sydney for a while
d now Mark's job offer sealed it. He'd known this was
the pipeline. The mega-successful CEO had hinted at it
hen he'd first taken on the job and since his relationship
ith Abby had entered a new dimension, he'd been secretly
ping for this outcome.

For the longer he spent with her, the harder it became
ignore the obvious. They were great as friends, stupen-
us as lovers—what if they got together for real?

The only way they could have that chance was if he
uck around in the one place long enough and it looked
if that time had come. Ironically, he'd looked forward
catching up on a regular basis with Abby once he'd re-
cated to Sydney, but never in his wildest dreams had he
ntemplated anything more between them.

He'd made that choice when he'd left her the first time
ound, had lived with the consequences since. But now
e rules had changed and he was in a position to offer her

so much more than he had as a wanderlust teenager wi
a lousy attitude.

Would she go for it? Would she want to trial a relatio
ship? Only one way to find out.

Whistling an old victory tune from a Sylvester Stallo
boxing movie, he headed up the beach towards his roon

He had plans to make for tonight.

Big plans.

Starting with organising a night for Abby she'd nev
forget.

CHAPTER TEN

'Where are we going?'

'Patience, Tara, patience.'

Abby pressed her lips together before slicking a topcoat Retro Rose gloss over them and stood back from the mirror. In a siren-red flirty strapless dress, matching strappy sandals and her hair mussed with enough mousse to ensure a 'just out of bed' look, she hoped Judd didn't stand a chance.

After tonight's thank-you celebration with Tom and Tara she had every intention of following up on the rain check he'd mentioned earlier that afternoon.

'I already told you we're just going for a drink to wind down after a hard day's work. We deserve it.'

Tara looked her up and down and Abby had the distinct impression she was being sized up. 'You're up to something.'

'Like what?'

Abby struggled to keep the grin off her face, knowing she had to get the supermodel to the intimate Lagoon Bar where Judd had organised the impromptu celebratory drinks before she blurted the truth: having a casual drink was a tad different from what they'd organised. Besides, she'd always been lousy at keeping secrets; unless she

counted the one where she'd hid her feelings for Judd f
the last eight years.

Tara folded her arms and grimaced. 'I don't know b
you're looking way too smug. And I have a feeling it h
nothing to do with the fact you're hooked on our reside
dreamboat photographer.'

'Look, just humour me, okay? Judd and I just want
to say thanks for making the wedding shoot so pleasan'

Abby turned back to the mirror for one final chec
hoping Tara bought her trite little story. The sooner th
all shared a drink, the sooner she could abscond with t
dreamboat and have her wicked way with him.

They only had two nights left on the island max and s
intended to make the most of them. Having Judd walk c
on her to take his precious business call this afternoon h
given her some valuable thinking time and she'd come
the conclusion that, no matter how she felt about him, s
had to focus on the here and now.

Judd wasn't a keeper.

As a friend, yes. As anything more? Hell, no!

It was the only reason she'd agreed to this fling in t
first place, knowing it couldn't go anywhere, knowing,
matter how she felt once he left for Timbuktu again, she
have plenty of time to get over him and resume a norm
life…as his friend.

'Okay, so I'm curious. Whatever you two have cc
cocted, how bad can it be?'

Abby noted the twinkle in the model's green eyes as s
picked up a sparkly silver evening clutch and tucke
strand of shining red hair behind her ear. 'On seco
thoughts, don't answer that. Let's go.'

Abby hid a triumphant smile. 'Great. Follow me.'

As they strolled through the lush gardens following a path lit by flickering torchlights, she inhaled, knowing the heavy scent of frangipanis perfuming the air would for ever act as a reminder of the incredible time she'd had with Judd on this island.

Who would've thought they'd have an island fling, when, for years, the only thing flinging between them had been the constant teasing barbs they'd fired at each other?

Now, just thinking about the night ahead made her pulse race and her heart respond in typical staccato fashion.

'The Lagoon Bar? This is a couple's hang-out. Won't I be a third wheel?'

Tara pulled up short as they reached the entrance to the dimly lit bar, digging her stilettos into the sand.

'This'll be fun,' Abby said, firmly propelling Tara towards the thatched door before she could flee.

Thankfully, the door swung open at that moment and Judd held it open, a naughty twinkle in his eyes as he locked gazes with her for an endless, loaded moment before nodding to Tara.

'Good evening, ladies. We've been expecting you.'

'We?' Tara's eyes narrowed as she followed them into the bar.

'All set?' Abby whispered to Judd as they fell in behind Tara.

'Yeah. They're going to love this.'

Judd's subtle jerk of his head pointed towards a small table situated on the lagoon's edge, screened from the rest of the bar by lush palm fronds and trailing fuchsia bougainvillea where the staff had laid out a tapas-style feast with an ice bucket containing the most expensive champagne on the drinks menu.

Tom sat at a nearby table, nursing a beer, a pensive expression on his face, rather unusual for him.

'Here we go,' Judd murmured, placing a hand in the small of her back and setting her pulse skyrocketing at the barest of touches as Tom looked up at the precise moment Tara first caught sight of the table and his face lit up.

Tara stopped dead and whirled towards her, a shrewd glint in her glittering green eyes.

'Is this a set-up? Because if it is, forget it. I can get my own dates, thank you very much.'

Before Abby could respond, Judd stepped in quickly. 'Tom's done a great job this week, too. When Abby told me about having a celebratory drink with you for your hard work I only thought it fair I invite Tom along, too. There isn't a problem, is there?'

Abby stifled a laugh at Judd's *faux* innocent look, especially when Tara melted beneath his goofiest smile.

'No problem,' Tara said, sending her blow-dried hair over her shoulder with a determined flick before striding towards the table.

'Nice save, Romeo.'

'Anything for you, Juliet,' Judd said, sliding his hand up her back to caress the bare skin between her shoulder blades, sending a shiver of anticipation down her spine as she silently praised her choice of strapless dress for this evening.

'You look beautiful, by the way,' he said, as if reading her mind. 'And those red shoes are way beyond sexy.'

She sent him a coy smile as she dropped her gaze to

where he was staring, wriggling her matching Retro Rose
toenails within her favourite shoes.

'They are pretty hot, aren't they?'

'Not half as hot as the woman in them,' he murmured,
brushing a soft kiss on the skin behind her ear, a kiss filled
with promise.

'Did you hear there's a storm coming tonight? Apparently the rain's going to bucket down in torrents.'

The gold flecks in his eyes glowed amber in the bar's
soft candlelight and her breath caught as his thumb trailed
across her bottom lip.

'In that case you'd better spend the night in my room.
After all, I am on a higher floor and we wouldn't want to
be flooded out. Besides, I feel a rain check coming on.'

'You're on,' she said, slipping her hand into his, already
counting the minutes till they could slip away. 'For now,
shall we see how our employees are getting on, spring our
surprise on them before making our escape?'

'Sounds like a plan.'

Tom and Tara were making small talk when Abby took
the seat Judd pulled out for her.

'Hey, Abby. You look great,' Tom said, not taking his
eyes off Tara for a second, and she smiled, knowing her instincts about these two were spot on. With a little luck she
had a feeling she and Judd wouldn't be the only couple
walking around with dazed expressions.

'Thanks. Nothing like Tara, though.'

Judd rolled his eyes and she gave a tiny shrug. Okay, so
she was laying it on a bit thick. She couldn't help it if she
was looking at the world through romantic-tinged glasses
at the moment.

'She's beautiful,' Tom said, a simple sincerity in his tone as Tara straightened her shoulders and sent him stunning smile before picking up the punch cocktail waiter had deposited in front of her.

'Do you think these two are up to something?'

Tom shrugged. 'Beats me, though looks as if they've gone to a lot of trouble so we should probably humour them. Besides, I agree with the boss. We've worked damn hard this week, why not celebrate a little? We deserve it

He raised his schooner in Tara's direction and she clinked glasses with him, resident flirtatious twinkle in her eyes while Abby smiled and took a sip of her own punch cocktail.

'How about a toast?'

Judd's hearty announcement startled the other couple who hadn't taken their eyes off each other since they' tapped glasses. It was almost as if such a simple action had opened their eyes, literally, and they were now casting co glances at each other while sipping their drinks.

'Go ahead,' Abby said, eager to drink up and leave th newly awakened couple to their own devices—screw th delectable feast they'd organised for them all to shar she'd rather feast on a seriously sexy photographer.

Judd raised his glass. 'Here's to the end of a successf shoot and the beginnings of a new future, for all of us.'

Her heart turned over at the serious expression behin Judd's joviality. His gaze hadn't shifted from her, the i tensity behind his stare trying to convey a message sh didn't understand—or was too scared to contemplate.

New future?

She wished.

But she'd given up wishing a long time ago, around the time her parents had never come back from one of their do-gooder treks and as far as sharing a future with Judd as anything other than friends, she'd be better off wishing for the moon.

'To all of us.'

Tom echoed Judd's toast and as they all raised glasses Abby tried not to squirm under Judd's penetrating stare. It was as if he was trying to tell her something with his eyes, trying to convey some mystical message she had no hope of deciphering unless he spelt it out for her.

Thankfully, Tom soon had Tara involved in some huge discussion about global warming, giving Abby ample opportunity to try and get to the bottom of Judd's little speech.

'Nice toast,' she said, inhaling as he leaned towards her, loving the faint musk combined with pure Judd that evoked memories of days gone by.

'Thanks.'

He shrugged as if uncomfortable under her praise, drawing her attention to the width of his shoulders beneath the open-necked white shirt accentuating his tan while he nodded towards the other two, who were flirting like mad. 'Looks as if you were right about these two.'

'Woman's intuition,' she said, finding herself leaning towards him, warmth radiating off him, and when he reached out for his glass and his forearm brushed her bare skin, she gritted her teeth in an effort not to groan out loud.

'You almost finished that drink?'

The urgency in his low voice made Abby look up and once she saw the blatant desire in his eyes, she had no hesitation in sculling the remainder of her cocktail and forgetting her intentions to grill him over his toast.

'I have now.'

She placed her glass on the table, her gaze not leaving his. The icy punch hadn't done much to quell the fire burning deep inside with Judd staring at her as if he wanted her right here, right now.

Heat sizzled between them, potent and fierce, obliterating everything but the need to make love till they were sated

'What about their surprise?'

She leaned towards him, using any excuse to place her lips an inch from his ear and whisper, enjoying seeing him stiffen when she blew gently. 'I know we thought we'd stick around and share it with them, but I'm a woman with a woman's prerogative to change her mind, don't you think?'

He smiled and trailed a finger across the back of her hand, raising goose bumps. 'I think you're a genius.'

He continued his trail up to her wrist before dipping under it, caressing her pulse point in slow, torturous circles. 'As well as the sexiest woman on the planet,' he added in a low voice before speaking up. 'Will you two be okay? I've got some shots Abby has to approve before tomorrow.'

Abby fought a rising blush and lost as Tara looked up and winked. 'Shots, huh? Well, don't let us keep you two from *work*.'

Tom didn't join in the wordplay. By the looks of his star struck expression as he glanced at Tara he was only too pleased to see the back of them. 'No worries. We'll be fine.'

'Great.' Judd pushed away from the table and helped her up, for which she was grateful considering her knees wobbled. It could've been the cocktail, but she knew better. He

kin prickled with awareness, reacting to his proximity
ınd leaving a rippling sensation in its wake.

'Though I think you two should swap tables. This one
over here seems much better.'

'We're okay right here…' Tara's words died on her lips
ıs Judd pushed the screen back, revealing the table cov-
-red in a staggering array of mouth-watering tapas. 'Wow.
Ʈhat's some feast.'

Abby smiled. 'It's a thank-you for all the hard work you
wo have done. So thanks, guys, it's been a blast working
vith you. Go ahead, enjoy. There's champagne in the
ʋucket and we've left strict instructions with the bar staff
o keep it coming for as long as you want it. Though we
ɖo have to work tomorrow, kiddies…' She waggled her
ınger at them and they laughed.

'Great, I'm starving,' Tom said, holding Tara's chair out
or her, his hungry gaze wavering between her and the
ood as if unsure which was the tastier delicacy.

Tara stood in a fluid, lithe movement and leaned over
ɔ give Abby and Judd a hug. 'Thanks for this. The crew
n most of the shoots I've done don't give a flying fig
ɓout anyone other than themselves. This is really thought-
ıl of you.'

'You're welcome,' Judd said, his smile genuine while
is gaze strayed to the door.

An anticipatory tingle raced down Abby's spine as she
ɪched towards him, giving him a gentle nudge with her hip.

'Right, we better get to work. See you guys in the
ıorning,' she said, barely managing a casual wave at the
ther couple while trying not to trip in her haste to fol-
ɔw Judd.

They'd just made it outside when he grabbed her aroun
the waist and pulled her close.

'Take a look at the sky. Do those look like stor
clouds to you?'

Abby cast a quick glance skyward, noting a billion sta
scattered against a midnight sky without a cloud in sigh

'Oh, yeah, definitely. Looks as if it's going to rain an
rain all night.'

His lips curved into a deliciously wicked smile. 'A
night, huh?'

She nodded, suddenly mesmerised by the glimpse
tanned skin in the V of his shirt. It looked good enough to tas
and all she needed to do was lean forward a fraction and..

'Then it's definitely time for that rain check.'

His husky murmur made her look up and she shivere
hypnotised by the intent behind his stare. Green flec
mixed with gold, both sparkling in the muted light fro
several flame-lit torches along the pathway, drawing h
deeper into the mesmerising hazel depths.

'Let's hurry,' she said, planting a quick, teasing kiss
his lips, the contact all too brief as she craved to lose herse
in his hot, steamy kisses all night long.

Judd didn't need to be asked twice.

He'd planned this evening to the nth degree since h
phone call that afternoon and nothing would go wron
He'd make sure of it.

Taking hold of her hand, loving that it felt so dan
right, he said, 'I've got a surprise for you.'

'I just bet you do.'

He laughed as she looked up at him from beneath h
lashes, a mischievous smirk playing about her glossed mout

'Come on. My room this time.'

He tried not to hurry, but like this afternoon they could barely restrain from breaking into a run in their haste to obtain privacy.

Abby's sweet laughter washed over him as he stabbed at the elevator button so hard it zinged, and he waited till the mirrored doors slid silently shut before silencing her with a kiss. He hadn't meant to touch her till they reached his room but his resistance was at an all-time low and all she had to do was glance in his direction and he lost it.

'Hey, they have cameras in these things,' she murmured, breaking the kiss to nibble along his jaw, dipping her tongue inside his collar, the merest flicker of her tongue against his skin making his hard-on twitch.

'You're right.'

He gritted his teeth, knowing he should stop her exploring him with her tongue, all too aware there wasn't one damn thing he could do about it as his body tensed with every teasing flicker against his damp skin.

Thankfully, the doors slid open with a loud zing and he slid his arm around her waist, all but dragging her the short distance to his room, sliding his room key into the slot at the speed of light and ushering her inside.

'Wow.'

She stopped dead, her beautiful blue eyes wide as saucers as she took in the scene before them.

'You like it?'

Nodding, she turned to face him, her smile lighting the room better than the countless candles covering every surface. 'It's incredible. Did you do all this?'

More than pleased with her reaction, he shook his head.

'The resort lent a hand. I wanted to go all out tonigh Make it a night to remember.'

The kind of night he wanted to repeat over and over wit her, if she'd let him.

Tugging her further into the room, he said, 'There's more

He had the pleasure of seeing her mouth open in a smal adorable O, the surprise turning her eyes a sparkling sapphir

'You remembered?'

Her voice came out on a wistful sigh as she squeeze his hand tight.

'Yeah, pretty hard to forget the night you told me yo idea of a perfect date,' he murmured, tracing her lips wit a fingertip, remembering very clearly being parked in h beat-up Mustang at the end of her street backing onto park after the grad dance, torn between wanting to repe the mind-blowing kiss they'd shared earlier that night ar hightailing it out of town.

Abby, his buddy, he could handle.

Abby, with stars in her eyes and romantic ideals dri ping from her lips, had scared the hell out of him.

'I can't believe you remembered.'

An unfathomable expression flickered in her eyes for moment before it disappeared as she reached up to cup h cheek.

'All this—' Abby's gesture took in the candles, the h pink gerberas scattered around the bed, the strawber sundaes, the chilled Kahlua on ice and the handmade truff chocolates '—is fabulous but you're all I need to make th a night to remember.'

He'd roughed it in the wilds of Africa, he'd faced angry elephant, he'd even been attacked by a cheetah onc t nothing made him feel so out of his depth as Abby's atant adoration at that moment.

He'd wanted to make tonight special before divulging e truth to her. He'd wanted to make it an unforgettable ght. But seeing the honesty in her eyes blew him away d he suddenly realised he was playing with fire.

This was Abby, the girl who'd befriended the town joke, ho'd stood up for him when other kids had teased him out his dad, who'd done countless small things to make s life in Pier Point bearable.

Would she buy his sudden turnaround?

Would she want him in her life beyond this week?

As more than a friend?

'Saying stuff like that can go to a guy's head,' he said, s hand covering hers and effectively pinning it to his est where his heart bucked like a wild animal.

'I'm counting on it.'

She slid her hand out from under his, fiddling with the p button of his shirt, not taking her eyes off his.

The button gave with a decisive pop and she laughed.)ops, looks like I've ruined this shirt.'

'Then you better take it off.'

The spark in her eyes lit his fuse in a big way, sending e blood pounding through his veins until he couldn't think ˙ anything but her fingers toying with him, everywhere.

'Need some help?'

'I think I've got it.'

Her hands went crazy as she wrenched his shirt open, nding buttons flying and scattering on the marble tiles ith several pings and he moaned as she leaned forward d planted her lips against his bare chest.

If he could have any wish it would start like this, wit the woman he wanted so much it hurt undressing him wit eager fingers and bedroom eyes.

He'd fantasised about this moment every waking secon for the last few hours, needing to assuage his hunger fe her with a drive that bordered on obsession.

Considering they'd already had sex, it should've take the edge off. Instead, his hunger grew every time he' glimpsed her smile while they'd worked, with every cc glance she'd sent him and now, with her exploring he chest like a woman who couldn't get enough, he was reac to explode.

'I'll go easier on the pants,' she murmured, her han flitting around the waistband of his trousers, driving hi crazy in the process.

Whatever happened to seducing her, of taking it ni and slow and making this more than memorable?

Damned if he knew and damned if he cared.

Her eager response was all that mattered now, that ar the fact that the woman of his dreams seemed to want hi as much as he wanted her.

'Shall I?'

Her tentative, whispered question, combined with he fingertips lightly skimming the sensitive skin of he waist, had him picturing icebergs and blizzards before h totally lost it.

'Go ahead, sweetheart.'

He drew in a sharp breath as she fiddled with the be buckle, the tinkle of metal unfastening, the rasp of leath and the smooth slide of a zip turning him on more than h thought possible.

When her fingers slid inside the waistband of his boxers and brushed his erection, he groaned, reaching for her blindly. In response, she leaned forward and ran her tongue along his collarbone, sending his libido skyrocketing and the last of his good intentions to take things slow flying out the window on the balmy tropical breeze.

She wanted him. He wanted her.

There was plenty of time for taking it slow later. Right now, blinded by insatiable lust, he had no other option but to satisfy the hunger raging through his body. Fast.

He dipped his head and kissed her, plundering her mouth with the desperation of a parched man finally slaking his thirst.

Abby moaned, her soft sounds exciting him further as she pressed her hips against him. God, he ached for her, eager to bury himself in her warmth, frantic to pleasure them both till they lay spent and gasping for air.

'Help me out of this,' she murmured, struggling to locate the zipper on her dress.

'Allow me,' he said, tugging it with so much force it almost came apart in his hand.

'That's better.'

She stared directly into his eyes as she shimmied out of the dress, allowing it to pool around her ankles in a sliver of red silk.

He broke the stare, unable to keep his eyes off the heart-stopping sight of the woman who meant the world to him standing in front of him wearing nothing but a skimpy pair of white lace knickers, a pair of seriously hot red shoes and a sexy smile.

'Shoes off?'

She wiggled her toes, all too aware of the power she had over him, and he growled, pulling her into his arms and nuzzling her neck.

'The shoes stay but you can lose these.'

Before she could utter a word, he'd ripped her panties off, and she laughed, a purely joyous sound that rippled over him in a seductive wave.

'At the rate we're going we'll have to buy each other a whole new wardrobe come morning.'

Her hand insinuated its way between their bodies, grasping his penis through the cotton and stroking along the length till he was forced to release his grip on her butt and lose the boxers in record time.

'You know I had visions of you draping your body in gerbera petals, eating strawberries off your breasts and drinking Kahlua out of your navel?'

She smiled and pushed him back onto the bed, straddling him in a heartbeat.

'I'm all for romance and foreplay, but how about we save that stuff for later? Right now I want you, Calloway. Real bad.'

Unable to keep the smug grin off his face, Judd ran his hands up her torso, starting at her waist and gliding upwards over smooth skin, circling her breasts, delighting in the tortured look that flickered across her face when he lightly skimmed her nipples with his palms.

'How bad?'

In response, she thrust her breasts into his hands, and he chuckled, tweaking her nipples, rubbing them, loving the soft, panting sounds she made as she leaned forward towards his mouth.

'This bad.'

She brushed a nipple over his lips and he obligingly enclosed the hardened peak with his mouth, sucking it until he writhed on top of him, taking him closer to the edge with each squirm.

'Protection. Now.'

He barely registered her demands as she settled over him, her slick entrance gliding over the tip of his erect penis in a slow, tantalising brush with ecstasy.

'Oh, man,' he muttered, reaching over to the bedside table and sheathing himself quickly, almost losing it completely when she slid down a fraction in an attempt to give him some room to manoeuvre, the slight movement brushing her liquid heat over him again.

'Definitely all man,' she said, inching her way down slowly, enclosing him, taking in every inch of him while wearing nothing but a confident smile and those horny red shoes.

'Oh, yeah.'

He grasped her waist, his hands fitting perfectly into her soft curves, content to let her set the pace while he tried to make this incredible experience last longer than a few minutes.

However, Abby had other ideas and she increased her tempo, tilting her hips forward, brushing her breasts across his chest, draping her silky hair smelling of frangipanis and ocean breeze across his face, driving him to the brink of losing control in a heartbeat.

'Judd… Oh, Judd…'

Closing her eyes, she arched back at the precise moment he climaxed, his pleasure heightened by her orgasm a second later as she cried out his name one last time before collapsing forward and smothering him in a welcome armful of warm, satisfied woman.

'Abby, sweetheart,' he murmured, cradling her close smoothing her hair back from her face, wondering if she found their incredible connection as unique and mind blowing as he did.

She was the most important woman in the world to him as a friend and now...

As her eyes fluttered open and a coy smile curved her lips upwards, the realization of how much she meant to him slammed into him with the force of a tropical cyclone.

He loved her.

More than a friend, more than he'd ever loved anyone before.

But he didn't do love. He didn't know how.

His whole life to date had been shaped by his burning desire to be free. However, he had a new burning desire and she was staring at him with a quizzical expression in her beautiful blue eyes.

'What's the funny look about?' She cupped his cheek tracing the curve of his jaw with a tender hand.

It would've been the perfect time to tell her how he felt how she made him feel. But he hadn't told her the truth about staying in Sydney yet and he didn't want to complicate matters until he'd come clean. Once she'd learned the truth, accepted his change of heart, maybe she'd welcome the truth about his feelings, too?

He could only hope. But for now he intended to make the most of the night with one incredibly sexy woman.

'Funny look, huh?'

Capturing her hand, he brought it to his mouth, nibblin

her fingertips before drawing her index finger into his mouth and sucking it, enjoying the look of sheer sensual shock that flashed across her face.

'Must be because I'm thinking about begging you to never take those shoes off ever again,' he said, joining in her laughter as she lowered her mouth to his, their kiss a slow melding of lips and tongues that notched up the heat between them all over again.

'Play your cards right tonight and you never know what might happen.'

Judd mentally crossed his fingers, hoping that come morning, she remembered how great they were tonight when he revealed his plans to her.

CHAPTER ELEVEN

For a smart businesswoman, Abby could be pretty dumb at times.

'Whatever we do on the island stays on the island.'

Had she really said that a few days ago? Had she been delusional at the time? Considering how Judd made her feel whenever he glanced at her, let alone touched her, probably.

It had seemed so simple at the time. Have a little island fling, enjoy sensational sex with a guy she knew almost as well as she knew herself and head back to the mainland at the end of the week, heart intact.

Unfortunately, her heart had other ideas and while she'd never let him know how she really felt, having him in her life as a friend would be a constant reminder of her foolishness.

Clutching the sheet, she wriggled onto her side, trying not to disturb Judd as she contemplated fleeing before he woke or staying for a few more precious moments.

Gazing at his sleeping form, she marvelled at how boyish he looked: long lashes curved against his cheeks, mouth relaxed into a semi-smile, dark flop of hair falling

over his forehead. If it weren't for the laughter-lines fanning out from the outer corners of his eyes, she could've
sworn he looked exactly how he had back in high school.

However, he wasn't a boy anymore and the man he'd
turned out to be wasn't quite what she expected.

And how.

Last night had been amazing, even better than the first
time they'd made love, yet she knew it had also been the
biggest mistake she'd ever made.

The first time she hadn't been in love with him, and
while it had been an incredible experience, she hadn't connected as they had last night where Judd making love to her
repeatedly had sent her body and soul soaring to heaven.
Before her common sense had kicked in this morning and
plummeted her back down to earth with a thud.

They could never go back to how things had been between them.

Last night changed everything and it scared her beyond belief.

His attempt at romancing her had sealed it. She'd been
blown away he'd remembered what she'd said all those
years ago, touched he'd gone all out to impress her. Though,
grand as his romantic gesture had been, it had nothing on
the expression in his eyes after they'd made love.

It had been the scariest thing she'd ever seen, her best
friend staring at her as if he never wanted this to end. For
both their sakes, she hoped she was mistaken.

His eyelids flickered open and he smiled that slow, sexy
grin that made logical thought impossible.

'Hey there. Sleep well?'

She nodded, unable to resist reaching out and trailing a

finger across his kissable lips. 'You know damn well ther
was little sleeping involved.'

His smile widened as he tried to nip her finger, bu
she was too fast for him. 'Yeah, you're right. And it wa
spectacular.'

She couldn't agree with him more. However, it wa
time to start disengaging, time to put up a few barriers be
tween them before they boarded the plane.

Aiming for casual, she dropped a quick peck on hi
lips. 'Yes, it was. But our little island idyll is drawing t
an end and I've got heaps of last-minute stuff to organis
today so this might be the last time we get any privacy t
ourselves and I'd like to say thanks for—'

'Hey, slow down.' He silenced her with a finger to he
lips and she resisted the overwhelming urge to lick it. 'A
this is our last day on the island I need to tell you something

A sense of foreboding crept over her, the same feelin
she'd had when Aunt May had broken the news of he
parents' deaths, the same feeling she'd had when Judd ha
left Pier Point first time around. Whatever had vanquishe
his smile couldn't be good.

'So, spill it.'

He ran a hand through his hair, sending ruffled spike
in all directions. 'When we get back to Sydney I'm hangin
around for a while.'

Her heart thudded at his words before common sens
kicked in. Judd's version of hanging around probably i
volved a few days longer than his usual snatched visits t
cities around the world and nothing like what she imagine
nothing like what had her so worried she was twisting th
sheet into knots before she realised what she was doing.

'A while?'

He nodded, looking uncertain for the first time all week. In fact, she'd never seen cocky Calloway appear uncertain about anything in his life and, combined with his announcement, it had her very, very nervous.

'I'm going to base myself in Sydney. I'll only do the odd freelance assignment, but basically I've accepted a full-time job there.'

'What?'

Her jaw hung open and he laughed, reaching over to place a finger under her chin and close it.

'But that's not the best part. I'm working for *Finesse* on an exclusive basis. Mark Pyman offered me the position of head photographer and I've accepted.'

She froze while he prattled on, every word hammering a new nail into her already fragile heart.

'Isn't that great? We're going to be working together a lot of the time. Not to mention hanging out.'

Oh, no.

This couldn't be happening.

Whatever happened to mending her heart in peace once he shipped out to whatever godforsaken place he was headed next?

Whatever happened to slipping back into their old friendship over time?

Worst of all, how could she stay immune to the guy and pretend she didn't have feelings for him when he'd be in her face almost 24/7?

'You're not pleased, are you?'

Abby frantically searched her brain for something to say, something other than the obvious, 'Why this? Why now?'

'Damn it, Abby, what's going on with you? I thought you'd be happy for me. Happy I'm sticking around?'

'Yeah, but for how long?'

Oops, her first thought had popped out and, worse, it sounded way more sarcastic than it had in her head.

'What's it matter?'

His bitterness stung as he swung out of bed, padding across the room and into the bathroom before she could apologise.

How could he look so delectable naked and so royally peed off at the same time? Shaking her head, she stepped out of bed, wrapped the sheet around her and followed him.

'Look, you just took me by surprise, that's all,' she said, raising her voice to be heard through the thick bathroom door. 'I'm sorry.'

A long, drawn-out silence greeted her before the shower turned on, effectively drowning out anything else she might have to say.

Great. Just great. Not only had she botched up big time by falling in love with her best friend, she'd also botched up their friendship with her over-the-top reaction to his announcement.

So the nomad was staying in town for a while? Big deal. As he'd said, what did it matter for how long? He'd soon tire of Sydney, he'd move on, just as he always did, leaving her more bereft, more broken-hearted than she'd ever imagined.

Friendship she could do; it was this lovers business she sucked at.

'I don't believe this,' she muttered, slipping her clothes and shoes on in record time—the shoes making her blush a matching shade—and heading out the door.

* * *

udd had the coldest shower on record to wake him up
properly—and to douse his libido that had hot-wired the
moment he'd first opened his eyes and caught sight of
Abby lying next to him all rumpled and sexy—and waited
till he heard the loud click of the main door latch before
stalking out of the bathroom.

What the hell had just happened?

One minute he'd woken to find Abby, a vision of post-
coital glowing woman, staring at him with what he'd
thought was tenderness on her face. The next, she was
colder than an Arctic blizzard.

If she'd given him half a chance to explain his motiva-
tion behind sticking around in Sydney, he would've told
her the truth. All of it. Instead, she'd acted as if she didn't
want to know him, let alone spend more time with him
back in Sydney, and it hurt more than it should.

He'd always known love was a crock. And he'd been
stupid enough to go ahead and fall for her anyway.

What was he thinking?

Unfortunately, he knew exactly what path his mind had
taken once he'd realised he loved her last night. He'd built
a cosy little scenario in his head that involved the two of
them having a relationship, his first real honest-to-God relationship in his life.

So much for that little fantasy. She'd meant it when she'd
said she only wanted an island fling, yet he'd hoped she'd
felt more. There had been times when the look in her eyes…

Dropping onto the bed, he picked up a pillow and buried
his face in it rather than punching the living daylights out
of it. Bad move. The pillow still bore the indentation of
Abby's head and he inhaled deeply, savouring the faint jas-

mine fragrance that filled his senses, the same scent tha
surrounded them when they made love.

Damn it, he'd had his fair share of women, but nothing
or nobody came close to the earth-shattering, climactic ex
perience of making love with Abby. Though it was far mor
than just the physical act between them and he knew it.

Whenever they were together, he felt as if he'd finall
come home.

She'd always had that affect on him, giving him a con
stant in his nomadic life. And now they'd taken their rela
tionship to the next level, he felt as if he could stay in th
one place for ever as long as she was by his side, and i
scared him. It scared him a lot.

Not that it mattered anymore. She didn't want him. He
reaction to his news sealed it.

So where did they go from here?

Abby zipped her suitcase shut, wishing she could compart
mentalise her emotions as well as she did her clothes.

Thankfully, the day had passed in a blur as she had woun
up the shoot, seizing on anything and everything to keep he
hands and mind active. The less she thought about what ha
happened the last week, the easier it would get, right?

Wrong. It would take a severe case of amnesia to wip
away her memories of her nights with Judd. And tha
wouldn't happen unless she stood under a coconut tree for th
next month and prayed one would fall on her head. Mayb
she should've done that earlier in the week—rather tha
giving her amnesia, it might've knocked some sense into he

'Can I come in?'

The balcony curtains parted as Judd stepped into th

oom, looking mouth-watering in camel-coloured cargo
ants and a white T-shirt that accentuated the breadth of
is shoulders.

'Remind me to get a second-floor room next time,' she
aid, hating how her heart leaped at the sight of him.

'And rob me of all this breaking-and-entering fun?'

Fun. Breaking and entering.

His words conjured up instant images of the first time
e'd strolled into her room wearing nothing but board
horts and a smile after the quickest dash in history to grab
ondoms—erotic, unforgettable images of the first time
hey'd made love that same night.

Folding her arms to hide the evidence of what those
memories were doing to her breasts, she said, 'What's up?'

He crossed the room and stopped less than two feet
way, invading her personal space with his potent pres-
nce, and it took every ounce of willpower not to reach
ut and touch him.

'I just wanted to say sorry for how things ended this
morning.'

She gritted her teeth, knowing they needed to have this
onversation but not looking forward to it.

'Look, I'm the one who should be apologising. You
were obviously excited about your new job and I wasn't
xactly doing high-fives with you.'

'That's okay.' He smiled, a soft, gentle upturning of lips
s he reached across and traced hers with a finger. 'What
want to know is why?'

She shook her head, needing to break his tenuous con-
act if she was to give him some sort of rational explana-
on for her behaviour. 'I guess you caught me off guard.

I'm so used to you not being around that the thought o
having you in one place takes some adjusting to.'

'It's because of what's happened between us this week
isn't it?' He dropped his hand, though his gaze lingered o
her lips a tad longer. 'You want to go back to being ju
friends and you thought my sticking around meant we'
still be lovers, too?'

Her heart turned over at the hurt lingering in his eye
What could she say? The truth, that she loved him an
wanted him as more than a lover and a friend, or some hal
hearted lame excuse that would drive an irreversible wedg
between them?

This was exactly why she shouldn't have gone crazy ar
shifted the parameters of their friendship. As for falling in lov
with him…her stupidity meter was off the scale with that on

'Come on, Abby, I need to hear you say it.'

He thrust his hands in his pockets, the simple actic
causing his T-shirt to pull tight across his shoulders, deli
eating every ripple and causing her pulse to race in th
process. 'I thought your responses to me over the last wee
were genuine, that you enjoyed it as much as I did. Wh
went wrong?'

She couldn't lie to him. She'd never lied to him befo
and there was no way she could start now.

'This week has been fabulous. What we shared w
amazing but it can't continue when we get back to Sydne

He reached out towards her and she held up her hand
stop him. 'Why?'

'Because you sticking around changes everything.'

He shook his head, the wounded expression in his ey
surprising her. 'Why? We're still best friends. And fro

hat has happened the last few days we're even better
vers. Why not give us a go?'

Her resistance wavered as he stared at her, the pleading
ok in his eyes boring directly into her soul. However, she
uldn't do this. Seeing him walk away in a month, a year,
aybe two, would be hard enough without having a full-
own relationship which is what she could see happening
tween them given half a chance.

Handling rejection had never been her thing courtesy
her flaky folks and, though she knew Judd would
ver intentionally hurt her, he'd do it anyway when the
anderlust he had running in his veins eventually bub-
ed up again.

'Because none of this has been real,' she said. 'We've
d a ball on the island but having a relationship based on
ore than friendship? It would ruin us. You're not a stayer,
u never have been and that's what I'd expect.'

Taking a deep breath, she decided to lay a few more
rds on the table. If he refuted her claims, maybe they had
hance. If not… Her heart turned over, already aching at
ving to go through this.

'Sure, you may want to stay in Sydney for a while, but
n you honestly say that isn't going to change? That you
on't want to take off when the urge hits or when the
ing gets tough between us or when the next big job offer
mes along? It's what you do. It's a part of who you are.
o you really think you can change that much?'

Whatever small hope she had harboured withered and
ed as he shook his head.

'I can't give you any guarantees,' he said, reaching for
r before thinking better of it, his hands dropping use-

lessly to his sides. 'You know I'm not that kind of guy. Yc know me better than I know myself most of the time.'

'And that's why we need to stay friends. But friends only

Saying the words out loud ripped a hole in her heart ar she blinked several times, hating the sting of tears as sh focused on the ocean view over his right shoulder.

Judd stared at Abby, willing her to look at him. Instea she looked away, her gaze darting around the room befo focusing on some distant spot.

Her words cut straight to the core. After this mornin he'd stupidly hoped they could still work this out, that he had an honest talk with her, they could come to son sort of agreement.

Instead, she didn't trust him enough to believe he cou change, that he wanted her enough to change, and she h no interest in giving them a chance.

Struggling to hide his disappointment, he said, 'If thai what you want, friends it is.'

'Okay, then.'

An icy fist wrapped around his heart and squeezed. Sl was right, of course. How stupid could he be? Being frien was so much easier than loving someone, but could I separate the two now that he'd been dumb enough to fa for her? Could he fall back into the old, teasing routi when every time she smiled at him he'd want to haul h into his arms, or every time she touched him he'd want tear her clothes off?

And what about the times she said 'I love you'?

When she'd said it on the odd occasion in the past, he taken it to mean something. They'd loved each other friends for as long as he could remember and she'd oft

rown the words at him, especially around birthdays and
hristmas, usually down the telephone while he'd been
led up in some jungle or other.

He'd treasured those words, knowing they were meant
an affectionate way rather than any great profession of
eper feelings. Yet this morning after his awakening, he'd
ddenly realised how much he wished she really meant
em. And how much he'd like to say them to her.

Like that would ever happen now.

'Right, I'll leave you to it.' He injected the right amount
coolness into his voice, unwilling to let her know how
uch she'd hurt him.

'Fine.'

Though, strangely enough, she looked anything but.

He shoved his hands into his pockets before he reached
t and enveloped her into his arms. He hadn't noticed the
rk smudges under her eyes till now, her fragility drawing
m under her spell when he should be putting as much
notional distance between them as possible.

'I'll see you later.' He turned and walked away, wishing
e'd call him back.

She didn't, and he silently cursed himself for being a
cker.

s the plane took off, Abby leaned back and closed her
es.

Her head pounded, her heart ached and she needed a
mforting hug like nothing else. Her best friend would be
od for that…and the instant the thought popped into her
ad she almost cried.

Judd was her best friend yet everything had changed and

she couldn't imagine telling him her deepest secrets any
more, let alone touching him.

The best she could hope for now was to bury herself i
work, considering the promotion was ninety-nine-poin
nine per cent hers anyway, and try to maintain some sem
blance of normality in her dealings with him at the offic

*'There's more to life than chasing some crazy dream je
and not getting attached to anything or anyone for fear
losing it.'*

Abby sat bolt upright, having one of those blindir
flashes of clarity that made her want to smack herself
the head. She'd said those very words to Judd when he
run out on her the first time around, when he'd been your
and dumb and filled with macho ideals.

So what was her excuse now?

She was doing the very same thing she'd accused hi
of. There was more to life than work and if she shut hi
out of her life because of her own stupidity at falling in lo
with him, she'd never forgive herself.

She'd been so cold towards him the last time they
spoken, not in the least surprised he'd changed his flig
and taken an earlier one to avoid her.

Friends didn't act like that: pretending they didn't car
deliberately sabotaging their relationship, withholding tl
entire truth...

She'd done all of the above and wasn't proud of it. Tl
was Judd she was blowing off, the guy who meant everythir
to her, and if she wasn't careful, she'd lose him complete.

Sighing, she pressed her fingers against her eyes, willir
the tears to vanish. She'd never felt so alone, had never fe
such a strong need to confide in someone. But that som

e was Sydney bound and probably didn't want to have
ything to do with her anymore.

She'd have to move past this and learn to get along with
n again, if not for the sake of her job, then for her sanity.

If being best buddies with Judd had been the best thing
er to happen to her, losing her heart to him could be the
orst, with the potential to slowly but surely drive her crazy.

CHAPTER TWELVE

JUDD surveyed his new office, filled with a strange sen
of pride. He'd never thought he'd see the day when
gave up his travelling lifestyle and took up roots in one ci
again. Then again he hadn't banked on becoming so b
sotted with Abby that he couldn't see straight half the tin
let alone think.

He clasped his hands behind his head and leaned ba
in the leather ergonomic chair, wondering how she
react when she heard Mark's news. Knowing Abby as
did, she'd probably tear strips off the guy. He knew hc
much she loved her job and Mark's offer would be t
good to refuse, but considering whom she'd be worki
with one-on-one…

Smiling, he glanced at his watch. She should be here a
moment and Mark had said he'd send her in to see h
once he'd presented the offer to her.

Oh, yeah, there would definitely be fireworks and, luc
for him, he'd have a ringside seat.

She might be singing the 'let's just be friends' tune,
he had every intention of changing her mind, starting w
a celebratory dinner to toast their new working relati

ip. Maybe if he was really, really lucky, she'd wear those
xy red shoes...

His body tightened in response as an image of Abby,
anding in his hotel room wearing lacy briefs, those hot
oes and a smile flashed across his mind.

Yep, no doubt about it, he had to talk sense into her and
tch the platonic plan she'd worked out. Either that or face
year of icy-cold showers, which wasn't fair considering
ustralia was in the grip of a drought and he should be con-
rving water. And never let it be said he didn't do his part
r the environment.

'Knock, knock. Got time for your boss?'

He sat up and automatically adjusted his tie as Mark
/man entered the room. For a CEO of a huge media con-
omerate he appeared surprisingly laid-back and lacked
e formality he'd expected.

'Come in, Mark. What can I do for you?'

Mark barged across the room and took a seat. 'This
fice okay?'

'Yeah, no probs.'

'Good.' Mark nodded, sent his BlackBerry a glare as it
eped and slid it back into his pocket. 'We didn't get
ound to finalising the length of your contract earlier. I
as thinking a year to start, see how it suits us both?'

Judd struggled not to squirm in his chair. Twelve months
asn't a huge amount of time in the grand scheme of
ings, but for a guy who'd spent the last eight years mov-
g around it sounded like a life sentence.

Crazy, considering this was what he wanted: a chance
settle down for a bit, to see where his life was headed,

to give Abby and him a chance, but having it spelled o⟩ in contract terms put a different slant on proceedings.

'A year sounds fair, but considering I haven't done fashi⟩ work before, could we leave the time frame open-ende⟩ Until I find my feet, see if it's a good fit for us both?'

Mark fixed him with a glare somewhere between di⟩ belief and admiration. '*Finesse* contracts aren't usual⟩ open-ended. You're not jerking me around? Or planning⟩ leave me in the lurch?'

'No way. I'm looking forward to the challenge of wor⟩ ing here. I just don't want to be tied into anything lon⟩ term. Call it a personal phobia.'

Mark paused and Judd could almost sense the whee⟩ turning in his head before the CEO said, 'This is high⟩ unusual but I'm trusting my gut instinct here and takin⟩ a chance you won't let me down.' He stood and head⟩ for the door, a grim expression on his face. 'Make su⟩ you don't.'

'I won't,' he said, but Mark had already left the roo⟩ hitting buttons on his BlackBerry as he stalked down t⟩ corridor.

This couldn't get much better.

He had a crack at a new job in a city he loved with⟩ woman who'd come to mean more to him than ⟩ could've possibly imagined. And he wasn't tied in⟩ anything so if it didn't work out, he could do as he⟩ always done.

Leave.

However, that wasn't on the agenda, not if he had a⟩ say in it. Especially if Abby came to the party as he hope⟩

* * *

bby stepped out of Mark's office, her head spinning.

When he'd said there'd be a 'huge deal' if Sapphire sland went well, he hadn't been kidding.

For a freelance fashion stylist to be offered every big job *inesse* had for the next two years was a dream come true. ot to mention the fact she wouldn't be tied into any long-rm contracts so she could still freelance, too.

She could hardly believe it and normally she would've mped at the chance. However, accepting the opportunity f a lifetime came with strings attached, huge strings, tied p in one giant bow around Judd Calloway's neck.

Mark had left her in little doubt that Judd was a coup to *inesse* and she'd be working closely with him if she ac-pted.

If she accepted… Damn, how could she refuse? Her job ad always meant everything to her. So what if she'd been mb enough to fall for Judd? She'd already told him they uld be friends only. Given a little time, she was sure ey'd slip back into their old camaraderie.

Taking a deep breath, she knocked on the last door on e left where Judd had his new office, according to Mark. he had to get this over and done with, make sure he under-ood exactly where they stood.

She'd barely had time to tug her favourite Dolce and abbana white suit jacket down before the door opened.

'Hey, I've been expecting you. Welcome to my new digs.'

Judd stepped aside and waved his arm in a flourish, hile she fixed a smile on her face, wishing her traitorous dy would calm down. The minute she'd caught sight of m wearing a charcoal pin-striped designer suit, of all ings, her heart had flip-flopped, her pulse had thundered

and a quick-fire heat she'd been sure she'd conquered an
left behind on the island flowed through her body like mol
ten magma.

'Nice,' she said, stepping into the office with its postcar
view of Sydney Harbour, funky stainless-steel desk an
matching ergonomic chairs.

Very minimalist, very sleek and so unlike anything she'
ever pictured the Judd she knew would go for.

'So you've had a chat with Mark?'

'Uh-huh.'

Perching on the end of his desk, she tried to act as
being offered her dream job—with her dream guy
ironically—happened every day.

'What do you think? I assume you're going to take it'

He tried to look nonchalant and failed miserably, h
steady gaze unwavering.

'It's a great opportunity. I'd be a fool to pass it up.'

His face lit up and he let out an excited whoo
'That's great.'

Crossing the room to perch next to her, his thigh brush
ing hers and sending tiny electric shocks up her stocking
clad leg, he captured her hand before she could mov
'We're going to be working very closely together. Ve
closely.'

She should've snatched her hand out of his the mome
his voice dipped to a husky murmur. Instead, she sat the
like a dummy, frozen, immobile, while he raised her ha
to his lips and branded her palm with a hot, lingering kis

The type of bone-melting kiss that sent electricity si
zling through her body at a rate of knots, the feel of h

arm lips a poignant reminder of what they'd shared on
e island, of what they could never have again.

'Not that closely,' she said, wrenching her hand out of
is and crossing to the window to put some much-needed
istance between them.

He didn't move, his casual stance screaming confidence,
nd she wondered what it would take to get through to him.

'After what happened on the island, I'm not buying this
et's just be friends" thing anymore. It doesn't make sense
onsidering how great we are together. The Abby I know
always up for a challenge, so what are you going to do
oout it?'

Abby gnawed on her bottom lip, knowing only one
iing would get through to him, but all too aware that in
lling him the truth she might drive an irreversible wedge
their friendship for ever.

'Give it to me straight, Weiss.'

The moment she heard him call her by her surname,
ipping into old familiarity, she knew she owed him the
uth. Either way, it would settle this once and for all.

'I'm not willing to take a chance on a relationship with
ou because I know where it will end, with you running out
n me and me picking up the pieces of a broken heart. Again.'

He paled beneath his tan. 'Again? What's that sup-
osed to mean?'

'You honestly don't have a clue, do you?'

Realisation dawned and he took a step towards her be-
re thinking better of it. 'You had feelings for me when
e were teenagers?'

She nodded, biting down on her bottom lip till she tasted
ood, not willing to blab the rest of the truth to him, that

'feelings' was a poor substitute for how much she love‹ him, had always loved him.

'Hell.'

He ran his hand over his face, as if trying to erase th‹ mistakes of the past. If only it were that easy.

'I didn't know. I thought we were just fooling aroun‹ that night, a couple of kids experimenting. You neve‹ said anything…'

And she'd kept her silence ever since, bottling up he‹ feelings all these years, not admitting she'd never got ove‹ her first kiss, her first love if she were completely hones‹

'What could I say? We were both young and I had n‹ idea if you felt the same way I did. Besides, you had place‹ to go, things to do. You were my best friend and I didn‹ want to stop you, to rob you of your dreams.'

'You did that for me?'

His tenderness was almost her undoing as she struggle‹ not to blurt out the rest.

'Of course. That's what friends do. They put the othe‹ person's feelings ahead of their own, no matter ho‹ much it hurts.'

She paused and balled her hands to stop from reaching o‹ to him. 'But not anymore. This time I'm taking care of me‹

He reached out to her, but she held up her hands and h‹ stopped. 'I'm sorry I hurt you and I'm sorry you had to g‹ through all that, but this time, will be different. I'm ne‹ planning on going anywhere any time soon.'

'That's what you say now, but how do you know?'

She shook her head, hating the devastation in his eye‹ hating the pain splintering her heart into tiny pieces. 'Mo‹ ing around is a part of who you are and I won't want to lo‹

you again, especially if we're involved in a relationship. And if we do give it a go either you'll feel stifled and end up resenting me, or I'll feel guilty for being the reason you're sticking around when you'd rather go. Ultimately we both lose and when you eventually leave, because you will, I'll be left to pick up the pieces all over again and I can't do it. I won't do it. I'm not strong enough.'

There, she'd articulated her fears, had come clean about her real feelings, but instead of a weight lifting off her shoulders, she'd never felt so shattered.

'All I'm asking for is a chance.'

She heard a hint of desperation in his voice and, suddenly, anger replaced her pain. Why was he doing this to her? She'd been honest with him, had hoped he'd get the message once and for all.

In a blinding flash, she knew how to get through to him, to ram her point home.

'You want a chance? Well, then, tell me how long you're planning on sticking around.'

The second his glance wavered from hers, she knew he'd won. Then why did it feel as if he'd ripped her heart out all over again and she was the biggest loser ever?

His lips set in a stubborn line before he replied, 'I'm not planning on going anywhere.'

Determined to end this before she started blubbering, she said, 'How long is your contract for?'

He stiffened and thrust his hands into his pockets. 'What's that got to do with us?'

'Everything. How long?'

Defeat dulled the gleam in his hazel eyes. 'It's open-ended.'

Hating how her heart sank when he'd already manage to break it without trying, she said, 'Let me guess. You idea, not Mark's.'

His barely perceptible nod was all the confirmation she needed.

'Well, then, there's your answer.'

She stalked across the room, her stilettos clicking agains the polished floorboards, short, sharp sounds echoing i the room, reinforcing the empty echo in her heart.

'You're wrong about me.'

Abby knew that tone; Judd had it down pat and used i to great affect when he wanted to get rid of someone h didn't like or was unable to resolve an unsolvable problem

She'd first heard it way back in high school when he' taken on the biggest bully and won without using his fist Who needed to resort to violence when the right tone combined with clever words, could cut someone down t size much quicker? Or when he couldn't figure out the an swer to a complex issue?

Pausing at the door, she turned to face him. 'Am wrong? Really?'

Without waiting for an answer, she walked out, wishin she had the guts to slam it as she'd just slammed the doc on any chance they ever had of a future.

CHAPTER THIRTEEN

ᴮBY lay the magazine across her desk, pleased with
ᴡ the photo shoot had turned out. The designers who
d paid big money to have their clothes featured in
nesse's Sapphire Island shoot would be blown away
th the results.

Usually, seeing the finished product of a shoot where
e'd had major input gave her a huge boost, not to mention
ense of satisfaction, but not his time.

As she stared at the pictures of Tara modelling the stun-
ɡ summer outfits, and tried not to dwell on the in-
dible bridal shots of her and Judd, pain wound its fingers
ɔund her heart and squeezed hard. Even now, a week
er, she couldn't forget the look in his eyes when she'd
lked out of his office, his pain a mirror image of her own.

Yet it had to be done and now she'd given her final an-
er to Mark, she needed to move on and concentrate on
r career. A career without *Finesse*'s lucrative offer.

She couldn't do it: spend countless hours working side
side with the guy she loved, trying to maintain a pro-
sional façade. It would be hard enough catching up
cially as friends considering the gulf that had opened

between them, and sadly, she had a feeling they'd never
capture the old Calloway/Weiss magic.

'Ready to go?'

Tara stuck her head around the door, looking way t
bright and bubbly for the mood Abby was in.

Nodding, Abby picked up her Hermes bag and point
at the latest copy of *Finesse*. 'Have you seen the spread ye

'Sure have. It's sensational. But then I'd expect nothi
less from working with a couple of pros like you and t
dreamboat.'

Abby muttered a noncommittal answer, grabbed
keys and headed for the door.

'Don't worry about keys. I'll drive.'

'Since when do you drive when scouting locations?

'Since now.' Tara poked her tongue out and slung an a
around Abby's shoulders. 'Come on. It'll do you good
sit back and relax, take in some of the scenery. You
looking like a misery guts these days and I can't stand

'Don't look, then,' she said, hating that Tara was rig
She couldn't stand her reflection in the mirror most mor
ings, considering her eyes were dull, her hair lacklustre a
her skin pasty.

Not a good look for a fashion stylist and, consideri
she'd turned Mark down, she needed to get her butt i
gear before her business went down the tubes along w
her love life.

While Tara hummed an old Bobby McFerrin tune,
lyrics along the lines of not worrying and being hap
Abby made a conscious decision to stop wallowing. S
needed to get back into the game and focusing on work w
a sure-fire way to do it.

'Speaking of the dreamboat, he's the photographer on is shoot.'

'What?' She stopped dead in her tracks and grabbed ara's arm. 'But he works for *Finesse* full-time. How can : be doing this one?'

Tara tapped the side of her nose and winked. 'Special signment, apparently.'

'Just great,' Abby muttered, releasing her grip and giv-g Tara an apologetic rub when the model winced.

'Thought you should know, as he'll probably be check-g out the location, too.'

Her heart sinking, Abby mustered a smile despite her isgivings. 'Thanks for the heads up. And it shouldn't be problem. We're both professionals.'

Now all she had to do was act like it.

dd glanced at the large green sign telling him exactly ow far it was to his destination, mentally counting down e kilometres as he had ever since he'd left Sydney's Cen-al Business District, the monotonous activity keeping his ind focused on the job ahead rather than mentally re-arsing what he'd say to Abby when he saw her.

The last week had been hell.

By turning down her dream job at *Finesse* she'd made r feelings more than clear and after she'd ignored his itial calls he'd finally realised there was nothing he could to broach the gap that had opened up between them and ade a conscious decision to leave her alone.

At least his work had proved to be fulfilling. Despite his rly doubts about working for a magazine, *Finesse* was a ass act, more than living up to its reputation as one of

Australia's top magazines. He'd thrived on every challeng so far, throwing himself headlong into long hours, anythir to take his mind off Abby. Unfortunately, work inevitab reminded him of her and he would've given anything share their mutual professional success together.

Perhaps after today he'd get that chance?

Patting the inside pocket of his jacket for the hundred time that morning, he sure hoped so.

As the car ate up the few remaining kilometres, drummed his fingers against the steering wheel, trying forget the last time he'd seen her.

Forget? Who was he trying to kid? Every time he clos his eyes the image of their last encounter would materialis flashing across his mind in a hazy kaleidoscope of painf memories. Her coolness, her stricken expression when he confirmed he hadn't signed a fixed contract, her pain wh she'd revealed how much she'd cared for him before…

That had been the hardest to take, the fact she'd love him all those years ago and he hadn't had a clue. Jeez, wh he would give for an ounce of her love now…

Shaking his head, he turned into a gravel drive and pull around the back of the secluded farmhouse, killing th engine and scanning the grounds with a practised ey searching for the perfect location for the perfect shot, tryi not to admit he was, in fact, searching for the perfect woma

And she was. In every way. It had just taken him long to figure out than most. Now he had to prove it to her.

Patting his pocket again and reassured by its contents, stepped from the car and strode towards the farmhou knowing that, whatever happened, he'd given it his best sh

* * *

'ara had been right. This place was perfect.

Abby climbed the stairs to the second floor, marvelling
t the Old World charm of the empty B & B. The peasant
tyle of the new designer who'd commissioned this shoot
vould look fantastic against this backdrop. She'd have to
hank Tara when she got back to Sydney, especially as
he'd been more than understanding at being blown off at
he last minute.

It would be hard enough facing Judd for the first time
ince she'd officially ended any chance of them having a
uture without having an audience and she'd needed the
ong drive out here to clear her head, marshal her defences
nd put her professional mask firmly in place.

She could do this.

She'd got over him the last time; she could do it again.

Hating the lump of emotion lodged in her throat, she
ook a slug from the water bottle in her handbag as she wan-
ered through some of the rooms, admiring the quaint fur-
ishings and fabrics, gasping as she opened the last door on
er left and stepping into what could only be a bridal suite.

'Wow,' she murmured, glancing around the room from
ne king-size mahogany four-poster bed draped in filmy silver
auze to the four-person spa standing elevated on a platform
o capture the mountain views. Throw in the exquisite antique
urnishings, the tiny embroidered cupids on the bedspread
nd the rose-moulded ceiling and the suite exuded romance.

Right now, it made her feel ill.

Turning her back on the inviting ambience, she angrily
wiped at the tears that sprang so easily to her eyes these days
nd slammed straight into the guy who had put them there.

CHAPTER FOURTEEN

'HEY, Abby.'

Judd captured her hands against his chest, steadying her from falling.

Abby stared at him, shocked by the treacherous reaction of her body wedged so closely against his: her heart pounded while heat streaked through her, an instant reminder of her foolishness when it came to this guy. Despite breaking her heart, he still had the power to reduce her to *this*.

'Let me go.' Her hands clenched into fists beneath his, ready to pummel his chest if she had to.

Ahhh...his chest. For one, all-too-brief moment she savoured having her hands clasped against the hard wall of muscle, her palms itching to explore the smooth flesh beneath the shirt, just as she had on the island.

'No. I've already made that mistake before and I don't intend to repeat it.'

'We both made mistakes. Letting me go was the least of yours.'

She wriggled out of his grasp, torn between a desperate need to run out the door and a strange compulsion to spend ust a few more minutes in his company. Not that she had much choice. She had to work with him on this job, so fleeing, no matter how much she wanted to, wasn't an option.

In response, he kicked the door shut with his foot, his eyes not leaving hers for a second. 'Just hear me out this time, okay? Surely as my friend, you can give me that much?'

'You don't play fair,' she muttered, whirling around to break his hypnotising stare.

'I'm not playing this time and I want you to believe it.' He spoke in a rush, as if he couldn't get the words out quick enough. 'I'm sorry for botching things up before. I owe you an explanation.'

'You don't owe me anything,' she said, trying to push past him and open the door.

'Please, sweetheart.'

His whispered endearment stopped her and she silently cursed the power he still had over her.

'Fine.'

She crossed her arms and leaned on the back of a chair, doing her utmost to appear as if she didn't care. 'The only reason I'm still here is that we have to work together, so hurry up. We've got a job to do.'

She couldn't fathom the intense gleam in his eyes, as if he knew something and she didn't, and she pushed off the chair, choosing to look out of the window rather than fathom what was going on in his head.

'What I have to say won't take too long,' he said, joining her at the panoramic window.

Heat radiated off him in palpable waves and, despite her best intentions, she almost leaned into him, craving the warmth of his embrace.

'Get on with it so we can get out of here.'

Despite her intention to keep her gaze focused elsewhere, her stare was drawn to his. Using all her willpower she resisted the pull of his hazel eyes as they sucked her in, willing her to drown in their enigmatic depths.

He reached towards her, and she instinctively shrank back, not willing to risk physical contact when his stare was doing enough damage to her equilibrium all on its own. ' didn't tell you the whole truth on Sapphire Island. I knew right from the outset that I'd be staying around in Sydney for a while. I'd already decided before I took the shoot.'

She'd been able to read him since their schooldays and in an instant knew he'd told her the truth. His sincerity was something she'd never doubted.

'Then why agree to the fling if you knew you'd be sticking around? Why would you do that to us?'

She swallowed, wishing she didn't have to hear the truth in its entirety, but knowing if she didn't, she'd never be able to move on with her life. 'You knew that's why I did it, because it wouldn't be permanent and you'd flit off to whichever ends of the earth suited and we could resume our old friendship. Why would you risk that?'

He had the grace to look sheepish as he turned away and leaned against the window frame, his gaze fixed on some point in the distance. 'That's a little more complicated to explain.'

'Try me.'

His head swivelled towards her in a second, the intensity of his gaze pinning her to the spot. 'You really want to hear the sorry story?'

She nodded, ignoring the ache that had seeped into her

bones and drained her of any residual animosity. She was past hurting, past blaming—all she had left was to settle this once and for all and look to the future. A bleak future without the love of her life.

He paused for a moment and cleared his throat. 'You know about my past and how I've spent a lifetime trying to escape it, but the real kicker? I've done it because I'm scared, bloody terrified, in fact. What if my father's weakness is hereditary? What if I turn out like him? So I run. I bury myself in work. I don't let myself get close to anyone. Except you.'

He reached out to her and took hold of her hand, and she didn't have the heart to snatch it away. His shattered expression accentuated his words and she knew he was speaking from the heart.

'I've depended on you, have done since the first minute we became buddies. You've been the one constant in my screwed-up world. After graduation night and that kiss I couldn't risk mucking up our friendship for what I'd put down to basic teenage desire, so I ignored what happened, focused on our friendship, and it seemed to work till Sapphire Island.'

He gripped her hand and she squeezed back, sending him a silent message to continue.

'I'd already made up my mind to stick around Sydney for a while because the running thing had worn a bit thin. Then seeing you again sparked things off between us in a way I'd never anticipated, we became lovers and all I could think was how great it was.'

He reached out and tilted up her chin. 'You feel it, too, right?'

Abby sighed. This was the part where she told a big, fat lie and ended this once and for all.

But she couldn't lie to him. She never could.

'It doesn't make a difference what I feel,' she said, shaking her head and breaking their tenuous contact. 'I appreciate you telling me all this now, but it doesn't change the fact you'll probably still run some time soon and I can't take that chance.'

'I thought you might say that,' he said, a surprisingly confident smile alleviating the concern on his face as he pulled a folded sheet of paper out of his top pocket. 'Here, this is for you.'

Abby unfolded the thick document, surprised to see a *Finesse* employment contract. She recognised it instantly considering she'd turned one down.

'I'm sorry, I can't work with you. It's just too painful,' she said, holding the contract out to him.

'Read it.'

'Why? I've already turned down Mark's offer. It won't make any difference.'

'I think it will.'

He continued to smile at her and it annoyed her beyond belief. So he'd unburdened his soul? Well, bully for him. It didn't change anything. It didn't ease the pain slashing her, swift and sharp and deep. And now he was trying to sweet-talk her into working with him? As if.

Knowing he wouldn't back down until she gave the contract a cursory glance, she scanned the document, her heart pounding as the fine print danced before her eyes.

'But this is your contract,' she said, flipping pages as her confusion mounted.

'Uh-huh. Check out the last page, particularly terms and length of employment.'

She quickly found the relevant section, read it and re-read it, blinking several times in between.

'But…but…this says you're a *Finesse* employee for the next five years?'

His eyes twinkled with triumph as he tapped the document. 'That's right. It's all there in black and white.'

Her pulse raced with the implication of what he meant, but she couldn't comprehend it, let alone accept it.

'*Five* years? No one signs an employment contract for that long. It's crazy.'

'Only if a person's crazy in love and crazy enough to want to be with his best friend for ever and crazy enough to want to marry her and never, ever leave her side,' he said, his eyes blazing with what could only be termed as love as he picked her up and swung her around and around till the room spun.

'You are crazy!'

She beat at his broad shoulders with her fists, unable to stem the tidal wave of joy sweeping through her body as the reality of what he'd just said, of what he'd just done by signing that contract, sank in.

He held her tight as she slid down his body, waiting till their lips were centimetres apart before kissing her.

'So come on, Weiss, put me out of my misery. Tell me you love me, too,' he whispered against the corner of her mouth, his warm breath sending familiar shivers down her spine.

Smiling, she traced the familiar contours of his face, stunned by the depth of feeling between them. 'I love you, too.'

He let out a whoop of joy and grinned, the same cher
ished smile she'd loved for ever.

'I'm never going to leave you. Contract or not, yo
know that, right?' He reached out and cupped her cheek
the tenderness in his eyes reassuring her as much as hi
declaration.

Abby didn't need convincing. In fact, she didn't eve
need a piece of paper proving he'd be sticking around fo
the next five years.

Judd loved her.

She loved Judd.

That was all that mattered, all that ever would.

Life didn't come with guarantees or time limits an
she'd take every precious second with him she could ge

'So you're never going to leave me, huh? Never is a lon
time, Calloway.'

'You better believe it,' he said, kissing her like a ma
with a point to prove.

EPILOGUE

JUDD laid down his camera and strolled over to his subject, rearranging the folds of her dress.

'Stop fussing. We've got loads of shots.'

Abby swatted his hand away as he slid it under the skirt's silky folds and caressed his wife's shapely calf.

'Can you blame a guy for wanting to look back on this day and remember it?'

She rolled her eyes, stilling his hand with a playful slap as it crept past her knee. 'I thought it was the bride who went to extremes on the big day. And don't forget we've done this before.'

'The fake island shoot doesn't count and as I recall I didn't take any photos that day.' He trailed his fingers over her thigh, enjoying the widening of her eyes, the slight glazed look that flitted across her exquisite face, relishing her passionate responses to his touch. 'Unless you count the ones I took when you were naked on our fake wedding night.'

'You didn't!'

She sat bolt upright before leaping to her feet, horror replacing the look of desire he'd glimpsed a few seconds earlier.

He laughed and swept her into his arms. 'You're right, I didn't. Had you going there for a minute, didn't I?'

'You're a bad, bad man.' She wrapped her arms around him, her eager touch showing how quickly she'd forgiven him for his risqué joke. 'First you leave me pining for you for eight years, then you strut back into my life and turn it upside down. The least you can do is give me a break and stop teasing me.'

'Like that's ever going to happen. It's a part of who we are.' He kissed her, relishing the slight tremble that shot through her body as she moulded against him. 'Oh, I almost forgot your present.'

She touched his face, her eyes glowing with love. 'I already have it right here.'

He dropped a kiss on her nose. 'Thanks, but you must see this. I got it especially for you.'

He took hold of her hand, trying desperately to keep from laughing as he steered her towards the back of the farmhouse. They'd returned to the quaint B & B for the quiet ceremony and intimate party where their guests could share in their joy.

It had been a lovely day, with a few close work colleagues mingling with ease while Tom and Tara, their witnesses, did their best to appear nonchalant while glued to each other's sides.

'My present's in there?' She cast a suspicious glance at him as they neared the barn.

'Sure is.' He threw open the barn door and pulled her close. 'Seeing as you've had a thing for me since high school I thought you might like to revisit some old memories. Particularly graduation night?'

Abby laughed as he tugged her towards an old Ford Mustang, an exact replica of the one he'd had as a teenager.

Running her hand over the gleaming red paint, she ducked around the bonnet and sent him a coy smile. 'Okay, so I had a thing for you back then. Though if memory serves correctly, *you* kissed *me* that night?'

His eyes glittered with promise as he strode around the car, pinning her against it with his body. 'Mere details. What's important is that we didn't get further than that kiss and I think it's time to remedy that. Care to take a ride to Pier Point before jumping in the back seat with me, Mrs Calloway?'

Laughing, she reached up and wound her arms around his neck. 'You're such a romantic.'

She kissed him, revelling in the knowledge that this man, her best friend, her lover and now her husband for real, still had the power to surprise her.

His head descended, blocking out the filtered sunlight as he brushed her lips in a kiss that promised for ever.

'And don't you forget it.'

BAD BLOOD

A POWERFUL DYNASTY, WHERE SECRETS AND SCANDAL NEVER SLEEP!

VOLUME 1 – 15th April 2011
TORTURED RAKE
by Sarah Morgan

VOLUME 2 – 6th May 2011
SHAMELESS PLAYBOY
by Caitlin Crews

VOLUME 3 – 20th May 2011
RESTLESS BILLIONAIRE
by Abby Green

VOLUME 4 – 3rd June 2011
FEARLESS MAVERICK
by Robyn Grady

8 VOLUMES IN ALL TO COLLECT!

www.millsandboon.co.uk

BAD BL☾☽D

A POWERFUL
DYNASTY,
WHERE SECRETS
AND SCANDAL
NEVER SLEEP!

VOLUME 5 – 17th June 2011
HEARTLESS REBEL
by Lynn Raye Harris

VOLUME 6 – 1st July 2011
ILLEGITIMATE TYCOON
by Janette Kenny

VOLUME 7 – 15th July 2011
FORGOTTEN DAUGHTER
by Jennie Lucas

VOLUME 8 – 5th August 2011
LONE WOLFE
by Kate Hewitt

8 VOLUMES IN ALL TO COLLECT!

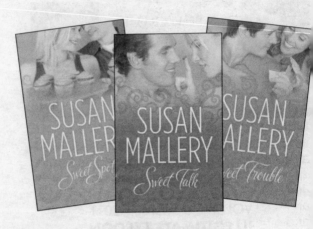